MAIN

BLIND

SUBMISSION

Nonfiction by Debra Ginsberg

About My Sisters

Raising Blaze:
Bringing Up an Extraordinary Son in an Ordinary World

Waiting:
The True Confessions of a Waitress

BLIND
SUBMISSION

A Novel

DEBRA GINSBERG

Shaye Areheart Books
New York

Published in the United States by Shaye Areheart Books, an imprint of the Crown Publishing Group, a division of Random House, Inc., New York.
www.crownpublishing.com

Shaye Areheart Books and colophon are trademarks of Random House, Inc.

Library of Congress Cataloging-in-Publication Data

Blind submission : a novel / Debra Ginsberg.—1st ed.
1. Literary agents—Fiction.   I. Title.
PS3607.I4585B56   2006
813'.6—dc22   2006013198

ISBN-13: 978-0-307-34604-9
ISBN-10: 0-307-34604-8

Printed in the United States of America

Design by Mauna Eichner and Lee Fukui

10 9 8 7 6 5 4 3 2 1

First Edition

*For all the writers who have yet to be published and
for the book lovers who will one day read their work.*

PROLOGUE

IT WAS THE FIRST MINUTE of my first day and my first impulse was to run. Just turn around and get the hell out of there as fast as I could. In that frozen moment between initial response and subsequent action, I stood mute, my vision tunneled to the desk in front of me. It was piled to toppling with files, pink message slips, newspaper clippings, and indeterminate scraps. A multi-line phone was half buried in the middle of this chaos, its angry flashing call buttons casting a blinking orange glow across the papers. What struck me with the greatest force, though, was the sheer number of words I saw in front of me. With the exception of the phone, every inch of the desk was layered in a dizzying collage of blue-black fonts and scribbles. And every word was screaming at me to pay attention and respond. This was my desk. This was my job.

I could feel the muscles in my legs twitching with the effort to keep still. I clutched the strap of my purse with one hand while the other gripped the to-go coffee cup I'd brought in with me. Fight or flight. Every cell in my body was held taut, waiting for the adrenaline rush. My mouth was dry and I knew I had bitten off more than I could chew. Inside my head, the voice of reason told me that this was only a job, not an invitation to walk off a cliff. But the much louder voice of instinct shouted that walking off a cliff was exactly what I was about to do. I was in the wrong place at the wrong time, it insisted, and I had to get out *now*. Before it was too late.

I *could* leave, I thought. I could back up and exit the way I came in and nobody would know I'd ever been there. The girl at the desk to my left hadn't even noticed my arrival. She was murmuring into her own phone, wrapped up in an intense conversation. There was nobody else in sight. Nobody to greet me or to welcome me to my first day on the job. Nobody to express alarm if I just bolted out of the office. It would be easy to simply disappear, go home, and reconsider the whole thing. And then, later, I could call and say that something unforeseen had come up, that I was terribly sorry, that I was unable to take the job, but thank you, thank you so much for your consideration. I could hear the conversation in my head—could hear myself murmuring the apology. In all likelihood, I thought, I wouldn't even have to talk to *her*.

I drew a deep breath and felt the muscles in my shoulders start to relax. Yes, escape was a possibility, and in it I found the comfort I needed to release the death grip on my purse strap and take a tentative step toward the mountain of words on my desk.

I knew then that I wouldn't leave, that I'd stay there come what may. I made an effort to push my misgivings to the farthest reaches of my consciousness and focus on why I was standing there in the first place. The truth of it was, despite my moment of panic, I wanted this job more than I could remember wanting anything. I wanted it with a single-minded desire I hadn't even known I possessed. I'd fought for it and I'd won it and nothing, especially not a few first-day butterflies, was going to stop me from taking it.

I took my second deep breath in the space of five seconds and felt my head start to spin with dizziness. I blinked a few times and swallowed hard. It wouldn't do, I thought, to start hyperventilating before I'd even had a chance to sit down. I took one more glance at what was now *my* overloaded desk, savoring my last few moments of stillness. And then, with one step forward, I moved into the fray.

ONE

IT WAS MALCOLM'S IDEA that I apply for the job at the Lucy Fiamma Literary Agency. Without his prompting, it never would have occurred to me. Which was peculiar, he pointed out, not only because I was about to become unemployed, but because of my almost fanatic love of books and anything to do with them. And it was true; I *was* a passionate reader, able to devour whole tomes in a single sitting. My unquenchable appetite for books was something I'd developed very early in my life. It seems a cliché now to say that books were a welcome escape from reality, but in my case this was the truth. It wasn't that I had a miserable or neglected childhood, but it *was* unstable. My single, hippie mother could never stay in one place ("place" being defined as various communelike encampments) for very long. She was on a relentless quest for enlightenment and never found it, unsurprisingly, outside of herself. Not that this stopped her from searching, or from dragging me with her. I had little in the way of continuity in my schooling and next to no contact with kids my own age. What friends I did make I soon had to abandon when my mother decided that a Buddhist retreat in Arizona was spiritually superior to an organic foods cooperative in Oregon, or that an artists' colony in California was morally preferable to a Wiccan enclave in New Mexico. My mother seldom had a man in her life to tie her down, and that included my father, whoever he was or might have become. My mother claimed she never even learned his name on the one night they spent together.

Books were the one constant in all this flux and I turned to reading whenever I wanted to be rooted and still. I loved my mother fiercely but never shared her enthusiasm for perpetual change. Nor did I fully trust the revolving groups of people (almost always women) she surrounded herself with. My mother chose to search for her truths in people and places, but I preferred to search for them in books.

But reading was only part of the thrill that a book represented. I got a dizzy pleasure from the weight and feel of a new book in my hand, a sensual delight from the smell and crispness of the pages. I loved the smoothness and bright colors of their jackets. For me, a stacked, unread pyramid of books was one of the sexiest architectural designs there was. Because what I loved most about books was their promise, the anticipation of what lay between the covers, waiting to be found.

Malcolm knew my passion very well. We met, after all, in the aisles of Blue Moon Books, the bookstore where I worked. I was immediately and embarrassingly attracted to him. He was extremely good looking—tall and tan with chiseled jaw and cheekbones—but there was something else about him that made me weak-kneed and fluttery and willing to drop all pretense of professionalism just to talk to him. He was a writer, I learned, which explained the depth of my instant crush on him. Malcolm was looking for a reference book that would help him get his novel published, so I pulled out several guides to literary agents and small publishers and went through every one of them with him, desperate to keep talking to him, about books, about his writing, and, not least, about whether or not he'd consider having coffee with me next door when I got my break.

"How is it you know so much about books?" Malcolm asked me when, to my trembling delight, he took me up on my offer. "Are you a writer?"

"Oh no," I told him, attempting to flip my hair in a sexy gesture without dragging it through my coffee. "That's not my thing at all."

"Really?" he said, nonplussed, raising one blond eyebrow. "Not even screenplays? Or poetry?"

"No, no," I said, giving him what I hoped was a beguiling half-smile, "I don't write at all. I *can* write, of course, if I have to. Like letters, and, um, I wrote papers in college, naturally, but, anything else, you know . . ."

It was a valid question. We were living near San Francisco, a city that seemed to contain, among many other things, a plethora of writers. To be more specific, I lived in Petaluma—the wrist-wrestling capital of the country—and Malcolm lived a little farther south, in Novato. For my mother, Petaluma had been at least three stops ago, but I'd come of age after we'd landed there and had just stayed. Despite the lack of panache our cities had, both Malcolm and I considered ourselves "Bay Area" denizens, although Petaluma, especially, was pretty far removed from the San Francisco Bay. Still, there were plenty of aspiring writers dotting my landscape. The ones I met came into Blue Moon, located in an otherwise bland strip mall in Corte Madera, searching for books on how to get into print and were usually doing something else to pay the rent. That "something" was often food service. Such was the case with Malcolm, as he went on to tell me, who waited tables in a high-end Marin County restaurant while he crafted his novel.

I was simply a book *lover,* I told Malcolm. I had no aspirations to write one myself. I was happy in my job as manager of Blue Moon Books, where I had unlimited access to the stuff of my addiction. I even liked Elise, the owner of the store, who paid me more than she could afford in order to keep me afloat and had always been more like a mentor and friend than a boss. Because I quickly developed a good sense of which books would sell well in the store, having read most of them, Elise had even put me in charge of buying for Blue Moon, a responsibility I truly enjoyed. I'd already been working at the bookstore for four years when I met Malcolm, but the job still felt as new and fresh as if I'd just started.

"It's like being a kid in a candy store," I told him.

Malcolm must have found this charming because, when we'd finished all the coffee we could hold and I reluctantly informed him that I'd have to get back to work, he asked if I'd like to continue our discussion over dinner. I couldn't believe my luck. The good-looking, confident guys never gravitated to me, especially not the guys who had Malcolm's level of sex appeal. It wasn't that I was unattractive myself. Although, like every woman, I found aspects of my face and body that are too long, short, wide, or narrow, I knew that I couldn't really complain. I'd even done some modeling, which had helped pay for college. So it wasn't my looks that turned off the self-assured, handsome men and drew in the socially insecure, less-than-anatomically-perfect, and vaguely desperate ones. There was something else about me, although I'd never been able to figure out what, that repelled men like Malcolm.

I'd complained about this to Elise on more than one occasion, most often after being hit on by dentally challenged musicians or would-be philosophers with marginal hygiene who'd wander into Blue Moon.

"You're easy to talk to, honey," Elise told me, after she finished laughing at my tales of woe. "And you don't have a bit of snobbishness about you."

"So that makes me a target?" I asked her.

"Not at all," Elise said. "These people—these guys—feel that they can trust you, open up to you. Hell, everyone opens up to you. That's how you can sell books that people didn't even know they wanted to read!"

"That's all well and good," I said, "but why can't a great-looking, successful guy open up to me, too?"

"Don't you worry, honey," Elise had assured me, "it will happen."

And, with Malcolm, it finally had.

It didn't take long for the two of us to become an item and for me to give Malcolm his own key to my apartment, which was where we ended up spending most of our time together. It was there, on the queen-size bed that took up the lion's share of my small studio, that we compared the notes of our days, where we shared our bodies and our dreams. Malcolm's dreams involved getting published and making it big as a novelist. My dreams mostly involved him. I wanted him to succeed as a writer as much as he did, and I was more than willing to support him in every way I could. If my social life was a bit limited (Malcolm made up most of it and Blue Moon accounted for the rest), I didn't mind. While I wasn't

and I regretted it almost immediately. My mother couldn't have cared less, for one thing, which completely undermined my purpose in getting it in the first place. I hated the way it looked for another thing and always ended up trying to cover it. Every time I looked at those wings I couldn't believe I'd been stupid enough to brand my own flesh.

Malcolm, however, thought my tattoo was cute—"Angel's wings," he called it—and made a point of kissing it whenever possible. "It's so conveniently located," he always said with a smile. But because we were usually in a state of undress when he delivered these kisses, I was usually focused on things other than my ill-advised tattoo.

My hair was another problem. Up or down? Barrette or free-flowing? At the best of times, I didn't know what to do with my wild mass of curls. It was a difficult color—mostly red, but with enough gold to allow me to classify it as *titian* when I was being both generous and literary about my appearance—and it fell halfway down my back. In the end, I twisted it into a librarian-type bun at the back of my head and hoped it didn't make me look too severe.

Makeup was an issue as well. I didn't wear much to begin with since, unlike many redheads, I had a smooth, almost olive, complexion, with eyelashes and brows that were dark enough not to need mascara. I searched through my pitiful supply of shadows and decided that none of them really matched the hazel of my eyes, the red of my hair, *and* the blue of my dress. I'd have to go bare, I thought, but made a vow to go shopping for both cosmetics and clothes if I got the job.

I was none too pleased with my last glance in the mirror. My legs looked overlong and pale under the dress, and my shoes were undeniably shabby. I didn't dare put on panty hose. Nobody wore panty hose anymore unless they were the thigh-high, my-boyfriend's-coming-over-with-a-bottle-of-champagne variety. And the shoes were just further proof that I'd gotten way too comfortable in jeans and sweaters and had smothered any kind of fashion sense I might have had. Overall, though, I was annoyed with myself for fussing so much over my appearance and didn't want to admit that I felt anything but supremely confident. Finally, I just ran out the door before I could change my mind about my hair, my outfit, or going to the interview at all.

As I drove in search of the office, which was nestled in the heart of lush, leafy, and very tony San Rafael, I tried to take my mind off my inadequacy by reviewing everything I knew about Lucy Fiamma and her agency.

Although I'd never met her, I'd heard enough about Lucy to feel like I knew her. Of course, I wasn't the only one who felt this way. Anyone who worked in any corner of the book business, from booksellers to aspiring writers, "knew" Lucy Fiamma in some fashion. At the very least, they knew her story.

Lucy had been a literary agent for a few years when she got the mother of all big breaks: the publication of *Cold!*, a memoir written by her client Karanuk, an Alaskan Inuit writer. *Cold!* described life in the dark frigidity of the Alaskan wilderness and went into detail about tribal customs and rituals. The emotional impact of the writing was intense, and Karanuk's descriptions were strikingly vivid. It was all those adjectives that reviewers fling around when they love a book: evocative, brilliant, riveting, powerful. For me, though, it was simply a *great* read. You couldn't help but feel the frost creep into your bones as you read through to the dramatic, chilling end. It was one of very few books I wanted to read again as soon as I finished it.

Karanuk and *Cold!* came out of nowhere (literally, in this case) and were a huge hit. There was nothing else out there like it. People who had never bought a book in their lives purchased a copy of *Cold!* At Blue Moon, I'd sell it to customers who claimed they hated reading, but just *had to have* this one. In addition to stirring up huge interest in the Inuit, Karanuk's book was the front-runner in what soon became a memoir craze. So many great books out there never get the kind of attention that *Cold!* did, so its success said quite a bit about what could happen when talent combined with luck. *Cold!* hit at exactly the right place at exactly the right time. The hardcover was on the *New York Times* bestseller list for two full years until the paperback took its place in permanent residence.

Naturally, *Cold!* found its way to Hollywood as well. The movie version won several Academy Awards, including Best Picture. Inevitably, a whole line of *Cold!*-inspired merchandise found its way to various outlets. There were *Cold!* dolls, *Cold!* fur hats, and even a *Cold!* line of frozen dinners. My personal favorite was the series of cruises around the Alaskan coast that promised glimpses of the scenery immortalized by the book. *Cold!* also became a required text in many university cultural studies classes.

But what made this appealing book even tastier was that the author was totally reclusive. He rarely gave interviews, and when he did, it was always to small, obscure newspapers or magazines. He almost never appeared in public, and the majority of his readers, myself included, had no idea what he looked like. The jacket photo on the original edition showed only a frigid landscape of snow, broken by a single stunted, leafless tree. There were no photos at all on subsequent editions. There was a big brouhaha at one point when Oprah picked *Cold!* for her famous book club and Karanuk turned down the invitation to appear on her show. Of course, unlike the other authors Oprah had selected, Karanuk hardly needed the sales or the publicity. The fact that he *wouldn't* make an appearance only added to his mystique.

After the Oprah incident, the one thing everyone wanted to know was when Karanuk was going to write the *next* book. I answered the same question at least once a week at Blue Moon:

"Say, you know that Alaska guy, Canoe? Kanuk? The *Cold!* guy? When are you going to get his next book?"

"As soon as he writes it," I always answered.

Lucy Fiamma was the woman behind Karanuk and his book. In various interviews, Lucy spun the tale of how she'd tirelessly shopped a partial manuscript of *Cold!* to disinterested publishers, meeting with a wall of rejections. "But I believed in it," Lucy was often quoted as saying, "so I never gave up." She'd finally convinced an associate editor at a small house to purchase the manuscript for "a song" with the promise that the finished book would be exquisitely written. A big publishing company bought the small house soon after and the associate editor was now one of its executive editors.

Unlike her author, Lucy Fiamma had no qualms about appearing in public. She accepted the ever-reclusive Karanuk's literary awards (of which there were several) on his behalf, always telling the same story of how she discovered her "frozen diamond in the rough."

After the huge success of *Cold!*, the Lucy Fiamma Literary Agency became one of the hottest spots for literary representation in the country, New York be damned. Despite the fact that her agency was located on the West Coast and not even *in* San Francisco proper, and that it wasn't attached to a larger well-established agency, Lucy Fiamma represented big-name authors from around the globe. Karanuk enabled Lucy to pick her shots, and according to *Publishers Weekly,* her books usually sold with big price tags attached. None of her books matched the success of *Cold!* (how could they?), but there were several best-sellers in the bunch and most of them were very well written. Still, and I'd always found this a little odd, few of Lucy's authors seemed to write more than one or two books before they faded from the literary landscape.

I'd gathered much of what I knew about Lucy Fiamma from Elise and from the various interviews I'd read, but also in a more personal way from Malcolm, who had submitted his manuscript to her agency several months earlier and was, for lack of a better word, a Lucy Fiamma groupie. He'd come over one night after work in a state of total agitation. Could I *believe* who had come in for dinner and sat at *his* table? he wanted to know. None other than Lucy Fiamma herself! They'd discussed writing, of course, because, well, he *had* to tell her he was a writer, didn't he, and she seemed so *nice* anyway, he didn't think it was a terrible imposition. She *loved* the title of his book, Malcolm stressed, and, could I believe it, she asked him to *send it in.*

I wasn't as starry-eyed as Malcolm—I'm not a writer, after all—but his excitement was infectious. I helped him create the "perfect" cover letter for his submission, gather clips of all his previous publications in little literary magazines, and put them together for maximum effect. Then there were five empty weeks while we waited for a response. Although Malcolm was quiet about it, I knew he was spinning scenarios of literary glory. As the days crawled by, I watched, pained, as his excitement turned to something much bleaker. Finally, a form letter appeared in the mail, tucked into the self-addressed stamped envelope that Malcolm had provided.

Although your novel shows much creativity and hard work, the letter began, *we regret that it does not meet our needs at this time and we are unable to accept it for representation. . . .*

At the bottom of the letter, there was a quickly scrawled line in blue ink.

Malcolm, it said, *you have a wonderful feel for setting, but your characters are flat! Work on the first 50 pp., try to get your reader <u>hooked!</u> Then I'd consider taking a 2nd look! LF.*

Malcolm held the letter in his hand for a long time, staring off into space while clouds of disappointment darkened his face. He was silent for so long, I started to get nervous and blurted out the first thing that came to mind.

"She uses a hell of a lot of exclamation points, doesn't she?"

Malcolm looked at me, a shadow of condescension crossing his features as if I had clearly missed the point. "She's right," he said. "The characters *are* flat. Very flat. Flatter than flat. I don't know how I didn't see it before. I'm going to rework it." He folded the letter and placed it carefully in his pocket. "She read it *herself,*" he said with more than a hint of awe in his voice.

Malcolm hadn't mentioned Lucy or her agency again until he cut out that want ad for me, but he'd been working on the manuscript like a demon. I knew none of its content aside from the title, *Bridge of Lies.* I was not allowed to read it until it was finished, Malcolm said, and I gladly went along because, although I hated to admit it, I was afraid. Afraid I would be disappointed. I'd read all of Malcolm's short stories and I liked them. But if I was totally honest with myself, I had to say that they were just okay. I'd started helping Malcolm with some of these stories, suggesting little revisions here and there, and he took well to my editorial comments. There was a lot of promise in Malcolm's writing and I could see that he was getting better. So I had every reason to believe that his novel represented a major breakthrough. I had every reason to believe it was *great.*

Thinking about Malcolm's novel gave me a twinge of doubt—the same twinge I'd felt when I'd first read the note he'd taped to the bathroom mirror. It didn't take a genius to figure out that Malcolm stood to gain by having me work for one of the best literary agents in the country.

He'd admitted as much, but he'd also pointed out that I hadn't given a whole lot of thought to developing a career, and that this job was an ideal place to start. He wasn't wrong about that—not by a long shot.

I forced my thoughts away from Malcolm and on to the road in front of me. I'd been driving for much longer than I should have been, considering the distance between my apartment and the office, and was starting to realize that Anna had given me plenty of unnecessary or incorrect information—the names of streets that were nowhere near where I needed to be, for example, and several left turns that should have been rights, or norths that should have been souths. If I had given myself only the half hour Anna told me it would take instead of the hour I'd neurotically opted for, I would definitely have been late. Finally, after doubling back at least twice, I found the famous Lucy Fiamma Literary Agency.

The office, as I'd been told, was an add-on to a spacious two-story home. About this, at least, Anna had been very clear. "Come around and park at the back entrance," she'd said. "The front door is to Lucy's house and you *cannot* go in there."

I felt a little like Alice in Wonderland, standing in front of the small white door, rubbing my sweaty palms on the sides of my dress, and waiting as one, two, three knocks went unanswered. I experienced a moment of total confusion before I turned the handle and just let myself in.

I was immediately surprised by the large size of the office. From the outside, it was impossible to gauge this breadth of space. Directly in front of me was a desk piled with papers of all kinds that looked to be the repository of all office items that didn't have a place. On my right, there were two more unattended desks in various states of disarray. One had the remnants of someone's lunch scattered across the surface and I could detect the smell of peanut butter. The other had several folders spread unevenly across the top. The fourth desk, to my left, which was the only tidy one in the room, was occupied by a dark-haired girl on the telephone, who jumped as I walked in and then motioned with her hand for me to stay where I was. From floor to ceiling, one entire wall of the office was taken up with books, all of which I assumed were titles sold by Lucy Fiamma. The whole room had a strange half-moon shape caused by the protrusion of a semicircular wall in the back. There was a closed door in the middle of this wall which, I assumed, led to Lucy's private office.

Frozen in place by the girl on the phone, I turned my attention to her end of the conversation.

"Yes, the first fifty pages," she was saying. "No, we don't need to see more than that." There was a long pause. "Well, five hundred pages is too much for us to read all at once. We'll be able to get an idea of the writing from the first fifty." Another pause. "No, she's not available at the moment, but I can tell you that she likes to have a look at the writing before she speaks to an author. No, we don't take e-mail submissions. Why don't you just send it in and— No, I'm sorry, she is *not* available." In the final pause that followed, her head sank lower and lower until it was almost resting on the desk. I could tell that she was being upbraided in a most pointed manner. The tirade on the other end continued for some time until, finally, she said, "Thank you, we'll look forward to reading it," and hung up.

She looked up at me then, an expression of abject despair on her face. The words *I hate my job* might as well have been printed on her forehead.

"Can I help you?" she said as she pulled herself out of her chair and walked over to me. She was painfully thin and the paleness of her skin made a stark contrast to the sheets of straight black hair that hung below her shoulders.

"I'm Angel Robinson. I'm here for an interview. I spoke to Anna on the phone. I'm sorry, are you Anna?"

"No," she said. Her wide gray eyes were too big for her face. Close up, they looked like windows onto a bleak, rainy day. I thought she might be older than I'd first guessed. Her skinny body was that of a little girl, but her face was lined and pinched.

"Anna's in the bathroom. She should be out in a minute. Do you want to sit down?"

I took a quick scan of the room and saw that there was no chair available that didn't belong to a desk. "I'm fine," I told her, wondering if she was going to offer her name. "Thank you, uh . . ."

"My name is Kel— I mean, Nora. My name is Nora."

"Okay," I said. "Thanks, Nora."

Kel-I-mean-Nora went back to her desk, where she busied herself pulling cards from three separate Rolodexes. I didn't know what to do with myself, so I stood there like a piece of driftwood for an uncomfortable minute or two until I heard a toilet flush somewhere out of sight and saw another young woman approach me.

"Hi, I'm Angel Robinson," I said, extending my hand. "Anna?"

"Yes, hi, nice to meet you," Anna said without taking my hand. Anna was the polar opposite of Nora. She was stocky and had bobbed blond hair tucked behind her ears and smallish, squinty blue eyes. Her cheeks seemed unnaturally flushed and she gasped a little, as if she were short of breath. She also had a rather unpleasant expression on her face that I put somewhere between petulance and condescension.

I noticed, with dismay, that both Anna and Nora were wearing jeans. Clearly, in spite of all that posturing in front of the mirror, I had overdressed.

"Lucy's in a meeting with Craig at the moment," Anna said, gesturing to the closed door in the middle of the round wall, "but she should be with you shortly. Why don't you sit down?"

It felt more like an order than a suggestion, so I backed myself into the chair belonging to the desk piled with the stacks of manuscripts. Anna hoisted herself onto the desk in front of me, her ample backside irretrievably crumpling several sheets of paper beneath it. One wrong move, I thought, and the whole show would topple to the carpet.

"So how did you hear about us?" she asked me. Something subtly different crept into her voice as she spoke. It sounded nasal and squeezed at the same time, as if she were trying to speak while someone sat on her stomach. It was slightly disconcerting.

"I saw the ad in the paper," I said. "But of course I've heard about Lucy Fiamma before. Who hasn't, right?"

"So you have experience in publishing?" Now there was a note of officiousness in her tone. I didn't like Anna already and I'd only known her for five minutes. Not a good sign, I told myself. I wasn't in the mood for what was turning into a pre-interview, so I answered her question with one of my own.

"Have you been working here long?"

"Yes, I've been here awhile already. About four or five months."

An intercom buzzed loudly on the desk and Anna leaned her entire body over the stacks of files to answer it, promptly knocking several piles to the floor.

"Yup," she said into the phone.

"Anna, am I going to get that subsidiary rights list today? These magazines are closing for the summer, you know." The voice sounded extremely unhappy. Anna's cheeks flushed crimson.

"I've got calls in," she said, "and I'm waiting for the copies to come back from Kinko's on the George manuscript and—"

"I don't want to hear excuses, Anna. Do I have to tell you how important subsidiary rights are? There's a reason we keep serial and audio rights, Anna. Not to mention *film*. Will the list be done today or not?"

"I don't think that's possible, Lucy."

"Then bring me what you've got now." The intercom disconnected with a loud click. Anna slid off the desk and stared down at the mess on the floor. She looked so miserable I jumped out of my seat and started gathering papers in an attempt to help her clean up.

"You don't have to do that," she snapped. "That was Lucy. I'll go tell her you're here."

I looked over at Nora as Anna stalked into Lucy's office, but she was steadfast in avoiding eye contact with me. Okay, I thought, so it's not exactly the welcome wagon around here. But I wasn't about to let it get me ruffled. They were obviously very busy and I was clearly an outsider. I heard the rise and dip of muffled voices coming from Lucy's office and then, unexpectedly, the sound of giggling. Anna reappeared, smiling but still ruddy. "You can go in now," she said.

Lucy Fiamma's office was unlike any I'd seen before. The circular room looked as if it had been designed with a specific purpose in mind, but I couldn't tell exactly what that purpose was. It was pristine, especially compared to the disarray of the outer office, without so much as a paper clip out of place. Adding to the overall effect of cleanliness and light was the fact that the entire room was done up in white, glass, and chrome. There was no window, but a generous amount of light streamed down from a large dome-shaped skylight cut out of the ceiling. The almost blinding whiteness of the wall, couch, chairs, and carpeting reminded me of something, an image just out of reach that I couldn't quite put my finger on.

"Welcome, Angel Robinson." Lucy Fiamma strode toward me and extended her hand. I noticed that her immaculately manicured fingernails were long, pointed, and ended with half moons of white polish. Her hand was small, soft, and very cold as I shook it. The rest of Lucy Fiamma was much more imposing. She was very tall, for one thing. I was five-four at last measure and Lucy towered over me by at least six inches. I had to look up to meet her smile. Her white-blond hair floated in a cloud around her face. It had the appearance of hair on which much time has been spent to create the impression of windblown effortlessness. She was wearing a peculiar combination of clothing: white capri pants, a lime green cable-knit sweater, and a red leather belt. The whole outfit was finished off with black leather flats. All the separate pieces were of very good quality, yet they were just wrong together. It was difficult for me to gauge Lucy's age; she had smooth, unlined skin, but her face had a vaguely unhealthy pallor as if she had just recovered from a nasty bout with the flu. Her mouth was big—or generous, if one wanted to be flattering about it—and filled with teeth that were on the large side, but, like everything else in her office, spotlessly white. Her eyes were laser green, with glittering gold flecks. I had no doubt she could speak volumes with the hypnotic stare she was fixing on me. All put together, Lucy was a striking woman, but there was something both unconventional and overwhelming about her looks. Perhaps it was the palpable sense of power that emanated from her, washing over me so completely that for a moment, I felt as if I were drowning in her presence.

"I'm so pleased to meet you," I said. "I've heard so much about you."

"Well, it can't have been too bad," she said, laughing, "or you wouldn't be here, would you? This is Craig Johnson, my right-hand man and the voice of reason in this office."

I hadn't even been aware of Craig's presence until Lucy introduced him. He was fairly easy to miss, so fair and slight he practically faded into the wall behind him. Craig looked as if he hadn't had a decent meal or a good night's sleep for some time. His eyes were sad and brown and his clothes hung lifelessly from his bony frame. So I was shocked when he said, "Nice to meet you, Angel," in a rumbling baritone. Craig had a radio star voice trapped in a milquetoast body. Just one more in a growing list of peculiarities here, I thought.

"Well, why don't we sit down and get started?" Lucy said, gesturing for me to sit on the couch. Craig positioned himself on a chair next to me, holding a legal pad on his lap. Lucy sat down next to me, so close our knees were almost touching, holding a small pad of her own.

"Now, where's your résumé?" she said to nobody in particular. "Nora!" she yelled toward the door. "Can I have this woman's résumé please?"

Nora appeared at the door and said, "It's on your desk, Lucy."

"It most certainly is not."

Nora shuffled over to Lucy's oversize glass desk, removed a sheet of paper, which I immediately recognized as my résumé, and handed it to Lucy.

"Nora, it would help me a great deal if you didn't *hide* these things, don't you think?" Lucy said. Nora simply sighed and left the room.

"Okay," Lucy began, "Angel Robinson. What a name! Surely that's not your real name. You must have changed it, yes?"

"No, no, that's my real name. From birth."

"Then maybe you *ought* to change it. I mean, *Angel* of all things. Quite a title to live up to, I'd think."

"Well, my mother . . . She saw me as her little angel, she said, when I was born, and so she thought, I mean . . ." I trailed off into an awkward silence. The truth was, I'd always been embarrassed by my name. It didn't help that the mega-bestselling book *Freakonomics* listed Angel as the number one "white girl" name that best indicated parents who were uneducated. I hoped Lucy hadn't read *Freakonomics* and resisted the urge to wipe my hands on my dress. My palms were slick with sweat and I could feel the prickle of perspiration on my lower back.

"Names are very important," Craig said suddenly. Again, I was startled to hear such a deep, sensual voice coming out of such a mouse of a man. I didn't know if I'd be able to get used to it. "My wife decided to hyphenate our names so that she could keep her own identity," he added.

"Hyphens are even worse," Lucy said dismissively, and then stopped short as if something important had just occurred to her. "Do you have a *husband*?" she asked me, her tone making *husband* sound a lot like *herpes*.

"No, no. I mean, I have a boyfriend—fiancé, actually—and he . . ." He what? I cursed myself. Is writing a book? Would love to be represented by you? How was it possible that I had spoken no more than a handful of words and was already in such a deep hole? And why had I referred to Malcolm as my fiancé? The two of us hadn't even come close to making any official plans to wed.

"Are you planning to get married sometime soon, then?" Lucy asked. "I mean, I'd hate to offer you a position and then have you disappear on a honeymoon or something. Or get pregnant. You're not planning *babies*, are you? Little Angels, as it were? Because we can stop right here if you are and not waste any more time. Time is money here and I don't have nearly enough of it to squander."

"Actually, we haven't really set a date." I could hear my own voice getting smaller in my throat. "And I haven't even begun to think about children."

"Good," Lucy said, "because this is an extremely busy office, and while I don't expect my employees to work twenty-four hours a day, there will be plenty of reading to do outside of the office and occasions when you may have to come in early or stay late. And as my assistant—" Lucy stopped herself short, her eyes narrowing, a new question working its way to her lips. "You understand that this position is that of *my assistant*?"

"Yes, of course," I said, but I was confused by her emphasis.

"Because if you are thinking of being hired as an *agent,* we should probably terminate this interview immediately."

"Oh no," I rushed to assure her, "I understand the position. And I'm not interested in agenting." I gave Lucy a broad smile to underscore my words, but I questioned, if only for a fraction of a second, just how truthful they were. *Would* I be interested in being an agent myself? Who knew? I hadn't even seen it as a possibility until that moment. I was surprised, and maybe even a little intrigued, that Lucy had. But no, I thought again, I could never—

"Good," Lucy said, drilling me with her laser eyes.

Nora entered the room once more. "Lucy," she said, "Natalie Weinstein's on line two for you."

"I have to take this," Lucy said, leaping from the couch. "This is a *very* important editor. I've been waiting for this offer."

Craig rose from his seat in tandem. "I'm going to make a couple of calls while you get this," he said. "I'll be back in a few."

"Fine, go, go," Lucy said. "You can make yourself comfortable, Angel. Have a look at all of our books." She made a sweeping gesture at the room around us and then sat down at her desk to take the call.

"Natalie, my dear," she began, "are we in business on this delicious book? I'd love to tell the author that you have won the prize. . . ."

My head had started to buzz and I found myself unable to focus on Lucy's conversation. I felt my interview had started badly, but I couldn't explain why. I distracted myself by looking around the room. There was a display on my left, a virtual shrine to Karanuk that I hadn't noticed earlier. Nestled between various animal pelts and a costume I assumed was native Alaskan garb was every edition of *Cold!* in print. Beside all the English editions in hardcover and paperback there were two shelves of foreign editions. I studied the spines for title changes. *Fa Freddo!* screamed the Italian title in red. The French copy was much quieter. *Le Froid,* it said in beige lettering. There was no exclamation point.

"No, it's certainly not a bad offer," Lucy was saying, "but this payout schedule is simply not going to work. Frankly, the author's no spring chicken, if you know what I mean. Is she going to live long enough to get this money? I can't say." Lucy flashed me a toothy grin. I smiled back and turned my head, afraid to be caught eavesdropping, even though she was clearly speaking loud enough for me to hear every word. But some poor writer's fate was hanging on the outcome of this conversation and it just seemed wrong for me to know how it would all turn out before the writer did.

"No, I'm not implying that she's ill," Lucy went on. "What I'm saying is that we might *all* be dead by the time this advance is paid out."

I turned my attention to another shelf of books. A slim volume caught my eye. I recognized it immediately as *Long Shadows,* the one book I'd always said I'd want with me on a deserted island. It was a short but densely written novel about three generations of women who were all writers. Through the different voices of her characters, the author gave a layered, intricate account of women, history, and the writing process. I'd first read it in college and still kept my copy where I could reach it easily, just to thumb through it. It was the author's first and only book. I reached over, almost involuntarily, pulled the book from the shelf, and felt its compact weight in my hand. I let out a breath I didn't realize I'd been holding and got a little light-headed.

I knew then that Malcolm was absolutely right about this being the perfect job for me. The author's mind was certainly where the seeds for great books germinated, but this was the place where they began to bear fruit. Without this agency, who knew how many books would have remained out of sight forever. I replaced the book on the shelf and realized that I really wanted this job. I'd been detached, even equivocal, when I'd first walked in the door, but after being surrounded by this flurry of literary activity for only a few minutes, I couldn't stop the flush of excitement from overtaking me. I wanted this job so badly I could feel my fingertips tingling with desire for it. I wanted—no, I *needed* Lucy Fiamma to hire me, and I scrambled frantically to come up with ways I could convince her to do just that.

Lucy was off the phone. "I see you've been admiring some of our books," she said.

"Oh yes," I said. "*Long Shadows* is one of my all-time favorites. I *love* that book."

"Yes, that was a good one," Lucy said. "One of my first. It's a pity the author only had that one in her." She gave an exaggerated shrug. "And of course you've read *Cold!*?"

"Oh, of course. It's a brilliant book," I said. "But you must know that," I added.

"Hmm," Lucy said, and rose from her desk. "Let me tell you a little publishing story, Angel. Since we're discussing brilliance. Of course, *Cold!* is a phenomenal book, no question, and would have done well regardless. But do you know what really made that book work? In terms of *market*?"

Several possible answers raced through my brain, but I settled for silence.

"What did it, I mean *really* did it, was the exclamation point on the title," Lucy said triumphantly. "And *I* am the one who put that exclamation point there. Indeed." There was a new note in her voice, something like, if this were possible, flirtatiousness. I was dumbfounded as to how to respond, but had developed an instant understanding of her fondness for exclamation points. I smiled like an idiot.

"Right," she said briskly, as if snapping out of a trance, "let's get down to this. I'm really running short on time now." She sat down on the couch and patted the space beside her. "I've looked over your résumé and your experience looks pretty good, but my concern is that you haven't had any direct experience in publishing."

"Yes, but I—"

"Which could actually work in your favor," she interrupted. "It means you have no preconceived notions about how things should work. Am I correct?"

I nodded mutely.

"Of course, in terms of *salary*, I'd have to take your limited experience into consideration. I'm sure you can understand. But let's discuss salary later, shall we?"

I couldn't figure out if Lucy meant that to be a rhetorical question, so, again, I just kept my mouth shut.

"I should let you know that this will be a very different environment than Blue Moon. As you've seen, we are very busy here. So you think you'd be able to juggle several tasks at once? Are you prone to feeling overloaded?"

"Oh no, I—"

"Well, let me ask you this. Say you're sitting here, answering the phone, and you get two calls at once. One is an associate editor at a small publisher you've never heard of who just wants to touch base with me. The other is an author whose book I'm about to sell. Say it's *Karanuk,* for example. Who do you put through to me and what do you say to the other one?"

I hesitated, unable to solve this Sphinx-like riddle with any kind of ease.

"Hurry!" she said. "You're not going to have time to mull this decision with two lines blinking."

"I put Karanuk through to you and let you know that the editor is on the other line," I said quickly. "Then I tell the editor that you'll be with her—or him—shortly."

Lucy smiled again, showing all her gleaming teeth. I exhaled and felt my shoulders relax a little, confident that I'd given the right answer.

"Wrong!" she said. "*Always* put an editor through first, no matter how small. That's where the money is. Without publishers, we have no business. That small-time editor could be a big-time publisher tomorrow. It's happened before and it will happen again."

"Oh," was all I could think to say.

"But you're obviously an author advocate. That's very sweet."

Craig had come back into the room in the middle of this interchange and seated himself with his pad once again. The two of them proceeded to ask me a series of questions, all of which seemed more or less standard, considering the position. Which books were my favorites? Why? Which popular books hadn't I liked? Why? What had I learned about publishing trends from my work at Blue Moon? How fast and how accurately could I read?

I answered all their questions with responses I'd prepared ahead of time, but part of me was removed from the interview and watching in dismay. I was quite sure I'd blown my chances with my answer to Lucy's editor/author question.

"Now . . . *Angel*," Lucy said, my name seeming to stick in her throat before she forced it out, "I must, of course, ask you why you've decided to leave Blue Moon. Doesn't Elise treat you well?"

"Oh no, it's not that at all," I said quickly. "Elise is wonderful! But she's closing the store." I felt a pang of sadness just saying it out loud. "I guess you didn't know."

"What a shame," Lucy said, shaking her head. "Although I've often told her she needed to do more to keep up with the big boys. Too idealistic—that's Elise's problem. What a pity."

"Yes," I said, "it's a real—"

"We could talk all day, I'm sure," Lucy interrupted, rising to her feet, "but I've really got to get back on the phone, and I have several other candidates to interview today. Really, we've had an overwhelming response from that ad, haven't we, Craig?"

"Overwhelming," Craig rumbled.

"What I'd like to do is to get your take on a couple of manuscripts," Lucy said. "Why don't you have Nora give you some things from today's mail and also something that we're working on now? She can give you the George proposal. I think that one would be good. You can drop off your notes if you like or fax them in. We'll talk again after that. How does that sound?"

"Great," I said, and shook her hand once more. "Thank you so much."

"Just one more question," Lucy said. "You're not a *writer*, are you? There's no place for writers here."

My mind stumbled over the irony of that statement while my mouth started forming an answer, but Lucy interrupted me once more. "I *have* made the mistake of hiring writers before. It doesn't work." She shuddered, as if remembering a bad dream. "We represent writers here, we don't create them. Is that clear?"

I had no difficulty responding this time. Of all the questions Lucy had asked me, this one had the surest answer.

"I have no talent for writing," I told her. "Reading is my passion." I thought about Malcolm and felt strangely guilty, as if I was somehow betraying him and lying to Lucy at the same time.

"Good, good," Lucy said, ushering me to the door. "What do you think of my office, by the way? Do you think you could be comfortable working in such a beautiful environment?"

"It's fantastic," I said, and as soon as the words were out of my mouth, I realized what her office reminded me of, the image that had been nagging for definition at the back of my mind. Lucy Fiamma's office was very much like an igloo.

AT THE SOUND OF Lucy's door shutting against my sweat-damp back, Nora and Anna simultaneously swiveled their heads in my direction. Nora looked completely wretched. Anna simply looked annoyed. Both of them raised their eyebrows, forming two sets of inverted parentheses, as if to ask me what the hell I wanted *now*. Standing next to Anna was a tall blond woman wearing a tailored gray suit and clutching a briefcase in one hand. She was, I assumed, the next "candidate" scheduled to interview with Lucy. She gave me a quick, questioning look as if to ask me what to expect, but I looked right past her. I meant to get this job and I wasn't about to offer someone else any help to take it from me, even if that help came from a simple smile. I turned toward Nora.

"Um . . . I . . . Lucy . . ." I drew back some of the oxygen that seemed to have been sucked out of my lungs and started again. "Lucy asked if you could give me some manuscripts from today's mail and the . . . um . . . the George proposal?"

Nora slid out from behind her desk and began riffling through a mail tub full of manuscripts. Anna got up as well, only to sit down again on the edge of the same desk she'd wrecked before. Both of them seemed to be intent on completely ignoring the woman in the gray suit.

"Guess it went okay in there?" Anna inclined her head toward Lucy's office. I smiled at Anna as politely as I could and hoped that would suffice as a response to the nosy question I had no intention of answering.

"This'd be your desk, you know," Anna said, patting the papers underneath her rump. "It's the closest one to her."

"Right," I said. "That makes sense." I looked away from Anna for a moment, not wanting to brand the image of her backside spilling onto the desk. If I managed to get the job, it wasn't a vision I'd want every time I reached for a Post-it.

"Does she want you to write notes? On the manuscripts?" Anna asked.

"Yes, that's what she said. And I'll fax them in."

"Do you know how to do that?"

"How to fax?"

"No, how to write a report."

"Oh. Well, I—"

"Make sure you put your name on it and the author's name. And what the genre is. The genre's very important."

"Okay," I said. "Thanks."

Anna turned toward Nora. "Don't forget to give her the George proposal, Kelly," she said.

Kelly? Who was Kelly?

"I'm sorry," I said to Nora/Kelly, "did I get your name wrong? I thought it was Nora?"

Nora/Kelly sighed heavily.

"It's my mistake," Anna said, an air of smugness hanging around her like a low cloud. "Her real name's Kelly, but we call her Nora. Lucy feels that Nora is a better name for her. So she's Nora here. Sometimes I forget. Sorry." Although she clearly wasn't sorry at all.

"I understand," I said, although I didn't.

Nora/Kelly looked at me as if she'd like to vaporize me on the spot. "Here are a few random manuscripts from today," she said through gritted teeth, "and here's a copy of the George proposal." She shot a poisonous glance in Anna's direction. "You should keep them separate. You can give me a call before you fax them in. Or you can drop them off. But we'll need them back pretty soon." I could tell she'd delivered this drill before. The phones were ringing and Anna had managed, once again, to vanish.

"I have to get that," Nora/Kelly said. "Nice to meet you," she added, and turned her attention to the phone.

"Um, excuse me?" I heard the gray-suit-woman say. "I have an appointment?" As I walked past her to leave, I thought I could see desperation flicker across her face.

When I opened the door and let myself out, the glare of daylight hurt my eyes. I hadn't realized how muted the light had been inside the office, even with all that whiteness. I felt weak and a little dizzy. A headache was starting to throb at the back of my skull. I clutched the manuscripts under one arm and my purse under the other and headed for my car, stumbling in the brightness like a drunk.

Lucy Fiamma
Lucy Fiamma Literary Agency

Dear Lucy,

I don't know if you remember me, but I came to the seminar you gave ten years ago at the college in San Francisco. Anyway, I'm writing to you because I have written a memoir and I would like you to represent it.

The book is about me and my cat, Hairy, and the years we spent together, developing recipes. This may sound odd, but my cat spoke to me and told me what ingredients to use and then we made the dishes. Since he doesn't have hands, I do most of the cooking, but he stands right there on the counter as we work. Together we developed many amazing recipes and stories. So I guess this is sort of a memoir/cookbook.

I am enclosing one of the best recipes here for you to look at. The manuscript is completed (it is 527 pages long) and I can send it to you right away.

I look forward to hearing from you.

Sincerely,
Clara Reynolds

Hairy Mac and Cheese

½ cup macaroni (cooked)

3 cups heavy cream

1 can Tuna

1 cup buttermilk

1 cup 2% milk

4 tbsp. melted butter

Combine ingredients in large skillet.

Sautee at medium-high heat for 20 minutes.

Serve hot!

Lucy Fimma Agency

Att: Lucy Fimma

Dear Ms. Fimma,

I am writing as to inquiry on my fiction book manuscript entitled ONE DARK NIGHT. This is a mystery thriller set in modern times but has an antiquity feeling.

I am looking for an agent to sell this book to publishers and I have read in the guide to literary agents that you have sold books of this type.

I am enclosing the first fifty (50) pages of the book for you to read and a self-addressed-stamped-envelope.

I have also sent this letter and the manuscript to ten other agents.

Thank you,

Robert Brownering

ONE DARK NIGHT

Chapter 1

It was windy a dark night raining. The street was quite for now except for the cars that drove down it no one ever saw the body lying under the curb. He body was dressed ornately because in the subsequent years before this happened he had made a lot of money selling Memberships in a Secret Society sort of like Insurance Salesmen but with riddles. Now he was shot through the heart once there was a brown ring around the wound with silvery dust on the edges. The second clue was the stream of blue ink that was running from his pocket into the storm gutter. The ink forbore to slowly trickle with alacrity across the dry cobblestones.

Above the street where the dead man laid was a late nite restaurant that served all the usual victuals to those who crept through its walls in the deepening hours that raced by in the dead of night. Two people were seated at the counter in the yellow glow. They looked a lot like that famous Hooper print from the 1920s The one person was a Cop and the other was a hooker prostitute, "Why don't I give you a ride home?" the Cop asked the prostitute by the name of Sadie who told him "I don't need a ride of the kind your going to give me."

They walked slowly outside into the warm dry night. The Cop looked into Sadie's eyes were rich in opaqueness the color of coffee. He thought she was beautiful so he didn't notice that as they exited the restaurant he stepped right over an important Clue to what would become the greatest act of subversion and to-

TWO

Lucy Fiamma
Lucy Fiamma Literary Agency
RE: PARCO LAMBRO (book proposal)

Dear Ms. Fiamma,

I am a well known Italian pastry chef living in San Francisco. I have been in this country since the age of 22 and I have taught myself English from reading books. The best books I have read are represented by you, especially *Cold!* by Karanuk. That book made a very big impression on me and it also made me realize that one man's story can be understood and felt by many, even if the experience of the man is new to most people. I, too, have a story to tell and this is why I am writing to you. I was a heroin addict for many years before I left my country. Heroin was a very big problem for young people in Italy in the 1970s and it probably still is. I had a group of friends I spent time with during these years and we hung out together in a park called Parco Lambro in Milano. I was able to quit, but I had to leave my home to do so. My friends were not so lucky. Many bad things have happened to them since then. My story is about the years I spent in the Parco Lambro and about my friends. It is also about how I managed to give up the drug and become successful here in America. It is a memoir. I am enclosing some pages from the book for you to read. I have never written anything before, but this story is from my heart. I have come to you because I know what good work you do and because Fiamma is an Italian name. I know that you will understand what I am trying to say.

Sincerely,
Damiano Vero

PARCO LAMBRO

By Damiano Vero

Everywhere there are lemons. Yellow rinds of lemons, old and new, rotting and fresh. Yellow pulp of lemons shining brightly on the green grass of the park. We need this fruit to clean our stuff. We only use the juice. Sometimes tourists come here and walk around, lost. They come with cameras in their hands and new shoes on their feet, looking for a photograph. They are confused by all the half-lemons squeezed out and left in the sun. If they look closer, they see more. Drinking fountains stained red with blood and the crunch of needles under feet, poking through the grass like an apocalyptic crop. This is when they leave the park, and maybe Italy too.

"We had a terrible time in that city," they will say when they return home. "It was not at all like the travel brochures say. You can't imagine what we found in this park."

There are no strangers in the park today. We are here today as we are every day. We are sitting and standing and lying where we fall. Now we are gathered together in a loose knot, looking over the still body of a young man who has collapsed on the ground. We've dragged him to a shady place under a tree and he lies there, unconscious. His face is beginning to turn the blue color of death. He is Luigi, our friend. We whisper over him and sway a little. Our voices swim slowly through the air, coming up from the bottom of a narcotic lake. We are trying to decide if Luigi wants to be saved. Soon he will be dead.

Soon is a changing concept in the park. Time is stretched differently here. It is elastic and free with a carnival shape. I have to sit down. The wet summer air is heavy with the sharp smell of lemons and it washes me down to the ground. I see someone moving towards Luigi, giving him something. But my eyes are closing and everything is moving very slowly. I can't tell what is happening. The sun is red and yellow behind my lids. I am warm for the first time in days.

When I open my eyes again, Luigi is sitting up, awake and angry. He wants to know who has come to his rescue and why?

"You ruined my high," he says. "Do you know how expensive that stuff was?"

Nobody speaks. The colors around me get brighter and then fade away. Green grass, blue sky, yellow lemons. This is our postcard from Italy.

FAX: 1 of 2
TO: Lucy Fiamma
FROM: Angel Robinson
RE: Reader Reports

Dear Lucy:

I enjoyed meeting with you yesterday and very much appreciate the opportunity to interview for a position in your agency. I have prepared reader's reports for the manuscripts that Nora gave me and plan to drop those off at your office by the end of the day. However, I thought I would fax the following report to you now, as I think this particular manuscript has some spectacular writing and shows a tremendous amount of potential.

I look forward to speaking with you soon.

With best wishes,
Angel Robinson

Title: PARCO LAMBRO
Author: Damiano Vero
Genre: Memoir
Reader: Angel Robinson

Author is Italian, living in S.F., and works as a pastry chef. This is his first book and he has no previous publishing credits. The story is a memoir about the author's struggle with heroin addiction in Milan in the 1970s. He goes on to describe how he overcame this addiction when he moved to the U.S. I believe there's much to recommend here. The author has an interesting way with language, which probably comes from his own internal translation of English. The pages we have here are very moody. The book opens with a gripping scene from the park of the title and goes on to describe the daily "habits" of the author and his group of friends; how they managed to support their addictions by stealing, etc. There are some great descriptions of Milan, and the author's struggles are related in a very compelling way. It's a sad story in many ways and definitely not how we Americans think of Italians. However, the second half of the story (at least how the author has described it) is much more hopeful—his hard-won success in this country, his efforts to help the friends he left behind, and so on. I think the writing is just great (I was hooked from the first sentence and didn't want it to end) and I also think it would have excellent market appeal for all the reasons listed above. I'd give it a strong recommendation.

I BEGAN MY JOB as assistant to Lucy Fiamma on Monday morning, five days after my interview with her. I walked into the office that day armed with nothing thicker or more durable than a sense of trepidation and the small cappuccino I'd purchased at the Peet's conveniently located less than five minutes from Lucy's office. I must have looked anxious because the girl making my coffee asked me twice if I wanted decaf and seemed almost troubled when I told her I had to have regular.

As I clutched my extra-foam cappuccino and made my way to my desk for the first time, I realized I had no idea whether it had been my interview, my reader's reports, or sheer desperation on Lucy's part that had convinced her to hire me. Anna had been the one to call me to tell me I'd gotten the job and that I should plan to start immediately. I hadn't even spoken to Lucy herself since the interview. I hovered over my paper-strewn desk for a moment and decided that it didn't matter. The job was mine and it started now.

"Hi, Angel!"

I turned toward Nora/Kelly, who, after a full five minutes, had finally noticed my presence in the office.

"Good morning," I said, infusing my words with as much perkiness as possible.

"How are you?" Nora/Kelly sounded almost hysterically glad to see me. She also looked hungrier than the last time I'd seen her.

"Fine, thanks. I'm ready to go. Is Lucy here?"

"She's on the phone, but she left a note for you on your desk."

"Okaaaay," I said, wondering how in the hell I was going to find a note from Lucy in that disorganized horror. Nora/Kelly returned her gaze to her own meticulously neat desk once again and started fiddling with loose Rolodex cards. Our moment of girlfriend-bonding was clearly over. I touched the edges of the files stacked highest on my desk. I had absolutely no idea what I was supposed to do with them or where they were supposed to go. I needed help. "Say, Kel— Nora, could you help me sort this a little?"

"I'm really busy right now," she said. "Lucy left you a note. And Anna will train you when she gets here."

"Great, thanks."

"And can you please just call me Nora? I'm Nora here, okay?"

"Okay, Nora."

Lucy had, indeed, left me a note. It was lying on the seat of my chair for lack of available desk space. I almost sat on it.

> *Welcome, Angel!!!! We're all so happy to have you on board! Your 1ˢᵗ task will be to sort through the papers on your desk and file them accordingly. Please try to have this done by noon. Anna is overloaded at the moment, but I've asked her to help you in this interim period. Try to use her as little as possible, though, and rely on your own smarts and organizational abilities to get started. I'd also like you to start making phone calls for me as soon as possible!!! Remember, NY is three hours ahead of us, so we need to make those calls by 2pm!! Anna can show you where my call list resides on the computer and I'll expect you to update it as per my notes. As everyone can tell you, the phone is the <u>lifeline</u> of this office, so please keep your calls as brief as possible and limit personal calls to <u>EMERGENCIES ONLY</u>!!! Your 3ʳᵈ assignment is to sort through last week's rejections and get them sent back to the authors as quickly as possible. And at some point today, I'd like to discuss your notes on the Italian book. Again, WELCOME!!!   —L.*

I made a place for myself on the chair and began sifting through the files. I stole a glance at Nora, who was busy trying to look as if she wasn't looking at me. The phone was ringing. It shrilled three times before Nora said, "You need to answer that. Lucy wants *you* to answer the phones first. Just remember, don't put anyone through to her unless it's someone she wants to speak to."

And how, exactly, was I supposed to know who she wanted to speak to? I gave Nora a look that I hoped would wither her and picked up the phone.

"Good morning," I said, "Lucy Fiamma Lit—"

"Is she there?" a tired man's voice interrupted.

"Ms. Fiamma is on another line at the moment," I said. "May I ask who's calling, please?"

"Who is *this*?" Now he sounded irritated as well as tired.

"This is Angel Robinson. I'm Ms. Fiamma's new assistant."

"Another one," he muttered. "Help me . . . How long have you been there, five minutes?"

I looked at my watch. "That's about right," I chirped. "May I ask who's calling, please?"

"This," he said, "is Gordon Hart. Of HartHouse Publishers. I am assuming you've heard of us?"

"Oh shit," I said, before I could stop myself. My first call was the head of one of the most well-respected publishers in the country. I bit my lip hard, hoping he hadn't heard.

"I take it you have," he said, and there was a smile in his voice. Lucky for me. "If it's not too much trouble," he continued, "would you mind very much putting *Ms. Fiamma* on the phone? No, no, on second thought, don't bother. Just tell her I won't be able to give her a decision today. She'll know what I mean. Thank you, good-bye." He hung up loudly in my ear and I felt a little sick.

"Who was that?" Nora asked.

"Gordon Hart," I said miserably.

"Oh my God!" Nora squealed. "Why didn't you put him through?"

"He didn't want me to."

"No, no, you've got to put *him* through. Don't you know that? You've got to go tell her. Go now, quickly!" Nora waved her skinny arms around wildly. She looked like an infuriated mouse. I couldn't tell how much of her hostility was pure bitchery and how much was self-protection, but I made a mental note to sort it out as soon as possible.

I had fever sweats and a hammering heart as I knocked on the door to Lucy's office. Craig opened the door a crack and leaned his face out. He looked flushed and disheveled, as if he'd been wrestling with something. "Don't knock," he said. "Use the intercom in the future." There was that teen idol voice again. If you put a large bag over Craig's head, I thought, he'd be utterly irresistible.

"I have a message for Lucy," I said, and Craig ushered me in. Lucy was sitting behind her desk, talking on the phone, and gave me a broad smile as I walked in. She was dressed in a blood-colored pantsuit with shoes to match. Her wild hair was restrained in a small knot at the back of her head. A large pendant, which looked very much like an amulet with a crimson stone in its center, hung from her neck. She gestured for me to come sit in a chair opposite her.

"Yes, my dear," she was saying, "I understand how traumatic this surgery can be, but at least you'll have one kidney left, won't you? And think of it this way, for a couple of days you'll have no kids to distract you. And you can take your laptop with you—get a little writing done. You are due to deliver your first draft, you know. What do you think?" She paused for the response, her mouth turning down as she heard it. "But the anesthesia is a small part of the process," she went on. I could hear an indignant voice on the other end of the phone rise by several decibels and Lucy looked at me, rolling her eyes. She covered the mouthpiece with one hand and as the voice ranted on she said, "What is it, Angel? Why are you sitting here?"

"Gordon Hart called," I whispered. Lucy's expression changed abruptly to one of sharp concern.

"Why didn't you tell me?" she hissed, and uncovered the mouthpiece. "Listen, Lorraine, I have to go now. We'll speak later. No, Lorraine, I can't, I've got one of the most important men in publishing waiting to talk to me. Bye." She hung up and turned to me. "What line is he on?" she asked, scanning the lines, none of which were lit or blinking.

"He's not on the line. He left a message."

"You *let him off the phone*? Why? Do you know how important he is?" She stood up and held her considerable height over me. Flanked against all the white of her office, she looked like a large, open wound. She seemed so angry that for a paranoid second I thought she was going to slap me. "Get him on the phone. Now," she said through clenched teeth.

"He said that he won't be able to give you a decision today," I said breathlessly.

"Just get him on the phone," she repeated. "We'll talk about this later."

I felt myself skipping out of Lucy's office as if the soles of my feet were burning. On my way out, I caught a glimpse of Craig's expression. It was one of amused pity.

I walked-ran over to my desk and picked up the receiver on my phone, only to realize that I was completely clueless as to where to find Gordon Hart's phone number, or *any* phone number, for that matter. I searched my desk, looking for a Rolodex, and found nothing. I did, however, manage to sweep several piles of paper to the floor, spilling what I could only assume were vital documents. My intercom flashed and screamed.

"Angel. Get Gordon Hart. On the line. Now." Lucy's angry voice penetrated my marrow. The useless and unwelcome thought that I was going to have to buy a better deodorant skipped across my brain.

"Uh, yes, I . . . just one moment, please." I brushed some more papers out of my way. "Say, Nora, could you maybe help me find the phone number for—"

"I'm really busy," Nora said, sighing. "But you might want to try turning on your computer. All the phone numbers are listed in the database."

I gave her a look of disbelief. I hadn't even seen the computer behind the reams of paper. Surely she had the number in one of the Rolodexes she was so intent on searching. I couldn't imagine why she wouldn't give it to me.

"Angel!" Lucy's voice shouted through my intercom once more. "I can't talk to Gordon Hart now. If you've got him on the line, tell him I'll get back to him."

As she finished this pronouncement, the phone started ringing again.

"You should get that," Nora said. "Lucy wants *you* to answer the phone."

"I know," I snapped. "Thanks for your help."

"Huh!" Nora favored me with a look of pure indignation and reached below her desk for something unseen. For a moment, I was sure she was going to pull out some sort of weapon, but instead it was a box of Slender-Aid diet protein powder, which she opened and proceeded to eat dry, with a spoon. I picked up the phone.

"Good morning, Lucy Fiamma Literary Agency."

There was a long pause on the other end of the line, punctuated by what sounded like heavy breathing. I tried again. "Lucy Fiamma Literary Agency. Hello?"

"Yes," a man's voice (and a smoker by the sound of it) finally spoke. "Lucy Fiamma, please."

"I'm sorry, she's on another line at the moment, can I help you?"

"She's reviewing my work," he said, "and I'd like to know when we'll be able to discuss it."

"Certainly," I said. "May I have your name, please?"

"Peter Johnson," he said. Proudly, I thought.

"Please hold," I said, and put him in limbo. "Nora?" I couldn't help myself, I needed her. "Peter Johnson's on the line. Should I—"

"He calls every day," Nora said, sniffing over her protein powder. "We keep rejecting him but he never goes away. His manuscripts stink of cigarettes. Ugh. He should really quit." Two other lines began ringing simultaneously. "You'd better get those," Nora said. "Lucy wants you—"

I punched Line 2. "Lucy Fiamma Literary Ag—"

"This is Lorraine. I need to talk to her now, please. Don't tell me she's on another line." Lorraine sounded as if she were weeping.

"Okay, please hold, Lorraine."

I punched Line 3. "Lucy Fiamma Agency."

"Yes, this is Fabio and I'm calling to confirm Ms. Fiamma's dinner reservations for this evening at Baciare Ristorante?"

"Please hold."

I stared at the three blinking lines in total dismay. The obvious choice was to put Lorraine (whom I assumed was the same Lorraine Lucy had been instructing to write through anesthesia) through to Lucy, but I was rapidly learning that the obvious choice wasn't necessarily the right one in this office. Occam's razor was turned on its ear here. I took a chance anyway and buzzed Lucy.

"Yes?" she said.

"Hi, Lucy, I've got Lorraine on Line 2 and Fabio from Baciare on Line 3?"

"Fabio!" she exclaimed. "Put him through."

Right. Fabio went to Lucy and I punched Line 2, dreading the conversation I was about to have with the weepy Lorraine.

"Hi? Lorraine? This is Angel Robinson, Lucy's new assistant. I'm really sorry, but Lucy's on a ca— conference call at the moment and she really can't get off. But she asked me to tell you that she'll call you back the minute she finishes." I didn't know where I was coming up with this and was vaguely surprised that I was able to lie with such ease.

"Sure," Lorraine barked, and hung up in my ear.

Peter Johnson was still blinking on Line 1.

"Mr. Johnson? I'm afraid Ms. Fiamma's unavailable at the moment. Can I help you?"

"Have you read my book?" he asked, coughing into the phone.

"Actually, I'm new here, so I haven't had a chance to—"

"We can still talk about it," he said. "Let me tell you the plot, if you've got a minute. It's a winner, I'm telling you. A real winner."

"Why don't I take your number, Mr. Johnson, and I'll make sure to deliver the message."

He coughed again and rasped out his phone number, promising that it was no trouble at all for him to call again and that he'd be happy to call tomorrow, and oh yes, congratulations on my new job at one of the finest literary agencies on earth. I hung up and stole a glance at my watch, sure that hours had passed since I'd first walked in at eight o'clock. I'd been there for exactly twenty-three minutes.

THE NEXT TIME I CHECKED, it was after one. Pacific time, that is. There was one clock in the office and it was set to New York time. Anna had arrived at nine but was only marginally more helpful than Nora in showing me around the office. She was, however, intent on telling me every detail of her eating habits. Instead of learning where Lucy's call list was, I learned that Anna had consumed eggs and bacon for breakfast. Rather than explaining how the filing system worked, Anna chose to tell me that she was planning a Chinese chicken salad for dinner, and what did I think of honey mustard dressing? Every so often, she'd throw out a bit of useful information, like where the filing cabinets were located, for example, or where I could find the manuscripts that were slated for rejection and had to be sent back to their authors, but these were delivered almost as afterthoughts. At least, thankfully, when I managed to unearth my computer and turn it on, Anna was able to direct me to the various databases of names and phone numbers that I'd be needing.

Craig spent most of the morning wearing a path between his desk and Lucy's office. When he was seated behind his folders and files, he was all but invisible. Aside from the brief conversation I'd had with him in Lucy's office, he hadn't spoken to me at all.

Anna must not have heard that I was to be the first person answering the phone, because, unless she was on a call herself, she leaped at it every time it rang. Her conversations were loud and she giggled often. These were not personal calls, either, because she put several through to Lucy, but she spoke to everyone as if she were a long-lost chum. I answered a few calls of my own, more successfully than the first, but still felt uneasy about the Hart episode. Lucy had not emerged from her office, and I expected to be called onto the sparkling white carpet at any minute for screwing up. When my intercom buzzed at one-thirty, I actually jumped.

"Angel, can you come in here now, please." Despite the *please*, it was clearly a command and she sounded none too pleased. I considered the possibility of being fired on my first day.

"Come, come, Angel. Sit down." Lucy was perched on her white leather sofa, holding a manuscript. I recognized the mass of curling blue script on the first page. I sat down on the edge of her couch and she gave me a look I could only describe as a "once-over."

"What have you come as, my dear?" she asked, her tone much less gentle than her words.

"Excuse me? Wha—"

"I mean, what are you *wearing*, Angel?"

I looked down at myself, as if I needed to be reminded of what I'd put on earlier, and saw a beige button-down shirt, jeans, and black mules. It was a very similar outfit to the ones both Anna and Nora were wearing. Obviously this was some kind of trick question. I had no idea what the answer was supposed to be.

"Um . . ."

"Oh, for God's sake, I don't have time for this," Lucy said with exasperation. "I want to talk to you about this Italian book." She handed me Damiano Vero's manuscript. My notes were clipped to the top and I saw that Lucy had written all over them. "Now, I gather that you really liked this, yes?"

"Yes, I thought the writing was great." I scrambled to switch gears in an effort to keep up with Lucy's broad jumps in topic.

"Well, it *is* very good, you're right, but I have some questions. First of all, it's set in Italy."

"Some of it."

"Yes, it's set in Italy and Americans are very xenophobic. They may not want to read about Italy right now."

"But what about *Under the Tuscan Sun?* Italy's always been seen as so romantic," I said. "Besides, when he gets to this country, he really cleans up his act. It's kind of an immigrant success story in a way." I was beginning to warm to the discussion. I'd almost forgotten about the files, the phone calls, and Nora's glowering looks.

"That's another thing. I don't think this should be a memoir. Memoirs—*especially* addiction memoirs—have become the wicked stepchildren of publishing lately. We're going to have to call this something else."

I watched as Lucy furrowed her brow in concentration.

"Let's pitch it as autobiographical fiction," she said finally. "That should cover all the bases." She gave me a sharp glance. "You should be writing this down, Angel." I looked down at my empty hands, debating whether or not to make a run for my desk for pen and paper. "Next time," Lucy stated, "come in here prepared, please. Now, is he still addicted? That would make a great angle. We could get him into rehab, give him interviews from a hospital or something."

"Actually, I think his point was that he's clean now."

Lucy shot me a disapproving look. "Well, we'll see what we can do about that. Much better if he *hasn't* cleaned up. This book could *be* his salvation instead of the book being *about* his salvation. Yes, yes, that's *much* better. What does he do?"

"He's a pastry chef."

"No, that's no good. Too many chef tales out there already. We're on the fourteenth minute of that story and the clock's ticking." She paused for a moment, tapping her Waterman fountain pen against the pages on her lap. "We'll just say he's unemployed. Impoverished and addicted. That's much better. Heroin and pastry don't make a sexy combination. This stuff about the park is fabulous," she said, flipping through the bent sheets. "Is the manuscript finished?"

"I don't know."

She sighed. "These are the things you really need to be paying attention to, Angel. Well, it doesn't matter. I can sell it on a partial with the right pitch. I can sell it as . . . an Italian *Trainspotting*. Yes, that's it. Unless you think the heroin thing is played out at this point. What's your take on that, Angel? You're young, you should know."

"I don't think so," I said tentatively. "It never really seems to be, you know, *finished* really."

"Has he contacted any other agents?"

"I'm not sure."

"Haven't you spoken to him?" She seemed appalled.

"No, I—"

"I left a note on your desk about this. I mentioned, specifically, that you needed to call him as soon as possible."

"I'm sorry, I didn't see it."

She stared at me hard, as if weighing my answer for the truth in it. "Angel, attention to detail is *paramount* in this office." I was a very small mouse to her great big cat, and there was nowhere to run. But as soon as I began to formulate some sort of verbal escape, Lucy shifted her tone once more. "This is very *filmic*," she said. "Yes, I definitely think so. Get him on the phone, let's sign him up before he goes somewhere else." I started to rise, but she held up her hand, palm out. "No, wait," she said. "Let's just see something first." She walked around to her desk and punched her intercom button. "Anna!"

"Yup?"

"Get Natalie Weinstein on the phone."

"Okay, Lucy. Is there anything else you need right now? I could get you a—"

"Natalie. Weinstein. Anna. Now."

Lucy positioned herself at her desk and motioned for me to come closer. "I want you to hear this," she said. I noticed that her voice had dropped an octave or two and had what I could only call a seductive tone washing through it. As soon as she was connected with Natalie Weinstein, Lucy began rearranging the items on her desk with her free hand. This was a pattern I would soon become very familiar with. Whenever she was on the phone, and that was a good portion of every day, Lucy compulsively stacked the notepads, paper clips, pens, and anything else that was on her desk. She moved the largest items into the center first, progressively piling on items as they decreased in size, until there was a small tower in the middle of her desk. Then she took them down, item by item, and placed them in the corners of the desk. If she was still on the phone at that point, she'd begin the process again. She repeated these motions over and over as she talked to Natalie Weinstein, and I became hypnotized, watching her hands move back and forth as her voice filled the room.

"It's really hot," she was saying, "and I thought of *you* first. I've got a virgin author here, came in over the transom. Yes, we *do* read our unsolicited manuscripts over here. Anyway, he's a divine Italian man with a blockbuster novel idea. Yes, I have the novel right here."

I watched the notepads stack up and come down.

"Well, it turns out he's written the Italian *Trainspotting*. Actually, it's more like *Trainspotting* meets *Under the Tuscan Sun*. Exquisite writing."

Up, down, up, down.

"He's a heroin addict and he's written the most vivid account of— Yes, I agree, there certainly is a market. Listen, Nat, this is *very* hot. He's still addicted. What? No, did I say addicted? *Recovery*. He's still in recovery. But it's—well, you know what a slippery slope recovery can be."

I watched her hand pick up a pen and begin writing a note.

"Yes, he's Italian. From Milano. Drop-dead gorgeous. You know how Italian men are."

She held up the note for me to see. *Do we have author photo?* it asked. I shook my head in the negative. She continued to write. *He'd better be good looking!* she added to her note.

"He's already working on a sequel. Actually, he has two more books in the works. We could have an antihero series character here. He's calling it the . . . let me find it here . . . yes, *The Horse Triptych.* What? Well, that doesn't matter, he can always change the title."

She offered me a dramatic eye roll.

"Yes, I will, Nat. I can't guarantee— Well, I can offer you an exclusive if— Fine, I'll have it on your desk tomorrow. You understand, I have to move on this right away. But, of course, I thought of you first."

Lucy hung the phone up abruptly and, snapped out of my trance, my eyes shot to her face. I was impressed and also a little frightened. Lucy was assuming an awful lot without having spoken one word to Damiano Vero. I had no doubt, however, that she would get everything she was asking for.

"And *that* is how it is done, Angel," Lucy said. She was smiling broadly, her teeth glowing in preternatural whiteness. "All right, Angel, get the author—what's his name again? Anyway, get him on the phone and then put me on with him. He's not going to know what hit him. I'm going to make him a star. And make sure to take the manuscript home with you tonight. It needs some work. Go over it carefully, fix it up, and have him make the changes. We've got to get this out in as perfect shape as possible. These editors are busy. They don't have time for books that need a whole lot of work from the outset, believe me." She drew a breath. "Right, I want to have it out by the end of the week, the latest. We'll need at least five more editors. I'll generate the list."

"But aren't you just sending it to Natalie Weinstein?"

Lucy looked at me with an expression of disbelief. "That would be a very big mistake," she said. "Now, go, go, we've got work to do." As I walked out of her office, Lucy added, "And find out about the other two books he's working on."

I paused at the door for only a millisecond. That was how long it took me to decide not to tell Lucy that the two books were figments of her imagination and not the author's. What did it matter? If she wanted two more books, he'd have to write them.

Damiano Vero had listed three phone numbers on his cover letter. The first gave me a busy signal and the second rang with no answer. I finally tracked him down on the third.

"*Ècco, sì!*" he exclaimed when I announced myself. "But I just sent it. So fast you are."

I smiled into the phone, thinking that this was the first happy phone conversation I'd had all day. "Lucy would like to talk to you," I said. "Can you hold a moment while I put you through?"

"Of course," he said.

"Lucy, I've got Damiano Vero on Line 1 for you."

"Who?"

"Damiano Ve— The Italian book?"

"Oh, him. Well, put him *through*, Angel. You're wasting time."

I sighed to myself as I punched the necessary buttons. At least, I thought, she didn't seem to have very good short-term memory when it came to my first-day screwups. My stomach growled and twisted, having had nothing to digest since the banana I put in it six hours before. After she'd polished off her entire box of protein powder, Nora left the office briefly to go collect the mail. Nobody else had made any kind of movement to take lunch outside the office, although Anna had pulled out a messy, smelly meat-laden sandwich and was eating it noisily at her desk. She felt my eyes on her and looked up at me.

"We don't take a lunch break here," she said. "I hope you brought something with you."

"I didn't know that," I said. "So, no, I didn't."

Anna shrugged and took a large bite out of her sandwich. Something that looked like mayonnaise oozed from the bread. She was still chewing when her intercom buzzed.

"Yeth, Luthy?"

"Anna, is your mouth full or do you have a cold? If you are ill, make sure you wipe down the phone after you use it. I shouldn't have to tell you. I need an agency contract for Damiano Vero now, please. And tell Angel to pick up Line 1 and talk to him."

"Angel," Anna said, nearly choking as she swallowed, "you need to—"

"Thanks, I've got it." I picked up my phone. "Hi, Mr. Vero. This is Angel."

"Please call me Dami," he said. "It's more easy."

"Okay. It's great to meet you. I really like *Parco Lambro*. I don't know if Lucy told you. It's very exciting."

"Oh yes," he said. "Very exciting. I had a good feeling about Luciana. I knew she would be the best person for this book. And she tells me that we will be working together, you and I. You are going to make some changes for me?"

"Yes, we talked about that. Of course, I'll just make suggestions and then whatever seems right to you . . ."

"*Bène*. Luciana gave me your phone number at home, but I think maybe we could meet at some point?"

Luciana? My home phone number? "Sure, that would be great. I can call you. . . ."

"*Bène*. I look forward to it. *Mille grazie*, Angel. Good-bye for now."

Before I could replace the phone in its cradle, my computer chirped with the sound of an instant message. I looked over at the rectangle of blue text and saw that the initials of the sender were AA. Anna.

Did she tell you about St. Lucy? the message read.

Did who tell me? I wrote back. I looked over at Anna. She was bent over her desk, looking very busy, clacking away at her keyboard. My computer sounded off again with another message:

LF. She likes to tell the new staff how St. Lucy is one of the patron saints of writers. They tried to burn St. Lucy but she was flame-proof. They had to stab her in the throat to kill her. She was Italian.

No, she didn't tell me, I wrote back.

I just thought it might help you with that Italian author, Anna responded.

I briefly entertained the notion that Anna might be insane and was debating a possible response to her last message ("thank you" just didn't seem appropriate) when Nora approached me with a large plastic tub full to the top with manuscripts and query letters.

"Lucy wants you to sort this," she said. "It's usually my job, but she wants you to get familiar with the submissions."

"These are just today's submissions?"

"It's not bad, really," Nora sniffed. "There are only about fifty today. Sometimes we get close to a hundred." She smiled. It was an expression that looked both awkward and foreign on her face. "Have fun," she said.

ANNA DROPPED A MANUSCRIPT on my desk, where it landed with a plop and a rush of air. "This is my reading for last night. It's a reject, but you should look it over. Lucy likes to get second opinions. I'm outta here, so I guess your training's done for the day. You can probably go now, too." I looked down at the manuscript and then up at the clock, subtracting three hours. It was six o'clock and my eyes were stinging. A hunger headache throbbed at the back of my head. Nora was gone. I could hear Craig's voice sounding from behind Lucy's door.

"Yes," I said, and gathered my purse, *Parco Lambro* notes, and several manuscripts to review, including the one that Anna had just dropped on me. "I have to eat something. I think I'm going to pass out." But I was talking to an empty room. Anna was out the door before I could finish my sentence. She had also left me without explaining what, if anything, I was supposed to do to close up or finish out the day. With a sudden rush of resentment, I realized that everything I had learned over the course of my extraordinarily long first day, I'd figured out for myself—in spite of, not because of, Anna's so-called "training." I tried to formulate a plan for how I would approach Anna, Nora, and even Craig in the coming days to elicit a little more help, but my brain was too hungry and tired to give shape to a single thought.

I stood up to leave, but a low-blood-sugar head rush kept me from moving until I could steady myself. The phone rang, loud in the now-silent office, cutting through my dizziness. *Answer it. Don't answer it.* If only I'd left a half minute earlier.

"Hello, Lucy Fiamma Agency."

There was static coming through the receiver and then a small voice speaking, it sounded like, from far away. "Ah, ook."

"Hello? Can I help you? Hello?"

"Ka." Crackle, hiss. "Oo."

"I'm sorry, I can't hear you. Hello?" There was more crackling and an extended hiss on the line. I was about to hang up when I heard it, faint but clear.

"Karanuk."

"*Karanuk?* Yes, please, yes, one moment please, just one moment."

I didn't bother trying to buzz Lucy with the intercom, opting, instead, to run to her office, knock rapidly on the closed door, and open it without waiting for a response. Lucy was seated at her desk, looking as fresh as if she'd just started her day. Craig was kneeling next to her (yes, *kneeling*), holding out papers for her to look at.

"Angel?"

"Karanuk," I blurted. "Karanuk's on Line 1 for you." Lucy lifted one of her boomerang-shaped eyebrows and stared at me, puzzled. "It's not a very good connection," I ran on. "He must be calling from Alaska. He's holding."

"Angel," Lucy said, "Karanuk lives in Los Angeles."

"Oh, okay. Um, he's on Line 1. And I'm going to go home now. Thank you."

Lucy shook her head, as if she couldn't quite believe what she was hearing, and picked up the phone.

"Thank you, Angel," Craig boomed, rising from his position on the floor. "We'll see you in the morning."

I backed out the door, gathered my manuscripts, and ran from the office as if my hair were on fire. *Stupid,* I cursed myself as I got into my car and drove home. *Stupid, stupid, stupid,* I thought as I unlocked my door and sat down on my bed. *Idiot,* I added, as I spread the manuscripts out in front of me and prepared to go through them. Although I'd relived the last five minutes of my day at least twenty times on my way home, I still couldn't believe that I'd been stupid enough to barge into Lucy's office, stammering like a fool. There was a dull but insistent ringing in my head.

On balance, I thought, I hadn't given a particularly stellar performance for my first day. I wondered, not for the first time, if I would even last the week. The ringing in my head persisted. I looked up. It was my phone.

"Hello, Lu— Um, hello?"

"Angel!" Lucy's voice slammed through the phone, hitting my brain like a mallet.

"Lucy?"

"Listen, dear, we hardly had a chance to chat and get acquainted today. You ran out of here so quickly." She gave a short, coughlike laugh.

"I know, I'm—"

"Anyway, dear, I wanted to welcome you and tell you that I think you have tremendous potential as a team player in our agency. Really, *tremendous*. I'm very pleased with your work on the Italian book and I think this is only the beginning. You've got a good eye and this is something we've been sorely lacking."

"Thank you," I said, exhaling the breath I'd been holding.

"And because there's been a lack in that area," she went on, "I want you to review *all* the submissions very carefully. You know, Anna's very sweet and she means well, but she clearly doesn't have your eye. I worry about what we're missing with her. Do you understand?"

"Um . . ." I glanced down at the rejected manuscript Anna had given me. Her reader's report was clipped to the top and started with, *This is a stupid idea. And boring.*

"So just *entre nous,* Angel, keep a close watch on what she's doing, all right?"

"Sure."

"Perhaps you can come in a little earlier tomorrow morning and we can have a quick meeting before the rest of the staff arrives. Because, frankly, Angel, I really can't spend this much time on the phone with you. I have dinner reservations."

"Sure, Lucy. No problem."

"You've brought the Italian book home with you?"

"Oh yes, I've got it—"

"Fabulous. I'm so excited about this book, Angel. See if you can make some inroads on it tonight. We'll discuss it in the morning."

"Okay."

"Again, I'm so pleased that you're joining us, Angel. I knew you were sharp the moment I laid eyes on you."

"Thank—"

"Just one more thing, Angel, and then I really must go. I realize that today was your first day and all, but I must insist that you dress a little more professionally. There's no need for a business suit or anything that formal, but I believe that jeans are too casual and send the wrong message. So no more jeans, all right, Angel?"

"No more jeans," I repeated thickly.

"Fabulous. I'll see you in the morning. Early. Good-bye, dear."

I replaced my phone in its cradle, tenderly, as if it were a newborn. The last thing I wanted was for it to wake up and start ringing again. I picked up the manuscript that Anna had so summarily rejected and stared at it, the words blurring in front of my tired eyes. For the first time that I could remember, I had a fully formed desire for an alcoholic beverage. But I had no time to think about when or where I might get one because, to my horror, the handle to my front door was turning, opening, and someone was walking in.

A handsome blond man stood in front of me, holding a bottle of wine in one hand and what looked like a very large manuscript in the other.

"Baby!" he said. "How was your first day?"

Malcolm. For a second, I hadn't even recognized him.

THREE

Lucy Fiamma
Lucy Fiamma Literary Agency

Dear Ms. Fiamma,

I am a writer seeking representation for my first novel, titled ELVIS WILL DANCE AT YOUR WEDDING. As per your recommendation in the guide to literary agents, I am enclosing the first fifty pages of the novel, a synopsis, and a self-addressed stamped envelope for your response. The entire novel is available if you'd like me to send it.

Although this is my first novel, I have published several short stories in literary journals over the last few years. Most recently, my stories have appeared in *Elephant Cage Quarterly* and *Flabbergasted*. I would be happy to furnish you with copies at your request. I am a graduate of the MFA writing program at California University. ELVIS WILL DANCE AT YOUR WEDDING was originally written as my master's thesis, but I have since revised it substantially.

The novel is about a road trip that takes place over a

twenty-four-hour period of time. The two main characters, Michael and Jennifer, drive from Los Angeles to Las Vegas, get married, and drive home again. They are a young couple and know very little about each other as they begin their journey into matrimony. Over the course of the novel, several secrets are revealed and they learn a great deal about themselves and about each other.

I understand that your time is valuable, so I'll keep my letter brief and hope that the writing will speak for itself. I look forward to hearing from you.

Sincerely,
Shelly Franklin

ELVIS WILL DANCE AT YOUR WEDDING

By Shelly Franklin

Chapter 1

Michael's eyes are the color of phosphorescent algae. They are so bright and so green that as Jennifer opens the back door and walks in, she speculates for a moment that the color is chemically induced. But love, Jennifer thinks, can do this too. Her thought is a bright spark in the darkened room. So, this glow is from love. This is what Jennifer chooses to believe as she approaches the man who will soon be her husband.

He is sitting in near dark and the TV is on without sound. He's left the windows open and the September air is warm and moist coming through the screen. Jennifer doesn't wonder why he has turned out all the lights. She knows he uses the TV like some people use food. For him, it's a nurturing lifeline. She glances quickly at the TV and recognizes a home shopping channel. An under-fed woman in red is selling golden angels on a chain for under twenty dollars.

"I'm sorry I'm late," Jennifer says, kissing Michael on the cheek.

"It's all right, Jen," Michael says, his voice a pan of melted butter. "We've got plenty of time. Las Vegas never sleeps."

Jennifer puts her arms around Michael's neck. His ocean eyes shine up at her and his mouth curves up into a smile. "Nervous?" she asks. She keeps her tone light because she can smell the fear on him, subtle but biting.

"Yeah," he says. His hands find a place in the small of her back and press in. "Aren't you?"

No, Jennifer thinks. She's not nervous. She's never been more sure of anything in her life. She says, "Do you have the rings?"

"I've got the rings, Jennifer. And, more importantly, I've got the car. Did you see the car?" He presses his lips on the side of her neck. He smells of the cigarettes he supposedly quit smoking three weeks ago and the mints he's chewed to disguise them. She can also detect the faint but unmistakable odor of alcohol.

"The car?" she asks.

"Go look outside," he says.

Jennifer breaks his grip, walks slowly over to the window. There is a candy-apple red Corvette sitting in the driveway. Even in the dark, it glows like a Pacific sunset.

"What's all this, Michael?"

"You like it?" He is smiling wide enough to swallow a small lake. "I rented it. For tonight."

"Why?" Jennifer asks him.

"Isn't it beautiful? I figure if we're going to do this, we're going to do it right. A classic car for a classic American experience. A wedding in Las Vegas. What do you say?"

Jennifer wants to be as enthusiastic as he is over this car, but she can't quite catch the same thrill.

Still she says, "It's great, Michael. When does it have to be back?"

"Tomorrow."

Jennifer raises her eyebrows in surprise. "Well then, cowboy," she says. "We'd better get going."

Title: ELVIS WILL DANCE AT YOUR WEDDING
Author: Shelly Franklin
Genre: Fiction
Reader: Anna

This is a stupid idea. And boring. The title is awful. The author has an MFA and she has had some things published in literary magazines, but otherwise no credits. This is a first novel. It's about a couple who drive to Las Vegas to get married. I don't think anything else happens. It's very slow and it's a dumb premise. The writing is dry and not evocative. I don't know where this is going. I don't know why Elvis is in the title. She doesn't say if she's sent it to any other agents, but I don't think it matters. This isn't our kind of thing. My recommendation is to reject.

Title: ELVIS WILL DANCE AT YOUR WEDDING
Author: Shelly Franklin
Genre: Fiction
Reader: Angel

Author is a graduate of the California University writing program, which has been producing many bestselling writers over the last few years, so I gave this (originally her thesis) a close read. I actually like the title. I know it's a bit wacky, but the novel is about getting married in Las Vegas. Who better than Elvis in the title? I also like the writing here. The author sets up a certain tension right away so we know, as readers, that there are already problems between these two people and that getting married might be a mistake. I didn't find the writing dry—quite the opposite. I read the synopsis and it's clear that the author knows where she's going with this material. She has a definite plot and structure, both of which will work, in my opinion.

The only possible problem I see is that the novel is written largely in the present tense. Although this works in terms of keeping us in the moment (and the novel does take place over the course of one day), it's also a bit confining and could become a little claustrophobic. However, I think this is easy enough to remedy if the author is willing to rewrite. I think there is potential here for a good book about contemporary relationships—always a topic of interest. I'd recommend contacting her right away to make sure she hasn't gone anywhere else with this and asking to see the complete manuscript.

MY FIRST DAY *at* work quickly turned into my first night *of* work. I read through my stack of manuscripts first, placing Shelly Franklin's novel at the top of the pile so as to rescue it from Anna's ham-fisted rejection, and then I turned my attention to editing *Parco Lambro.* I was surprised by how easily the work came to me. It was as if I knew, instinctively, which words to move around and shave off to uncover the picture Damiano wanted to create. I could hear his voice in my head as I read and sensed the story he meant to tell. I responded with marks from my red pen. I'd never really done anything like this before, unless you counted the minor editing I'd done on Malcolm's stories, but it felt entirely natural to me—unlike the other first-day tasks I'd fumbled through. The biggest bonus, though, was that I was truly enjoying myself.

Malcolm hovered around me as I worked, careful not to interrupt me at first, but growing increasingly impatient as the hours stretched on. It was clear he wanted a full report of everything I'd experienced at my new job, but I explained to him that he'd have to wait for the blow-by-blow account.

"She has to have this *tomorrow,*" I told him, pointing to Damiano's manuscript.

Malcolm came up behind me and put his hands in my hair, stroking my neck. "Are you sure?" he asked, his voice heavy with seduction. "You've been at it so long, baby."

"Malcolm, please . . ."

"Fine," he said, dropping his hands and his attempt to sway me. "Then I guess I'll make you some coffee."

"That would be great," I said.

The next time I looked up it was close to dawn and Malcolm had passed out, fully clothed, on my bed.

I WAS ON MY WAY TO the office a few short hours later, and by the time I made it in, still long before nine o'clock, Lucy and Craig had already generated a list of ten top editors for *Parco Lambro*. In the meantime, Lucy had sent a copy of the unedited manuscript overnight to Natalie Weinstein, to whom she'd promised an exclusive. Natalie Weinstein would have it exclusively for exactly two days, but according to Lucy, that was long enough. "She knows this business," Lucy told me. "She knows that I can't let a hot manuscript languish on her desk."

While I walked Damiano through my revisions on the phone ("We need this yesterday, Angel," Lucy told me. "Make sure he gets it to you by tomorrow or type it up yourself. On your own time."), Lucy pitched his book to her ten editors. Because she wanted me to hear her make these pitches ("You need to learn how this is done, Angel."), I put Damiano on hold several times to run to her office, paper and pen in hand, and listened to her conversations in progress:

"Well, I can't give you an exclusive, you understand, Charles. However, I *can* guarantee that you will be the first to receive it. If you'll give my assistant your home address, I can overnight it to you there."

"I'm telling you, Katherine, I've really never read a manuscript with so much raw power. Of course, this is why I thought of you first. I know your talent for keeping such emotion fresh on the page."

"Yes, Julia, he's extremely marketable. Think dark and sexy."

"I thought of you immediately, Frank. This is bigger than genre—it's a sweeping social comment. What? Yes, I agree, we certainly do need one."

Periodically, during the course of these conversations, Lucy would hold up notes for me to read.

Where is author photo?!!! one said. *Need it NOW!!!*

Are edits finished? asked another.

And then there was, *Start pitch letter.*

I nodded and mouthed "Okay" after the last note, but I had absolutely no idea what she wanted. As I sat down at my desk, I gave a look around the office at my coworkers and debated who might be able to help me. My prospects weren't so hot.

"Damiano," I said into his perpetually holding line, "Lucy's really got a *lot* of interest and she wants to go out with this as soon as she can. Do you think you can get this done by, um, tomorrow?"

"*Bella,*" he said after a pause. "Okay. I can call you later? How do I send it? And please call me Dami."

The sound of my intercom cut off my answer before it left my mouth. "Angel, have you begun that pitch letter? I'd like to see it, please."

"Listen, Damian—*Dami,*" I whispered into the phone, "why don't you call me after you've made some more of these changes? And then you can just, um, e-mail it to me at home. I'll—I'll just print it out."

"*Grazie,*" he said.

"And a photo," I added hurriedly. "Do you have a photo you can e-mail? Of yourself?"

"Not really, but—" he began, but my intercom buzzed again and I rushed him off the phone. After assuring Lucy that I'd have a pitch letter for her momentarily, I took a chance on the possible kindness of strangers and approached Craig.

"How are you doing, Angel?" he asked. Craig looked particularly scrawny in a blue polo shirt that was a size too big and brown pants that had seen better days. As he pushed his spectacles back on his nose, I was reminded of Woody Allen minus the irony. But that voice! It resonated in the center of my body and made my heart skip. Craig's wife, I thought, was obviously a lights-off kind of gal.

"I—I'm okay," I said. "But I wonder if you could give me a hand with something. Lucy wants me to—"

"Draft a pitch letter for the Italian book?" Craig asked.

"Right," I said. "And I don't . . ." I trailed off, not wanting to admit to Craig that I didn't have the vaguest idea how to start such a thing.

"There's a template on the computer," Craig said. "But if you want an example to follow, I've got one here somewhere." He slid open a meticulously neat file cabinet beneath his desk and pulled out a sheet of paper. "Here you go," he said. "But I'll need that back when you're finished with it."

"Sure," I said, but hesitated.

"You're going to have to jump right in, Angel," he said, and the sound of my name in his mouth made my throat constrict. "It's the best piece of advice I can give you. Don't be afraid to get wet."

This was, oddly, the warmest, most encouraging thing anyone had said to me since I'd started, and it immediately endeared me to Craig, who was, nevertheless, frowning as he uttered it.

"Okay," I said, giving him a high-wattage smile. "Right you are."

I returned to my desk and scratched out a one-page letter that included a brief description of *Parco Lambro,* heavy on superlatives, and a short paragraph stating why "Dear—(Ed.)" absolutely had to have it. I copied the sign-off on Craig's sample letter, which was "As always, Lucy Fiamma." And I supposed she was. Always Lucy, that is.

It took Lucy less than ten seconds to decimate my letter with razor-like flourishes of her fountain pen. *Redo as per my notes,* she wrote on top. *This reads as if a (small) child wrote it.*

I felt a flush spread up my neck as I read her comments and my ears began to burn with humiliation. I realized that I hadn't really been stung by Lucy until that moment and I found it particularly painful. The escape fantasy I'd envisioned for myself during my first five minutes on the job flared in my head. Craig must have sensed this somehow, because just as I was contemplating how long it would take me to gather my purse and exit, an instant message from him appeared on my screen.

Don't take it personally.

I sat down at my desk and typed one back. *I'll try not to,* I wrote. *Thanks.* I looked over at Craig, hoping for some kind of visual affirmation, but he was already on the phone, murmuring something about overdue royalties into his headset.

I rewrote the pitch letter five times. Each draft came back to me (via Anna, Nora, or myself as we took our turns through Lucy's office) with more strike-throughs and margin notes than the last. Lucy made corrections on her own corrections. Finally, I received a copy that stated, *Enough already—we're out of time. Let's get this done!* I looked at the changes and realized that the final copy was almost identical to the original I'd given her.

I returned Craig's sample pitch letter to him and hovered at his desk until he looked up at me and asked, "Is there something else I can help you with, Angel?"

"Well, actually, um . . ."

"The letter's fine. Is that it?"

"No. I . . ."

"We're kind of busy here, Angel."

I realized that I was sweating profusely and had no idea why I was finding it so difficult to broach a subject that should have been discussed and put to rest after my initial interview.

"I don't, uh, ha-ha, know exactly what my, um, salary is here, Craig." I gave him a big smile, hoping it would cover my conversational flailing. "I was sort of wondering if you could fill me in. You being the money guy and all."

Craig leaned back in his chair and, for a moment, a strange look passed across his washed-out features. If I hadn't known better, I could have sworn it was a kind of indictment—as in, why would I be so presumptuous as to assume I was actually going to get *paid* for this opportunity? The look passed quickly, before I could positively identify it, and Craig gave me a weak smile in return. He leaned over his desk, grabbed a scrap of paper, wrote *25K* on it, and handed it to me.

"And this is . . . ?" I searched his eyes for an answer.

"Yearly." He'd lowered his voice to a kind of Shakespearean actor's whisper.

"Okay," I said, staring at the paper, dividing it by twelve, subtracting taxes in my head, and coming up with much smaller figures.

"Most people who start in publishing make much less," Craig said. "This is a very generous starting salary. She has a lot of faith in you."

"Right. Of course. Thanks," I said, and went back to my desk. I'd barely seated myself when my intercom screeched once more.

"Angel!"

"Lucy?"

"My office!"

Before I could get more than one foot in her office, Lucy barked, "Copy and circulate," and thrust a memo at me.

We are not running Gap ads in this office!!!! it screamed. *Professionalism is paramount to the success of this operation! I must insist that, from now on, there will be NO JEANS worn to work! Please adjust your wardrobes accordingly! LF.*

I had, of course, already adjusted my "wardrobe" and was wearing a pair of khaki pants I'd pulled from the depths of my closet earlier that morning. Anna and Nora, however, were still clad in denim. Nora's reaction to the new "no jeans" directive was to fold and refold the memo until it was an extremely small square. When Anna read her own copy, she shot a pointed glance in my direction and turned to her computer. Two minutes later, I received an instant message from her:

LF has requested that we dress more professionally. No more jeans. Just so you know.

I held up my copy of the memo, but Anna's eyes were fixed on her computer screen.

Okay, I typed back. *Thanks for letting me know.*

Any idea why we can't wear jeans anymore? Anna sent back. *I'm just wondering because jeans were fine until today. Just thought you might know.*

My guess is as good as yours, I typed. I hoped that would be the end of it, but I suspected that Anna was just getting started. The phone started ringing again and she leaned back in her chair, sulkily refusing to answer it.

"Lucy Fiamma Agency."

"Listen to *you,* all professional!"

Malcolm. Damn it. "Hello there," I said, lowering my voice by several octaves.

"'Hello there'? You know who this is, right? Your boyfriend? The man you left lonely and unfulfilled in bed this morning?"

"Yes, Mal—of course I know who it is." I was whispering, which had drawn Anna's attention. I swiveled my chair away from her so that she couldn't see my face, but that put me squarely in Nora's sights. I was learning that privacy was at a real premium in this office. "I can't talk now," I breathed into the phone. "I'm not really supposed to get personal calls here, anyway."

"Well, you're not answering your cell phone."

"Of course I'm not answering my cell phone. I'm *working.*"

"Angel, why do you sound like someone's standing on your hair?"

"I have to go," I told him.

"Wait, I'm calling to see if you want to go out to lunch. I can come get you—"

"No, no, I can't. I have to get off now—"

"Why *not?*"

I was desperate to get Malcolm off the phone, and although I was staring down at the note-covered surface of my desk, I could feel the heat of Anna's stare on me. "It's really busy here," I told Malcolm, trying to sound calm. "We're trying to get that book ready. You know, the Italian guy—the one I was working on last night."

"Who *is* this guy?" Malcolm asked. "Is he somebody famous or something? Why so much attention?"

"He's got a good book," I muttered.

"Has to be more than that," Malcolm huffed. "He must be some kind of stud or something. Is he? Angel?"

"I don't know, Malcolm!" I lowered my voice again. "I really have to go now." Two more lines were ringing and Anna refused to touch them.

"What about dinner, then? I'll cook."

"Great, great," I said. "I'll see you then. Good-b—"

"Angel, wait."

"*What?!*"

"Your mother called."

A long second passed, suspended and fraught. "Couldn't you have mentioned that first?" I whispered finally.

"Well, excuse *me.*"

"I have to go," I said, and hung up on Malcolm, jamming my finger on the next call line button.

"Lucy Fia—"

"Angel, *bella!*"

"Hi, Dami, can you—" I thought about putting him on hold to answer the other calls and, in an instant, decided against it. As far as I could see, Damiano Vero was now my top priority. Nora would have to get her face out of her protein powder and pick up the phone. "Never mind," I said. "How are you?"

"*Bene,*" he said. "But Angel, a couple of things. I don't have a photo. Is it so important?"

"Well, Lucy thinks . . ." I trailed off. How to tell him that she'd already pitched him as some kind of Johnny Depp–meets–Benicio Del Toro? To be honest, her ongoing descriptions of dark, brooding Italian sexiness had become my own mental picture of Damiano. Not that the dark look meant anything to me, particularly. For a moment, I debated asking Damiano to describe himself, until I realized how absurd that would sound.

"Lucy thinks it helps," I finished. I thought about Karanuk and wondered what the real reason was that nobody knew what he looked like. Was it possible he was so unattractive that Lucy had actually kept him hidden on purpose? Perhaps this was why she was so obsessed with seeing Damiano's photo.

"And if I don't have one?" he asked. He sounded amused.

"Well," I repeated, "Lucy thinks it helps."

"Okay," he said. "The other thing . . . *Penso che* . . . uh, sorry . . . I think I need some help tonight, Angel. With the book."

"Sure," I said. "How about if I call you when I get home? It'll be quieter there and then we can go over it. Does that sound okay?"

"*Bellissima,*" he said. "That's wonderful. *Mille grazie,* eh? You are very kind, Angel."

"You're most welcome," I told him, and hung up smiling. It was only later, after dozens more calls and a sheath of memos from Lucy, that I remembered I'd told Malcolm we'd have dinner together and that the editorial session I'd promised Damiano was probably going to ruin those plans.

At five o'clock, with a good hour of office work yet to go, I sneaked into the "employee bathroom" (a guest bathroom tacked onto the office, which Nora had informed me it was *her* duty to keep clean, as if that were some kind of prize) and called Malcolm on my cell phone.

"Hey," I whispered when he picked up, "it's me. Listen, I'm sorry about before. I just can't . . . I mean, it's really crazy here."

"Must be," he said.

"What did my mother say?" I asked. "Did you talk to her?"

"A little," he said. "I'll tell you about it at dinner."

"Right. About dinner, Malcolm. I'm going to have to take a rain check."

"Why?" he asked. "Does the Italian guy need his shoes shined?"

"Don't be like that," I said. "Do I need to remind you that *you* were the one who advised I apply for this job?" I ran the water in the sink to drown out the sound of my voice.

"I'm sorry," Malcolm said. "I didn't mean— Angel, what's that noise? Are you hiding in the bathroom?"

"Shhh," I breathed into the phone. "She'll hear."

Malcolm gave a perfunctory sigh and said, "Okay, I get it. No dinner. But I'm coming over anyway, okay? Later."

"Okay," I said. "I'd better go."

"Angel?"

"Yes?"

"Love me?"

"Of course," I said. I waited for him to tell me he loved me, too, but I lost the connection before he got a chance.

As I closed the bathroom door and made my way back to my section of the office, I saw that Anna and Nora were in a huddle at Nora's desk. Before I could sit down, both of them looked up at me, wearing identical bemused expressions.

"What?" I said.

"Check this out," Anna said, gesturing to a letter in Nora's hand. I approached Nora with caution and read over her shoulder. Anna stood behind me, too close, as if she were guarding me. The single line of type on the paper was streaked as if someone had spilled water on it.

I am your next star author. The manuscript is on its way. Get ready.

"Hmm," I said.

"Kind of weird, don't you think?" Anna asked.

"Certainly a *novel* approach," I said, trying for levity.

Nora held the page away from her, between her thumb and forefinger, as if it smelled bad. "What am I supposed to do with this?" she asked. "There's no return address or anything."

"Then don't do anything!" Anna said cheerfully.

"Whatever," Nora said, and tossed the page into her reject pile.

Anna shrugged and I headed back to my desk, where there were several more demanding tasks screaming for my attention.

WHEN I GOT HOME, there were two notes and the still-unopened pinot noir from the night before sitting next to my telephone. The first one, slid under the bottle, said, *Drink me, I deserve it.* The second was scrawled with my mother's name, Hillary, and a phone number. I didn't recognize the area code, but I picked up my phone and dialed it, anyway. It rang five times before my mother picked it up and breathed, "Greetings," into the receiver. I could barely hear her. It sounded as if a hurricane were blowing across the line.

"Hillary!" I shouted. "Where are you?" One of the very first things my mother had taught me was to call her by her name and not by any modification of the word *mother*. I'd never even thought of her as *Mom*.

"Is that my Angel?" she sang into the phone. "Hello, darling."

"Where are you?" I repeated.

"I'm in the most beautiful place, Angel. You really have to come here. You must come. It's gorgeous. Trees and fresh air and—"

"But *where*?" I persisted.

"Near . . . it's near Seattle, Angel. Is that so important?"

"Well, it certainly would be if you wanted me to come visit," I said. "Everything okay? I haven't heard from you for a while, Hillary, I was starting to worry." This wasn't nearly the first time I had taken the mother role on the phone with mine. Nor, I suspected, would it be the last.

"Darling, don't you know by now that I will always be fine? Have a little faith, daughter. How are you?"

"I'm fine. Actually, I'm good. I just got a great job, Hillary. I'm working with Lucy Fiamma—she's a literary agent. I'm sure I must have mentioned. . . . Do you remember *Cold!*?"

"What? No, it's not at all cold here, Angel. Look, honey, I have to tell you something. I've found the most wonderful group of women. They are descended from actual *Amazons,* can you believe it? Anyway, we're planning a ritual cleansing, sort of a female sweat-lodge type of thing, and I would really like you to join us, Angel. You need to get in touch with your inner Amazon."

The only Amazon I was likely to get in touch with was the dot-com version, but there was no way of telling my mother this without sounding sarcastic and faithless. Sooner or later she always found the Wiccans, eco-feminists, or sculptors disappointing and moved on, but while she was in the throes of community ecstasy, there was nothing I or anyone else could say to dim her enthusiasm.

"Hillary, did you hear what I said about my new job?"

"What new job, sweetie?"

"I'm working for a literary agent," I almost yelled into the phone.

"Terrific!" A rush of static filled the phone and her next words were partially drowned out. All I heard was, ". . . to take care of yourself."

"What? I can't hear you, Hillary."

"Listen, honey, I have to go to a goddess meeting now. I'm running out as we speak. But I really want you to come up here, Angel. It's important. I'll call you later, okay? We can talk more then."

"Hillary—" I began, but she was already gone. I tried to imagine what a goddess meeting might entail, but stopped myself when I started envisioning a grotesque ceremony involving menstrual blood. Well, she was okay. That was good at least.

I looked at the bottle of wine, fighting an urge to open it and drink it down. I wished Malcolm were beside me and took immediate comfort in the knowledge that he'd be showing up soon. The last two days had worn me down and talking to my mother had just polished me off. Malcolm, I thought, would make a perfect balm. I'd be ready for him when he arrived, I thought. But first there was *Parco Lambro*. I picked up the phone and dialed Damiano's number, which, by now, I knew by heart.

WITH MY HELP, Damiano managed to finish his revisions by the end of the following day, and by the end of that week, all the editors on Lucy's list had received a copy of the manuscript. Despite the fact that Damiano had not managed to come up with a single photograph of himself, a point Lucy bemoaned constantly ("We're screwed if this author isn't mediagenic, Angel!"), every one of them wanted to buy his book.

Natalie Weinstein, who I could actually hear yelling through Lucy's telephone receiver, came in first, with an offer of one hundred thousand dollars, hoping vainly to preempt the others. Lucy then used Natalie Weinstein's offer as the "floor" with which to start an auction. Natalie was representing Weinstein Books, her own small imprint at Gabriel Press, which was, in turn, part of the behemoth Triad Publishing Group. *Parco Lambro*, like all of the books she acquired, would be a direct reflection of her taste and style; her name would be embossed on the spine of the book along with the author's. And she wanted this one badly.

I was amazed by how quickly the level of excitement escalated. Although the editors had enough time to do a surface read, how could each and every one of them have had the time to really feel the writing— enough to be so captured by it that they just *had to have it*? The answer, I believed, was Lucy herself. There was something about the way she spun that book, some mojo she managed to send through the phone that snared them completely.

"It's all about *buzz*, Angel," she told me. "You have to create it. You have to make it happen."

This, I was learning, was Lucy's particular genius, if it could be called that. There was something hypnotic or bewitching about the way she worked. I felt a little like the sorceress's apprentice as I traipsed back and forth from her office, watching her cast the spell.

Lucy gave the ten editors less than a week to prepare for the auction ("Have to keep it fresh," she said, "so that they stay ravenous"), during which time she debated endlessly whether or not to throw a few more into the mix. "I'm just wondering if Susie Parker might not just love this book," she'd say. And, "You know, we haven't yet tried Nadia Fiori. She *is* Italian." Ultimately, she hooked three additional editors, with more frantic overnight deliveries, to make a baker's dozen. I was sure that had she wanted to, Lucy could have involved half the editors in New York, along with many heads of houses. Gordon Hart was among those heads, and he called a few times during the course of that next week, never once actually speaking to Lucy on the phone, but managing to communicate with her through me.

"Are you still working there?" he asked every time I answered his call. "This has got to be a new record for her." That was another thing about Gordon Hart: He never referred to her as *Lucy*; it was always *she* or *her*. His tone was always extremely dry and crisp. It was difficult to tell on the phone, of course, but although he was clearly authoritative, Gordon Hart sounded like a relatively young man. Because he never seemed to be available when I called HartHouse for Lucy, I ended up logging quite a bit of phone time with his various assistants, most often Jessie Hill, who had recently been promoted to associate editor. It was Jessie who told me that Gordon Hart sounded young because he was only in his forties; he was the grandson of HartHouse's founder. It was also Jessie who told me that Gordon and Lucy went "way back," but she didn't explain in what way.

The day before the auction, Lucy circulated a memo through the office:

> *As you are all aware, we will be auctioning the Italian book to-morrow morning. Therefore, I would like to ask that you arrive to work a little earlier than usual—*
>
> *Angel and Anna—6 am*
> *Nora—7 am*
> *Craig—8 am*

It is very important that you remain sharp, so get plenty of sleep tonight! If all goes well, we will have cause to celebrate!!! and you may go home early, at about 4 or 5. —L.

It occurred to me that Lucy might be one of those people who didn't need to sleep. I'd read about this syndrome somewhere. It went beyond garden-variety insomnia. There was a certain chemical in the brains of these individuals that kept them up and functioning on a fraction of the sleep that the average person needed, and when they did fall asleep, it was into the deepest sleep state. They had far fewer dreams than normal and never remembered the ones they did have. I made a mental note to research this further.

Anna, who had said not a word about the early-morning summons, beat me to the office the following morning. When I arrived, at six exactly, shivering, miserable, and clutching the strongest coffee I could find, she was already at her desk, computer fired up, a cherry-and-cheese Danish combination laid out on her desk. I stood still and stared at it for a moment, paralyzed with cold and exhaustion. Anna's face flushed carmine.

"It's for Lucy," she said, pointing at the pastry. "In case she needs something to keep her going."

"I don't suppose there's an extra one?" I asked, hoping I sounded sly and conspiratorial instead of tired and desperate.

Anna furrowed her sandy eyebrows into a misshapen **V**. "No," she said, "but you can have this." She thrust a fax at me and turned her attention back to her artful arrangement of Danish.

"What's this?" I asked her, but I was already reading it.

Your next bestseller is on the way. I hope you are ready. I am your next star author.

"Isn't this the same one who sent Nora that weird letter? When did this come in?" I asked, searching the fax for information and finding none.

"It was here when I got here," Anna said.

"Makes you wonder, doesn't it? I mean, if the manuscript is that good, why don't we have it already?"

But before Anna could answer me, Lucy's voice, shouting "My office, please!" came flooding through our intercoms.

I came in behind Anna, who had shoved her way in ahead of me, which was a good thing because the sight that greeted me temporarily stole my breath.

Lucy was standing in the middle of her office, arms and hands raised in a steeple above her head, exhaling expansively. She was dressed, head to toe, in blinding white. Her ensemble started with a white cashmere turtleneck, included a long string of pearls, an ankle-length white wool skirt, and white suede spike-heeled boots, and finished with a white Pashmina, which she'd draped insouciantly over one shoulder. Her hair, already a whiter shade of pale, floated loose around her face and seemed, like the rest of her, to be electrified. The brilliant green of her eyes and the scarlet cut of her mouth provided the only color in the entire office. For a brief, overtired moment, I thought I'd entered Narnia and was face-to-face with the White Witch.

"Yoga!" she barked, releasing her arms. "You should try it."

"I'm not as flexible as you are, Lucy," Anna gargled, sounding as if a small animal had lodged itself in her throat.

"Flexibility is a state of mind," Lucy said, and gave me a long, sweeping gaze. "What about you, Angel? Surely you could maneuver those long legs of yours into a few yoga postures?"

"Uh . . . yoga . . ." I managed, still entranced by the scene before me.

"All right, enough small talk!" Lucy snapped, moving toward her desk. "Are we ready?"

"All set for round one," Anna answered. I could hear her trademark smugness edging into her tone. "Would you like me to be first on the calls?"

"Don't be ridiculous," Lucy said. "I'm going to need both of you on the phones and then Nora when she gets here."

"Okay," Anna said. "And I've brought a pastry for you, Lucy." A weird, almost-smile appeared on Anna's face.

"What makes you think it would be appropriate to *eat* during an auction, Anna?"

"Well, I wasn't . . . I mean, you could . . ." Anna's face looked like a puzzle on the verge of coming apart. I felt an unwanted stab of sympathy for her. A short, bright silence filled the room for an instant and then the phone rang.

"Got it!" Anna squealed, and ran from the room. Lucy gave me a Cheshire grin. "You may leave my office now, Angel," she said. And then: "The Italian book. It begins."

When I returned to my desk, there was an instant message from Anna waiting on my computer:

Feel free to take the Danish.

Thanks, I wrote back, *I might.* Although we both knew that I wouldn't.

"Doesn't she look great?" Anna asked out loud.

"Who?"

"Lucy! Her outfit. She always wears white to her auctions. She says it brings her luck. I think she looks smashing."

"Right," I said. "Smashing."

"And just a tip," Anna sniffed. "Don't go into her office unless she calls you. Usually, she likes to be alone in there until the auction's over. Also for good luck."

"Okay, got it," I said, and picked up a ringing line.

"Good morning, Lucy Fiamma Literary Agency!" I realized, after the words were already out of my mouth, that I sounded almost hysterical. There was a distinctive coughing on the other end of the phone. Peter Johnson again. His timing was impeccable.

"Good morning. Ms. Robinson?"

"Mr. Johnson?"

"Yes!" he splutter-coughed into the phone. "You recognize my voice!" I stopped myself from telling him that of course I did. He called every day and I had somehow been assigned, after dispatching him on my first day, to be his personal rejection slip. If I hadn't answered his call, it would have been put through to me, anyway. Nora also slid his manuscripts over to me as soon as they arrived in the office, glad to rid herself of the task of sending them right back. Part of the problem with Peter Johnson was that he never failed to include a self-addressed stamped envelope with his submissions. He had to be answered. He also had to be rejected. His novels, or what we saw of them, ranged from bad to worse. They were tedious thrillers with rehashed plots and purple prose, and he seemed to have an endless supply of them for our review. The next one, he kept insisting, was the winner. But I didn't have time to hear about another one; I had to get him off the phone.

"Mr. Johnson, I'm going to have to call you back if that's okay. It's very busy here this morning."

"I just need a minute of your time, Ms. Robinson. I've got something here I think is—"

"Great, we'll be happy to look at it when you send it in."

"I don't think you understand." He was breathing very heavily and I hoped he wasn't working himself into some kind of fit. "I have a book that Ms. Fiamma is *definitely* going to want."

"That's great, Mr. Johnson. We look forward to reading!"

"Let me tell you—"

"Thanks so much! Have a great day."

The moment I hung up on Peter Johnson, every phone in the office seemed to explode with sound, and they just kept ringing. I didn't even notice Nora slink in at seven, and at some point, Craig just seemed to materialize at his desk. As Anna had predicted, Lucy remained sequestered in her office, communicating with us via intercom or e-mails. She never sent instant messages and I began to think that either her computer hadn't been set up for them or she simply didn't know how. There was one tense five-minute period during the third round of bids when, with every line blinking, Lucy seemed to vanish from her office and none of us could get her on the line. Anna stated that Lucy was probably inside her house "centering herself."

I placed several calls to Damiano as the day wore on and Lucy gave him updates on how high the bids were getting. I heard none of these conversations, of course, I merely placed the calls, but every time I got Damiano on the phone, he got more excited, awed, and, finally, disbelieving.

At about three o'clock, Lucy emerged from her office and stood, taller than usual it seemed to me, in the middle of ours.

"The deal is done," she said. "That Italian pastry chef is now a very wealthy man." Lucy had sold Damiano's book plus a sequel (she'd decided against the idea of a trilogy) for half a million dollars. The sheer magnitude of what she'd accomplished gave me gooseflesh.

Lucy clapped her hands briefly and then put them on her hips. "Congratulations, everyone. Well done." She looked over at me. "Let's just hope he can deliver," she said. "His new editor's about twelve years old. And she's no hand-holder."

FOUR

Lucy Fiamma
Lucy Fiamma Literary Agency

Dear Ms. Fiamma,

It is here.

Although I am sure that you receive many such claims, I am writing to tell you that I am your next star author and am ready to take my place in your literary heaven. I do realize that this is a rather grandiose statement, but I have the goods to back it up.

Rather than wasting any more of your time with this letter, I am enclosing a few pages from my novel, BLIND SUBMIS-SION. I am convinced that once you read them, you will agree with me that this novel has the potential to be a huge bestseller. It's a real winner.

Should you wish to see more (and I know you will), please contact me at ganovelist@heya.com

Happy reading!

BLIND SUBMISSION

Chapter 1

Alice wrapped her scarf around her neck to stave off the chill of the late winter morning. The pale sun looked like cold butter in a hazy sky as she raced down Fifth Avenue to get to the office by nine o'clock. Alice thought about stopping for a coffee to warm herself and decided that there wasn't time. She had only been working for Carol Moore, New York's most successful literary agent, for a few weeks and it was important that she stay in her boss's good graces. It wouldn't do to rock the boat at this stage of the game. Later, when Alice made herself indispensable, there would be time for maneuvering.

As she rode the elevator to the fifteenth floor, Alice thought about how easy it had been to land this job. Before she'd been hired, Alice's only publishing experience had been serving lunch to editors in the Manhattan restaurants where she worked as a waitress. She had learned plenty by listening to their conversations as she leaned over them with plates and glasses, but none of that could be put on a résumé. So Alice had fabricated jobs on her application and had bluffed her way through her interview. Carol Moore was both tough and smart and Alice had been sure that her made-up jobs wouldn't pass muster. However, if there was one thing Alice had learned in her twenty-seven years on earth, it was how to lie well. She kept her secrets closely guarded under the blonde halo of her hair. Her fake experience passed under the agent's radar and she convinced Carol Moore to hire her. Of course, the part that was true, the part that had probably tipped Carol Moore over the edge, was that Alice was driven and ambitious and that she desperately wanted the job. What Carol Moore didn't know was *why* and, if Alice had anything to do with it, she never would.

When Alice arrived at the Agency, the office was already a hive of activity. The phones and faxes were humming as Carol

Moore's well trained staff took their places at their desks. Alice observed her co-workers as she greeted them. There was Jewel, a tall, stunning natural blonde who could easily have made a career in modeling if she wanted to. According to Carol Moore, Jewel's good looks had always been more of a hindrance to her than anything else. Jewel was simply too smart for a career on the runway, Carol said. As a woman with secrets of her own, Alice found this difficult to believe and thought that Jewel probably had some sort of hidden disfigurement or weakness. Every woman had something in her past she was ashamed of. Alice planned to find out what this was and use it to her advantage.

There was Ricardo, Carol Moore's office manager. Ricardo was an extremely well-dressed and very handsome man who was, according to Carol Moore, as smart as Jewel. Ricardo kept the office lively with jokes and imitations of movie stars and was always very polite. Ricardo had a photograph of a wife and daughter on his desk, but Alice had looked at the photo and decided that it had come with the frame because the only woman Ricardo ever spoke about lovingly was Carol Moore herself. Yes, Alice thought, Ricardo too had something to hide. Everyone, Alice knew, had something to hide.

And then there was Carol Moore herself. Like Jewel, Carol Moore was very beautiful. Alice thought she had the look of an older Grace Kelly. Alice had researched Carol Moore before she applied for the job, so she knew that Carol had been a force in the literary world for almost thirty years, but she was carrying those years very well. Alice also knew that Carol Moore had grown up practically destitute and had worked very hard to obtain her position of power. And Carol Moore *was* a powerful woman. She represented famous writers from all over the world, some of them Nobel Laureates. When Carol Moore called, publishers listened. Alice was counting on that.

In their meager beginnings, Alice and Carol were similar. During her interview, Alice had implied, without ever seeming to, that she and Carol Moore shared a certain struggle. Alice was counting on Carol to feel drawn to her as a protégé and as someone Carol wanted to make in her own image. That would suit Alice very well indeed. Alice had cut off relations with her own mother long ago in an act of cruel finality and had never known much about what it meant to be a good daughter. But she was a quick study and planned to play on every maternal instinct Carol Moore possessed.

For now, Alice had positioned herself as close to Carol as she could. She hadn't minded at all that her title was that of assistant. For Alice's needs, her position was, at the moment, perfect. She was close to Carol, close to the files, and, most importantly, the receiver of all the mail that came into the office. On all three fronts, Alice had made excellent progress. Besides, Alice didn't plan to remain Carol's assistant for very much longer. She had started laying plenty of groundwork. Everybody Alice had ever known, both biblically and in less physical ways, who counted in any way or who could be useful in any way now knew where Alice was employed.

There was much excitement in the office when Alice took her place at her desk and began to prepare a list of the day's appointments. Carol Moore had just agreed to represent Vaughn Blue, an internationally known rock star. Vaughn was writing a memoir of his life in the business, much of which involved the sex and drugs that the music industry was known for. Although the book would tell all and name names, Carol Moore was most excited by the fact that Vaughn Blue was a brilliant writer. Vaughn Blue was something of a genius. He held a PhD, which he had completed before he broke onto the music scene, and his book would appeal both to celebrity hounds and book critics. The fact that he was one of America's sexiest men didn't hurt either.

Alice finished preparing her list and took it to Carol Moore who was on the phone and swaddled in Versace couture. Carol smiled at Alice and beckoned for her to sit on the chair opposite Carol's desk.

"I have a special assignment for you today," Carol Moore told Alice.

"Terrific," Alice said. "What is it?"

"Vaughn Blue is coming by the office to sign his contract at around noon," Carol said, "and I'd like you to take him to lunch. My treat, of course. I'd love to go myself, but I already have lunch scheduled with a publisher who will probably want to buy Vaughn's book! So what do you say? How does lunch with a rock star sound?"

"Fabulous!" Alice panted. "I'm so excited!"

Alice hoped she wasn't laying it on too thick in an effort to conceal her distaste. Dining with one of America's sexiest men would have held much more appeal if that man wasn't also a writer because, in her deepest heart, Alice hated writers. This was one of her secrets.

That she was a writer herself was another.

I rubbed my eyes, taking them off the pages in front of me. The words had been slipping and blurring and I struggled to retain focus. It was very early and I was very tired, but I had to keep reading. This, after all, was "the bestseller" that had been promised by letter, by fax, and now by submission from our "next star author."

After the author's admitted "grandiose" claims, I'd fully expected the manuscript to be awful. Because I thought I'd be able to reject it quickly, I hadn't even bothered to read it the night before, electing instead to get some much-needed sleep. But I was surprised to find that it wasn't awful at all. Strange, yes, and maybe even a little unsettling, but definitely not out-and-out bad. I read the cover letter again. There was no return address, no phone number, and no name. Was the anonymous-author conceit supposed to tie in to the novel itself? Or was it just to keep us interested enough to ask for more? I leaned over, stretching and touching my toes in an effort to get more blood flowing to my brain so that I could think a little more clearly.

It had been six weeks since I'd started working for Lucy. Every day of those six weeks had felt like an eternity in itself, but all put together they seemed to have raced by, giving me a strange split perception of the passage of time—a perception only reinforced by Lucy.

It had only been a few weeks since the sale of *Parco Lambro*, for example, yet she acted as if the auction were a distant memory. Although she'd sold two more projects since then, neither was auctioned or came close to generating either the excitement or the cash of Damiano's. Still, the first of those two, a comic novel about a vampire-hunting dog ("*The Dogs of Babel* meets *The Historian*," as Lucy had pitched it), had sold for a respectable seventy-five thousand dollars and the second, a cultural history of lawn ornaments, had gone for fifty thousand. I'd brought both projects to Lucy's attention. The first had come directly from my reading pile and I'd rescued the second from a stack of rejections that were due to be returned when the cute photo of a garden gnome on the cover letter caught my eye.

But Lucy didn't seem to take much satisfaction from either of those sales and was getting edgy, asking every day if I'd found something that could compare to *Parco Lambro*. "It has to have power," she told me. "Self-help is bread and butter and nonfiction's hit or miss. I need something that will make them cry. When they cry, you know it's going to be expensive." I wanted to deliver for her. I, too, wanted to make them cry.

I passed my eyes over the manuscript in front of me again. It wasn't going to bring anyone to tears, I thought, and it needed some serious work, but it *was* different from anything else I'd seen lately. Despite its clumsy prose, there was something captivating and even subtly dark about it. And then there was the fact that it was set in a literary agency, something that added a whole other level of weirdness to it. The author's anonymity *had* achieved its desired purpose, I decided; it had gotten my—our—attention. The author had obviously submitted before, probably even to us, and had figured out how to keep from getting rejected instantly. And now I'd read the manuscript. And it wasn't bad. It had potential, I decided, and so I'd pass it on to Lucy.

While I booted up my computer to write the report, I gave a backward glance at my bed, where Malcolm was sleeping soundly. And why shouldn't he, I thought. Everyone but doughnut-makers and hospital workers were sleeping at this hour of the morning. My eyes itched with fatigue as I stared longingly in the direction of my pillow. Malcolm's body was a long shape deep under the covers. I could see only a bit of gold hair and the sloping edge of one cheekbone over the top of the fabric. It took a tremendous amount of will not to abandon my post and crawl in next to him. I didn't sleep until sunrise anymore, or even close to it. These predawn hours had emerged as the only time I had to get caught up on the avalanche of work that fell on me every day.

A big part of that catching up had to do with Anna. Her reading had become my reading and her reports were starting to become a big problem for me. I'd already rescued two good novels from the reject pile that she thought were "stupid" and "boring," two of her favorite adjectives. She was, rightly, convinced that I was undercutting her opinion by championing her rejects. Anna felt that once she'd put the kibosh on a manuscript, my function as a second reader should only be to support her. Of course, Lucy had made me the second reader on Anna's manuscripts for the exact opposite reason. All this had served to deepen Anna's hostility toward me. When I wrote my own reports on her rejects, I had to get very creative, writing in a fashion that would seem to support Anna's statements without pointing out what she'd missed, while implying that she was completely wrong in her assessments without appearing to do so at all. It was starting to become an exhausting process. It occurred to me once again that Lucy should just take Anna off the reading list altogether. But it seemed to me that Lucy got some sort of weird pleasure out of the growing conflict between Anna and me over the reading pile. During my first few days at the office, when Anna had still been chatty with me, she'd told me that Lucy was "grooming" her to become another agent in the office. Considering the fact that Lucy seemed to find the very thought of another agent in the office repugnant, I suspected Anna was not only an inadequate reader but delusional as well. Besides, if Lucy wanted to groom anyone to be an agent, she'd look to *me*.

I put Anna out of my mind, rubbed the cold out of my fingers, and started hitting the keyboard.

Title: BLIND SUBMISSION
Author: ?
Genre: Fiction
Reader: Angel

This is an interesting piece. It came in unsolicited through the mail, but the author, who is anonymous at this point, lists no phone number or address and only has an e-mail address as a contact. I suppose this adds some intrigue, since the novel is set in a literary agency (!!!), but it also means we know nothing about previous publishing credits, etc. My guess, judging from the writing, is that there aren't any. The author didn't provide us with a synopsis, either.

What this novel seems to be is something of a reverse "insider revenge" novel or, as the *New York Times* calls it, "bite-the-boss fiction." Here, instead of having a bitch-from-hell boss and a long-suffering assistant, we've got a manipulative assistant with a hidden agenda—something like *The Nanny Diaries* or *The Devil Wears Prada* but darker and told from the other side. I think the idea has potential, but I've got a couple of concerns. One is the setting. While I like the idea of setting a novel in a literary agency (the fact that it's close to home notwithstanding), the conventional wisdom is that books set in the publishing world don't sell. My other concern is the writing, which just seems a little stiff. And, although it feels as if the author also wants to come out right away with mystery and intrigue, the pacing is slow and the characters don't really stand out, especially the main character, Alice, who is supposedly "a woman with secrets." The writing is not particularly descriptive and, when it is, the descriptions are awkward. "The sun looked like cold butter," for example. The dialogue, too, seems a bit forced.

However, while these aren't minor details, they are workable. I think we should ask to read more (the author says there *is* more) to see if the pace picks up and if the writing gets stronger. If the author is willing (and able) to revise, this novel could be quite promising.

By the time I printed out the report, the small clock on my desk read 6:30 A.M. Lucy had succeeded in training me to function on New York time, and I couldn't help thinking that people in that city were already at their desks and working. Time was getting short. I had to be at the office at eight and I had a half-hour drive ahead of me. The last manuscript in my pile, a memoir from an Alaskan hairstylist titled *Perm-or-Frost,* was going to have to wait. I didn't have high hopes for it, anyway.

As usual, the sound of my morning shower and hair dryer did nothing to interrupt Malcolm's slumber. Watching him sleep had become something of a pattern for me. Before I started working for Lucy, he'd spent an average of four nights a week at my apartment, but since my first day, he'd come over every night, whether he was working late shifts at the restaurant or not. Not that this meant we were actually spending more time together. It was more like we were spending more time *next to* each other. My nights were consumed with reading. Malcolm watched TV. Or slept. Or pointedly reread his own manuscript.

Malcolm's novel; another thing I was going to have to deal with soon, I thought. Despite his protests that I was the major beneficiary of my new job, Malcolm had wasted no time in bringing his hefty manuscript over to my place. Of course, he hadn't demanded, or even suggested, that I take it to Lucy, oh no, he'd just sort of placed it on the floor beside the bed, so that I could "look it over, you know, to give it the final polish."

Right around the time of the *Parco Lambro* auction, Malcolm casually mentioned, "You know, whenever you want to take a look at my manuscript, Angel, please feel free. You've clearly got the magic touch."

"Let's wait a bit," I told him at the time. "It's too early for me to—"

"I'm just *saying,* Angel, if you want to look at it—"

"Right, of course."

"And I've started working on something else, by the way." He gave me a canary-eating cat smile and dropped his voice to a seductive whisper. "I'm really excited about this new one."

"Really? That's great."

"You're an inspiration to me, Angel. Since you've become the Mistress of Literature, I've been very productive. And notice, I'm not asking you to look at this new one."

"I know, Malcolm. I'll look at *Bridge of Lies*. I promise."

But I hadn't looked at it and wasn't sure I wanted to. Malcolm had stopped mentioning his book over the last week or two, but his silence felt heavier and more demanding than his "suggestion" that I read it. I knew I'd have to give it to Lucy at some point, but what would she think if this novel turned out to be less than stellar? And what if she gave it to Anna to read? I shuddered at the thought. There wasn't going to be an easy way out of this one. I felt a tiny flicker of resentment flare in the back of my brain. I couldn't help wishing that Malcolm hadn't put me in this position so soon, despite the guilt that wish brought in its wake. After all, if it hadn't been for Malcolm, I wouldn't even have this job. And, despite its challenges, I really did love my job. I'd never worked as hard in my life, but I'd also never experienced the kind of anticipatory rush I felt every time I sat down at my desk. Working for Lucy was . . . *extreme* seemed a fitting word. And with extremes, you had to expect both big highs and low lows.

I searched my closet for something presentable to wear and, as I did every morning, cursed Lucy's no-jeans policy. My new schedule didn't allow much time for things like laundry, so my wardrobe offered little in the way of acceptable items. I grabbed my last pair of borderline-clean pants and threw them on. I had no time or inclination to give myself a final inspection in the mirror and told myself that it didn't matter. In all the time I'd been working there, there had not been a single visitor to the office.

I heard Malcolm stir and sigh as I gathered my purse, manuscripts, and keys. I bent down into an awkward kneel by the bed so that my face was level with his.

"Hey," I whispered. "I'm on my way out. See you later?"

Malcolm smiled, his eyes half-closed, and reached out his arm to cover my shoulders. I could feel the enticing warmth of his skin through my shirt. He brushed the tips of his fingers across my cheek.

"Mmm, you smell so good," he said, deepening the corners of his smile. He pulled a strand of my hair free and rubbed it between his thumb and forefinger. A lewd gleam crept into his eyes. "Got a minute before you leave?"

"I really, really don't," I told him, and hoped that the regret in my voice sounded genuine.

"You sure, Angel?" he said, pulling me gently toward him. Our lips met for one moment before I lost my balance and slipped off the edge of the bed, dropping my purse and keys and kicking paper as I tried to find purchase on the floor.

"Baby, are you okay?" Malcolm looked down at me, laughter dying in his throat as we both saw that I'd fallen on his manuscript, tearing a couple of pages and flipping the rest across the floor.

"I'm so sorry," I said, quickly shoveling it back into place. "I just—"

"It's okay," he said. "Leave it." His smile had vanished and his voice had gone cold. I could hear everything he wasn't saying as clearly as if he'd been yelling it at me. *Go ahead, step on my work. That's what it means to you. That's what I mean to you.*

"Malcolm, I'm sorry. I didn't mean to—"

"Better go," he interrupted. "You'll be late." He turned away from me and burrowed under the covers.

"Malcolm—"

"Don't let it worry you, *Angel*." His voice, muffled by sheets, was almost a growl. "You've got more important things to do."

I allowed myself only a second to debate whether or not I should attempt to make things right by falling onto the bed next to Malcolm and burying my face in his neck. But I *was* going to be late and my desire not to be overwhelmed my desire for him. I'd have to make time later, I told myself, and gathered my things once more. And then, fighting with myself all the way, I collected Malcolm's pages from the floor and put them in with my pile. At the very least, I owed him enough to take the manuscript with me, even if I wasn't ready to give it to Lucy yet. If he heard me rustling, Malcolm gave no indication, and then I was out the door. It wasn't until I was already on the road that I realized I'd forgotten to say good-bye to him.

UNLIKE ALMOST EVERYONE I KNEW, I loved my morning commute. I felt as if the time I spent in my car was the only real time I had to myself— the only time when I didn't have to answer phones, respond to memos, or talk to anyone else. For a half hour in the morning and a half hour in the evening, I allowed myself just to think—to sort through the minutiae of my days and organize it all appropriately. It usually went all to hell once I set foot in the office, but that wasn't really the point. What was important was that I got a few uninterrupted minutes to just let my mind trip and wander wherever it wanted.

It helped, of course, that I had attractive surroundings to look at while I drove. As soon as I crossed the line out of Sonoma County into Marin, the dry, rural feel of Petaluma gave way to lusher scenery on either side of the road. The closer I got to San Rafael, the greener and better tended the streets became. San Francisco's famous fog was romantic and all, but I didn't mind trading it for the warmth and sunlight on the other side of the Golden Gate Bridge.

As I wound my way through the exclusive real estate that was San Rafael and my guilt over Malcolm's manuscript started to fade, my mind latched once more on to the anonymous novel, which was sitting next to me on the passenger seat, its presence as large as that of any person. It occurred to me that the author might have sent the manuscript out to several literary agents. If it *had* gone out wide and I hadn't chased it quickly enough, I'd risk some pointed wrath from Lucy. Nothing got Lucy more excited or more irritated than when a potentially hot author had his or her manuscript circulating among several agents. Of course, the fact that an author *had* interest from other agents went a long way to making that author hot, regardless of the potential book's content.

And hot was what Lucy wanted—what Lucy craved. Immediately after the sale of *Parco Lambro*, she'd circulated a memo (which I'd drafted ten times before she approved it) that said, *While our recent auction was a success, we cannot afford to sit back and take a break. We need to redouble our efforts to bring in more of the same. This office cannot support all of you without a healthy flow of cash. Remember time is $$$!!!! I expect you all to use yours wisely.*

Of course, I suspected that none of us was making the kind of money that would drain Lucy's coffers. My own probationary salary was barely a living wage after taxes. I'd done a little research and discovered that even starting salaries at New York publishers were a little higher. Elise had been paying me a little more, but I'd expected to take a dip in salary when I started working with Lucy. I just hadn't realized how lean things would become. Lucy had, however, called me into a meeting with Craig in her office after *Parco Lambro* and, with a great flourish, presented me with a bonus.

"I believe in incentives," Lucy said. "And although some might say that this is a foolish move, I believe you've earned this. And *I trust you, Angel*. Craig? Will you do the honors?"

Grimacing as if he'd eaten something rotten, Craig handed me a check for one thousand dollars. "Congratulations, Angel," he said. "And just so you know, there are no taxes deducted from this check. This is not part of your salary. You'll have to pay taxes on it separately."

"I—I don't know what to say," I said.

"'Thank you' is always appropriate," Lucy offered. "There's more where that came from, Angel, if you know how to get it." She took a dramatic pause. "And I think you do."

Of course I did. Like Skinner and Pavlov before her, Lucy was conditioning me. Every time I pressed the right bar, I'd get a fat check. Find another Damiano Vero. That was the message, but it wasn't one that Lucy needed to send. The desire was already alive in me. There was something surprisingly seductive about the rush of excitement *Parco Lambro* had created in me, and it wasn't about the money. It was very much like a drug, I thought. The intensity faded soon after the event, but enough of the memory remained to make me want more. I supposed it had to be the same for Lucy and was at least part of what gave her that insatiable drive.

I FOUND THE OFFICE EMPTY when I let myself in and realized that, despite the fact that I'd stopped for a cappuccino on the way over, I'd arrived ten minutes earlier than usual. I settled myself at my desk and flipped on my computer. There were multiple notes from Lucy in my in-box. At the top of the pile was her daily memo itemizing the tasks that were most important the moment she'd thought of them the previous evening, but that would probably change as the day went on.

Angel—

Today's Top Priorities:

1. Report on reader's reports.

2. Chase Elvis!!!!

3. Find salon (as in SF Chron) and make appt. (Where is my blue pen?)

4. I need complete list of all projects in development/in submission/due for delivery/pubbing in the next two months.

5. Calls!!!

It was a list of labors worthy of Hercules. The only items that were missing were "Kill Hydra" and "Clean Augean stables." Which actually wasn't a bad idea for a business book for one of our authors, I thought. I made a mental note to run it past Lucy; something like *Twelve Tasks for Better Business* or *Twelve Rules for Commercial Success.*

I wondered once more how Lucy was able to do it. How was it possible that she'd accumulated so much for me to do before the day even began? Not to mention the fact that I needed to crack the Da Vinci Code to figure out what each item on the list actually meant. I'd worked out that #3 was a request to make her a hair appointment at a salon that the *San Francisco Chronicle* had just named the hottest spot in town, but I couldn't quite grasp how she wanted me to chase Elvis. And, of course, the phone was already ringing.

"Good morning, Lucy Fiamma Agency." My voice sounded gravelly and tired. I cleared my throat and heard his trademark coughing on the other end of the phone. Peter Johnson.

"Hello, Angel. How are you?"

I wondered when I'd become Angel to him. He'd always been meticulous about calling me Ms. Robinson before.

"I'm fine, Mr. Johnson, how are you?"

"Please call me Peter," he wheezed. "I think we know each other well enough at this point." He lapsed into another coughing fit. He had a point, I supposed, although it had been a few days since I'd spoken to him last. I couldn't remember exactly when I'd sent his most recent rejection or if there was one just about to go out.

"Okay, Peter. You must be calling about your manuscript. I wrote you a note and sent it—"

"No, no," he rasped. "I got that. And thank you, Angel, for your kind words. But that's not why I'm calling." He took a breath and choked on it, hacking once more into the phone. I bit my lip with impatience and a little remorse. My "words" on his last rejection letter had been anything but kind. I'd tried my best to imply, without being nasty, that Lucy would never accept his work for representation. Apparently, he hadn't quite gotten the message.

"I'm calling because I'd like to give you one more chance. I need to tell you something. I've—" He interrupted himself with more hacking.

I couldn't stop myself from sighing into the phone. He wanted to give *us* one more chance? What was he talking about? How many different ways could I tell him no?

"You know, Mr. Johnson, I really don't think—"

"Please hear me out," he gasped, but I couldn't. I didn't know whether it was fatigue, impatience, or just irritation that got me, but I decided that it was time to put Peter Johnson out of his—and my—misery for good.

"Mr. Johnson, I think it's only fair I tell you that Lucy Fiamma has seen your work and it's just not right for her. She's not the agent for you. I'm sorry."

"You don't understand," he said. "You're not listening."

"Please," I begged him. "Do yourself a favor, don't send us anything else." There was a quiet pause. For a second I thought he'd stopped breathing altogether.

"You're making a mistake," he said. "And you are *not* Lucy Fiamma."

"I'm sorry if you—" I began, but Peter Johnson hung up on me. I stared at the receiver for a moment, stunned. He'd always been unfailingly polite. But so had I until this moment. I felt a twinge of discomfort. But really, what could he expect? I debated looking up his phone number and calling him back, but the phone shrilled again and I picked it up, assuming he'd beaten me to it.

"Fiamma Agency." I waited for the sound of labored breathing.

"Angel? Is that you?"

I was momentarily thrown by a woman's voice on the other end of the phone. "Uh . . . This is Angel Robinson. May I help you?"

"Angel, it's Elise."

"Elise!" At that moment, I realized how much I'd missed her. Our daily confabs, swapping customer stories and discussing books, came rushing back to me on a wave of instant nostalgia. And it wasn't just the easy camaraderie I had with Elise that I missed, it was her good nature, her lack of hard edges, and her centeredness. I missed the quiet enjoyment of working for her. It had been less than two months since I'd last sat with her at Blue Moon sharing quips and coffee, but it felt like the farthest reaches of the past.

"How are you, Angel? I haven't heard from you since you left. I thought I'd catch you at home this morning, but Malcolm said you were already at work." I'd forgotten that she knew Malcolm. I met him in her store, after all. She'd always been very protective of me when it came to him, telling me to watch my heart, not to give away too much of myself—even if he *was* one of the best-looking men she'd ever met. I'd almost forgotten all of that.

"I'm so sorry, Elise. I keep meaning to call you, but by the time I finish work, it's so late and then I don't remember . . . I'm sorry."

"You don't have to be sorry, Angel, I just wanted to see how you were doing. How's the job? Tell me honestly. She treating you okay?"

"Great!" I said too perkily. "Busy, you know. We just sold an amazing book by a new author. You'd love it, Elise." I wondered at my sudden desire to hold back the less pleasant details of my job to present the best possible face. Oddly, I felt as if Elise, who'd been both friend and mentor, had become an outsider.

"Really? That's wonderful, Angel. If I know you, you're doing an amazing job. I suppose you don't have very much free time, though, do you? I was hoping maybe we could get together for lunch or coffee. I've got something to show you—well, give you, actually. I found it when I was clearing out the store. I think you'll find it very interesting."

It was a nice idea, but I'd never be able to find the time to have lunch with her unless I took a vacation day, and Lucy had made it clear that I didn't have any of those coming to me for at least a year. Even the weekends were booked solid with reading.

"Maybe I could call you when I get home? We can set something up then." I was eager to get her off the phone before Lucy caught wind that I was on a personal call. "I'm so glad you called, though. It's great to hear from you."

"Are you sure you're okay, Angel?"

"I'm fine, great. I'll speak to you later. Bye, Elise." I hung up the phone and exhaled so hard, spots started dancing in front of my eyes. Elise was the second person I'd hung up on in the space of ten minutes. I sensed that this was to be a day of extremes.

"Angel!"

I startled and jumped at the sound of my name. I turned my head in the direction of her voice and had to stifle a gasp. Lucy was standing in the doorway of her office, clad only in a large, fluffy white towel.

"Glad you're finally here," she said. "It's going to be a very busy day today. I need you to start making calls now."

I couldn't answer, paralyzed by the sight in front of me.

"Is there a problem, Angel?" she asked.

"Um . . ."

Lucy shifted her position and the unthinkable happened: The towel sprang loose and fell to the floor before she could catch it. I lowered my eyes instinctively but not before the vision of her nakedness seared my retinas.

"Goddamn it!" I heard her curse. And then, "My calls, Angel! Now!"

FIVE

I SAT AT MY DESK, head down, eyes glued to my keyboard, for several minutes after I heard the click of Lucy's office door shutting. That was as long as it took for me to try, and fail, to erase the image of a naked Lucy from my brain. I wasn't exactly shocked at her lack of modesty. Like many memsahibs before her, Lucy didn't think much about revealing herself to her servants, and I'd often arrived at the office early enough to see her in various states of undress. This was the first time that I'd actually seen her unclothed, though, and it was a little much to take on an empty stomach. Perhaps I was just exhausted, I thought, working so many concentrated hours on so little sleep that I'd started hallucinating. Yes, that was it—I'd imagined the whole thing. But why, then, were the details so remarkably clear? It appeared that my vision had breast implants, for example, and I couldn't understand why my brain would choose to hallucinate those. The back of my throat was dry and scratched as if there were something small and sharp poking into it. I felt a little dizzy and slightly nauseated. I needed to drink something. As I bent toward my purse for my water bottle, my intercom buzzed, shrill in the empty office.

"Angel!"

"Yes, Lucy?"

"Why am I not yet on the phone? Is nobody working in Manhattan today? Some sort of holiday I'm unaware of?"

"No, Lucy. I mean, yes, I'm—"

"Did I not ask you to begin calling several minutes ago?"

So I hadn't imagined it. I waited a second, almost hearing the impatient thrum of passing time.

"Angel, is there something wrong with you today?"

"No, Lucy."

"Then why the *fuck* am I not on the phone at this moment, Angel?"

There was something about the way Lucy cursed, some sort of stiff nuance she placed on the word *fuck,* that took all the teeth out of it. It wasn't as if Lucy couldn't sound nasty, far from it. She could make almost any word sound like the vilest epithet when she placed the right venomous emphasis on the syllables. But she shaped those words like daggers herself, they didn't start that way. Words like *shit, fuck,* and *bullshit,* which she used with intermittent frequency, were already loaded, but I never recoiled when she cursed—unlike the times when she hurled my own name at me like a weapon.

"I'm sorry, Lucy, I'm calling right now." I moved to pick up the receiver on my phone.

"Too late! Put the phone down and come in here now, please, Angel. There's something else I need to discuss with you immediately."

"Okay."

"And bring your reading."

I realized I'd started perspiring. I could feel beads of moisture on my upper lip and the soles of my feet were tingling. It took me a second to identify the combination as my body's own response to fear.

I gathered up the *Blind Submission* manuscript and a pad of paper to take notes. Malcolm's novel stared up at me from its position in my bag. In a fit of guilty impulsivity, I grabbed it and added it to my stack. My morning at the office was already so strange and unsettling that trying to push my boyfriend's book hardly seemed uncomfortable. I knocked on Lucy's door, standing outside for as long as possible before she shouted, "Come *in,* Angel!" and I had to enter.

"I'm quite serious when I ask if you need medical attention today, Angel. First you walk in on me when I'm practically naked—please try not to do that again, by the way—and now you are just standing there. What is wrong with you?"

I took a deep breath and looked over at her. She was fully dressed, wearing a brown leather vest with a matching skirt, a chunky turquoise necklace, and a bright yellow turtleneck. The outfit did nothing for her complexion, but it was so much better than what I'd seen underneath. I could feel relief flooding my body like warm water. I was so relieved, in fact, that I decided to let her maintain the illusion that *I'd* walked in on *her*. It appeared she was capable of embarrassment after all.

"I'm so sorry, Lucy," I said. "I guess I'm a little tired today. I haven't been getting much sleep lately."

Lucy scrutinized me for a moment, one eyebrow arching, as if she was trying to decide between two responses.

"What you do in your *private* life is entirely up to you, Angel," she said, and again I noticed her particular talent for making the mundane obscene. "But I must insist that it not infringe on your job," she continued. "I'm sure you can understand my feelings about this. Perhaps you should save your late nights for the weekends, hmm?" Malcolm could certainly attest that my late nights had nothing to do with anything private and everything to do with the office, but it didn't seem wise to mention that with Lucy's eyebrow still arrowed in my direction.

"Right," I said.

"*Although,*" she said, stretching out the syllables, "I suppose you're young, aren't you? And there's a boyfriend, isn't there? A fiancé, no?"

"Yes, but—"

"No need to be prudish, Angel. Not for my benefit. Just the two of us girls here now." She grinned. "Angel, you're blushing! Well, isn't that sweet?" That seductive tone had worked its way into her voice again. Was she flirting with me? I had no idea how to respond. I was sure that the burn on my cheeks was deepening to a nice shade of scarlet. "You must be an angel after all," Lucy was saying. It sounded like a quote, but I had no idea from where. "All right, sit down," she said abruptly. "Let's get to it."

I sat-fell into Lucy's white couch and she left her desk to come sit beside me, turning so that her softly booted knees were just touching mine. I made a show of reassembling the manuscripts on my lap so that I could shift away.

"Not yet," she said, watching me shuffle the papers. "We have another matter to go over first."

"Okay," I said, pulling my notepad closer.

"No," she said. "No notes for this conversation. In fact, Angel, I'm going to have to ask you to keep this in strict confidence. This is a very sensitive issue and I wouldn't be discussing it with you at all if I didn't feel I could trust your judgment completely." She grinned at me again, showing all her white teeth. They seemed shinier than usual.

"Of course," I said. "I mean, of course I won't say anything."

"It's about Anna," she said, and stopped, waiting for my response.

"Okay," I said.

"I'm wondering," Lucy continued, leaning in closer, "if I should let her go."

"Oh," was the only response I could muster.

"The thing about Anna is that, although I believe her heart's in the right place, she's just not that sharp. Do you know what I mean, Angel?" Her tone implied that I should not only know what she meant, but that I should agree. I wasn't happy about the position that put me in.

"Um," I said, stretching for time.

"Don't be coy, Angel. I know for a fact that you've noticed what she misses with the reading."

"Well, I—"

"And, frankly, I'm not confident that she's detail-oriented enough for her other work, either. Although that could be fixed. The reading is the lifeblood of this office, Angel, I'm sure I don't need to tell you that. You can't train someone to have an eye. And that's what you have, Angel, it's why I hired you despite your naïveté and obvious lack of experience."

"Oh, yes. Thank you." Had I just thanked her for insulting me or had I agreed with her about Anna? The conversation was fast getting away from me.

"Now, Angel, even though I rely on your judgment, you cannot be the only person in this office with an eye for what will sell. I need every member of my staff to be as sharp."

"Right."

"Craig has plenty of responsibility outside of the reading, so I can't expect the same kind of volume from him. And Nora, well, that's another topic altogether, isn't it? I'll have to address that later. But Anna is clearly falling down in this area. So, my question to you is: Do I let her go? Do you feel the quality of her reading is getting better or worse?"

"Oh, Lucy, I'm not sure I'd be the best person to help you decide. . . . I mean, I . . ." I trailed off and looked down at my hands, as if what I should say next might be written there. It occurred to me that Lucy might be fashioning another one of her tests, along the lines of the "Do you put the author or editor through to me first?" question from my interview. Perhaps this was her way of separating the girls from the women? Some sort of office *Survivor*, perhaps? If that were the case, it was a particularly distasteful test. Lucy was waiting for an answer and I opened my mouth to speak. What came out of it next was a complete surprise to me.

"I don't think her reads are getting any better," I said. "I was just thinking this morning how she seems to be rejecting most of her manuscripts without really reading them carefully."

"Yes," Lucy said, and leaned back into the couch, an unpleasant grin spreading across her face. "I thought as much. So your recommendation would be to let her go, then?"

"No, I didn't—"

"You're pretty confident, aren't you, Angel? Only here a few weeks, and already you're suggesting I fire one of your superiors."

Up to that moment, I could safely say that I'd never felt my jaw drop. But it fell open then, independent of any will on my part, while the words that came to my mind—*What are you talking about?*—remained tangled and unspoken in the back of my throat.

"Oh, don't look at me that way, Angel," Lucy said, waving her hand. "You've got the killer instinct. That is not a disadvantage in this business. However, you'll have to put a leash on your ambition for a bit longer. I'd like to give Anna a chance to redeem herself. In fact, I'd like *you* to give her a chance. I want you to work with her, Angel. Let her know what she should be looking for and what she's missing. I've invested quite a bit of time and money in that girl, and I'm not willing to throw it all away just yet. Do you understand?"

"Yes," I said, although I didn't.

"Of course, I'll have to let her know that she's in a probationary period as far as the reading goes. We'll have a staff meeting when everyone gets here—draft a memo about that, please—and then perhaps I can see you and Anna together in my office." It wasn't a question.

"What time would you like to have the staff meeting?" I asked. Lucy looked over at me as if I'd lost my mind.

"The usual time, of course, Angel."

This meant that I'd have to make one up. We hadn't really had an organized staff meeting since I'd started the job.

"Now," she said briskly, "this brings me to my next point, and I have to say I'm somewhat disappointed in you, Angel." She reached down and plucked a manuscript from a pile on the floor. I recognized it as Shelly Franklin's novel, *Elvis Will Dance at Your Wedding.* So that's what "Chase Elvis" meant, I thought, and was seized with a quick panic. I'd given Lucy the manuscript weeks ago, but in the heat of Damiano's auction and everything else that had happened since I'd read it, I'd forgotten to ask her about it. I'd forgotten to anticipate, remind, and otherwise order Lucy's thoughts—a failing she was sure to pounce on.

"This," she said, waving *Elvis* in front of me, "is one of the very manuscripts you feel is better than Anna has given it credit for. Why, then, has it taken *so long* to get to me?"

"But—" I began, and stopped myself before I could say something stupid. I *had* given it to her right away, I just hadn't remembered to remind her of that fact. I couldn't figure out if I was guilty or innocent. "I did pass that on to you a while ago," I finished weakly.

"But I'm only seeing it now!" she exclaimed. "How do you account for that?"

Several insubordinate responses flashed through my brain, but I opted for the safest path, which was just to say, "I'm sorry, Lucy, I thought you'd read it already."

Lucy stared at me for a second, her gimlet eyes flashing, and then moved quickly to another thought. "Fine," she said, "I'll let it go this time, but really, Angel, you need to be more careful. I don't have to tell you. Anyway, let's just discuss this piece—and give me the short version, Angel, we're running out of time here."

"Um, well, it's . . . uh . . ." I remembered the manuscript well, but it was a struggle to pull the words out of the thickness in my brain. For one flashing second, I was sure I was going to pass out.

"The *short* version, Angel." Lucy leaned toward me so close that for the first time I could see that she had tiny lines around her mouth into which her brick-colored lipstick was bleeding. I was starting to feel that Lucy was about to eat me like a predator with its fallen prey and I forced myself out of my haze.

"Right, right. I think this one is really good. *Elvis Will Dance at Your Wedding,*" I said. Lucy wrinkled her nose. "I know, I thought the title was too long when I first saw it, but it really does conjure the perfect image of what she's trying to get across here."

"Which is? Fiction or non?"

So she *still* hadn't read it, I thought.

"Fiction. Road-trip novel about a couple who drives to Las Vegas to marry. Good writing, very evocative. Voyage of discovery about themselves, their relationship. It's literary, but not too. Still has mass-market appeal. It comments on the state of modern love—no, actually, it's *post*modern love and marriage in the new millennium. *Wild at Heart* meets *Leaving Las Vegas.* But more upbeat." I'd come back to myself, finding all the right words, throwing them out in a rush and creating the kind of hot energy I loved. I could see that Lucy was warming to it as well. We were on a roll.

"Credits?" she asked.

"A few little lit mags. She's got a master's from California University, though."

"*Pretty Feet,*" Lucy mused, referring to the last bestseller written by a California University MFA graduate. A quirky little novel about a young woman with enormous misshapen feet and her quest for love, *Pretty Feet* had been a solid fixture on the *New York Times* bestseller list for almost a year.

"Exactly," I said.

"Intriguing," Lucy said. "Has she contacted other agents?"

I bit the inside of my cheek and lied through my teeth. "No, we're it. Would you like me to call her? To get the rest of it, I mean."

Lucy gave an exasperated sigh. "You haven't done that yet? Come on, Angel, you have to take some initiative. You don't need my permission to call an author to request more material if you like something. That should just be a matter of course at this point, no?"

"No. I mean yes. Yes, of course."

"And you really like it?" she asked.

"Very much."

"As much as the Italian book?"

"Yes, but in a different way."

"Good! What else do you have?"

"This," I said, and thrust *Blind Submission* at her.

"Can you be more specific?" Lucy said, a cold edge of condescension creeping into her voice.

"Sorry. It's a novel set in a literary agency. Anonymous author." I smiled for effect. "Kind of fun."

"Really?" Lucy asked, taking it from me. "And how long have I been waiting for this one?"

I was sweating again. "Just came in," I said.

"Hmm," Lucy mused. "And you like it?"

"I think it needs some work, but it's got potential," I said.

"And have you written notes to that effect?"

"Yes," I said. "Of course."

"Fine, I'll read it right away," she said. "Is that it? Are we finished?"

"Yes, that's it," I said, standing up. I felt as if I'd been sitting on that couch for days. Time got completely distorted in Lucy's office. It really *was* similar to Narnia in its way.

"What's that?" Lucy asked, pointing at Malcolm's manuscript, still in my arms, which I'd just decided I shouldn't show her. But there was no escaping it now. Lucy's eyes missed nothing.

"It's . . ." I filled my lungs with air. What the hell. "My fiancé is a writer? And a big fan of yours?" Now I was forming my sentences as questions, the first sign of the conversationally weak and lame. Lucy was not going to help me at all with this one, I could see. She looked bemused. "Anyway," I went on, "he's written this novel. . . ."

"Have you read it?" Lucy asked me.

"No, I haven't."

"Then why in God's name should I waste *my* time reading it, Angel?"

"I've read his other work and I think it's good. I thought it might be hard for me to be objective about the novel, though, if I read it before, you know, I gave it to you. But I totally understand if you're too busy. I mean, he could have sent it in—he did, actually, send this to you once a long time ago, and you encouraged him to rewrite, but if he sent it now, I'd be the one seeing it first anyway probably and then—"

"Just give it to me," she snapped, and so I did. "This is a big favor I'm doing for you, I hope you realize," she said. "I hope *he* realizes." She glanced at the title page. "*Bridge of Lies,* is it? Interesting. Why are these pages torn like this? Looks like the dog ate it." She looked up at me, irritation creasing her features. "You're still standing there, Angel."

"Yes, okay, your calls. Thank you, Lucy."

"Get me Nadia Fiori first, please. We still have to settle the schedule on the Italian book." She was already at her desk, positioning her notepads and pens for their inevitable stacking and unstacking, as I left her office.

I DECIDED THAT THE "usual" time for a staff meeting should be at nine A.M.—lunchtime in New York—and placed a copy of the memo on everyone's desk. It would have been much simpler, of course, to just tell Anna, Craig, and Nora that there was a meeting, but Lucy insisted we have memos for every activity.

"What's this about?" Anna asked me, holding up her copy of the memo. For a paranoid moment, I was sure she'd somehow heard my earlier discussion with Lucy. She looked uncharacteristically pale and worn out. She'd gained some weight in the last couple of weeks and it wasn't sitting well on her. There was a gauze bandage on her left hand and wrist.

"I'm not sure," I told her. "What happened to your hand?"

"Cut myself making chicken," she said. "Spent all night in the emergency room."

"Why didn't you call in?" Nora said, materializing as if from nowhere. Nora's long hair was pulled back, accentuating the sharp line of her jawbone. She'd lost the weight Anna had gained recently, and its absence looked even worse on her. The half-circles under her large eyes looked as if they'd been drawn in charcoal. I wondered if I looked as unhealthy as my coworkers. It wasn't a pleasant thought.

"Can't call in," Anna said. "It's just a few stitches. Only twenty. I missed the vein, anyway."

"Well, at least it wasn't a paper cut from all the reading you've been doing," Craig said as he made his way to Lucy's office. "I'd hate to think you got a work injury at home." Anna, Nora, and I gave him matching perplexed stares.

"It was a *joke,* ladies," he said, his rich voice covering us like honey. "You know, ha-ha? Never mind, then. Join me for the staff meeting, won't you?"

There was a fair bit of shuffling around before the four of us found comfortable places to sit in Lucy's inner sanctum. Her office wasn't particularly well designed for meetings since the couch provided most of the seating and actual chairs were in short supply. Craig took his position on the one large chair in the office, while Anna, Nora, and I settled into the couch, all of us trying to keep our arms and elbows as close to our bodies as possible so as to avoid touching our neighbor. Lucy was seated at her desk, surveying the scene, and when we'd finally assembled and were sitting still, she said, "This is lovely and you all look very cozy, but there's one problem here." Nobody ventured to ask her what that might be. "Who is going to answer the phones?" she said.

Anna sprung up like a jack-in-the-box. "I will, Lucy!" she gulped.

"Anna, what *is* that on your arm?"

"I had a little accident last night. It's nothing, really, just a few stitches."

"Did you bandage that yourself or did you see a doctor about it?" Lucy asked.

Anna gave Lucy a puppyish smile and said, "No, I went to the emergency room. Thanks, I'm fine, really."

"Do you realize how much bacteria there is at a hospital?" Lucy said. "I hope you aren't carrying in some kind of staph infection. These are close quarters, you know. You might have thought of that before coming in to work today."

Anna sank back into the couch, her color rising to a bright red hue. Embarrassment was written all over her face, but I could see the hard, angry edge underneath it. I read her thoughts as one word: *bitch*.

"Nora, it will have to be you, then. No, don't leave. Come and take my place over here. You can answer the phone at my desk." Nora looked stricken. "And Craig, I'll take your place and you can sit next to the patient over there on the couch. I can't afford to take the chance." Craig moved without a word, his face expressionless, and Nora, moving with all the speed of someone approaching the guillotine, seated herself at Lucy's desk. The phone rang immediately, as if sensing her presence there.

"Lucy Fiamma Literary Agency, may I help you? Yes? Hi. Can you hold, please?" Nora pushed the hold button on Lucy's phone and looked up. "Lucy? It's Susie Parker for you?"

"Nora, we're in the middle of a staff meeting here."

"So shall I—"

"Yes, Nora, and do it now." Lucy sighed heavily and muttered, "No sense, that girl." She adjusted a notepad on her lap while Nora dispatched Susie Parker. "I don't know why these staff meetings take so long to get going," she said. "Really, it ought to be a simple thing. We're going to have to learn to be more efficient here, people, if we're going to keep the coffers full. I realize that we've made some impressive sales in the last few weeks, but we cannot stop, slow down, or look back. I shouldn't have to spend time getting a meeting like this started. You all should be ready to go the minute you arrive. Angel, I'd like you to draft a plan for how we can improve the efficiency of these meetings. Please have it to me for review before the end of the day so that I can go over it."

Staff meetings more efficient, I wrote.

"Now," Lucy said, "our first order of business is the reading." She took in a deep breath. "As you are all aware, the reading is key to the success of this business. . . ." Despite myself, I began to glaze over. I'd heard Lucy say the same thing so many times, I'd reached a saturation point. My brain could hold no more. I was heading into a full-scale drift until the sound of my own name reeled me back in.

". . . and Angel informs me that you are not keeping up your end of the reading, Anna. Apparently, you've rejected several projects that were worth keeping or at least worth passing along to me. Now, I don't know if this is because you feel you're overloaded with work and don't have time to do your reading carefully or if your judgment is impaired. Which is it, Anna?"

I felt as if I'd been slapped. Although I was sure she knew what she was doing, I couldn't imagine what good Lucy thought would come of pitting me against Anna in front of the entire staff. It was becoming more and more difficult to figure out what constituted a good work performance in this office.

"I wasn't aware that my reading was so bad," Anna said, shrinking into herself as she cradled her bandaged arm. "Angel never mentioned it to me or I would have done something about it." Anna gave me a look of undisguised hatred. There was nothing I could say and no denials I could offer that would mitigate the damage, so I opted to remain silent.

"Is that true?" Lucy asked me. "You haven't kept Anna in the loop on this?"

"No. I mean yes. I've just taken . . . I didn't think—"

"So the answer is no," Lucy said. "In all fairness to Anna, then, perhaps we should start over here." Lucy graced Anna with a smile.

"Perhaps the problem here is that Angel is unaware that she should be sharing information," Craig said. "We're a team here, after all." With that, Craig managed to make *me* the problem, and as I glanced around the room, I could see that everyone was giving me similarly poisonous looks. So Craig was no friend of mine. That much was clear.

"We are indeed a team," Lucy said, "and we need to start working as one. To that end, I'd like you to work with Anna on the reading, Angel. Perhaps you can share some of that insight you've got with her. I'll let the two of you decide how best you can accomplish this, but I'd suggest you get together at some point after work and create a plan. Maybe you can have dinner together? I understand that Anna's quite an accomplished cook."

Sure, I thought, right after hell froze over.

"Good, that's decided," Lucy said, without waiting for a response. "Now we can move on to my second order of business, which is *money.* If I am going to continue to pay all of your salaries, we need more of it. Angel has just been discussing a manuscript that looks as if it might be promising. Another *Pretty Feet,* or so you said, correct, Angel?"

"The Elv— Yes, right," I said.

"Good, so let's hope your instincts are as sharp as they were on the Italian book. But regardless of whether or not that one turns out to be something, we need to start getting more creative about increasing revenue. In our search for the next hot book, we seem to be neglecting a very important source of possible sales. Can anyone tell me what that is?"

"Subsidiary rights?" Anna asked, hope threading its way into her voice.

"That's not what I'm talking about, but yes, that is another front we've been neglecting. Which you should know, Anna, since you've been in charge of sub rights for the last two months. But what I'm referring to now is *our authors.* The ones we already have."

"Option books," Craig said.

"Exactly," Lucy said. "We have a number of authors out there who are not producing second or third books. They need to be contacted and, if necessary, they need to be given some direction on what to do next."

"I could compile that list for you, Lucy," said Anna. As sorry as I was for my part in Anna's earlier embarrassment, her sycophant approach to Lucy was starting to nauseate me.

"No, your plate's full of sub rights to attend to, Anna. And by the way, I'd like to see an updated list of what you're working on right now, please. Angel will generate the list of authors and possible projects. In the meantime, I have two authors in mind who can be contacted immediately." Lucy took a dramatic pause. I noticed that Craig was smiling as he jotted notes on his legal pad. I wondered if there was something I was missing because I couldn't understand what he might be finding so amusing.

"Karanuk!" There was a collective intake of air at Lucy's pronouncement. "Yes, that's right, Karanuk has begun work on a new book. I've spoken with him recently and he's ready to move forward. However, he needs a little . . . *encouragement,* shall we say." She cleared her throat and plucked some nonexistent lint from her skirt. "Angel, I would like you to call him and offer him whatever he needs to get going."

"You want me to call Karanuk?" I asked her. My heart had started thumping so hard that I coughed over the last syllable of his name.

"Yes, call him. You know how to operate a telephone, do you not? Why do you look so frightened, Angel? He's just a *writer,* you know. After all."

"Does he have pages you want him to send?" I managed to ask.

"He has a title," Lucy said. "He's calling the next one *Warmer.* At least that's what he's calling it now. What do we think of that title?"

"Sounds great!" Anna gushed. "A perfect follow-up."

"I like it," said Nora. "Sounds, you know, *warm.*"

"Maybe *Warm* would be better. Without the *er,*" Craig offered.

"Yes, with ellipses," said Anna. "Instead of, you know, the exclamation point."

I watched Lucy's face as they spoke. By the time it came around to me, I knew exactly what she was thinking and exactly how to respond.

"I guess it would depend on what kind of book he's planning to write," I said. "You wouldn't want him to spoof himself."

"No, you wouldn't," Lucy said. "Good, then. You'll call him. Now, the second author I have in mind is Stephanie Spark."

"*Eat, Treat, Defeat!*" Anna practically shouted.

"Exactly," Lucy said. "As I'm sure you all know, that was a fabulous book. The meditations were excellent, but the diet was what really sold it. People lost thousands of pounds on that diet."

"I was one of them," Anna said. "Of course, I put some back on, but that wasn't the fault of the book or the diet. I should go back on it again."

"Yes," Lucy said. "Anyway, one of the reasons the book did so well was because the author took her own diet very seriously. Too seriously, in fact. She now suffers from anorexia. I think there's a story to be told here about the so-called success of dieting and where it can lead from the standpoint of a bestselling diet book."

"Good idea," Craig said.

"I could call her," Anna said. "As someone who's tried her diet—"

"No, I want Nora to handle this one," Lucy said.

"Why? Why me?" Nora squeaked, shocked out of her customary silence.

"Well, isn't it obvious?" Lucy asked, scanning Nora with her eyes. "You're anorexic yourself, aren't you? You must understand the mind-set, surely."

"What? What? I am not! Why would you say that?" Nora flailed her arms as if someone were trying to pin them down. She started shaking her head back and forth, on the verge of hysteria.

"There's nothing to be *ashamed* of, Nora," Lucy said, her tone clearly indicating that there was. "There are treatments for this kind of thing, you know."

"I can't, I can't, I can't," Nora said, and started to cry. I felt as if I were watching a train wreck. I was horrified, but I couldn't look away. Neither, it appeared, could Anna or Craig.

"Nora," Lucy said, her voice slow and measured, "if you are unable to participate in this meeting, perhaps you should take a break. I'm trying to run a business here."

Still sobbing, Nora bolted from Lucy's chair and disappeared into the main office. After a minute of uneasy silence, punctuated by the sound of the bathroom door slamming shut, Lucy stood and reclaimed her own seat.

"Totally unprofessional," she said. "This is the problem with these *girls*, Craig." Craig shrugged and raised his palms as if to deny culpability. "I ask you, was that performance really necessary?" I almost expected Anna to answer because she seemed to love skewering herself on rhetorical questions, but this time she wisely left it alone. Lucy sighed heavily. "Well, I suppose you'd better go see to her," she told Craig. "More time wasted. And I suppose we'll have to adjourn this meeting until later. Angel, you've got work to do. Anna, you stay here, I need to talk to you."

"Okay," Anna said. "I'll get the door." The look of self-satisfaction on her face annoyed me more than I wanted to admit.

There was a small tempest hovering over Nora's desk when I walked back into the office. Stacks of manuscripts sat on her chair, on the floor, and in the middle of her desk. Spilled Rolodex cards lay scattered on her computer keyboard and an assortment of rubber bands, paper clips, and pens decorated the remaining space. Nora was bent over the mess, emptying the contents of her top drawer into a large canvas bag. I watched as she threw in a jar of mustard, a container of protein powder, a hairbrush, a spoon, and a small notepad decorated with iridescent hearts. Craig sat in pacific calm at his own desk, attending to a file. Not only was he not "seeing to her," as Lucy suggested, he wasn't even looking at her. I felt a jolt of panic followed by a stab of guilt. Panic because she was obviously quitting and her workload would no doubt fall to me. Guilt because my panic wasn't even slightly tempered by any sympathy for Nora. I wondered if I should talk to her, offer some words of encouragement, or try to convince her to stay. But I'd already decided that it wasn't really my place. I wasn't Nora's buddy and I wasn't her boss. And it wasn't like anyone would do the same for me. It was clear that we were all on our own here, despite Lucy's constant assertions that we were a team. I was the only one watching *my* back in this office. Besides, judging by the speed with which Nora was moving, it didn't seem as if any kind of supportive gesture would make the least bit of difference. The phone rang and I leaped to answer it, glad for the excuse to shift my attention.

"Lucy Fiamma Agency."

"Yes," a small voice said, "this is . . . my name is Shelly Franklin? I sent you a manuscript a while ago? I don't know if you've seen it?"

"Hi, Shelly!" I said, sounding ridiculously upbeat to my own ears. "This is Angel Robinson, Lucy's assistant. I was just about to call you!"

"Oh. You were?" Her voice became more timid and I could barely hear her.

"Yes, I really like your novel. Lucy's reviewing it right now."

"Oh." She sounded almost disappointed. Not a good sign.

"We were wondering if you've sent this novel to other agents? You didn't mention that in your letter."

"Oh, I didn't? I was calling because I was wondering if I enclosed a self-addressed stamped envelope? If I forgot, I can send one in?" she whispered.

What was it about these authors? Every one of them seemed loony in his or her own way. "You did send one in as I recall," I said, my voice rising as hers dipped, "but we really don't need it right now because we'd like to see the rest of the novel."

"The rest?"

"You have the entire novel written, don't you? You did say that in your letter."

"Yes, I've written it."

"Can you send it to us?" I asked her. I realized I was almost shouting into the phone. There was obviously something wrong with this woman and I scrambled to try to figure out what it was.

"Okay," she said. "I'll send that out today. Thanks."

"Can I just ask you, have you sent this novel to any other agents?" I asked before I lost her.

"No?" she said, and hung up. I stared at the phone, as perplexed as I'd ever been. I'd have to call her back and I didn't relish the prospect. I looked up and saw Nora standing over me with a pile of manuscripts. She was dry-eyed, but tear-tracks stained both sides of her face.

"This is my reading," she said. "Now it's your reading. You'll have to go get today's mail."

"Okay," I said. "I'm really sorry."

Nora leaned in so that her face was close to mine. "She's cruel," she whispered. "It's one thing to be tough, but she's *cruel.*" She straightened up and turned to walk out. Craig's voice caught her before she could reach the door.

"Nora, if you leave now, I'll assume you're quitting. And if you're quitting, I'll need you to sit down for an exit interview," he said.

Nora shot him a look potent with hatred and misery. When she spoke, her voice trembled under the weight of unshed tears. "My name is Kelly," she said. "Kelly. *Kelly.*" She walked out, closing the door behind her, and Craig didn't try to stop her.

As if on cue, Anna emerged from Lucy's office before the dust from Nora's—*Kelly's*—exit could settle and walked over to my desk.

"Lucy wants me to ask you if you've called Karanuk yet," she said. "And we're supposed to have a meeting about my reading. But she wants me to read this first." She held up a manuscript for me to see. I recognized it immediately. Malcolm's novel.

"Hey," Anna said, noticing the unoccupied and disheveled desk for the first time. "Where's Nora?"

SIX

THE PHONES WERE RELENTLESS, ringing and flashing in an unremitting assault to my senses. If I hadn't known better, I would have sworn that Nora contacted every unpublished author who'd ever sent us a manuscript and instructed them to call right after she made her exit. Even Craig, who almost never picked up the phone, was forced to put on a headset and catch the calls that Anna and I couldn't get to. Lucy had voice mail on her phone system but hated the idea that any caller would ever hear a recording. It was unprofessional, she said, and gave the idea that we were a small, struggling agency. She wanted a live human to answer every call, even if that human had to spend the next ten minutes getting the caller off the line. Which is what Anna, Craig, and I did for the better part of two hours after Nora left.

"Just the first fifty pages and a self-addressed stamped envelope," I could hear Anna saying over and over again. Lucy hadn't emerged from her office since the staff meeting, and I wondered if she even knew that Nora had left. Surely, if she did, she would have called another meeting to discuss it.

I'd taken one break, if it could be called that, to retrieve the day's mail from the nearby postal store where Lucy had the agency's account.

Again, as if N— Kelly had planned it this way, there was an unusually heavy load. I dragged three full mail tubs to my desk and was frantically trying to separate the submissions from the catalogs, letters from editors, bills, and the usual choice items. Prospective authors sent in an astonishing array of ridiculous gifts in an effort to catch Lucy's attention. Most sent chocolates (Ghirardelli, Godiva) or money (cash stapled to cover letters), but others got more creative. Since I'd started working at the agency, we'd received a variety of animal pelts from writers trying to copy Karanuk's work, hand-painted mugs (stating *World's Best Agent* in gold glaze), theater tickets, gift certificates, and lavender-scented soap. All of these items had to be returned immediately, of course, along with their accompanying manuscripts. Nothing got a project rejected faster than when it had an attempt at bribery attached to it. Wading through all of this had been N— Kelly's job, and now it was mine. Whatever sympathy I'd had for her was fast dissipating as I struggled under the weight of my additional workload. Could she not have waited until the end of the day? As if she'd heard my thoughts and sent the gods to punish me, I caught my finger in an unusually stubborn clip and tore enough of the skin that I started to bleed on a manuscript.

"Damn, damn, damn," I whispered, smearing the cover letter in an effort to save it.

"Angel!" Anna's voice, high pitched and frantic, sliced through my consciousness. I dropped the manuscript into my own take-home pile and turned to Anna, trying to hide my bleeding finger, but she had already seen. "What are you doing?" she hissed.

"I cut—"

"Never mind! I need you to get the phone." I didn't ask her why she couldn't get the screaming thing, just turned and punched the line.

"Lucy Fiamma Agency," I said.

"Angel, is that you? It's Dami."

"Dami! Hi!" I was absurdly happy to hear from him and I was sure he could tell from my voice, which had turned high and squeaky. Anna must have heard it, too, because I could see her glowering at me from the corner of my eye.

"How are you?" he asked.

"I'm fine," I said. "How are *you*? You must be so thrilled about your book."

"It's amazing," he said. "I can't believe it."

"Well, believe it," I told him. "It's really going to happen. Do you need to speak to Lucy? If you hold on a minute, I can put you through. We've been really busy here today."

"I love to speak to Luciana, but I called now to talk to you," he said.

"Oh. Is there something you need help with? I can—"

"No, no, Angel. I want to come to the office today to thank you in person. I have something for you and Luciana. We have to celebrate."

"Oh." For a moment, I had no response to give him. I'd never seen a visitor of any kind in the office, let alone an author. Lucy had some local authors on her list, but most of her clients lived far away. I should probably ask her first before I extended an invitation to Damiano, I thought. On the other hand, I was almost positive that she'd nix the idea immediately. Lucy couldn't tolerate any kind of interruption of the workday unless she created it herself. And although I seemed on my way to becoming a liaison between her and her authors, I sensed that the last thing she wanted was for me to have any kind of personal relationship with them. Still, I was eager to meet Damiano. After spending so much time with him on the phone, and working through so much of his writing, I felt as if I already knew him. To hell with it, I thought. If Lucy complained, I could always plead ignorance. After all, I'd never received an *explicit* instruction not to allow an author into the office without permission.

"Well, it would be great to meet you," I said at last. "When were you thinking of coming by?"

"I'm coming from the city," he said, "so it takes me a while to get to you. The traffic, the bridge, you never know. So I'll be there sometime this afternoon."

"Okay, I'll let Lucy know," I said, although I had no intention of doing so. I didn't want Anna to hear, either, and had lowered my voice to a near-whisper. "Do you need directions?"

"Not to worry, Angel," he said. "I know where you are. *Ciao, bella.*"

"Who was *that*?" Anna asked as soon as I'd hung up, but I pretended not to hear her and picked up the phone again. My intercom line was flashing. Lucy had been silent long enough.

"Hi, Lucy."

"Angel, have you spoken to Karanuk yet? I'd like a status report on that."

"Not yet, Lucy. The phones have been crazy today."

"*Prioritize,* Angel," she barked, and hung up.

I hated to admit it to myself, but I was scared to call Karanuk. Despite what Lucy had said about him being "only a writer," I was intimidated by the very thought of him. What could I possibly say that would be helpful to someone of his literary stature? I had no idea what approach I was supposed to take with him. I could try fawning and cajoling, which would be preferable to a tongue-tied stammer, I supposed, but that didn't seem to be what Lucy had in mind. At any other time, the opportunity to speak to Karanuk would have seemed to me like a great honor. At this point, however, it was another fumble in a dark room.

As I dialed, I clung to the hope that I'd get voice mail or even an assistant, but no. Karanuk answered his own phone on the first ring with a simple but firm, "Karanuk."

"Hi, Karanuk?" (*Mr.* Karanuk? I had no idea.) "This is Angel Robinson? I'm Lucy Fiamma's new assistant? Lucy asked me to call you?"

"Yes," he said.

Yes . . . what? I thought, but forged ahead, anyway. "Lucy's very excited about your new book and she wanted me to ask you how—I mean when—she'll be able to take a look at the manuscript?"

"I don't have anything to show her," he said abruptly. I was sure he was going to hang up on me.

"Okay, do you know when you might have something? I think what she meant was just an outline or proposal, not the whole thing, of course."

Karanuk laughed, the first display of any kind of emotion since we'd begun talking. For a laugh, however, it didn't have much mirth. Like his voice, it was deep and strong, but devoid of accent or inflection. For someone who wrote as eloquently as he did, that absence of feeling seemed very odd. Which reminded me that I'd said nothing to him about his work.

"I'm a huge fan of *Cold!*, by the way," I said hurriedly. "It's one of the best books I've ever read."

There was a brief silence and then he said, "I live in Los Angeles. I'm not very cold anymore. Things are much warmer here and much different. My shape has shifted. I'm suffering the fate of a Klondike bar in the Sahara. There has been a melting process. Additives . . . plastic components . . . One does not know which way to proceed."

So he was off his head like almost every other author, I thought. But he'd given me an opening and I felt the jolt of an idea zip through my head.

"Oh, is that the theme of the new book?" I asked. "It's terrific. Displacement. Loss of self. Man out of his element. Disconnection from culture and reality under the hot sun of . . . of . . ."

"Celebrity," he said, and paused for a beat or two. "What did you say your name was?"

"Angel."

"Angel," he repeated. "You are her assistant? She has had many assistants. She needs much assistance."

"Yes, I've been here about . . ." I couldn't remember how long I'd been working for Lucy. Five minutes? Forever? They were the same thing here. "I've been here awhile."

"And you are a writer yourself?" he asked.

"Oh no, no. *No.* I don't write at all."

"But you know how a writer thinks," he said.

"Well . . ."

"I will send you pages. You can tell her that."

"That's great! If I can be of any help at all, please let me know."

"You have been of help already. That's why I am sending the pages to you."

"Great! And the working title is *Warmer,* is that right?"

Karanuk let out another mirthless laugh. "No," he said. "This book does not have a title. That's her title. If I wanted, I could compile an entire book with her proposed titles."

"Oh, okay. Well, it sounds fantastic. We can't wait to see it." As I hung up, I realized that, like Gordon Hart, Karanuk had not once referred to Lucy by name. Their relationship was obviously a very complicated one, and I didn't want to spend time trying to figure it out. Instead, I allowed myself a minute to revel in the pure excitement of the fact that I'd soon be reading a new work by Karanuk before anyone else. There was a new title forming in my mind already. *Thaw.* I hoped he'd like it.

"Angel!" My intercom shrieked, punching a hole in the first moment of silence we'd had all day. "My office. Now." I stood up too fast and knocked into my desk, bumping my forgotten cup of coffee and spilling it all over my pants.

"*Shit,*" I hissed. Anna and Craig swiveled their heads simultaneously to look at me. I caught the shadow of a smile forming on Anna's lips. Craig raised his eyebrows in surprise. As if cursing were a novelty around here, I thought.

"Angel!" she shouted again, and I ran to her office, the scent of old cappuccino rising off me in waves.

"I asked you about Karanuk," she barked before I could get all the way through the door. "What is the status, Angel?"

"I just spoke to him," I said.

"And?" She sat at her desk, imperiously straight, tapping her Waterman pen against a stack of notepads.

"He's sending pages."

"He's *what?*" Lucy got up and walked around to where I was standing, not stopping until she came within inches of my face. Her closeness was unnerving. I felt cold and naked in her gaze of lusty anticipation.

"He's sending us pages for the new book. He didn't say how much, but he asked me to tell you that he's sending it in soon."

"Really, did he," she said, but it was not a question. "And did he happen to tell you what his idea for this book is?"

"Um, yes, he's writing about his experiences since leaving Alaska and how that has changed his life."

"How did you manage that, Angel?" Lucy's voice had dropped considerably and was softer than I'd ever heard it. I watched myriad expressions dance across her face like shifting clouds. In her eyes, which were boring into me with laserlike precision, there was surprise, something that looked like pleasure, a hint of annoyance, and self-satisfaction all at once. It was as if she couldn't decide to be angry or pleased that I'd done exactly what she'd asked me to do. Before I could answer her, though, she seemed to catch herself and draw all the emotion out of her features. "Good," she said. "I'll expect it shortly, then." She inhaled and wrinkled her nose. "What is that awful smell?"

I looked down at my wet-stained pants. "I had an accident with my coffee," I said, attempting a smile.

"That's disgusting," she said, backing away from me and heading back to her desk. "Children have accidents, Angel. Have Nora get you some soda water or something when she goes out for the mail."

If only she hadn't mentioned it. Now I was stuck having to be the messenger. "About Nora," I said. "She's gone."

"Well, send her out again when she gets back. What's the problem?"

"No, she's gone for the day. I mean, she's gone for good. I think she quit. She took all her things. . . ." I was frozen in place by Lucy's stare of unvarnished bitterness.

"These *girls*," she spat. "And after all I've done for her. You have no idea what I go through here. I need some *men*. Get me Craig. And bring Anna in here, too. What are you waiting for, Angel? Go!"

BY THE TIME he showed up at close to five, I'd completely forgotten that Damiano had said he was coming to the office. I was as surprised as Anna and Craig when a knock came on the door, which rarely opened during the course of the day. It was Anna who finally registered the sound and sauntered over to let him in. Damiano stood at the door, his face obscured by a giant basket filled with pastries and cakes and elaborately tied with gold and silver ribbon.

"Are you FedEx?" Anna asked, puzzled.

He lowered the basket and gave Anna an equally perplexed stare. "Angel?" he asked, disbelief in his voice. It was only then that I realized who he was.

"I'm Anna," she said, making no move to let him in.

"I'm so sorry," he said, grinning broadly. "Good to meet you. I'm Damiano."

"Ohhh," Anna crowed after one beat too long. "The Italian book. Well, come in." She turned around to me and waved her hand in my direction. "That's Angel," she said. "We didn't know you were coming. Lucy didn't say—"

"I'm sorry," he repeated. "This is a surprise visit. I wanted to come to thank you all in person for my great good fortune." He held the basket out to her. "These are for you all," he said. "I make them all myself. Something for everyone."

"Wow," Anna said, wrapping her arms around the basket and giving the pastries a look that could only be described as loving. Craig got up from his desk and came around to shake hands with Damiano.

"Very nice to meet you," he said. "I'm Craig. We've talked on the phone."

"Yes, yes. Luciana calls you 'the man with the money.' It's nice to meet you." He turned to me then and walked the short distance to my desk, where I sat, paralyzed, trying to figure out if I could smooth my hair without being noticed and wishing desperately that I didn't reek of spilled coffee. At least my finger had stopped bleeding.

"Angel," he said. *"Finalmente."* He leaned toward me but didn't extend his hand for shaking. I stood, awkwardly, unsure whether to offer my own hand. Somehow that gesture seemed too formal. He was shorter than I'd imagined—we stood almost eye to eye—but he held himself in a way that made him appear taller. He was olive-skinned and slender and his eyes were the color of dark red wine. His hair, thick and black with strokes of gray at the temples, was cut short but not buzzed. He had a decent five o'clock shadow darkening his jaw and it suited him well. He was a good-looking man, no question, but in a way that was not at all obvious.

"You have red hair," he said to me. "I'm surprised!"

"Well, I don't really sound like a redhead on the phone," I said idiotically, and made a move to shake his hand. He grabbed it instead and kissed me on both cheeks. He smelled delicious, like marzipan, chocolate, and citrus.

"*È vero,*" he said. "I saw a blond angel when I talked to you." I could feel the prickly heat of a blush spreading across my cheeks and could do nothing to stop it. A sidelong glance at Anna showed me that her color had risen, too, and that she looked extremely put out. Damiano's visit was already feeling like a runaway train and I had to do something to redirect its course.

"You know, we should probably tell Lucy that you're here," Anna said in a very loud voice. "Don't you think, *Angel?*"

"Of course," I said, and turned away from Damiano's amused gaze. "Lucy?" I said into my intercom. "Damiano Vero's here to see you." There was a second or two delay before my intercom flashed back. She wanted me to pick up the phone and I realized I would have to listen to a tirade with Damiano standing right in front of me, no doubt hearing every word of it.

"Lucy?"

"He is *here?* In the *office?*"

"Yes, Lucy."

"*Why?* And why was I not informed?"

"Nobody knew he—" I looked up at Damiano. One corner of his mouth was turned up in an ironic smile.

"DAMN IT!" she screamed.

"Should I tell him—" There was a loud click in my ear and she slammed her receiver down. Anna was smirking. Damiano looked bemused. I had no idea what to tell him.

"Any trouble finding us?" I asked him, stalling.

"No, not at all," he said.

"How . . . how did you know where we were?" I was seized with a sudden fear that I'd inadvertently given him our physical address during one of our conversations.

"Luciana told me where you are when I spoke to her. Is it okay?"

At that moment, Lucy sailed out of her office and with a toothy grin presented her hand to Damiano as if she were accepting a dance in a Victorian ballroom.

"*Buon giorno,* Damiano Vero!" she said. Her voice was high and fluty, a tone I'd never heard from her before. "In the flesh," she added.

"Luciana, *piacere*," he said, and moved to kiss her cheeks. There was an awkward moment when it became apparent that he wouldn't be able to reach her face gracefully, but he made a quick recovery by taking her hand and kissing that instead.

"Well!" she exclaimed. Her flustered schoolgirl tone was becoming a little grotesque. "You *are* a handsome man, after all. You should have sent a photo, Damiano, I could have gotten you even more money! Yes, indeed." She raked him with her eyes. "You're the best-looking heroin addict I've ever seen!"

To his credit, Damiano didn't flinch, nor did his expression change. I, on the other hand, was in a sweat of reddened embarrassment for him.

"I assume you've met my staff," Lucy continued, waving her hand in our direction. "And to what do we owe the honor of your presence today?"

"I bring a gift." He gestured to the basket that Anna was still holding. "I made some sweets."

"Charming," Lucy said, and took the basket from Anna. "Very sweet of you."

"I am so grateful to you all," he said, but looked directly at me. Lucy, missing nothing, followed his gaze and raised her eyebrows.

"Delicious, isn't he, Angel? Pity you're already spoken for." I felt my stomach clench and had to lower my eyes. The heat on my face had reached fever temperature. "I'll put this lovely basket in my office," Lucy was saying. "Why don't you come with me, Damiano? Since you're here, there are a few things we should discuss."

"*Bene,*" Damiano said, and started to follow her. "I almost forgot," he said, and walked back to my desk. "I have this for you," he said quietly, and pulled a CD jewel case out of his jacket pocket. He laid it on my desk and turned quickly to go after Lucy. I looked up, sure I would find a disapproving scowl from Anna, but she'd missed the whole interchange and was staring, bereft, as Damiano's basket disappeared into Lucy's office. I grabbed the CD before she could see it and tossed it into my purse. For all I knew, it was merely a copy of his manuscript on disk, but something told me that it wasn't for public consumption. My computer chirped with the sound of an instant message. Anna.

Well, I guess that's the last we'll see of those cakes.

I'm sure she'll share, I wrote back.

She won't. Nothing ever comes out of there once it goes in.

Just as well, they don't look too slimming, I wrote, and immediately regretted it. Now she'd think I was implying she was fat. I looked at the clock. It was just past eight in New York. It was to be a day without end, as the persistent twitter of Anna's instant messages reminded me.

Guess I'm reading your boyfriend's ms tonight, she wrote. *I'll try to be gentle.*

Just be honest, I typed, striking my keyboard with more force than was necessary. And skip the lame attempts at humor, I thought to myself.

Will do, she sent back. *Anything special I should know before I start reading?* She wasn't letting it go. I looked at the clock again and over at Lucy's closed door. Through it, I could hear the rise and dip of her voice mingling with Damiano's. I was suddenly and unbearably tired.

Yes, I replied to Anna, *I'm exhausted. I have one more thing to do and then I'm heading home.*

Before she had a chance to respond, I covered my last base of the day and sent an e-mail to the anonymous author of *Blind Submission.* I wasn't about to risk letting that one get away from me like I had with Shelly Franklin.

To: ganovelist@heya.com
From: angel.robinson@fiammalit.com
Subject: BLIND SUBMISSION

Dear "g,"

Thank you very much for sending the opening pages of BLIND SUB-MISSION to us. We have now had a chance to review your work and, on behalf of Lucy Fiamma, I'm happy to say that we are sufficiently intrigued by your pages and we would love to see more! In fact, if the entire manuscript is finished, please send it along as soon as pos-sible. If you could let us know whether or not this novel has been submitted to other agents, that would be great. Could you please give us a call at 510-555-7666? We'll look forward to reading!

Many thanks,
Angel Robinson
Lucy Fiamma Literary Agency

I hit the SEND button on my computer, turned it off, and started gathering my substantial pile of take-home reading. But before I could get out the door, the phone started ringing in one final cruel burst of sound. Anna, head bent over some imaginary work at her desk, pointedly refused to answer it and so, with a loud sigh, I lifted the receiver.

"Good *evening*, Lucy Fiamma Agency."

There was laughing on the other end. "Still there, are you?" Ah, Gordon Hart.

"Hello, Mr. Hart." I looked at the clock. It was closing in on nine in New York. "We could say the same for you! It's very late there, isn't it?"

"No rest for the *wicked*," he offered. "I'm sure you're familiar. I'll assume she's still there as well, then?"

"Well, actually, she's . . ." I looked over at Lucy's closed door. Once again, I was faced with what I'd secretly dubbed the Lucy Challenge. Did I put the very important (and consistently elusive) Gordon Hart through to Lucy and, in the process, interrupt her conversation with her newest, brightest author, or did I take a message and risk her possible fire-breathing wrath? And then I realized that Lucy would like nothing better than to look as important and powerful as possible in front of Damiano by cutting him off to take a call from one of "the country's most important publishers." As soon as this thought occurred to me, I decided that I simply didn't want to give her the pleasure. It was a small thing, possibly even petty, but it gave me a substantial feeling of satisfaction.

"She's actually not here at the moment," I said. "But I can—"

"Really?" he said, and laughed again. "How *unusual*. But not to worry, I don't really need to *speak* to her. I was calling to leave a message. I'll be out of town next week and I wanted to make sure she knew that. I will call her back when I return. Let her know, will you, Ms. Robinson?"

"I will," I said.

"Good," he answered, and hung up.

Gordon Hart wasn't the only one who didn't want to talk to Lucy. Before she could emerge again with enough new work to keep me at my desk indefinitely, I grabbed my things and hightailed it out the door.

I LAY IN MY BED, awake and unmoving, Malcolm's warm body wrapped around me in the wordless intimacy of flesh against flesh. I could feel his slow, even breaths in my ear and his lips against my cheek. I reached my hand out in the dark to stroke his arm, my fingers tracing the swell of his shoulder, and he stirred, pulling me closer to him.

"Can't sleep?" he whispered into my hair.

"I guess not." I sighed. "Didn't mean to wake you, though."

"I wasn't sleeping," he said. He lay silent for a while and I was sure that he'd drifted off. I closed my eyes, hoping for the sleep that wouldn't come. "Do you want to talk?" Malcolm asked. "You've been so quiet." It was true; this was the longest conversation we'd had since he'd arrived hours earlier.

I'd found my kitchen nearly empty when I got home from work and realized that I couldn't remember the last time I'd gone shopping for food. Too tired to go out again but too hungry not to eat, I found myself staring into my refrigerator at an old carton of eggs that had expired the week before, wondering if they were still safe. I considered what would happen if they weren't. Perhaps they'd make me sick, I thought; maybe even sick enough to be hospitalized. And hospitalization was a perfectly legitimate reason to take a day off. I figured I couldn't lose. I had the eggs in my hand, ready to scramble, when I realized the horrible nature of my logic. Clearly, hunger and exhaustion were making me crazy. Because only a crazy person would consider making herself dangerously ill in order to miss work. In a fit of self-preservation, I turned instead to a stale box of crackers and polished them off while I unpacked manuscripts and laid them out for reading. But the thought of doing more work was so overwhelming, I found myself close to tears. I cued Damiano's CD in my stereo and was contemplating a hot bath when Malcolm knocked on my door.

I didn't ask him why he hadn't let himself in with his key because I didn't care. I was just so glad to see him. No, glad wasn't it, exactly . . . I was *hungry*. For him. He walked in and I grabbed him and pressed my face into his chest.

"Hey," he said as I clutched at him. "I'm sorry about this morning."

"Forget it," I said, and lifted my face for his kiss. Neither one of us had spoken another word until now.

"Want to talk about it?" Malcolm repeated. "Might help."

"My job . . ." I started. I closed my hand around his wrist as if to anchor myself. "I don't know if I'm going to make it."

Malcolm shifted beside me, separating his limbs from mine. "What do you mean?" he asked. "I thought you were doing so well there."

"I am," I said. "I mean, I think I am. You never know with her."

"You're not getting along with her?"

"That's not it, exactly," I said, and struggled to pull the right words out. I wished I could transfer my thoughts to him without having to verbalize them. "There's just so much pressure. And it's getting really weird in the office. One of the girls I work with quit today. She just walked out."

"But people quit all the time," he said. "What's so weird about that?"

"You don't understand. . . ." I sighed. I didn't know how to explain how casually cruel Lucy had been to Nora—*Kelly*—and how I'd just accepted it, even going so far as to blame N— Kelly herself.

Malcolm propped himself up on his elbow. I could feel his body tensing next to me. "Make me understand," he said. "I'm asking because I want to know. I care about what's going on with you."

He *did* want to know, I thought. He was concerned. He loved me. I should be able to tell him everything, otherwise what kind of relationship did we have?

"I saw her *naked* this morning," I told him. "I got to the office and she came out in a towel and told me to start making her calls. And then the towel fell off. Ugh."

"Are you talking about Lucy?" he said.

"Yes, Lucy. Totally naked. I nearly had a heart attack."

"What, she bent over to pick up the soap or something?"

"I wasn't in her *bathroom*, Malcolm. She came out into the office in a towel and it fell off. And then *she* accused *me* of walking in on *her*."

"Oh, come on," Malcolm said, and laughed. "You're exaggerating, right?"

"Not in the slightest."

"Well, maybe she was embarrassed, A. Did you think of that? And did everyone else see this, too? Because that would have been even more embarrassing."

"No, nobody else saw it. She went back into her office, and when I went in there again, she was dressed."

"I think you're making a big deal out of nothing, Angel. The poor woman—"

"Poor woman? Are you kidding? There's nothing poor about Lucy Fiamma! Poor *me* is more like it."

"Okay, okay," he said. He waited a moment and then laughed. "So," he said, "is she hot or what?"

"Very funny," I answered.

"Okay, no jokes about naked bosses. What else is bothering you?"

"It's just . . . difficult," I said. "And it doesn't seem to be getting any easier." I'd lost my desire to share the particulars with him. Laid bare in my own bed, I felt overexposed.

"You're not thinking of quitting, are you?" he asked, his voice soft and serious.

"And if I was?" It came out sounding testy.

"Well, you haven't exactly given it much of a chance. And I know you love it. I've seen how involved you are. You're into it, admit it."

"I do love the work. Some of it, anyway. Just not all of it. And not all the damn time." I thought about telling him about the expired eggs and decided against it. He clearly wasn't in an empathetic mood.

He reached over me and fumbled around my bedside table until he found the stereo remote. "Let's have a little music, shall we?" he said, and clicked it on. I felt my whole body stiffen when the strains of the first song, "Angel" by Jimi Hendrix, washed over us in the dark. Damiano's CD. In my haste to drag Malcolm off to bed, I'd forgotten to take it out.

"What's this?" Malcolm asked.

"A new . . . a new CD I got."

"Hmm," he said, and curled around me once more. "You're not still mad about my novel, are you? You should just forget about it, okay, Angel? It's important to me, but not more important than us."

"I'm not mad at you, Malcolm." I hesitated before I went on, measuring my words. "I gave her your novel today," I said at last. "She's going to read it." *After Anna got to it,* I added silently, but I sure as hell wasn't going to mention that to him. There was a long pause. Because he was lying so close to me, I could tell that Malcolm actually stopped breathing for a few seconds.

"Really?" he asked finally.

"Yes, but Malcolm, I don't know if she's going to want to take it. You understand that, right?"

"Of course I understand it," he said, "but . . ." He hesitated. Jimi Hendrix gave way to the next song, Tom Petty singing "Angel Dream (No. 4)."

"But what?"

"Haven't you told me how much she respects your opinion? If you tell her it's great, don't you think that makes a difference? Seems like it's made a big difference for a few writers already."

"But I haven't read it, Malcolm. She'd know I was biased. This way I'm being fair."

"What do you mean? You told her it was your *boyfriend's* book?"

"Of course."

"Why 'of course'? What the hell, Angel? She didn't have to know the connection. Wouldn't it have made more sense just to give it to her without telling her who I was? It's not like you haven't been doing that with all the other assholes who send their crap in. Now she'll think I'm just trying to get a free ride off my girlfriend. She won't even *read* the thing."

"Hey," I said sharply, disentangling myself from him and sitting up. "You're *welcome.*" There was a pointed silence and then Malcolm sighed, reached up and gently pulled me back down next to him. And that was when it occurred to me that he had a point. I could feel my face get hot with guilt and I was glad Malcolm couldn't see me in the dark. I sighed, hearing the sound of my breath between us.

"I'm sorry," Malcolm said quietly. "I didn't mean . . . I just thought you'd want to read it yourself. You know, before . . ." We lay still for a moment and then Malcolm folded his arms around me and put his hands in my hair, tickling the back of my neck with his fingers. He brushed his lips across my mouth and throat, moving downward, covering the angel wings on my breast with a long, exquisitely sweet kiss. For that moment at least, all was once again right with the world.

"Thank you," he whispered. "I mean that."

I put my arms around him and sighed again, this time with pleasure.

"Want to talk about anything else?" he asked.

"Mmm," I sighed. "No, no more talking. Just keep . . ." I put his hands back in my hair. "Keep doing what you're doing."

Malcolm did that and more, moving his hands across my back and his lips along my neck. He covered me with his body and I could feel the heat of him all the way to my bones. All the while, Damiano's CD continued to play in the background. "She Talks to Angels," "Maybe Angels," "Angel of Harlem," and more angels after that.

Malcolm stopped kissing me midway through "Angel of Mercy" and looked at me. I could just make out the glimmer of his eyes in the dimness.

"Where did you say you got this CD?" he asked. "They're all angel songs."

I supposed there was nothing quite like stating the obvious.

"Um, well, an author sent it to me. A wannabe."

"Really?" he asked. "That's a little overboard, isn't it?"

"You'd be surprised," I said. "Some authors will do anything to get published."

And then he covered my mouth with his own.

SEVEN

To: angel.robinson@fiammalit.com
From: ganovelist@heya.com
Subject: Re: BLIND SUBMISSION

Dear Ms. Robinson,

Thank you for your kind reply. Although this may sound a little "over the top," I am not surprised that Ms. Fiamma has taken an interest in my work. I believe, as you do, that this novel has the potential to be a blockbuster. A real winner, as it were. To answer your question, I have not submitted this manuscript elsewhere. Ms. Fiamma's agency is known to be among the very best in the country and that is why I selected her. I do not plan to submit elsewhere.

Having said that, I prefer to remain "anonymous" at this point for reasons I cannot disclose at the moment. Please assure Ms. Fiamma that, when the time comes, there will be no problem concerning my identity.

In the interest of retaining this anonymity, I will send the manuscript to you via e-mail. To that end, I've attached another chapter. Enjoy!

With best wishes,

G.

BLIND SUBMISSION

Chapter 2

Carol Moore was throwing a party at the office to celebrate the entry of yet another book onto the *New York Times* bestseller list. This one was a first novel by Svetlana Vladic, a book the *New York Times* called "a modern *Anna Karenina.*"

Alice settled the bottles of Dom Pérignon in their ice buckets and suppressed the rage that had been building in her all day, all week, for her entire life. Svetlana Vladic was nobody—a pale, washed-out, passionless holograph of a woman. She'd lucked into this success and it tore a hole in Alice's heart. Alice had to admit that the book was good. No, the book was great, but the author wasn't. It was insanely unfair for someone as uncharismatic as Svetlana Vladic to have achieved this kind of glory.

Alice ground her teeth. The mask she wore in the office— that of model employee who wanted nothing more than to please her boss and her boss's clients—was slipping. What was under the mask was considerably uglier and Alice couldn't afford to show it. Yet.

Alice thought about the rejection letter she'd received from Carol Moore only days ago. Of course, Carol hadn't known that Alice was the author she was rejecting. Alice had submitted her own novel under a false name and had given it to Carol, telling the agent that it was some of the best fiction she'd ever read. Carol was inclined to believe Alice because Alice had proven herself to have an excellent eye.

"If you recommend it," Carol told Alice, "I'm sure it must be wonderful."

The ax fell soon after. Carol had called Alice into a private meeting and told her that she was sorry, but the novel was just not good enough for her to sell. "I understand that you were very fond of this one," Carol told Alice, and regarded her with a questioning look, as if she couldn't really comprehend why Alice had liked the novel so much, "so I read it very carefully. But it's just not for me. Perhaps you'd like to work with this author? You could make some suggestions and then we could take another look at it?"

Alice had to take a minute to gather herself after that. Her disappointment and anger flooded her like a tidal wave and she wasn't sure she could keep her face from showing it. Passing her own work on to Carol anonymously had been a calculated risk. Had Alice told Carol that she was the author, Carol would not have been able to read the pages objectively and might even have started looking into Alice's background. Alice couldn't afford that. Had Carol liked what she'd read, none of that would have mattered.

Damn her, Alice thought bitterly. Carol's rejection, however innocent, wounded Alice to her core. Carol had no understanding of what Alice felt. She could never understand what it meant to want something so badly and for so long that every day without fulfillment killed you a little more. And then to know that what you wanted would never happen the way you wanted it . . . To know that really, underneath it all, you weren't any good . . . Alice was again filled with red anger.

Finally, when she was able to contain herself, she told Carol, "I don't think so. If it isn't good enough for you, I don't think we should waste our time on it."

"Were you wanting to represent it yourself?" Carol asked. "Did I misunderstand? Because it's a little early for you to be taking on projects of your own. You understand, don't you, Alice? But we should talk about that if it's something that concerns you. I am certainly willing to work with you. In time, you could be a fine agent."

Alice tried to twist her bitterness into a smile. "You are very kind, Carol," she said. "I really appreciate it."

"Listen, I know how tough it is when you're just starting out," Carol said. "Especially if you're a woman. It's supposed to be easier now, for women, but it isn't. As I'm sure your mother told you—"

"I don't have a mother," Alice said, her words bitten off and strangled.

Carol's eyes widened. "Everyone has a mother, dear."

"Well, not me," Alice said. She could feel her hands turning into fists. She didn't think she could stand it if Carol kept this up.

"I'm sorry," Carol said, "I didn't mean to—"

"It's okay," Alice interrupted, "it's just . . . It's okay. Of course somebody gave birth to me. But I've been on my own forever. I've never had a woman I could look up to. Not until now, anyway." Alice's fists were so tight she could feel her manicured fingernails beginning to break the skin of her palms.

"That's very nice of you to say," Carol said. There was a pause between the two of them. Carol looked down at the letter opener on her desk and then back at Alice. "Listen, Alice, I tell you what I'll do—I'll write your author a long letter and make some suggestions." A tiny flicker of hope danced through Alice's head. Carol managed to extinguish it with her next words. "Perhaps that way it won't seem as harsh. And then there's always the option of trying again after a rewrite. Although, frankly, I'm not sure it would help too much."

"Great," Alice said, her rage threatening to explode in her brain.

Later, Alice had been forced to mail herself Carol's rejection letter. That letter was the point of a knife in Alice's heart. Now the success of yet another undeserving author had driven the knife clean through.

It was time for a new plan. As Alice picked up the phone to call Vaughn Blue's personal number, she knew exactly where she was going to start.

The arrival of *Blind Submission*'s second chapter couldn't have come at a worse time. The theme of ego-crushing literary rejection it illustrated so well wasn't so strange in and of itself, but the fact that the very same theme was playing out in my own life (and at my own agency) made it uncomfortable—even disturbing—to read. Of course, it wasn't my own work that had gotten rejected; it was Malcolm's.

Deep down, although I didn't like to admit it, I never truly believed that Lucy would agree to represent Malcolm. I had no concrete reason for my doubt, but I didn't need one. I was starting to develop an instinct about how Lucy would react—almost as if part of my unconscious was wired into hers—and it told me that Malcolm would never find his way into her pantheon of published authors. I'd certainly been no help at all. He would have been better off just sending it in himself.

The first sign that I was right came when Anna, perpetually behind in her reading, finished Malcolm's book in record time. Naturally, she didn't share her opinion of it with me. I assumed she'd disliked it (if she'd actually read it), or at least said she did, because that was the way things went in this office. Allying herself with me would do nothing to promote Anna's cause. Of course, Anna's reaction, whatever it was, was immaterial. The manuscript went to Lucy next and then, a day or two later, Lucy called me into her office.

She was sitting at her desk, wearing a lavender dress, gloves, and a hat to match. I'd quickly gotten used to Lucy's bizarre outfits, but this one, which was some sort of post–Henry Higgins' Eliza Doolittle, was stunning on many different levels.

"Do I strike you as someone who has a lot of spare time on her hands, Angel?"

The hat actually had a veil.

"I'm sorry, I don't understand what you mean, Lucy."

"I mean, do you, Angel Robinson, feel that I, Lucy Fiamma, have the time to *fuck* around with *bullshit*, or do you think that my time is possibly more valuable than that?"

"Of course your time is valuable, Lucy."

She was wearing white stockings. Not panty hose. Stockings.

"Well, then, Angel, why have you taken up my time with this?" She tossed Malcolm's book onto the carpet at her feet and waved her hand at it in disgust. I bent, almost involuntarily, and picked it up. I realized what a mistake I had made and cursed myself for being so stupid. Although it hardly mattered, I had to know—had to ask the question.

"Was it the writing?" I asked in a small voice.

"His writing is *okay*," Lucy sniffed. "But there's no plot! It's some sort of literary exercise, destined, at best, for midlist. You know what midlist is, don't you, Angel?"

"Yes, Lucy, I—"

"Let me put it this way," she continued. "If this book were a film, it would be going straight to video. Do you understand me?"

"Lucy, I—"

"What I don't understand is why you would risk your career over a man. Can you enlighten me, Angel? You're so smart in other ways."

"I don't know what you mean, Lucy." My voice was cold, if not loud, and I could feel ice spreading across my middle. I was angry, but I was also afraid. Afraid of Lucy and afraid that she was right. She so often was.

"He must be something," she went on, lowering her voice. "Is that it, Angel? Is he some kind of divine lover?" A green gleam entered her eyes. I debated making some kind of comment about the inappropriateness of her remark, but she started speaking again before I had the chance. "You're young, Angel, but you have to understand it's imperative that a girl—no, a *woman*—with intelligence like yours not give up yourself for a man. Or for anyone. We've been so conditioned to believe that we are nothing without men that we forget our own power. I would hate to see that happen to you, Angel. It would be a terrible, terrible waste."

She was completely sincere. Her ability to couch cold barbs in warm truth was another one of Lucy's singular talents. She'd tear you down in a heartbeat, but, at the same time, she'd be laying the foundation to rebuild you. What always got me was her accuracy. She could find the sore spot and press in relentlessly, but she was also able to find the unshakable strengths and tease them out. I knew that she was right about Malcolm. I *did* define myself through him. Until I started working for Lucy, my plans for my own future were dependent on Malcolm's plans for his. I'd merely been trying to fit myself into his vision. Of course, this wasn't his fault at all—it was mine. I found myself confused into silence as I stood in front of Lucy. She kept talking, her voice becoming soft and lugubrious as she went on.

"Now, I realize that you've put yourself in rather a tight spot with this man and his novel by giving it to me, so I've done you a favor." She removed her hat and placed it, with great care, on the edge of her desk. "I've called the boyfriend," she said. It took me a moment to realize that she was talking about Malcolm. "And I have given him some very good advice as to how he can improve his chances of becoming published. I know you understand how valuable such a discussion can be and I know that you are aware that this is something I *never* do. The authors I represent don't need the kind of advice I've given him free of charge and those who do need it I wouldn't represent in the first place."

Lucy pursed her lips and waited for my reaction, which was awhile in coming because I had to spend a few moments trying to figure out when she'd made the phone call and why Malcolm hadn't mentioned it to me.

"That was very kind of you, Lucy," I said at last. "I'm sure he really appreciated it. I know I do."

"Yes," Lucy said, and smiled broadly. The softness, however, was gone from her voice. "I'm sure I've spared you quite a bit of discomfort."

"Thank you, Lucy. I owe you." As soon as the words left my lips, I regretted them. Yes, I owed her for hiring me in the first place, but I'd more than proved my worth. If it hadn't been for me, she'd never have seen *Parco Lambro;* Anna certainly wouldn't have pulled it out of the pile for a second look. No, Anna's specialty was finding cute books about kitties and puppies and the occasional travel guide, nothing that required any actual *reading* or thought. Still, I should have read Malcolm's manuscript before I'd given it to her. That was my mistake. One I wouldn't make again.

Lucy had me fixed in that stare of hers again. "Yes," she said. "You owe me, Angel. You certainly do." She seemed to mull this for a moment and then snapped back into the mode I knew so well. "Now, let's get on with it. I don't even want to think about how much time we've wasted on this."

My heart sank at hearing Malcolm reduced to "wasted time."

"What we need to talk about," Lucy went on, rising from her desk and striding over to her couch, "are *these*." She picked up two manuscripts from the pile on her coffee table and held them out. One was *Blind Submission* and the other was *Elvis Will Dance at Your Wedding*. "Now, *this* is how you should be using your talents, Angel. Come on, sit down."

I settled myself on the couch, trying not to sit so close that we were touching. "My first question," she said, pointing to Shelly Franklin's novel, "is can you make this one work? Because if you can, it could be one of those literary darlings. Well, *I* can make it one of those literary darlings, at any rate."

"That was my thinking, too," I told her. "The author's willing to work, definitely, so I think—"

"Good! Make sure she has an agency contract by the end of the day." She tossed the manuscript at me and I caught it before it could slide off my knees to the floor. "Now, this . . ." She trailed off as she glanced over my original notes for *Blind Submission*. ". . . is very interesting." I was surprised to see actual excitement on her face.

"You like this one, Lucy?"

"Is there a reason I shouldn't?"

"Well, the writing's a little weak . . . I thought . . ."

Lucy raised her eyebrows in an exaggerated expression of surprise. "The writing is not overly literary, if that's what you mean. But I think the style suits the concept here, Angel. And I believe this has the potential to be an extremely commercial novel if it's presented correctly. Didn't you mention *The Nanny Diaries* in your notes? In any event, it would be nothing for you to retool the writing, would it, Angel?"

"Well, no, I suppose I could—"

"Of course you could." She leaned in close to me, her green eyes probing mine. "But yes, I like it and I find it most amusing that it's set in a literary agency. Don't you, Angel?"

She was leading me somewhere, but I couldn't tell where. My growing sense of discomfort told me that it wasn't a place I wanted to go.

"It's interesting," I said. "But what about the fact that books about publishing don't usually do well?"

"Nothing sells until it does, Angel. That's the rule of this business. Who cared about the Inuit before Karanuk? Did anyone, aside from myself, believe that *Cold!* was hot? You have to make it happen, Angel."

"Well, that's certainly true," I said. "But how do you feel about this anonymous thing? It's a little cloak-and-dagger, don't you think?"

Lucy's smile looked like an incision in her face. "I'm willing to play along," she said. "It might even add some glamour . . . some danger . . . to the package. The anonymous author worked for *Primary Colors,* didn't it?"

"Yes, but his *agent* knew who he was, right?"

She sat up straight and her demeanor changed again. She'd run out of patience. "Why am *I* trying to convince *you?*" she barked. "Didn't you give me this novel in the first place?"

"Yes, but—"

"Has the author contacted other agents, then? Have we lost it already?"

"No, in fact—"

"Well, then, get on it, Angel."

I tried to stand, but Lucy reached out and grabbed the fabric of my sleeve as if to pull me back down. The movement took both of us by surprise and she let go as quickly as she'd reached for me. "Is there anything else you want to tell me about this novel, Angel?"

"I don't think so," I told her. I still didn't know what she was driving at, and it was starting to make me very anxious.

"Are you sure? Nothing to tell me about the protagonist? The assistant who is also a *writer* and who sends in her own work *anonymously?*"

I stared at her for a moment, my mind a complete blank, but then it finally hit me—hard. "You don't think *I* wrote this, do you?"

"You needn't sound so shocked, Angel. Isn't that what you'd think if you were in my position? And it's not as if something like this has never happened before. I can't tell you how many aspiring writers I've had to wade through in this office. I didn't think you were one of them. But if it is you, I'd advise you to tell me now. Because I'll find out, Angel. You know I will."

"Lucy, I have no aspirations to write, none at all." I was almost laughing at the absurdity of it. "I can't write, anyway! I'm hopeless at it."

"Well, I don't believe *that*," Lucy countered. "Nobody who under-stands writers the way you do would be a hopeless writer herself."

I shrugged and offered her a limp smile. "What can I say?" I offered. "I love books. I'm a reader. I can't write, Lucy, that's the truth. And I cer-tainly didn't write this." I waved the manuscript in front of me. Lucy tilted her head to one side, studying me, the movement giving her the look of a large bird. She removed one glove and then the other, placing them carefully on the coffee table in front of her.

"I hope you're not upset about your boyfriend's novel, Angel. Are you?"

Lucy's look had changed to one of concern and I wondered whether or not it was genuine. I decided that it was.

"I'm disappointed," I told her, "but not upset."

"I may have been a little harsh earlier," she responded, "but, Angel, you realize now how very difficult it is to sell even excellent projects. There's just no room for those that don't have at least the potential to be great. I hope you know that had I seen any possibility in that novel I would have considered taking it on."

"I do," I said.

"I see so much potential in *you*, Angel. I hate to see you squandering your talent. I'm looking out for *you*, dear. I believe you have an extremely bright future ahead of you."

Dear? Since when had I become a "dear"? But I believed her. Her tone was suddenly so soft, soothing, and laden with feeling that I wouldn't have been surprised if she went on to tell me she loved me.

"Thank you, Lucy." My voice cracked over the last syllable of her name. Her unexpected burst of sentiment had actually choked me up.

"I am investing in *your* future, Angel. I do hope you realize that. You have a wonderful opportunity here—so much room to grow."

I wondered again if she truly meant what she was saying, but there was nothing in her tone to suggest otherwise. "Thank you," I repeated because I'd lost track of what she'd said and this seemed like the only appropriate way to respond.

"Well, all right then," she said. "You'd better go back to work."

I left her office thinking I'd be able to do just that, focus on my work and shrug off my guilt about Malcolm's rejection, but I was mistaken. When I got back to my desk, the second chapter of *Blind Submission* was waiting for me in my e-mail in-box.

I WAS WIDE AWAKE, editing Shelly Franklin's novel, when Malcolm let himself into my apartment after his shift that night.

"I need to talk to you," I said.

"Mind if I take a shower first?" he answered. "It was a very long night and"—he sniffed the sleeve of his white shirt—"I think I've got at least seven different wines on my shirt. I stink."

I didn't want to wait. I had to talk to him about Lucy before it could fester in my brain any longer. "It's about your novel, Malcolm."

Malcolm sat down on one of the two chairs in my apartment, not on the bed next to me. I could see resignation lining his features but also, under that, a small glow of hope. I hated that I had to extinguish it and hated that he'd put me in the position of having to do it.

"What about it?" he asked.

"Lucy gave it back to me today. She's not going to represent it."

"I know," he said. "I thought maybe you were going to tell me she changed her mind."

It took me a second to realize why he knew and then it came back to me. Lucy had said she'd called him. Like a good author, he'd put his phone number and address on the cover page of his novel.

"Why didn't you tell me she called you, Malcolm?"

"Haven't exactly had the chance, have I?" A twisted, mirthless grin spread its way across his mouth. "You're not what I'd call available these days, Angel."

"What's that supposed to mean?" I put down Shelly Franklin's manuscript and capped the red pen I held in my hand. I needed to get up, but I was too tired to move. I was feeling very defensive and didn't think my bed was the right arena in which to deflect an attack. Malcolm was leaning back in the chair, his legs spread out in front of him. He looked worn out and exhausted but stubborn and ready to fight.

"You're a little caught up in work, aren't you?" he said. "Always so damn busy, so very, very important. Anyway, Angel, it doesn't seem as if you're particularly interested in what happens to me and my career. I think being rejected by your boss makes that pretty clear. If you'd taken just a little time out of your fascinatingly busy schedule to give your *fiancé* a little help—to *read* his damn book—like you give to every other nobody-writer who sends in a manuscript, perhaps it wouldn't have been rejected in the first place. Did that ever occur to you?"

"Fiancé?" I asked. "When did you become my fiancé?"

"Is that a joke, Angel?"

"No, it's not. When it suits you, obviously, we're engaged. But I don't remember having a discussion about this recently. When is the last time we talked about our future, anyway?"

Malcolm sat up in the chair, his face darkening with anger. "That's not really the point, is it, Angel? I think you're only bringing this up now to get out of taking responsibility for what you've done. You shafted me and you don't want to admit it."

"What are you talking about? The only reason I applied for this job in the first place was because of you."

"You might want to rethink that," he said softly. "It seems to me you've got a whole other agenda working here. I don't—" He stopped and looked down at his hands, flexing them. He cleared his throat. "I don't know what's happened to you, Angel. Since you started working at that place, you've become a different person. I mean, even *Lucy* cares more about me than you do. At least she took the time to call me."

"Don't read too much into that!" I snapped at him. "She did that for me."

"See what I mean?" he said. "You're becoming a real bitch."

We were both stunned silent after that one. Malcolm and I had disagreed from time to time, but we'd never had a fight like this. And we had never even come close to name-calling. He might as well have slapped me. I felt tears, hot with anger, welling in my eyes. If he was affected by them, Malcolm gave no indication. He stood up and headed over to the door. "I can't deal with this," he barked, and stalked out, slamming the door behind him.

FOR A LONG TIME after Malcolm left, I lay staring at the door as if I could erase the last hour by sheer force of will. My eyes filled, emptied, and filled again. The Malcolm I knew was sweet and loving and, for the past two years, had been my best friend. I didn't recognize the angry, bitter person who had just left my apartment.

The phone rang and I leaped up, convinced it was Malcolm calling to apologize, or to tell me that he loved me, or that it had all been a huge misunderstanding.

"Hi," I breathed into the phone, breathless enough to sound like a 900-number phone-sex operator.

"Angel?"

I was so shocked that the voice I heard belonged not to Malcolm but to Damiano that for a moment I just said nothing.

"I'm sorry," he said into my silence, "I must have the wrong number."

"No!" I said, much sharper than I'd intended. "This is Angel."

"I'm very sorry, Angel. It's so late. I woke you?"

"No," I said, pushing the hair off my forehead and trying to get my bearings. I was sliding between my office persona and that of weeping girlfriend and couldn't find any kind of conversational purchase. "I'm— I mean, it's okay. I'm not sleeping."

"I shouldn't have called," he said. "But I thought . . ."

"You thought what?"

"I didn't really see you before. When I came in to the office."

I had become very familiar with Damiano's broken English, and because I'd spent so much time with his words and thoughts through *Parco Lambro,* I was usually able to understand what he wanted to say before he finished speaking.

"It's okay," I told him. "You didn't have to . . . You came to talk to Lucy, anyway, right?"

"Sì, but . . . Angel," he said, "I don't know how to say it." There was a long pause while he formulated the correct words. "I have to thank you in some way. I know how much you have done for me."

"You don't. I mean, you have, Damia— Dami. You have thanked me."

"I just thought to call you and tell you, but . . ." He sighed into the phone and muttered something in Italian under his breath I couldn't catch. "Now it is so late and I have disturbed you. *Mi dispiace*. I'm sorry, Angel."

"Dami, it's really fine. It's okay. Thank you."

"I should find a better way than to call so late at night. I've made you sad."

"What?"

"You sound sad. That's the right word, no?"

For a heartbeat I considered what it would be like to tell him he was right, I was sad, but not at all for the reasons he thought. I had the sudden, strong feeling that he would understand, that he'd be able to read me as I'd been able to read him. It was tempting, but then, in an instant and for so many reasons, completely impossible.

"Yes, it's the right word. But I'm not sad, just . . . tired."

"I know, I am so sorry to call. I will find a better way to thank you. Good night."

"Good night, Dami."

"Sleep well, Angel."

I PREPARED FOR BED and lay down in it, but sleep was far from coming. There was no comfortable spot in my bed, no fold or corner that didn't continuously remind me of Malcolm's absence. When I couldn't stand it any longer, I reached for the phone, preparing to call Malcolm and act like the helpless, dependent woman I'd always hoped I'd never become. I couldn't tell if it was a last vestige of female pride or the fact that I saw her phone number tucked under the phone, but at the last minute, I decided to dial not Malcolm but my mother.

The phone rang so many times I was almost hypnotized by its steady sound. There was no answering machine, of course, and so I just held on, waiting and hoping. I was about to give up when she finally picked up and I heard her voice.

"Hello?"

"Hillary?"

"Angel? What's wrong?" There were some things, despite the distance and the differences in our worldviews, that my mother just didn't have to be told. "Are you in trouble?"

I couldn't imagine what my mother's definition of trouble might be, so I didn't try. "No, Hillary, I just wanted to talk to you—see if you were okay."

"I'm fine, love, never better. I'm glad you called. I was going to call you, honey. I was going to tell you that I'm moving and I don't know if I'll have access to a phone where I'm going."

"Didn't you just get there, wherever you are?"

"Well, I've been here long enough, that's certain. I'll have to tell you about it another time. Anyway, I've met these two amazing Inuit women and I'm going with them to Alaska."

"Alaska!" The first thing that came to my mind was the cover of *Cold!*

"It's still the United States, Angel. Don't sound so alarmed. But we can talk about that later. I want to know what's wrong with you. You haven't told me. Is it Malcolm?"

I wasn't surprised that she knew, but I wasn't glad, either. I knew what was coming.

"You're losing your center, Angel, I can feel it. Men will do that, especially this one."

"I don't know why you don't like him, Hillary."

"Why don't you ask yourself why you think I don't like him, Angel? I guarantee you'll find the answer if you look for it. What's he done to you? And why have you let him?"

"Nothing. Look, it's fine, okay? Never mind. I just wanted to talk to you, that's all. I'll call you— When are you leaving the Amazons?"

"I'll be here until the next new moon, so I have about three weeks yet."

"All right, I'll call you before the next new moon, then, Hillary."

"Angel, you know what will make you feel better?"

"What?"

"Read a good book, my love. From the time you were a tiny little thing, a good book worked better for you than antibiotics."

I started laughing because there was nothing else to do at that point. Maybe she was right. Maybe it had been too long since I'd read a *good* book.

I picked up Shelly Franklin's manuscript again and got back to work.

It was well past two when I stopped and finally turned off the light. Some time after that, I heard Malcolm's key turning in the door. He came inside very quietly and sat down next to me on the bed. He smelled like shampoo and soap and he'd changed into soft, fleecy clothes. As he bent over me his hair brushed my cheek. It was still wet.

"I'm sorry," he whispered.

"So am I," I said, reaching up and pulling him close to me.

Malcolm took off his clothes and slid into bed next to me. We turned to face each other and touched each other carefully, hesitantly, as if either one of us could shatter the other with the wrong move. We fell asleep like that, skin to skin, no space between our bodies. But the emotional distance between us was wide and full of everything we'd left unsaid.

EIGHT

MEMO

To: Angel
From: LF
Re: BLIND SUBMISSION

Let's discuss.

Jackson Stark, Lucy's new hire and replacement for Nora/Kelly, edged toward me and gingerly placed Lucy's glaring memo on my desk.

"Uh . . ." he began.

"Thanks, Jackson," I said.

"Um, yes. Sure. You're welcome."

"Okay," I said, knowing that there was more. I looked up at him, waiting. The scent of his cologne (lush, expensive, but way too liberally applied) engulfed me. He was twenty years old, a fact Lucy had shared with all of us, and didn't have enough facial hair to justify the razor burn on his smooth cheeks. He was wearing a silk shirt festooned with paisley patterns and black, tight-fitting designer jeans. He'd been working with us for three weeks and had worn jeans every day. There had not been a single mention or memo from Lucy regarding his attire in all that time. I wondered if it was because he was male or, likelier, she was waiting for someone else (me? Anna?) to blow the whistle on him. It was Craig who had dug Jackson's résumé up from one of his mysterious files and called him in for an interview. Perhaps he'd been hired simply because he was male. On one of Lucy's memos to Craig during the interview process, she had written simply, *No more girls!!!!*

"I think she wants to talk to you about this," Jackson said, pointing at the manuscript.

"Okay, great. Thanks, Jackson."

He sighed and glided back to his desk. He rearranged his already ordered stacks of paper for a moment and looked over at me once more, concern darkening his eyes.

"I think she wants to talk to you about it, like, now."

"Got it. Thanks, Jackson."

"You're welcome."

Hearing this interchange, Anna looked up from the peanut butter sandwich she was eating and raised an eyebrow in my direction. "Whathat?" She pointed to the memo. I wished she wouldn't speak with her mouth full. It was really starting to annoy me.

"Memo from Lucy," I said.

"Whabout?" Anna asked.

I shot a disgusted look in her direction. At least swallow, I thought. "I don't know," I snapped, but of course I did. I hadn't given Lucy a progress report on *Blind Submission* for a few days and I knew she was expecting a revised, edited manuscript *yesterday.* It had been some time since anything even worth a second look had come in, and Lucy was starting to make plenty of noise about the "dry spell." It didn't seem to matter to her that Karanuk had sent the first couple of chapters of what was sure to be a gigantic sale (not that I'd had a chance to read it—Lucy had snatched it off the pile the moment it arrived in the office) or that, after I finished the Damiano Vero–style edit I was doing on Shelly Franklin's novel, she'd be able to sell *Elvis* for plenty of money. In fact, an auction seemed likely for that one. But Lucy still seemed hungry—ravenous, even—for more. It wasn't about the money. She had an insatiable, constant need for the next big thing. And *I* was the one who was supposed to deliver that to her. I'd become the miller's daughter of my favorite fairy tale, spinning a roomful of straw into gold overnight. Unlike the miller's daughter, however, I didn't have Rumpelstiltskin showing up to help me.

"Um . . . Angel?" Jackson and his cologne were at my desk again.

"Jackson?"

He pointed at Lucy's note. "I think, um, I mean, she, um, like, asked that you see her about that."

"I got it the first time, Jackson," I snapped. From the corner of my eye, I could see Anna's brow furrow with surprise and I felt Craig's disapproving glance from his corner of the office. I couldn't find it in myself to care. For his part, Jackson didn't seem to mind my tone at all. He nodded affably and made his way back to his desk.

"Angel!" Lucy shrieked into my intercom.

"On my way," I answered. I detected a whiff of satisfaction coming from Anna's desk as I jumped up from my chair.

Lucy was sitting on her couch, tapping her Waterman pen impatiently against her corduroy-clad knees, when I entered her office. "Finally!" she said. She didn't wait for me for me to sit down before she started. "What's going on with that novel about the literary agency?"

"I—"

"Have you spoken to the author? Do we have the complete manuscript? Do we have revisions?"

"No," I said. "And no."

"Why not, Angel?"

"The author wants to remain anonymous. I don't have a phone number. And I've been working on the *Elvis*—"

"Still?"

"Yes. But I don't have much to work with on the other one. And are you sure you want me to put so much time into it before we get an agency contract?"

"We don't *have* an agency contract yet?"

"No, but—"

"You'd better get one, Angel."

"Okay, I'm on it."

I got as far as her door before Lucy stopped me again with a question. "How are you and the boyfriend doing?" she asked. "Everything all right there?"

Why she'd ask, I couldn't tell and didn't want to know. The truth was things were not really all right with Malcolm, even if they weren't exactly all wrong. We were spending fewer nights together for one thing. We were getting along fine, but since our argument over his novel, there was a kind of emptiness between the two of us that neither he nor I seemed to be able to fill. This was most evident when we were physically close. It was then, when we were actually touching each other, that I noticed the space between us, as if there was a charged layer of air, a force field, keeping our bodies from joining the way they had before. I wanted to get back whatever we were missing, but I didn't know how. My growing fear, too, was that it had never been there in the first place. None of this was anything I wanted to share with Lucy. Despite the fact that she suddenly sounded all warm and girlfriend-y, the last thing I wanted was to get into a discussion about my love life with her. "Everything's fine," I said.

"Is it? Well, I'm happy to hear it."

"Thanks, Lucy." I thought she was finished then, and I was half out the door before she called me back yet again.

"Angel?"

"Yes, Lucy?"

"I'd like you and the boyfriend to join me for dinner." Although her words indicated an invitation, I knew Lucy well enough to realize that she was issuing a command. I didn't relish the thought of spending more personal time with her than I already did, but turning down dinner was no more an option than refusing to answer the phones. Why she'd want "the boyfriend" there was a mystery, but I was sure I'd find out soon enough. In the meantime, I'd have to make a show of being excited at the prospect.

"That would be great, Lucy."

"Good. Saturday at seven."

"Okay. Great. Um, which restaurant?"

Lucy looked at me with an expression of supreme exasperation. "At my *home*, of course, Angel." She tapped her pen again. I'd come to hate that sound. "You're still in my office, Angel. Is there something else? If not, I believe you've got a writer to chase."

"Okay," I said, and finally, I managed to escape.

To: ganovelist@heya.com
From: angel.robinson@fiammalit.com
Subject: BLIND SUBMISSION

Dear G,

Thanks so much for sending the new material. You haven't mentioned whether or not you have a completed manuscript. In any event, Ms. Fiamma would like to discuss representing you! Could you please give us a call at 510-555-7666 as soon as possible?

Many thanks,
Angel

I hit the SEND icon on my computer and let out a sigh. The anonymous bit had gone on long enough and was starting to wear very thin. We were *interested*; wasn't that what the author wanted? What was the point of carrying on this way? I hoped the next e-mail from our mystery author would have more information and I'd be able to stop playing this guessing game. If not, I'd have to start pressing the author harder, and I wasn't sure I knew how to do that. That hard-bitten agent approach was really much more Lucy's style than mine.

"Go ahead and send the whole thing in, then."

I swiveled my head in the direction of Jackson's voice. I wasn't the only one—Anna was also staring at him, her mouth open in amazement.

"Yeah, it sounds really good," Jackson went on. "Okay, thanks. Bye now."

"Who was that?" I asked Jackson as he hung up the phone.

"Um, just a writer who wants to send something to us." He sounded defensive, but also slightly indignant.

"And you decided to tell him to send the *whole manuscript?*" I thought about checking my tone, which had suddenly become very sharp, but decided against it. It wasn't as if Jackson hadn't been trained—I'd seen to that myself after witnessing Anna's methods first-hand. Why he'd suddenly decided to tell an author to send in hundreds of pages was beyond me.

"But it sounded really good," Jackson said.

"If it's good, we'll ask to see more," I told him. "You never tell them to send the whole thing in first. Haven't we been over this?"

"But—" Jackson began, and found himself cut off by Craig.

"Angel, can I see you for a moment, please?"

I thought about how much I'd like to tell Craig that he could see me quite plainly from where he sat, but instead I got up and walked the short distance to his desk. Craig pulled out several drawers of the tall filing cabinet next to his desk so that we'd be partially obscured from view. This was what constituted privacy in this office. Of course, any-one within earshot (Anna, Jackson) could *hear* everything that was being said. Which, I suppose, was Craig's point.

"Don't you think you're being a little harsh with him?" Craig said, lowering his voice to a movie-star whisper.

"It seems pretty basic," I answered in a whisper of my own. "Telling callers to send in the first fifty is sort of the rule of thumb here, isn't it? I know *I've* told him."

"You're getting a little ahead of yourself, don't you think, Angel?"

Craig's eyes, normally washed out and vague, were alive with brown sparks I'd never seen there before. He was actually angry, and I sensed it didn't have as much to do with me as it seemed.

"What do you mean?" I asked him.

"There's only one boss here," he hissed. "And you're not her."

That set me back—literally. I moved away from Craig as if I'd been pushed. "I'm sorry," I said. "I thought when you asked me to train—"

"Exactly," Craig snapped. "I asked you to *train* him, not pass judg-ments on his character."

"I never—"

"Do you really think you are so far above the *little people* already, Angel Robinson? Have you forgotten where you came from only a few months ago?" Something caught Craig's eye then and he lowered his gaze to the vicinity of my chest. "Or where you've been?" he added ominously.

I raised my hand to my chest instinctively while looking down to see what Craig was staring at, and discovered that I'd managed to pop one of the buttons on my shirt, exposing a generous bit of bra and breast. And that damn tattoo. I clutched my lapels together, blushing furiously and trying desperately to regain some sense of dignity.

"Excuse me, Craig?" was the best I could come up with.

"Jackson's a good kid," Craig rasped. "You can go back to your desk." He slammed his filing cabinet drawers shut and bent over his desk, leaving me to plod the awkward steps back to my own. I avoided looking at Jackson at all but couldn't help seeing Anna's face. She was wearing a twin version of my embarrassed blush, and for a moment I was completely confused. Was it possible that she felt bad for me?

As if to answer that question, Anna sent me an instant message as soon as I sat down.

It's not your fault. I've told him the same thing. C doesn't like having his territory invaded.

I felt like a kid passing notes in high school. *I'm not invading anyone's territory,* I wrote back, deleting as I went.

He's pretty protective of Lucy.

I deleted the message and looked over at Anna, eyebrows raised. The red color in her face was fading, leaving pinkish splotches on her cheeks. She nodded meaningfully.

"Do you have a safety pin?" I asked her.

"Sure!" She began rummaging through her desk drawer. "What do you need it for?"

Why did she have to know everything? "Just got a problem with my shirt," I stage-whispered.

"Hmm," Anna mumbled. "Thought I had one in here . . ."

"Never mind," I said, watching her unwrap an ancient Tootsie Roll she'd found in the detritus of her desk drawer. "I'll just use a stapler." I reached for the heavy stapler on my desk and angled it to try to bind my gaping buttonhole.

"Angel!" Although I'd heard it countless times, Lucy's voice in my intercom always made me jump, and I just missed stapling my shirt to my exposed flesh.

"Yes, Lucy?"

"My office, please!"

She was holding out a pink memo when I walked in. "Give this to Craig, please," she said. "And Angel?"

"Yes, Lucy?"

"Have you contacted that author yet?"

"I sent an e-mail, yes."

"Why didn't you call, Angel? You know we don't take e-mail submissions here."

"There's no phone number, Lucy. Remember I told you? It's all anonymous?"

She sighed in exasperation. "Well, then, I hoped you asked for one. Now deliver that to Craig, please."

"Okay." I glanced at the memo. *C—my office. —L.*

"Angel?"

"Yes, Lucy?"

"How's the new one doing? Jackson?"

I could feel the flush spread across my face. Lucy couldn't have heard my conversation with Craig unless she'd bugged the outer office (not such a far-fetched prospect, really), but it was far likelier that this was just another instance of her psychic melding. Sort of the mental equivalent of the synchronized menstrual cycles that women get when they live or work in close quarters.

"He's fine."

"You seem unsure of that, Angel."

"No, he's doing fine."

"Because if he isn't doing a good job, it's on your shoulders. You trained him, yes?"

"Yes."

"Good."

I left her office and handed the memo to Craig, who glared at me, grabbed a folder from his desk, and stalked off to see Lucy. I could feel the throb of a headache starting at the base of my skull. It was going to be a bad one, I could tell. I leaned over to get the one-hundred-count bottle of aspirin I had started carrying in my purse and almost tripped over a large FedEx box sitting on the floor next to my desk.

"What's this?" I asked Jackson, who was looking over at me.

"Just came for you while you were in with her," he said. He waited a moment before hopping over to my desk like an eager kid on Christmas morning. "Open it!" he said. "Aren't you going to open it?"

I had to smile in spite of myself. It was almost quaint that he found an unopened box so exciting. Although I hated to admit it, Craig was right—I *had* been too harsh with Jackson. After all, unlike Nora/Kelly, Jackson was actually trying to work with me instead of against me. "Okay," I said. "But you realize it could just be some really big hate mail from a disgruntled author we've rejected."

"No, it can't be," he said. "Those people don't know this address."

He was right. I made another mental note: *Jackson. Smarter than he looks.* Not to be left out, Anna had also made her way over to my desk, and I opened the box with both of them staring at me in anticipation and pulled out its items one by one. Everything was packed with great care, which was a good thing because the first item was a small glass fishbowl. Inside it was a frantic fish swimming in a sealed bag of water. There were two other items in the box, a large package of fresh angel-hair pasta and a bottle of Angelica liqueur. There was a postcard taped to the bottle.

Angel—
Something for your desk, something for your appetite, something
for your dreams.
Tuo Damiano

I turned the postcard over. It was a photo of Angel Island, the park in the middle of the San Francisco Bay.

"Wow," Jackson said. "What kind of fish is that?"

"It's an angelfish," I said.

"How do you know?" Jackson asked.

"There are a lot of angel-themed things out there," I told him. "When you grow up with a name like Angel, you get to know them pretty quickly."

"Huh," Anna said. "Guess you've got a real admirer there." She looked as if she'd swallowed something extremely bitter. "Nice work, *Angel*."

"You have to hand it to him," I said, more to myself than to anyone else. "He's incredibly creative." It was the most thoughtful gift I'd ever received from anyone, and I was so moved by it that I couldn't even concern myself with Anna's venomous glare. "Guess I'll put my fish in some water."

I filled the fishbowl with water from the bathroom sink, flipped the fish into it, and took my seat at my desk. An unsettling silence descended on the room after Jackson left to pick up the mail. There was no sound at all coming from Lucy's office and the phones were uncharacteristically quiet. Anna shifted in her chair, her cheeks slightly puffed out, as if she was getting ready to expel air. After a second or two, she started pecking halfheartedly at her keyboard and humming. There was something vaguely familiar about the tune, but I didn't recognize it until she started adding lyrics, one painful off-key word at a time.

"'Just call me . . . angel . . . of the . . . mor-ning, ba-by . . . hmm, mmm . . .'"

Trust Anna, I thought, to know a Juice Newton song. "Angel of the Morning" was probably the only angel song Damiano *hadn't* included on the CD he'd made for me. The only reason I recognized it at all was because my mother used to sing it to me. I felt an unfamiliar pang of sentimentality as I remembered how my mother used to brush my hair, always long and forever tangled, when I was little. It was always a lengthy procedure since there was always so much of it to get through, and my mother liked to style it, braiding it and curling it as she sang that song, imbuing the corny lyrics with special emphasis. But hearing the song in Anna's throat was torture, a perversion of a very sweet memory, and I didn't know how much longer I could take it.

Mercifully, after one more chorus the phone rang and I lunged to answer it.

"Lucy Fiamma Agency."

"Angel?"

"Malcolm . . ." He never called me at the office and I was first surprised, then dismayed (*no personal phone calls*), and finally, guilty (he couldn't possibly have known about Damiano's gift, could he?), all in the space of the two seconds it took to say his name. "What is it? What's wrong?"

"Nothing's wrong, Angel, I just wanted to speak to you. I just wanted to talk."

Just wanted to talk? Was he crazy? "Malcolm, you know I can't talk." I lowered my voice to a whisper, knowing that Anna could probably hear every word, anyway. "I'm not supposed to take personal phone calls here. You know that. I thought something terrible happened."

"Something terrible *has* happened. I haven't seen you for a couple of days. That's terrible. Why are you still whispering? Even people in the CIA make personal phone calls from time to time, Angel."

"I can't talk now."

"Of course not. All right, just thought I'd try—so kill me for that. I'll talk to you later."

"Malcolm, wait."

"What?"

The phone rang and Anna picked up the line. Even so, I lowered my voice until I could barely hear myself.

"Are you working Saturday night?"

"I work every Saturday night, Angel. Why?"

"Lucy's invited us to dinner."

"What? I can't hear you."

"Dinner with Lucy. She wants you to come."

"Angel, can you please speak just a little louder? I can't hear a word you're saying."

"Lucy has invited us for dinner," I said, raising my voice more than I meant to, the words coming out just as Anna put down her phone. So much for keeping that a secret.

"Really?" Malcolm said. "Okay, I'll get the night off. What time? What do you think I should wear?"

I sighed into the phone. "I'll call you later, okay? I really can't talk now. All right?"

"Okay, great! Call me. I'll see you later anyway, right?"

"Okay." Malcolm sounded disproportionately happy about this dinner invitation, and I found his happiness depressing. It was all backward and upside down. We were supposed to be on the same page, but it seemed as if Malcolm and I were reading from entirely different books. I wondered when that had happened. My computer trilled with the sound of an instant message from Anna.

Damiano Vero holding for you on Line 1.

I glanced over at her as I picked up the phone, but she was keeping her head down, buried once again in the chaos that was her desk drawer.

"Hi, Dami!" I said too brightly into the phone. "Thank you *so* much for your package. It's so . . . I don't know what to say. It's really beautiful."

"I'm so glad," he said. "I didn't know what to do else."

"I have my little fish right here," I said, watching it flick its tail back and forth in tiny flashes of color.

"*Bene,*" he said. "I'm so glad."

"Thank you," I said. "Again." I waited for him to say something else, having run out of words myself, but he didn't, and after a moment, the pause between us stretched into weighted silence.

"I was working on my book," he said finally.

"Do you have— I mean, is there something I can help you with?"

"It's stupid," he said, and laughed mirthlessly. "I was just— It was a part of my life that was so difficult. I thought to call you. I don't know why."

I wanted to tell him that he didn't have to have an excuse to call me, that I enjoyed talking to him, that although I hadn't experienced a fraction of what he had in his life, I still felt as if I understood what he'd been through. But it wasn't exactly true; Damiano was a client of Lucy's and I was on her clock. The phone was ringing again and Anna was pointedly not answering it.

"Damiano, I'm so sorry, I have to—"

"I know, I can hear it, the phone. Go, go. *Ci vediamo,* Angel," he said hurriedly, and hung up. I punched Line 2.

"Lucy Fia—"

"Angel, hi. Listen, is this dinner formal or what? I want to make sure that—"

"I *don't know.*" My voice came out sounding high and shrill. I brought it down to a stage whisper. "I *can't talk,* Malcolm."

"Fine," he said, and hung up. I'd barely had time to draw my next breath before I heard the sound of Anna's next message on my computer.

You don't have to whisper about dinner with Lucy. I know she likes you better than me.

I felt a nauseating mix of revulsion, pity, and guilt churning in my stomach. I started to type a reply to Anna's message but stopped myself. This was the height of ridiculousness. We were separated by a few feet and there was nobody else in the office.

"Anna, I really don't think it's about who she likes better. I don't know why . . . I mean, I'm sure it—dinner—is work-related."

"Well, whatever," Anna said, her face flooding pink. "I'm just saying you don't have to feel bad. Or hide it from me. I should probably try to learn from you, in fact." She gave a small, uncomfortable chuckle. "Dinner with the boss. Good way to get ahead, isn't it?"

"Anna, I didn't ask—"

"It's *okay.* Come on, we're on the same team here." The phrase "honor among thieves" danced through my head. I shrugged in a palms-up gesture of surrender, as if to say I couldn't argue her point. "You know what would be really great, Angel?"

"What's that, Anna?"

"I'd love it if . . . I mean, if you would . . ." She stopped, flustered, her color rising dramatically. If the concept hadn't been so absurd, I'd have sworn she was getting ready to ask me on a date. "It would be great if you'd let me make dinner for you sometime." So it *was* a date she was angling for. My headache had come on full force despite the aspirin. "Oh, jeez, I'm sorry, Angel, that didn't sound right at all!" I could almost feel the heat of her red face at my desk. "I just mean it would be great to get together outside of work, you know. And I *am* a pretty good cook, so . . . Anyway, I feel like we kind of got off to a little bit of a bad start, maybe, and I'd like to sort of change that." She took a deep breath and exhaled noisily. "What do you think?"

I thought that I wouldn't be able to get through a meal with Anna unless I had several alcoholic beverages. What did we have in common aside from the job? I also sensed there was something other than a desire to be buddies that was festering behind Anna's invitation. Of course, I couldn't tell her any of that, nor, for the second time in one day, could I refuse. She and I both knew that if I turned her down after that pathetic plea, I'd be the world's biggest bitch.

"Sure," I said. "That would be great. Maybe when things quiet down a bit around here."

"Well, we can't wait for that, can we?" Anna said. "Hopefully, that will never happen! But yeah, okay. Thanks, Angel."

She was really laying it on thick. I repressed the urge to throw my stapler at her. "No problem. Sounds like fun."

"We're the only girls in the office now," she said, and gave me an exaggerated wink. "We have to stick together." Female anatomy, I thought. I stood corrected—she'd found something else we had in common. "And I *know* some things, Angel. Things you don't know. I could share them with you."

"What?"

"Shhh!" she said, shutting me up just as Craig exited Lucy's office. She put her head down and started typing. After a few seconds I got an instant message from her saying, *I'll tell you later.*

"Where's Jackson?" Craig barked from his desk.

"It's okay." Anna laughed. "He's only gone to get the mail. He hasn't quit."

Actual humor. Score one for Anna, I thought.

If he heard, Craig gave no indication. "Angel, can I see you for a moment, please?" His tone was now much more solicitous. I prepared myself for another bait-and-switch. This was turning out to be the day for them. Craig didn't bother pulling out the filing cabinets as I approached. "You can sit, Angel," he said, and as I positioned myself across from him, Jackson reappeared at the door, staggering under the weight of a full mail tub.

Craig looked over at Jackson for a second and then back to face me. "I've got some good news for you, Angel."

I gave Craig a big, if forced, smile. He seemed strung tight enough to be on the verge of a breakdown. I decided it would be wise to be as careful as possible with him. "Good news is always good," I said, wondering if Anna was listening.

As if on cue, the phones began ringing. Jackson and Anna went for separate lines and began talking. The office had come alive again.

"Your official probation period isn't up yet," Craig began, "but Lucy's decided to jump the gun a bit here and give you a raise." He looked up at me, waiting for a response. My intuition told me that it had better be an effusive one.

"Really? That's great!"

"Yes, well, you don't even know how great yet." Craig cleared his throat. "Lucy's been very impressed with how quickly you've assimilated in the office and with your reading. Guess that bookstore experience really paid off for you. Anyway, as you know, Lucy believes in rewarding good work, so she's made the decision to substantially increase your salary." He scribbled a figure on a piece of paper and slid it over to me. I stared at the numbers, utterly confused.

"But Craig, that's what I'm making now, isn't it?"

"No, Angel, that's not your new salary. That's the amount of your raise."

I could feel my eyes widen. The room seemed very bright. Craig was looking at me impassively, a slight twist in the corner of his mouth. This clearly hadn't been his idea, and I was sure that he had even lobbied against it.

"But . . . but that's double what I'm making now. Is that right?"

"Yes," Craig said. "I take it you're pleased?" I could only nod. My throat was dry and I didn't trust myself to speak. I could move into a place with an actual bedroom. Hell, I could probably even move out of Petaluma and closer to the city—maybe Berkeley. I could buy shoes and still have enough left over for dinner. And I could actually start making some inroads on my student-loan debt. That bill had been hanging over my head like the sword of Damocles since the day I'd graduated. I'd never allowed myself to get so excited about money. I was like a kid who'd just been told she could eat the cake, the ice cream, *and* the candy bar. It was a little overwhelming.

"There's one condition, though," Craig said.

Of course there was. This was Lucy Fiamma country, after all. "Oh?"

"Like any intelligent businesswoman, Lucy would like to protect her investment. And this is a rather large investment, I think you'd agree." I nodded again. "So, bearing that in mind, the condition is that you commit to your employment here for a period of two years from this date. Should you leave *voluntarily* at any point before that time, Lucy would expect you to return the difference in salary that she is offering you today."

It was as if she were offering me a book contract, I thought. If the book wasn't written and delivered within two years, she'd expect the advance to be returned. Only, in this case, I was the book. I didn't know if it was legal, but it was certainly interesting, and all that money was almost irresistible.

"Wow," I said after my heart rate slowed. "That's really amazing."

"I'll have the contract written up by the end of the day," Craig said. "You can sign and Lucy can countersign. I'm also a notary public—I don't know if I mentioned that before—so we won't have to take it out anywhere. You'll get a copy, of course, for your records. I take it you accept the terms?"

I stared into Craig's eyes, searching for a glimmer of the fire I'd seen there earlier, but there was nothing but the bleached effect of driftwood. "Can I sleep on it tonight? Just because, you know, it's a good idea to think things through."

"Lucy will need an answer today," Craig said. "Really, Angel, what's to think about? She's being absurdly generous here. And it's almost like a guarantee of employment. You know what the job market is like these days. *Especially* in publishing."

I closed my eyes for a moment, wanting to let Craig's rumbling Barry White voice wash over me. Looking at him simply ruined the effect.

"Okay," I said. "You're right, of course. I'm . . . I couldn't be happier."

"Good. And there's just one more thing."

"Yes?" I said. Craig leaned forward, grimacing, and for a moment I thought he was going to tell me that the whole thing was a joke, ha-ha.

"Lucy would like to give you the first year's raise in a lump sum."

"So—"

"Yes, all at once. Also, although this is a raise, Lucy will pay it to you as if it were a bonus, so we won't be taking any taxes out of it. Again, you'll be responsible for those. I can have a check ready for you by the end of the week. And, of course, the same terms apply. Should you leave before—"

"I think I understand, Craig. I'd owe it all back. Got it." I was actually counting it in my head, visualizing piles and piles of green dollars laid out on my bed.

"I'll write it up, then?" Craig said.

"Yes, thank you. Thanks so much."

"Don't thank me," he said. "It's all her."

There was an instant message and an e-mail waiting for me when I returned to my desk. The instant message, from Anna, read: *Congratulations.*

I didn't stop to think about her bionic hearing or what were the implications of her knowing about my huge pay increase, because the e-mail message demanded my immediate attention.

To: angel.robinson@fiammalit.com
From: ganovelist@heya.com
Subject: Re: BLIND SUBMISSION

Dear Ms. Robinson,

I am indeed pleased that Ms. Fiamma would like to offer me representation. I assure you that when the time is right, I will happily sign on with her. Rest assured that I will not be submitting elsewhere. You have my word. I thank you for getting in touch and look forward to our correspondence.

I will be sending you more text shortly. I am, just now, putting a few finishing touches on a key scene.

With best wishes,
G.

The e-mail struck me as both pompous and cheesy, a dreadful combination. I found I was really beginning to dislike this author, which didn't bode well for the manuscript. I mean, really, "ganovelist"? **Great American Novelist**? There was also something about the language of the e-mail that struck me as very familiar, but I couldn't place it. The whole thing—the manuscript, the e-mails, and the secret identity—was really starting to grate on me. It occurred to me that I should have rejected the manuscript when I'd had the chance, before Lucy even saw it. But then I had the unnerving thought that even if I *had* rejected it, the author would have found a way to get back in. It had become very clear that this particular author knew a little too much about the way things worked at our agency.

"Peeuwww!" Jackson was going through the day's mail. He held an envelope away from his face with one hand and made fanning motions with the other. "This one stinks!"

"What is it?" Anna asked.

"This manuscript smells terrible," Jackson said. "It reeks."

"Smokers," Anna said, and I nodded in agreement. "Their work smells so bad you don't even want to open it, let alone read it. You'd think they'd know that and open a window or something before they print it out."

"Yes, but if they knew . . ." It was right there, edging into my mental field of vision. I reached for it—

"Knew what?" Jackson asked.

—and grabbed it. "Peter Johnson!" I exclaimed out loud.

"Smokers knew Peter Johnson?" Anna asked. "What are you talking about?"

"When's the last time we heard from him?" I asked Anna.

"Who's Peter Johnson?" Jackson asked.

"Yeah, it's been awhile, huh?" Anna said. "He used to call every day, didn't he? Did you finally chase him off, Angel? I haven't seen one of his manuscripts for a long time. What was the last one? Wait, I remember, it was that awful one about the Russian spy who . . ."

I tuned her out as she went on. I knew exactly the last time we'd heard from Peter Johnson—it was the morning I'd given Lucy Malcolm's novel and started that whole mess in motion. He'd hung up on me, but not before giving me his usual speech, which sounded exactly like the words I'd just read in that e-mail. The mystery author had Peter Johnson's literary DNA all over him. And hadn't he said, in that last conversation I'd had with him, that he was giving *us* another chance? It had to be him.

"Hey, Jackson, can you do me a favor?" I said when Anna's breath ran out.

"Sure, what do you need?"

"Can you see if you can find an address or phone number for Peter Johnson in the submissions log? He's submitted so many times, we must have a record of it somewhere. He practically has a log all to himself."

"Why do you want to contact Peter Johnson?" Anna asked. But before I could answer her, my intercom vibrated with the sound of Lucy's voice.

"Angel? Can we talk?" She sounded like a bad imitation of Joan Rivers. She knew Craig had talked to me about her "absurdly generous" raise and she was waiting for a response. I knew what she wanted. I punched the button on my intercom.

"On my way," I said, and prepared to go fawn and grovel.

To: angel.robinson@fiammalit.com
From: ganovelist@heya.com
Subject: Re: Edit notes

Dear Ms. Robinson,

Thank you for your speedy response to my work. I have already made some of the corrections you suggested in the opening chapters. Let me also say that I am pleased to be working with you, but I'd just like to make sure that Ms. Fiamma is, in fact, the person who will be representing this novel? Before I send you the next installment, I'd like to go over some of your notes for my own clarification. To wit, you say that there should be "more intrigue right up front." Is it not intriguing enough to place a frustrated writer in a literary agency where she can only hope to usher in the works of other writers? Perhaps not. Perhaps you are suggesting that there needs to be a dead body? I need to kill someone off, as it were? If so, I can arrange that, but I may need a few more chapters to do it. Is this the direction you'd see as best for this novel?

You also say Alice needs more dimension and asked me to define what it is that Alice wants. The answer is: everything. At this point, her goal is to attain as much power as possible and she will be ruthless about obtaining it. She's also a frustrated writer in search of the perfect novel. She wants a bestseller and she doesn't care what she has to do to get one. Perhaps that aspect is not coming across as clearly as it should. (By the way, I appreciate your compliment about how I've gotten the details right where it comes to describing a literary agency. My research has paid off!)

As far as the Carol Moore character, I will try to "flesh her out," as you say. She is a very powerful character. Indeed, she holds the power that Alice is looking for, and that should come across for the reader. In your notes, you didn't mention whether or not you felt that Carol Moore was sympathetic or not. You did mention that it's important to have the protagonist be somewhat likable, which takes care of Alice (I assume she's not likable enough?), but I'm curious as to your take on Carol, the agent, since she's a very important character as well.

I will look forward to your reply, Ms. Robinson. You can expect my next installment shortly, along with corrections on what I've already sent.

With best wishes,
G.

Blind Submission, p. 68

Carol Moore held a staff meeting every morning. In addition to conducting the business of the day, she also liked to get caught up on the manuscripts that her staff was reading and allowed everyone the time to discuss whatever they thought was important. "Fresh ideas are crucial," Carol said. "And I have hired all of you because you all have excellent ideas on how we can better serve our clients." To make everyone feel comfortable and to encourage casual dialogue, Carol ordered muffins and coffee for every staff meeting. Alice noticed that Jewel ate at least three muffins every morning. It was starting to show, Alice thought. Those thighs of Jewel's weren't getting any slimmer.

Carol seemed especially excited for today's staff meeting. "It's easy to keep believing that this is just a business like any other," Carol was saying, "but the truth is that this is art. What our authors do is incredibly important and influential. It means something and their books make a difference in the world. It's so important for us to get them out there—to do what they can't do themselves."

Alice found herself drifting off as Carol spoke. Carol was right, of course, books were important, but it was too painful for Alice to listen to Carol's adulation of other authors.

"Can you stay here for a moment please, Alice?"

Alice came to attention in time to notice that the meeting was breaking up.

"Of course, Carol," Alice said, shutting the door behind Jewel and Ricardo.

"Vaughn Blue is very happy with the work you've been doing for him," Carol said once Alice was sitting down again. Alice's heart started beating a little faster and she searched Carol's face for an indication that Carol might know the real nature of Alice's "work" with Vaughn Blue. But Carol looked very happy and there was no sign that anything was amiss.

"For that matter," Carol went on, "I'm very happy with the work you've been doing. You are a real asset to this agency, Alice."

But not a good enough writer to be represented by you, Alice thought bitterly. What she said was, "Thank you, I appreciate that, Carol."

"I'm giving you a raise," Carol said, "and your own office. It's the small one next to mine, but it will be your own office. I think you've earned it."

"I don't know what to say," Alice said. "You're too good to me, Carol."

"Just carry on," Carol said. "You're doing a marvelous job."

Alice left Carol's office and prepared to move into her own. Yes, she was grateful to Carol, but not in the way Carol thought. And she would carry on, but not in the way Carol planned. She would carry on skimming the cream off the top of incoming proposals and manuscripts. She would carry on raping Carol's files and slowly undermining the efforts of her staff. She would carry on sucking ideas from out of Carol's clients' heads and then convincing them that those very ideas were completely unmarketable. She would carry on playing Vaughn Blue as expertly as he played his own instrument. And she would carry on letting Carol think that her greatest ambition was to become just like Carol herself. Very soon, Alice's careful planning would bear fruit. And Carol had just made it easier for Alice to do what she needed to do.

NINE

———

To: angel.robinson@fiammalit.com
From: ganovelist@heya.com
Subject: Quick question

Dear Ms. Robinson,

I hate to bother you on the weekend, but I am wrestling with what may be an important decision, and since you have been so very helpful already, I was hoping you could help me resolve it.

It occurs to me that my novel might be—or become—a little claustrophobic. What I mean is that the setting rarely strays from the inside of Carol Moore's agency. Do you think that this gets too confining? I was thinking that perhaps Alice could attend some kind of literary event outside the agency? Perhaps a book signing, for example. Or perhaps even a cocktail party honoring one of Carol's authors? That would add a little color and then the reader would also get a chance to see what Alice is like outside the agency.

What do you think?

With best wishes,
G.

I tapped my fingernail on the edge of my computer keyboard, debating whether or not to return G's message. I didn't want this author to think I was available 24/7 for editorial advice. Clearly, G didn't mind bothering me on the weekend—the e-mail was proof of that. On the other hand, G had known, somehow, that I'd check my e-mail on the weekend, so what was the point of pretending I hadn't? Once again, mystery G had managed to unsettle and irritate me at the same time. I wondered if I had developed some kind of literary stalker. Or was I just being overly paranoid? No, this was an author who knew just a little too much—who'd submitted manuscripts one too many times. I was almost positive now that it was Peter Johnson, only I hadn't yet been able to get in touch with him to confirm my hunch. The only twinge of doubt I had about my theory was that Peter Johnson wasn't really a good enough writer to have produced *Blind Submission*. But who knew—maybe all those rejections had actually sparked some kind of latent talent. Whether it was Johnson or not, though, it would have to wait. I turned off my computer and snapped it shut. I had a dinner to prepare for.

I DECIDED TO LET MALCOLM DRIVE us to Lucy's house for dinner. I didn't know if Lucy was planning to serve anything alcoholic, but if she did, I knew I'd be partaking. I'd never been much of a drinker—anything harder than the occasional glass of wine in a restaurant tended to make me ill—but if ever there was an occasion that called for an altered state of consciousness, dinner at Lucy's house was it. Malcolm was happy to be the designated driver for this soiree, and he laughed when I told him why.

"I don't think I've ever seen you drunk, Angel," he said, and winked at me. "Might be fun."

"I didn't say I was planning to get drunk," I told him, although I realized that I probably was.

Once we were in the car, I allowed myself a closer look at the clothes Malcolm had come up with for dinner. I'd never seen him dressed quite like it and didn't even know he owned such attire. Given his heroine worship of Lucy, though, it was entirely possible that he'd sneaked off and bought something just for this evening. His outfit looked like a cross between something you'd see in the pages of *Esquire* and *Cat Burglar Quarterly.* He was wearing a tight-fitting black silk T-shirt tucked into equally form-fitting black pants, which were neither jeans nor slacks but a happy blend of the two. All this was finished with sleek black loafers and *The Matrix*–inspired sunglasses. Altogether, his garb was slightly ridiculous, but it worked in a big way. The long-sleeved T-shirt outlined and clung to every line of muscle of his arms and chest, and the pants were not tight enough to be vulgar, but not loose enough to disguise what was underneath them. His thick blond hair and naturally tan skin nicely set off all the black he was wearing, and the perfect amount of stubble decorated his jaw. He was hot—no question about it.

After discarding several outfits as unworthy (and flashing back to my first interview with Lucy), I'd finally settled on the only black dress I owned. It was on the short side, the hem coming to mid-thigh, and cut so low in front that the angel-wing tattoo on my breast was plain to see and impossible to cover. But it was an excellent combination of casual and elegant and the best I could hope for, so I threw a gauzy scarf around my neck, draped it over my décolletage, and called it even. I hadn't gotten a haircut since I'd started working for Lucy, and had taken to wearing my hair in a sloppy twist in the office. It had gotten quite long and very curly, so rather than torturing it into some kind of fancy do, I just let it fall loose down the back of my dress.

Malcolm had purchased a big bouquet of red, yellow, and orange roses for us to give to Lucy and I held them on my lap as we drove into San Rafael. He was good with flowers and I couldn't argue with his statement "You can't show up empty-handed when someone invites you to dinner, can you?" but I felt somewhat put out, anyway. I should have remembered to get something, I thought, not to mention the fact that I was a more worthy recipient of those roses than Lucy.

"It's like taking coals to Newcastle," I told him as I buried my nose in the blooms. They were exceptionally fragrant. "People send her flowers all the time."

"Common courtesy," Malcolm said. "And you're welcome, by the way."

"So what do you think she'll serve?" I asked in a weak attempt to change the subject. I pulled down the passenger-side visor and checked out my reflection in the mirror. It was time to apply more lipstick.

"Who knows?" Malcolm said. "I'm sure it'll be good, though."

"Why are you so sure? God, I hope it's not some Alaskan thing, like roasted caribou or whale ice cream."

"Come on, you know she doesn't eat that stuff in real life," Malcolm said.

"What do you mean, 'real life'? She's all over the *Cold!* food. She tried to get Karanuk to write a cookbook once, did I tell you that?"

"Yes, you mentioned it," he said. I couldn't see his eyes behind his super-cool shades and that bothered me.

"I told you about his new book, right?"

"Yep."

"Did I tell you that he's going to call it *Thaw*? Like I suggested?"

"Really? That's great, baby."

"Lucy says she's trying to talk him into coming up here for an appearance. Top secret. Like only half a million people will know about it. Can you imagine how many books that would sell? So far he's not biting."

"Maybe *you* could talk him into it," Malcolm said. "He seems to really like you from what you've said. That would be some coup, huh?"

"Hmm." I pondered the scenario for a moment. Karanuk showing his face for even the briefest of appearances would be a bigger media event than J. D. Salinger showing up on David Letterman. I hadn't even thought of it as a possibility until Malcolm mentioned it, but planted now, the idea started to grow on me. It had weight, dimension, and infinite potential. At the very least, I could feel Karanuk out, see if he'd be amenable to the suggestion. It was worth a shot. I let myself drift into the daydream of a huge Karanuk book party. We could have ice sculptures that melted down during the event, signifying the "thaw" and the return to the unmolded shape of nature. . . . I bolted upright in my seat. I was thinking *exactly like Lucy*. It was as if she'd beamed the thoughts straight into my brain. I shook myself, literally, and looked ahead.

We were close to Lucy's house and I could feel the adrenaline surging as it did every time I approached the office. And then I realized that I wasn't driving. My stomach gave a sick little flip. I hadn't given Malcolm directions. How had he found his way here without them?

"Malcolm?"

"Baby?"

"How the hell did you get here?"

"I drove, love. You know, foot, gas, all that."

"No, Malcolm, I mean, how did you find it? I didn't give you directions. And you've never been here before. Have you?"

"Shit," Malcolm said softly.

"What? Tell me now."

"Look, I'm sorry, Angel, I didn't want you to know. . . . I'm so stupid."

"Malcolm, what the hell are you TALKING ABOUT?" I was yelling almost out of control, and I didn't even know why.

"I followed you, okay?"

"*What?*"

"A couple of times . . . When you first started working and you seemed so stressed out and I was just worried about you, okay? You were so tired—you're still tired all the time—and I just wanted to make sure you got there safely, okay? And it was always so off-limits, I wasn't allowed to call, to come take you to lunch, you know? Like it was some kind of white slavery ring or something." He let out a nervous giggle, incongruous next to his outfit.

"But how did you follow me without my seeing you?"

"Angel . . ." He took a long and very dramatic pause. "You don't see anything except what's right in front of you or inside your head anymore. You're so focused, a herd of elephants could sneak up on you. Of course you didn't see me. I don't think you saw anything."

He wasn't wrong. There had been many times I'd arrived at the office without remembering how I'd gotten there. But his following me—sneaking behind me—gave me a cold, nervous feeling in the pit of my stomach, and I couldn't shake it.

"You know, Malcolm, I don't know whether to think this is sweet or just totally creepy."

"Just trying to look out for you, Angel." He let out a long sigh and pushed his shades back on his nose.

"Look out for me or spy on me?"

"Why would I need to spy on you? How does *that* make sense?"

"I don't know!" I said, my tension and frustration coming through my voice. "It's weird, okay? It's just a weird thing to do."

"I'm sorry I didn't tell you earlier, I should have," he said. "I guess it *is* a little weird." He giggled again and I realized I really didn't like the sound of it.

"Yes, it is. Listen, Malcolm, next time just— Damn, we're here already." Malcolm pulled into Lucy's long, gravel driveway. I realized I'd never even looked at the front of the house before because I always entered through the back entrance. There was one other car in the driveway, a tired-looking Honda Civic. I happened to know that Lucy owned a silver Jaguar (I'd placed several calls to her mechanic, auto detailer, etc.), even though I'd never actually seen her drive anywhere, so I knew the car wasn't hers. It didn't belong to any staffers, either. Fabulous, I thought, a mystery guest. "I guess it's too late to back out now," I told Malcolm as we got out of the car.

"Come on, A, this'll be fun," he said, but he wasn't looking at me anymore. He'd fixed his gaze on Lucy's mansion and was striding toward it.

"Hey, want to wait for me?"

Malcolm turned slightly and hesitated. He looked annoyed. "I guess you want to give her the flowers?" he said.

"No, Malcolm, why don't you?" I said, shoving them into his hand. A couple of crimson and yellow petals dislodged and fluttered to the ground. Malcolm's eyes narrowed to gold slits. "What's wrong with you?" he hissed.

I chose to ignore him and stared at the front door, which was white, thick, and decorated with a giant silver knocker fashioned in the shape of Alaska, complete with Aleutian islands. I picked it up with some difficulty as it was incredibly heavy and let it fall against the door. There was no sound from inside. I tried again, still to no avail. I looked at Malcolm, telegraphing my instant panic with wild eyes. I could feel perspiration begin to seep through the thin fabric of my dress.

"You might want to try this," Malcolm said, pointing to a doorbell on the jamb. "Clearly, the knocker is just for show."

"Clearly," I said, and jammed my finger into the bell. There followed a resounding ring from inside the house. "That must be our Angel," I heard echoing toward me, and the sweat froze under my arms.

The door swung open and Lucy appeared inside it, her lightning-colored hair fanned out around her face, her arms spread wide as if to hug us both. She was wearing a black dress that was frighteningly similar to mine, although hers was no doubt a Donna Karan or Dolce & Gabbana or something like that (I'd made a few pricey boutique phone calls for her, too) and mine was a designer-less fourteen-hour special from Robinson's (which was about as fancy as I got). Lucy was taller than I was and therefore her dress was even shorter on her, showing a truly horrifying amount of pale, albeit firm, naked thigh. I hoped she wasn't planning to bend over at any point in the evening because I didn't think I'd be able to stomach a glimpse of whatever she'd thrown on for underwear. The scoop of her neck was slightly lower than mine as well, exposing the tops of those full-moon breasts I'd had the displeasure of glimpsing that morning in the office. Her shoes were just as startling—high satin heels ending with straps that laced all the way up her calves. She'd finished the ensemble off with a few pieces of silver jewelry similar to ones I had in my own jewelry box. It was disconcerting to see them on Lucy because—and I felt terribly ageist even thinking this way—they just looked too young for her. So, despite the fine quality of her jewelry and clothing, and despite the intensity of her looks, her getup had a mutton-dressed-as-lamb feel to it, as if she were intentionally dressing up as a much younger woman.

"Welcome!" she exclaimed, and to my horror, smothered me in a Chanel-soaked embrace. "And this must be the boyfriend! Malcolm, is it?" Lucy released me and turned her attention to Malcolm, whose face had turned the deep reddish-brown color of barbecued meat.

"It's wonderful to meet you. In person," he said, and thrust the roses out in front of him. "Thanks so much for inviting me tonight. It's really a pleasure. We brought— These are for you. For your house."

I'd never seen or heard Malcolm be so awkward. Lucy fixed him with an expressionless gaze, as if waiting to see just how deep a hole he could dig himself into. I would have felt sorry for him had I not been so irritated by his transformation into a stuttering marionette.

"Lovely," Lucy said as Malcolm trailed off. "Let's see if Anna can find some water for them. Follow me, will you?"

Anna? So she'd been invited after all. I wondered why I hadn't seen her car in the driveway and then realized that she must have parked in the back. Which still left the presence of the Honda unexplained.

"Angel, I don't believe you've seen my house before, have you?"

As Malcolm and I fell into step behind Lucy, I tried to catch his eye without being obvious about it, but he was marching ahead, a glazed look on his face. Lucy's house was huge, even more spacious than it appeared from the outside, and looked very much like an extension of her office space. We went from the foyer to the living room, which had light wood floors covered with an assortment of white rugs, and was furnished with chrome-and-glass tables and a blizzard of white furniture. In all this whiteness, there was not a single visible book.

"I don't think we need to go up there, do we?" Lucy said, waving her hand when we reached the free-standing spiral staircase in the center of the house.

"It's a beautiful staircase," Malcolm said reverently.

"I like to think of it as inspirational," Lucy said. "Shall we move on?" As she turned to continue her brisk tour, I was reminded of *Charlie and the Chocolate Factory.* I half-expected a team of Oompa-Loompas to march in and start singing a ditty about her inspirational staircase.

She took a left turn through an arched doorway and led us into a vast open kitchen, beyond which was a simple, sunlit dining area. Anna was standing in the kitchen, bent over a platter of what looked like cold cuts. A few feet past her, rising from a white-upholstered dining-room chair, was Damiano Vero.

"Damiano!" Lucy said brightly. "Your Angel has arrived!"

As my eyes scanned the varying levels of discomfort on every face but Lucy's, I knew one thing was certain: From this point until the day I died, I'd remember this as my life's most uncomfortable moment.

Lucy broke the silence, but not the tension, with her next gambit.

"Anna," she said, "can you relieve Angel's man here of his roses and put them in some water please?" It was then I realized that Anna was not at Lucy's house in the capacity of guest. I saw now that she was wearing a white shirt, black pants, and an apron tied around her waist. As unfathomable as I found it, she was to be our server.

"Sure," Anna said, her voice a small, strangled thing in her throat. "Hi, Angel."

"Hi, Anna."

"I'm Malcolm," he said, handing her the roses.

"So you are," Lucy chimed in. "Damiano, meet Angel's *fiancé*." Damiano looked both shocked and stricken at Lucy's announcement. I watched with helpless dismay as he struggled to regain his composure while Lucy forged ahead. "Malcolm, this is Damiano Vero, author of what is going to be a *major* book. But I'm sure Angel's told you all about him, hasn't she? They've spent so much time working together."

"Not really," Malcolm said, finally finding his voice. He shook Damiano's hand with quite a bit of force. "Angel keeps her work pretty well under wraps, actually. But congratulations, you must be very excited. I'm also a writer." He stole a nervous glance at Lucy. "It can be a rough road to travel."

"*Piacere*," Dami said. "I only just started with the writing. I owe Angel so much. She saw something in those pages to give to Luciana. They made a miracle together."

I could feel the heat of Malcolm's stare at my back as I leaned in to receive Dami's double-cheek kisses. "It is so nice to see you again, Angel," he said softly. He was the only person in the room who wasn't dressed in black. He'd opted instead for a light blue linen shirt over khaki pants. Rather than looking too casual, his quietly understated clothes made the rest of us look wildly overdressed. As his lips brushed my face, I could smell the same intoxicating citrus-sweet scent he'd worn when he came to the office. He backed away, fixing me with those purple-brown eyes of his. It was only the second time I'd seen him in person, but the visceral connection between the two of us was strong. All the time I'd spent talking to him on the phone and reading him, absorbing his words, his feelings, his thoughts, and his experiences made me feel as if I'd fallen right into his head. It was a strange familiarity—like déjà vu.

"Hardly a miracle," Lucy was saying. "It practically sold itself, didn't it, Angel?"

Lucy was on a fishing trip and she'd trained me very well. I bit down on the lure. "Oh no, that was all you, Lucy. That auction was brilliant," I said.

"I'll bet," Malcolm said. "Maybe one day I'll be as fortunate."

"Maybe you will, indeed," Lucy said, raking Malcolm with her eyes. She put her hands on her hips and assessed him as if he were livestock, one corner of her mouth turning up in a half-smile. For a moment she looked . . . *carnivorous* was the only word to describe it.

"Would anyone care for a drink?" Anna had appeared in the midst of our throng, holding a tray of cocktails no less.

"I thought martinis would be in order for this evening," Lucy said. "Please, help yourselves."

"Thanks," I said, and grabbed one from Anna's tray. As I did, I raised my eyebrows as if to ask her what the hell she was doing, but I got only a flat stare in response. I took a long sip from my martini and nearly choked on it. It was too strong and I hated gin, but I held my breath and swallowed more.

"I'll have one," Malcolm said, and took a glass from Anna's tray. I shot him a meaningful look, but he ignored me. Anna moved on to Dami, who said, "No, *grazie*. If you have a little mineral water?"

"Well, of course," Lucy said. "I forgot that you're in recovery. Although it's not like martinis and heroin really have much in common, do they, Damiano? Surely you can allow yourself a little now and then?" She plucked the olive out of her own glass and deposited it in her mouth. "Really, it's practically food."

"*È vero,*" Dami said, laughing. I marveled at his graciousness and his ability to retain his sense of humor around Lucy. It was truly a talent. "That's not the reason," he went on. "I don't like the juniper taste of the gin. The other . . . It has been a very long time. It's all in the past now."

"Hmm," Lucy mused. "Well, that's not particularly sexy, is it, Damiano? When this book hits, and it will hit big, I assure you, you may have to sex up that whole heroin thing." She turned away from Dami and focused her laser stare on Malcolm. "There are so many facets to an author's work," she said. "Don't you agree?"

"I'm sure," Malcolm said. "I'm looking forward to experiencing some of those." He gave her a dazzling smile. I hadn't seen such a big smile from him in quite some time, which explained why I hadn't noticed until now that he'd recently whitened his teeth.

"Yes," Lucy said. "You've got some looks, Mal. It's a pity you're only a waiter. If we could find you some kind of platform . . . take advantage of that face . . ."

"Thank you," Malcolm said. "I really appreciate that."

Appreciated *what*? Why was he thanking her? For that matter, why was he still staring at her with that shit-eating grin on his face? I finished my drink in one long swallow and reached for another. The alcohol was having no effect that I could sense and my nerves were winding tighter and tighter. I caught Dami's eyes over the rim of my glass. He gave me a knowing look full of humor and empathy, as if we were coconspirators— the only people in the room who got the joke.

"We should eat," Lucy announced. She gestured to Anna, who was standing behind a long marble island in the kitchen. "Anna will man— or should I say *woman*"—she laughed at her own joke—"the buffet table. Help yourselves, everyone. Malcolm, I see that your glass is empty. How are you on bartending?"

Lucy led Malcolm back into the living room, which was apparently where the bar was located, and I made my way over to Anna's buffet station, Dami following close behind me. Laid out for us, on a variety of white platters, was every kind of meat I'd ever seen and some I hadn't. Folds of ham, turkey, roast beef, and pastrami sat alongside a plate of veal cutlets and chicken wings. There was a ring of crackers decorating a mound of pâté, but no bread and not a vegetable in sight, unless you counted the parsley garnishes. It was either some kind of crazed Atkins fantasy or the embodiment of a vegetarian's worst nightmare.

"Would you like some meat?" Anna asked me.

"Anna, what are you doing here?" I whispered.

"You think you're the only one who can come to her house?" Anna whispered back, piling flesh onto my plate. "There's not as big a difference between me and you as you think, you know. We're both working."

"What do you mean?" I stole a glance at Dami, who stood a polite distance away, allowing me to have a semi-private conversation with Anna.

"At least I'm getting *paid* to do this," Anna huffed.

"What do you mean?"

"You know," she hissed, "you ought to be a little nicer to her. You've got some attitude going."

"Anna, wha—"

"Here you go. I made the chicken, by the way. You should try it."

"I'll have some chicken," Dami said, appearing beside me. I watched as Anna fumbled a few wings onto his plate. "This is a very interesting dinner," he said, and looked at me, barely contained laughter straining at the corners of his mouth. I stared at him and found myself having one of those out-of-body experiences. For one moment, everything around me seemed like an elaborate fiction. Lucy, Anna, Malcolm, this ridiculous festival of meats—all of it became somebody else's work, the play of an insane writer. I felt as if I'd been following along, but my script pages had suddenly run out and I could no longer find my place. In that elongated disconnected second, I looked at Damiano and felt anchored. Somehow he knew, could sense what I was feeling, and his eyes told me he was right there with me. I wanted to stay inside that moment of clarity forever, but, too soon, I felt myself back inside my own skin, blinking my staring eyes, my heart beating double. It was the booze, I told myself. But I wasn't drunk. Not even close. What had he said about dinner? How was I supposed to respond?

"Yes," I said, hoping that would cover it.

"Is she always like this?"

"She?"

"Luciana."

I took another swig of my martini, finishing it. That made two full drinks. When the gin finally caught up with me, it wasn't going to be pretty. Damiano was waiting for an answer and I didn't know which one

to give him. I teetered on the brink of an honest response but held myself back. He had just substantially increased his net worth thanks to
Lucy. If I were in his shoes, I'd be focused on the positive with her. He
was an author, a *client,* after all. I felt I couldn't yet trust him with the
contents of my head, even as his wine-dark eyes were telling me I could.

"She has a beautiful house, don't you think?" It was a lame deflec-
tion and Damiano saw right through it. He shrugged and moved toward
the dining-room table. "*Sì, sì,*" he said. "Spectacular." He gestured
toward a set of glass doors, through which I could see a large, completely
empty deck. "It's too bad there are no chairs outside," Damiano said.
"Outside would be nice."

The two of us sat down at Lucy's vast dining-room table. Damiano
positioned himself opposite me so that I could either look down at my
plate or at him. Those were my only options. I heard Lucy's laughter,
high and girlish, coming from the living room.

"I didn't know you were . . . *agganciata,*" Damiano said. I looked at
him, uncomprehending. He pointed to his left fourth finger. "To be married," he said.

"Engaged?" I said. "I'm not."

"But Luciana—"

"She's mistaken," I said.

"Do you listen to the CD?" Damiano asked after a minute, his voice
lower than it needed to be.

"I do," I told him. "I like it very much." It was true. In the last few
weeks, with more and more nights alone, I found myself playing Damiano's angel-themed CD late at night, using it to usher myself into sleep.

"And how's your *pesce?*" His smile was so bright it lit my face.

"You mean the fish?"

"*Sì,* the fish."

"He's very pretty, Dami. I leave him at the office, since I see more
of him there." This was true, but the main reason I left the fish at the
office was to avoid having to explain it to Malcolm. "It was such a sweet
thing for you to do," I added.

"It was nothing," he said.

"How's the writing coming?" I asked him. "When you called the other day, you wanted to tell me something, didn't you? I feel like it's been awhile since we talked about your book. I . . . miss it."

Damiano smiled. "I don't think anybody understands it like you do," he said. "Would it be okay for you to look . . . ? I know how busy you are. You have been . . . I don't know the word. *Ispirazione.*"

"Inspiration," I said softly. "It's the same in English. I'd really love to read it, Dami."

"*Bravo,*" he said. He smiled again. "I should do something for you. You have done so much for me."

I thought that the right thing to say was that I was just doing my job and that there was no need for him to repay me in any kind. But when I tried for those words, they became a dry wedge stuck in my throat.

"I would love that, too," I said, and felt a solar blush spread across my entire body. I ran one hand nervously through my hair as if that could dissipate the heat. Damiano watched me with the same knowing look he'd been wearing all evening.

"Your hair," he said.

"I know," I said, trying to laugh. "It's a mess. I couldn't figure out—"

"No," he said. "It's like a fire. Like the tail of a comet running down your back."

I looked up sharply as he finished the sentence. Lucy and Malcolm had suddenly materialized at the table, as if they'd been beamed in. I hadn't seen them coming at all. Malcolm held a fresh drink in his hand. His face looked dark and I couldn't read the expression in his eyes.

"Good!" Lucy proclaimed, apropos of nothing. "Let's sit. I have an announcement to make." She seated herself next to me and pulled her chair in close to mine. Malcolm took my other side, across from Damiano, and gulped his drink. So much for my designated driver. It was time for me to stop my own drinking for the night.

"A toast!" Lucy said, raising her glass. "Damiano, pick up a glass at least, will you?" Damiano obliged, lifting his mineral water. "Now, to books and all things literary." She drank greedily and we followed suit. "Angel!" Lucy exclaimed.

"Lucy?" I felt as if I were back in the office. My hand twitched at my side, ready to pick up a pen and write a memo on the spot.

"As you know, I travel to New York at least once a year." She swept her gaze over Malcolm and Damiano. "The heart of publishing is still in New York and it's important to have face time with these editors."

"But you're so successful in California," Malcolm said. I thought I detected the hint of a slur in his words. "And with the Internet and everything, is it still so important to be in New York? I mean, you're so well known. Seems to me they should come to *you*."

I was so embarrassed at Malcolm's unadulterated idolatry, I could only look down. My plate of meats glistened up at me.

"Well, that's terribly kind of you, Malcolm, and all ego aside, it's probably true. However, to answer your question, I do indeed have to go. But I find New York exhilarating and there's always something to learn, isn't there? None of us can say we're ever at the end of our learning curves, can we?"

There was a murmur of assent at the table, although I suspected that, like me, Malcolm and Damiano had no idea what she was going on about.

"*At any rate,*" Lucy went on impatiently, "the point of my mentioning this is not to give any of you a lesson in publishing. What I wanted to say was this: I have decided to take you, Angel."

"Take me?"

"Yes, on my upcoming trip to New York. You will accompany me to the Big Apple. Gotham. The City That Doesn't Sleep. I know you've never been there, but surely you've heard of it, yes?" She gave a tinkling little laugh into her glass, as if I should find that very funny. "Anyway, Angel, I'm taking you to New York with me. That's what I wanted to say. You've earned it."

"Wow, Lucy, I don't know what to say." I'd found that saying I didn't know what to say was an excellent time-filler, and I lingered over the words, playing for as many seconds as I could until I could figure out the response she wanted and align it with the one that came from my gut.

"What an honor for you, Angel," Malcolm said. "That's so very generous of you, Lucy."

Lucy nodded and tipped her head to one side. She was fixing Malcolm with a very peculiar look, as if she'd stepped in a pile of dog crap and then decided to flirt it off her shoe. I turned my head slightly to gauge Anna's reaction to all of this, but she'd vanished. Damiano's head was bent down toward his plate, but I could see his lips pursed tightly against a grin he was barely holding at bay.

"I'm very excited, Lucy. Thanks so much."

"Honestly, Angel, you don't sound very excited. You should know that I've never taken *anyone* to New York with me, let alone my assistant."

Malcolm was glaring at me. Damiano raised his eyes to meet mine.

"I'm just overwhelmed, Lucy. It's so . . . such a great opportunity for me."

"Exactly," Lucy said.

"Luciana, what is it you do there in New York? I'm so new to all of this, I don't know." Damiano shifted his entire body toward Lucy, his considerable charisma ratcheted up to full power, as though she were the most fascinating creature in the world. And he did it for me because he could see how I was struggling. It was an absolutely heroic save. Because he was focused on Lucy he couldn't see my eyes, but I sent my gratitude through them anyway as Lucy launched into a discussion of how she met with editors and publishers and pitched new projects. She talked about how exhausting the meetings were, scheduled back-to-back because every editor in New York wanted to see her. And then there were the parties, of course. There was always some kind of book "happening" in New York. She had several New York–based authors, she said, who had opted to go with *her* instead of the many well-known New York literary agents, and she always made time to see them. She was a native Californian, Lucy said, but she felt as if she had a New York sensibility. And at least she didn't hail from Southern California—she'd never be able to overcome *that* prejudice. At least those in the north had a little more credibility. Did Damiano find that as well, coming from Italy? Wasn't there a north/south split there as well? Which was somewhat surprising, considering that Italy was so much smaller than California. Her people, she said, hailed from northern Italy originally. . . .

As she went on, Damiano occasionally interjecting an Italian phrase or exclamation, I stole a glance at Malcolm. His face was still dusky and he leaned forward in his chair, clinging to Lucy's every word. At some point, he felt my stare and averted his eyes slightly to look at me. I looked for the complicity that couples are supposed to have, that unspoken communication borne of shared experience, but he was offering none of that. He looked impatient and vaguely annoyed with me.

I turned my attention to Damiano, who was still leaning toward Lucy, making a pitch-perfect show of being completely fascinated by everything she was saying. Like Malcolm, he felt my gaze and, for the briefest of moments, his eyes caught mine. Desire hit me then, with the force of a piano falling from a skyscraper. It wasn't something as simple as attraction or as ladylike as longing. It had no relation to romance. It was wanton desire so strong it was painful. And it was Damiano I desired—probably had desired from the moment I read the first page of his book. I felt the weight of this realization as a physical sensation and it threatened to suffocate me. Damiano saw everything in that second— my shock, my sudden comprehension, the nakedness of my desire— and his eyes sparked with recognition.

". . . and Angel's been working on something very interesting, haven't you, Angel? I'm going to blow their socks off with this one."

I turned to Lucy's voice, but I was well and truly lost. "The Las Vegas novel," I said, scrambling. "It's looking really good."

"Not that!" Lucy snapped. "Our mystery manuscript."

"Oh," I said. "That."

"Yes, *that*. We're taking it to New York, Angel! I have a feeling it will be the talk of the town."

I was filled with sudden, unstoppable dread. I knew Lucy had been intrigued enough by *Blind Submission* to keep pushing for more, but what I hadn't realized was how much stock she'd put into its ability to sell. Now she was taking it to New York—and me to keep it company. And I would be stuck with an anonymous author I was starting to hate and a manuscript that was probably going to drive me crazy. The worst part was that I'd brought it all on myself. I'd given her the manuscript in the first place because I wanted so desperately to please her and to give her something to sell.

"It's terribly exciting, don't you think, Malcolm?" Lucy was saying.

"Exciting?" Malcolm seemed lost.

"Angel's work," Lucy said. "Surely she—"

"I don't know," Malcolm said, flustered, his color deepening. "Angel doesn't . . . I don't know."

"Really?" Lucy said, and her eyebrows lifted in surprise. Malcolm bit his lip. Damiano leaned backward in his chair, his glass half-raised as if stopped in the middle of a toast. Lucy's expression was neutral, but her eyes glittered. I felt the tension settle inside me, clenching and twisting. The silence was becoming unbearable, a looming entity unto itself. I couldn't understand why nobody would speak. I cleared my throat and all three sets of eyes turned to me, waiting.

"I'd love another drink," I said.

I GRIPPED THE STEERING WHEEL at ten and two and stared straight ahead, petrified that I'd do something to alert the police that my blood alcohol level was way past the legal limit. Not that I was blurry, fuzzy, or felt even slightly drunk. The excess adrenaline in my body had somehow acted as an antidote to the gin, and I felt more sober than I had before my first drink. Which was a great deal more than I could say for Malcolm, who was completely potted and slouched in the passenger seat next to me. We were ten minutes from my apartment and hadn't exchanged a single word in the last twenty. The air between us was charged and smoking with resentment.

"I can fuggen drive, you know."

"You can't even fucking talk, Malcolm, let alone fucking drive, okay?"

"You've got a mouth on you, Angel," he said. "Better things you could be doing with it. Or maybe you already have."

"What are you talking about? Never mind, don't tell me. I can't believe how drunk you are."

"I'm not fuggen drunk, all right? And what if I was? How could you blame me? The way you treated me over there."

"The way I treated you? Now you have to tell me what you're talking about because you're not making any sense, Malcolm."

"You know what happened, Angel. You fuggen know."

I saw the events of the evening unfold as a series of still frames on the black night in front of me. How Lucy had moved closer and closer to me throughout dinner until our legs were touching, her cold thigh pressing into mine. How Malcolm had taken his dialogue with Lucy from shameless flattery to overt flirtatiousness to something approaching lewdness. How every time I tried to eat, I choked on the meat. How Lucy ate a good portion of several animals with gusto. How Malcolm drank and drank and how Lucy encouraged him to have still more. How Anna stood in the doorway between the living room and dining room, shooting daggers with her eyes, until uncountable minutes later, Lucy told her, "You may leave now." How Lucy presented us with dessert, a giant angel food cake in a spun-sugar basket, and explained that Damiano had baked it especially for me. How Lucy had invited us all to the deck for cigars. *Cigars!* How Malcolm had gladly accepted her offer, although he'd never smoked a cigar in his life, and left Damiano and me sitting at the table. How Damiano had leaned so close to me, I could feel the small hairs on my arms stand up with gooseflesh. How he had said, "Can I call you?" and how I knew exactly what that meant. How I told him, "I can't," and how he'd said, "I understand." How I'd watched Malcolm and Lucy through the glass deck doors. His gesturing hands, loosened with gin and vermouth, drifting ever closer to her until they touched her arm, her hand, her shoulder. How Damiano watched this tableau with me, saying nothing for a long time, then standing, telling me he had to go. How the rest of it happened very quickly—Damiano leaving, Lucy pressing foil-wrapped cake into my hands, telling me we'd be going over "our New York schedule," ushering me and Malcolm out of her big white door, my taking the keys out of Malcolm's pocket, starting the car, not believing, even now, that any of it had actually happened.

"I know you made a fool of yourself," I told Malcolm. "But I don't know why."

"*You* made me into a fool," he said.

"I didn't do anything."

He exhaled heavily, his liquor breath filling the small space inside the car. I rolled down my window. "Did you shleep with him?"

"Shleep? With who? What does that mean?"

"Angel, for fugg's sake. Don' play dumb. Did you have sssexxx? With that Italian cook. Junkie. Writer. Whatever. Did you?"

I was trembling, with anger or guilt or surprise or some combination of all three, and had to steady myself, knuckles white on the steering wheel, before I could answer him. "What are you talking about, Malcolm? Do you even know what you're saying? How ridiculous you sound?"

"You think I'm so stupid, *lover*? Think I don't have eyes in my head? *Angel* fuggen food cake? Your hair. The tail of a comet? I mean, Jeesusss. Did you think I missed that?"

"That doesn't mean anything."

"He's the one made you that CD with all the angel songs, izzen he? I knew it." He spit the last few words out with bitterness I'd never before heard in his voice.

"I edited his manuscript, Malcolm. I helped him get a lot of money. He's grateful, that's all. I didn't sleep with him. When you sober up, you're not even going to believe you said that to me."

"Edited his manuscript," Malcolm repeated slowly, his words losing their slurs. "His book. *His* book. Might as well have had sex with him. It's the same thing for you, anyway."

"That's not fair, Malcolm, and you know it. So Lucy sold his book and not yours. So what? That means I slept with him? And what were *you* doing with Lucy? Touching her, flirting—no, not flirting, *drooling* all over her. Jesus, Malcolm, she's my *boss*. And she's . . . God, she's *Lucy Fiamma*." I heard my voice go higher and higher as I went on and wondered if Malcolm would see what I thought—that I was protesting too much. He'd seen the way I'd looked at Damiano and he'd known what it meant. *Might as well have had sex with him.* Was that so far off?

I screeched to a stop. We had made it to my apartment, hydroplaning on a sea of gin, without being killed or arrested. I offered a small prayer of thanks. Malcolm and I sat in the still car for seconds or minutes, both of us lost in our own confused and tangled thoughts.

"Seems like you were pretty close to her yourself," he said finally. Suddenly he didn't sound drunk anymore, just mean and tired.

"So you think I slept with her, too? Go ahead, say it, Malcolm. That would just be the perfect end to a perfect night."

"Did you? Don't act like it's so far out, okay? I saw how close she sat to you. I think you turn her on, Angel."

"Malcolm . . ." I sighed. "That's just fucking disgusting."

I leaned back, resting my head on the seat. Malcolm was half-turned toward me, his eyes glassy, his hands lying limp in his lap like two dead birds. I remembered how handsome he'd looked at the beginning of the evening. He looked unraveled and lost now, as if he were wearing someone else's clothes. And I probably looked the same.

"Why are we doing this?" he asked.

"I don't know," I answered.

He reached over to me, his arms covering mine, his hands searching for their place in the tangles of my hair. He leaned in to kiss me, but I moved back and away from him. I couldn't do it. Not then. I gathered my purse and unlocked the car door, leaving the keys in the ignition.

"You okay to drive home?" I asked him.

Malcolm stared at me for a long moment. Even in the dark of the car, I could see the complex interplay of emotions crossing his features.

"So it's like that, is it, Angel?"

"Just for tonight," I said.

"Why? You have more *work* to do?"

"Malcolm, please." I was practically begging him. "Are you sure you're okay to drive?"

He got out of the car, came around to the driver's side, and, very formally, opened my door and gestured for me to exit. I slid out and he took my place, slamming the door behind him. He started his car and gave me a last look through the rolled-down window. "Yes, Angel," he said, "I'm okay to fucking drive."

He pulled out faster than he should have, spraying gravel bits into the night behind him, but I could tell that he was in complete control. I stood there watching, purse in my hands, my eyes stinging with fatigue, until his taillights disappeared down the road.

TEN

To: angel.robinson@fiammalit.com
From: ganovelist@heya.com
Subject: Blind Submission pages

Dear Ms. Robinson:

As usual, your comments have been most useful. May I say that I am beginning to truly enjoy working with you. I understand the need to make the prose more "vivid," as you say, and, no, I don't take offense. Please review the attached pages and let me know if they fit the bill. I believe you will find them most stimulating. I do hope that they will continue to please Ms. Fiamma as well. I look forward to hearing from you as always.

G.

Blind Submission, p. 102

Alice waited naked on the bed.

The hotel was in Midtown Manhattan and nice, but not too. It wasn't so fancy that it would draw too much attention.

Nobody would suspect that Vaughn Blue would stay in a place that was just "nice." Here, disguised, he would be someone who looked like Vaughn Blue, not "the" Vaughn Blue, sex-godrockstar. And that was exactly the way Alice wanted it. She wasn't about to become some groupie slut with her face in the tabloids. She had much bigger plans than that.

Still, it was true that when they'd had that first lunch at Michael's, at Carol's request, Alice had found him almost irresistibly attractive. His skin was olive colored and his eyes were the color of ripe plums. He was in some twelve-step program due to an obligatory rock star addiction to heroin, so he didn't drink any alcohol and remained happily coherent. But it was his undeniable charisma that appealed to Alice the most, and her excitement grew to the point that she could hardly stand it. It was a happy coincidence that Alice found herself physically attracted to a man she planned to seduce. Attraction was unnecessary but in this case it was a definite bonus.

Vaughn hadn't wanted to talk about his book at first. He seemed annoyed that Carol Moore hadn't come herself. It took little time, though, for him to warm up to Alice. Alice knew the power of her looks and how to make the best of them. But more than that, Alice knew the power of power and that power was the strongest aphrodisiac there was.

Vaughn was intelligent and he could write, which set him apart from almost every other celebrity author. Alice ignored that aspect of him—the writerly part of him that she couldn't help but detest—and focused on her growing attraction.

She soon got Vaughn off the topic of his book and on to better things, like when he might meet her again and where. He wanted some more feedback about his book, Vaughn said. Alice said, of course, and pointed out that there were several hotels where they could have such a discussion.

The first time had been amazing—a surprise to Alice, who was hard-pressed to allow herself any pleasure at all. They hadn't talked at all—they'd just gone at each other like two animals. Then there was a second time—slower, deeper, and afterward, Vaughn had talked a little about his life. There was another book, he told her. One he had written long ago. Nobody had read it. Nobody. Until he'd met Alice, he'd never felt he could fully trust anyone. Would she consider reading it?

Yes, Alice had told him. Oh yes.

Now here she was again, every bit of clothing stripped from her lithe body, her hair laid out like a golden net on the pillow, the insistent throb of anticipation in her loins.

She didn't have to wait very long.

A tapping came on the door and Alice opened it. Vaughn Blue stood in the doorway wearing a hat, sunglasses, and a false beard. He looked ridiculous, but he didn't look like Vaughn Blue. He licked his lips when he saw Alice and told her she looked like Lady Godiva. Alice asked him what he was waiting for and why wasn't he already naked?

Celebrities were always smaller than you thought when you saw them in person, Alice thought as she tore Vaughn's clothes from his body. But not Vaughn, who crashed into her larger than life.

They rolled on the bed together, their musky sweat blending and dripping onto the sheets. Vaughn bit Alice's breasts and licked her neck. Alice dug her fingernails into the flesh of Vaughn's shoulders. She pushed her hips up to meet his and he reached around to her back, pressing in with the palms of his hands, tickling her skin with his fingers. Alice moaned with pleasure. She grabbed his huge manhood and drove him inside her where she was wet and steaming. It was so good, she thought, as he plowed her like a ripe field. So very, very good as he filled her and honeyed fires coursed through her body. She wanted it to never stop, even as wave after wave of ecstasy crashed against her.

Vaughn pulled out of her trembling body and raised himself, glistening, on the pillows. He laced his fingers into her hair and held on.

"Don't stop." Alice panted.

"I have to look at you—I have to." He sighed. He ran his hands along her breasts, cupping them. He took one finger, traced it around the circle of her right nipple, and stopped.

"I never noticed this before," he said.

Alice quickly raised her hand to her breast as if to rub it off—the tattoo she'd had put there long ago when she was so much more hopeful about everything. It was a small but exquisitely detailed tattoo of Alice in Wonderland, sitting under a magic mushroom. "It's nothing," Alice said. "Nothing."

"It's beautiful," Vaughn said, "like the rest of you." He leaned down and kissed the Alice on Alice's breast.

"Let me in now," he said.

And Alice did.

So. It had been Malcolm all along.

He was due to show up at my apartment within the hour and I was finding it difficult to sit still and wait for him. I could feel anger vibrating through my body, working its way into the muscles of my jaw and shoulders, forming knots so tight they felt like bone. I watched the clock, counting off the minutes as a way of distracting myself. For perhaps the hundredth time, I felt my hand go up to my breast and curl around that cursed tattoo—the biggest mistake I'd ever made—as if I could tear it out with my fingernails. I forced my hand down but couldn't do anything about stopping my mind from going back there—to the tattoo and everything it had come to mean.

I suppose I must have known from the beginning—from its very first pages—that the literary agency in *Blind Submission* was modeled on Lucy's. It was such an obvious conclusion but I wouldn't allow myself to draw it. It could have fit the profile of dozens of other literary agencies as well, I told myself. Having only worked with Lucy, how could I be sure?

When the chapters first started coming in, I was so focused on the clumsy prose that I didn't see how clear the links were between the characters and their real-life counterparts in Lucy's office. But as the writing started to improve with my notes—and it *was* getting better—it became apparent that Carol Moore was based on Lucy, that Jewel was based on Anna, Ricardo on Craig, and Alice on me. But these were parallel-universe versions. Anna, of course, looked nothing like the beautiful and graceful Jewel. Craig was miles away from the suave sophistication of Ricardo. Like Lucy, Carol Moore was a brilliant and powerful literary agent, but in every other respect she was exactly 180 degrees removed from Lucy. Carol Moore was pleasant, even-tempered, magnanimous, gentle, and philanthropic. Lucy was . . . well, none of those things.

But it was the character of Alice that became the most disturbing to me. She was conniving, rapaciously ambitious, mean-spirited, and manipulative. And she was a writer. In all respects, she was the exact opposite of me. In my edit notes I'd been prodding the author to create a more nuanced version of Alice. It was one of the first rules of fiction that one couldn't have an entirely unlikable protagonist and expect to have a successful novel. But even as I told the author this, I started to wonder if I wasn't just trying to defend *myself*. Because my hunch was proving true: Whoever was writing the novel knew me. And not just in passing.

All this was compelling at first. Perhaps, in a narcissistic way, I even found it a little thrilling. But by the time I went to Lucy's party, the parallels were just too close and too many for comfort. And even as I tried to get in touch with Peter Johnson, I had the sinking feeling that it wasn't him after all.

I'd called Mr. Johnson at home after Jackson unearthed his number for me, only to hear the phone ring and ring, nobody picking up, no answering machine to take a message. I tried again the next day and the day after. On my fourth attempt, somebody finally answered, but it wasn't Peter Johnson, it was a woman who identified herself as Mr. Johnson's nurse. Peter Johnson had passed away, she informed me. He'd been ill for some time. She asked me who I was, and when I identified myself, she gave a sad sigh. He'd been waiting for so long for a call from my agency, she said, it was all he ever talked about. How very unfortunate that his ship had come in after he'd taken leave of this world. I offered hurried sympathies and got myself off the phone as quickly as possible. Although it was completely irrational, I couldn't help but feel that I was somehow responsible for Peter Johnson's demise. Anna's comment, "If only *all* our annoying writers would die as conveniently," only made me feel worse.

Along with regret that I hadn't been nicer to him the last time I'd spoken to him, Peter Johnson's exit left me totally confused. I told myself to just work on the manuscript like I would any other. It wasn't as if I didn't have enough going on at the office or, after Lucy's horrendous dinner party, in my own life to keep my mind occupied. Besides, *Blind Submission* was *only a book*. No, not a book, a manuscript. Hardly even a manuscript, for that matter—it was mostly a series of e-mail attachments. Plus, it needed work. It wouldn't be readable, much less salable, without my help. Whoever was writing the thing had to know that—better than he knew *me*.

But there were all those "coincidences" between the events in *Blind Submission* and the corresponding ones in my life. There was only one person who knew all the details well enough to write them. Alice's work was rejected—and so was Malcolm's. I got a raise—and so did Alice. I worked with Damiano—Alice worked with Vaughn.

Still, I wasn't sure—didn't want to admit it—until I read *that scene* and knew that Malcolm was the author of *Blind Submission*.

There could be no other explanation, no other author. Alice's torrid (and purplishly overwritten) sex scene with Vaughn perfectly mimicked Malcolm's accusation that I was sleeping with Damiano. Vaughn himself seemed like a copy of Damiano, down to the heroin and the color of his eyes. But that wasn't all—not by a long shot. What made my heart race and the tips of my fingers go cold was the description of the sex itself. Who else but Malcolm would know exactly how I—and, by extension, Alice—liked to be touched? But it was the tattoo-kissing that really got me. That little intimacy was *ours*. He'd given Alice an Alice in Wonderland tattoo to mimic my "Angel's wings" that he had kissed so many times. Reading it made me feel physically ill. If Malcolm was writing this novel—and it had to be him—everything I thought I knew about him and everything I thought I understood about our love for each other was wrong.

The funny thing was, before I read those pages I was actually feeling bad about the way I'd been treating him.

A day or two after Lucy's party from hell, Malcolm had called me, contrite. He said he was sorry, that he shouldn't have had so much to drink, he didn't know what had gotten into him, it was an awkward situation and he felt uncomfortable, surely I could understand that, couldn't I? And I could. What I *couldn't* understand was why he was suddenly so apologetic. The Malcolm I'd known before I started working for Lucy might have admitted he was wrong, might even have been conciliatory after a disagreement, but would never have groveled, especially before *me*.

He suggested that we have dinner together and I agreed. I asked him to give me a week or two and then we set a date. He seemed pleased and a little surprised, as if he hadn't expected it to be that easy.

And why *had* I made it so easy? I told myself that it was because I loved Malcolm and I wanted to mend the tears in our relationship and keep it together. But the real truth of it was simply that I felt guilty. I felt guilty that Lucy had rejected Malcolm and that I'd put him in the position of being humiliated. And I felt impossibly guilty about my feelings toward Damiano. Nothing had actually happened between the two of us or had even come close to happening, but Damiano had crept into the space inside me where only Malcolm had been for so long. I couldn't deny that attraction or its power. I'd been physically faithful to Malcolm, but the accusations he'd thrown at me the night of Lucy's party stung with the ring of truth. In my desire, I *had* cheated on him. And that was a betrayal of the man I loved.

But then I read the scene and everything I thought I believed went into a mad tailspin.

My first impulse was to call Malcolm and pour out my outrage over the phone, but I forced myself not to. I let it simmer for a couple of days, turning it around in my mind, looking, again, for reasons why he couldn't be the author, trying to recapture my trust in him. I was hoping that by the time he came over for the dinner we'd planned I'd have had some kind of revelation, but I didn't. Instead, I just felt my anger and confusion grow until my entire being was saturated with it.

This was the state I was still in as I waited for Malcolm to show up for the dinner that was supposed to mend all our fences. When, finally, I heard his knock at my door, I found my legs so stiff with tension, it was difficult to even walk across the room to open it.

The first thing I saw when I opened the door was the giant bouquet of I'm-so-sorry flowers Malcolm was holding in front of his face.

"What's the matter?" he asked before he'd even gotten both feet inside.

"Why are you doing this?" I said, sounding much more dramatic than I'd intended.

"Doing what?" he said, but his face paled immediately and he looked as guilty as sin.

"You know what I'm talking about," I said. "Don't make me go round and round with it, okay? I just want to know why. What do you think you're going to get out of this ultimately? How long do you think you can keep it going?"

"Angel . . ." He hesitated and looked down at his feet. The flowers seemed to visibly wilt in his hand. "I really don't know what you think . . . what you mean." He shrank away from me. The sight of it made me sad and furious at the same time.

"Come *on*," I said. "Stop it. When were you going to tell me? Were you going to tell me at all? She wants to sell it. She's *going* to sell it. You know that! How long do you think you can be anonymous?" My voice had risen to a screechy pitch.

I watched as Malcolm's face changed from pale to flushed. His eyes, which had been downcast and clouded, snapped and sparked. He'd been almost cowering but now stood up straight, filling his chest with air. "What the hell, Angel?" His voice was angry, no longer hesitant. "I. Do. Not. Know. What *you're talking about!* Make some sense."

"*Blind Submission*," I said. "I know you're the author. I've read that chapter, okay?"

"Say *what*, Angel?" Malcolm looked at me, his face a wild mix of competing expressions, as if he didn't know whether to laugh, cry, or throw up. He opened his hands and raised them palms up, dropping the flowers on the floor. They landed heavily, making a splayed pattern of stems and blossoms at my feet. "You're crazy," he said. "'That chapter'? Do you hear yourself? You've gone nuts, Angel."

I went on, fueled by days of compacted anger, insisting that he was the only person who could have written the manuscript. He remained adamant that he hadn't and forced me to go over every detail of it with him. He made me say it out loud—made me talk about Damiano and how I was sure that the sex scene between Vaughn and Alice was another accusation. His face grew darker when I brought up Damiano and then twisted into a grimace when I stumbled over the description of the sex scene and, finally, the irrefutable evidence of the tattoo.

"You think you're the only woman who likes it a certain way, Angel? And please, can you possibly believe that you're the only chick with a tattoo on her tit?"

I was stunned. I felt like those cartoon characters that have the floor give way underneath them but remain suspended in the air for several seconds before they fall. But Malcolm didn't need a response from me; he wasn't finished with his own commentary.

"Do you think I'd have such little pride that I'd send an anonymous novel to be edited by *you*?" he said. "Do you think I have as little faith in my own talent as you do? I'm an *artist,* Angel. You've never understood that. How could you think, even for a moment, that I'd do something like that?"

"Because—"

"How do you know it's not your boy Damiano? Maybe that's your mystery author. Seems he knows quite a bit about you, doesn't he?"

"You can't still think—"

"I'm not sure what I think anymore."

"Damiano doesn't need to sell another book!" I spat. "He's already writing a very good one for very good money."

"Unlike me, right, Angel? Isn't that what you meant to say?"

We stood staring at each other for several long seconds. I didn't know how to answer him or whether or not he was right. My eyes started to fill, but I was so confused about what was going on, so unsettled by all the strange turns my life was taking, that I didn't know whether I was crying or whether my eyes were watering at the strain of being open too wide and too long. I looked away from him, down at the mess of spilled flowers at my feet. I didn't know what to say. I didn't even know how I felt anymore.

"You think I need you, don't you, Angel?" Malcolm said. The edge of indignation in his voice was sharp and grating. "Well, I don't. I don't need your help and I don't need your pity."

"No," I said softly. "You certainly don't."

"That's right," he said, his tone growing more forceful, "and I'll tell you something else, *baby* . . ." He paused, drawing and puffing himself up, honing in. "*You* need *me*."

"And what's *that* supposed to mean?"

"I've been carrying you since I met you, Angel."

"Carrying me?"

"Seriously, do you think you'd be where you are now without me? If I hadn't pushed you, you'd probably be out on your ass without a job, let alone a career. And then where would you be? With me, that's where. It's not like you have anyone else to support you."

"I don't remember you supporting me, Malcolm. I've been supporting myself just fine for years."

"I'm talking about emotional support, Angel. It's been only me since I've known you."

"What's that supposed to mean?"

Malcolm shrugged. "I'm just saying . . . for the last couple of years, you've had nobody but me in your corner and you haven't even looked for anyone else. And I think . . . You depend on me. That's all I'm saying."

That was all he was saying, all right. Not one word about love.

"Thanks for clearing that up, Malcolm," I said. "Maybe it's time for all of that to change." My voice was shaking.

"What do you mean?" he asked, a slight catch of doubt puncturing his self-righteousness.

"I think we should . . ." My whole body felt unbearably cold, encased in ice, but my heart was racing. I could hardly believe the step I was about to take, and I faltered on the edge of the gangplank.

"You think we should break up?" Malcolm was incredulous. "Is that what you're saying?"

"Yes, I guess that's what I'm saying." I'd started trembling. The two of us stood frozen in the chill of my words for a moment and then Malcolm took a step closer to me, leaning down so that I had no choice but to look into his angry eyes.

"I don't think you know *what* you're saying, Angel, but I'll tell you something: When you wake up and think about this for a second, you're going to realize what a huge mistake you've just made."

"I think you'd better leave now, Malcolm." I had to get him out of my apartment before I could change my mind and take everything back. I could feel myself on the edge of it as it was. It wouldn't take much to send me over.

"There's one thing you should know, Angel."

"Just *go*," I said, praying that he would before the ice melted and I dissolved in tears.

Malcolm shrugged and turned to leave. "I'm not your guy," he said as he made his exit. "You should look somewhere else."

I didn't know whether he was referring to our relationship or to *Blind Submission*, but he was long gone by the time I thought to ask him.

⁓

TEN DAYS TO GO until Lucy and I left for New York. As I made my way to the office in the dawn's early light, I anticipated that every one of those days would be jammed with appointments made, canceled, and remade; memos and e-mails to various editors, assistants, and heads of houses; and endless flight and hotel reservations, again made and remade until they arrived back at their original formula. From the moment Lucy had announced her New York trip and the fact that she was taking me with her, these booking details had become all-consuming. As we counted down to liftoff, Lucy became more and more obsessive and micromanaging about her schedule, the travel, and anything else related to the trip. Three days earlier, I had been instructed to give her a twice-daily weather report from New York ("And make sure it's the *city* of New York, Angel, I don't need to know skiing conditions in the Adirondacks") in addition to any late-breaking TSA reports about what one could or could not bring onto airplanes.

Of course, none of this work was supposed to interfere with my usual load, namely finishing my edit of Shelly Franklin's novel so that it would be ready for Lucy to sell (for a small fortune) in New York and the now-almost-impossible task of working on *Blind Submission*. The sheer magnitude of my workload did have one advantage: It kept me from thinking too much about what a shambles my personal life had become.

———

CRAIG'S CAR was the only one in the driveway when I pulled up to the office. I'd hoped I would be the first to arrive so I could get a jump on Lucy's endless list in relative quiet, but Craig had also been putting in crazy hours since we'd started planning our trip to New York, so I wasn't exactly surprised that he'd beaten me to work.

I steeled myself for the day ahead, gathering my bag, the endless pile of manuscripts, and my still-steaming coffee, and got out of my car backside first in order to gather everything I needed to carry in.

When I straightened up and turned around, Damiano was standing in front of me, a sudden mirage holding a vase full of calla lilies, and I jumped, a muffled yelp of shock coming from my throat, dropping my coffee and a good portion of the manuscripts I was holding.

"Damiano! You scared the life out of me!" My heart was pounding and skipping and my knees felt unsteady.

"I'm so sorry, Angel, I thought you heard me come up. Here, let me help you." He leaned over to pick up my papers at the same time I did, and the two of us bumped heads, fumbling through a scene that could have been in any number of date movies. "Sorry, sorry," he said again, and started to laugh. Our faces were very close, and when I raised my eyes to his, I was pulled in again by the sheer force of my attraction. A wave of heat rushed up my neck and into my face. I could feel myself starting to sweat. I lost my balance and started to tip over. Damiano reached out to steady me, and when his hand touched my arm, it felt like an electric shock. I had to stand up, pull myself out of this narrowing orbit of desire before I lost it completely.

"Do you have an appointment with Lucy?" I asked him when we were both standing with a comfortable distance between us and I could trust my voice again. It was a stupid question because if Damiano had an appointment with Lucy, I'd have been the one to arrange it, but it was the best I could come up with.

"No, not exactly," he said. "I have the contracts to sign and I thought to bring them in with these." He gestured to the vase of lilies, which he'd picked up again. He was wearing a white sweatshirt and blue jeans and looked as if he'd just finished shooting a Levi's print ad. I could hardly stand to look at him. It was so much easier when I talked to him on the phone and didn't have to deal with this rush of blood in my veins.

"You could have sent the contracts in," I said. "You didn't have to come all this way."

"È vero," he said, and the look on his face grew clouded. "But I wanted to bring the flowers, too. I wanted to say thanks for dinner." One corner of his mouth turned up in a half-smile and he looked at me questioningly, as if there was some subtext I should understand. But it was all too dangerous and I was too exposed, and we were both within the gravitational pull of planet Lucy.

"Right, dinner," I said, trying to make my voice light and flip. "That was quite a party. I can see why you'd want to thank her for that."

Damiano knit his eyebrows in confusion and the smile faded from his face. He couldn't understand the bitter tone that had crept into my words and I couldn't blame him. I couldn't explain it myself.

"Well, I guess you'd better come in, then," I said. "No point standing out here."

"Angel," Damiano started, "did I do something to offend you? At the party . . . I'm sorry if I—"

"No, no, Dami, not at all. I didn't mean—"

"Because I didn't know you had a—"

"Boyfriend. I don't. I mean, I did, but I don't. Anymore."

I turned my eyes away from him, desperate to extricate myself from the tangled threads of the conversation.

"Okay," Damiano said finally. "Should we go in?"

"Yes," I said, feeling as if I was answering more than one question.

Craig looked up sharply as we entered, his expression changing from annoyed when he saw me, to surprised when he saw Damiano, to disapproving when he realized we'd come in together.

"Good morning," Craig said. "Good to see you, Damiano. Angel, Lucy's been waiting for you. She needs—"

"I know," I said, and made my way over to my desk. There was a note waiting on my chair, Lucy's favorite location for memos she didn't want me to miss. *GORDON HART!!!!* it screamed. *WHEN AM I SEEING HIM?!?!? PLEASE FINALIZE TODAY!!!!*

"Fine," Craig said. "Damiano, can I help you with something?"

Damiano looked from Craig to me and back to Craig again. He wore the same bemused expression I'd seen on his face the last time he'd been in the office. There was absolutely nothing about this little pig's house of bricks that intimidated Damiano in the slightest.

"I would like to see Luciana," Damiano said. "I come bearing contracts and flowers."

"Contracts, terrific!" Craig said with false brightness. "I can take those for you."

"*Bene,*" Damiano said, and shot me a sidelong glance full of amusement, "but I prefer to give the flowers to Luciana if that's okay."

I saw Craig's face redden. "Right. I'll take you in," he said, and stood so abruptly he knocked into his orderly desk, disrupting a few of his piles.

"*Grazie,*" Damiano said, and followed Craig to Lucy's door. I could hear the rise of Lucy's voice as they both entered, but couldn't make out what she was saying as Craig shut her door immediately afterward. As soon as Damiano disappeared into Lucy's igloo, I could feel some of the tension leaving my body. What had possessed me to blurt out that I'd broken up with Malcolm? My head was swimming and my intercom was already screeching.

"Oh Damiano, ha-ha, you're just a riot! Angel?"

"Lucy?"

"Gordon Hart?"

"Right now, Lucy."

"Please!" and she clicked off, still warbling over Damiano.

I fished the aspirin from my purse and picked up the phone, dry-swallowing three tablets as I dialed Gordon Hart's phone number. He wouldn't be there. He was never there unless he was the one calling, especially if Lucy Fiamma was on the line for him.

"Gordon Hart."

I was so shocked to hear his voice, I just stammered, "Uhh, uh . . . he . . . hello," into the phone.

"Ah," he said. "Angel Robinson, I presume?" I could hear the smile in his voice again—the same smile I'd heard the first time we spoke.

"I'm so sorry," I said. "I'm just surprised that you answered your phone."

Gordon Hart laughed. "Yes, we do that sometimes," he said. "Just to spice things up. What can I do for you, Ms. Robinson? Does *she* need to speak with me?"

"Um, actually, no," I said. "I'm just trying to finalize her schedule for New York. She'll . . . actually, *we* will be there the week after next, and I wanted to make sure we had a date and time settled for when the two of you will meet."

"I'd love to help you, Angel, I really would, but I have no idea when I'm meeting with her. Sarah, my assistant, takes care of these things for me. She's the keeper of my time. Frankly, I don't know how she does it."

"Of course," I said. "Sure." I was loath to let him off the phone. I had no idea when I'd be able to get him again.

"Tell you what, though," he said. "I *am* capable of writing a note, and I promise I will give Sarah one as soon as she returns. I'm expecting her back within the hour, and I'll be sure to have her call you and set the whole thing up, all right?"

"That would be great," I said. "Lucy's anxious—"

"I'm sure," he said, clipping his words. "Tell me, Angel, will we be seeing you as well when you come to New York?"

"Um . . . I don't know," I said, surprised by the question.

"Well, I hope you'll have the chance to come by," he said. "It would be nice to meet you."

"Thanks," I said. "That would be terrific."

"Take care," he said, and hung up.

I replaced the phone in its cradle. Gordon Hart wanted to meet me. One of the most important men in publishing. I couldn't stop the grin from spreading across my face.

To: angel.robinson@fiammalit.com
From: ganovelist@heya.com
Subject: Re: BS/edits

Dear Ms. Robinson,

As always, your editorial suggestions were very good; clear and to the point. I am in complete agreement with you with one exception. I don't believe that the sex scene between Vaughn Blue and Alice is, as you say, "overly graphic and cliché-ridden at the same time." You may be correct that there are one or two overly familiar tropes in my description of Alice's feelings (perhaps I'm not as adept at describing a woman's sexual response as I thought!), but I have to take issue with your assessment that it is too graphic. Alice is a voracious character—a consumer. It makes sense that she would "devour" Vaughn Blue. Alice doesn't even know exactly how Vaughn can help her, she only knows that he is a means to an end. She may fall in love with him, complicating her goal, in which case she might become slightly more tender. What are your thoughts about that? Every novel needs a good love story, doesn't it? At any rate, I will "tidy" the sex scene, but won't "clean" it, and then I'll send it back to you.

For now, I am enclosing more text for you. You'll see that I've heeded your advice to "speed things up" and now everything is starting to move much faster.

I will look forward to your comments as always,

G.

Alice was on her way into the daily staff meeting when Ricardo called her over to talk to him. Alice had big plans for this staff meeting and was mentally preparing how she was going to present "her" novel to Carol Moore for representation. This was the one Carol was going to take; the first of many moments for Alice to shine.

Alice hated having her thoughts interrupted and was annoyed to be sidetracked by Ricardo, but she kept her composure. It was very important to Alice that everyone in the office see her as calm and placid as a summer sea. Despite the fact that Ricardo would ultimately be as disposable as a kitchen sponge, Alice had to give him her attention.

"Yes, Ricky?" Alice said. Ricardo hated being called Ricky and Alice knew it. It was a game they played regularly now. Ricardo would correct Alice and Alice, affecting a Scarlett O'Hara attitude, would claim to have forgotten. Alice waited for Ricardo to play his part in the game, but this time he didn't. He looked disturbed, Alice thought. His smooth, caramel-colored skin was covered by a light sheen of perspiration and his shirt was rumpled. Normally, Ricardo was extremely careful about the way he looked and dressed.

"Alice . . ." Ricardo trailed off, looking very uncomfortable.

"Well, what is it?" Alice asked, with an impatient tone that reflected how she really felt.

"I know that Carol was very impressed after your interview for this job. Even though you didn't really have any experience, she liked you enough to hire you," Ricardo said.

Alice knit her brows together, a gesture that Vaughn had described, just this morning, as "charming." She had no idea where Ricardo was going with all of this, but his nervousness indicated it was somewhere that she wasn't going to like at all.

"Yes?" Alice said, and cursed herself for not sounding more solicitous. "I mean, of course I was thrilled when Carol hired me. But I do have experience, Ricardo."

"Do you think Carol Moore got to where she is today

because she's a stupid woman?" Ricardo asked. He was now perspiring quite heavily.

"Of course not."

"So didn't you think she would check your references and your experience?" He didn't wait for an answer. "And didn't you think that she would discover that almost all of it was made up?"

"I don't know what you're talking about," Alice said. Her fingertips were starting to feel cold and an icy sensation was starting to spread through her body like slowly melting snow.

"Of course you know what I'm talking about," Ricardo said. "The point is that Carol liked you so much that she decided to hire you even after she discovered that you'd lied at your interview." He paused and Alice waited for what was coming next, showing no expression. Her usual plan for a situation like this was to start showing some leg, some breast, or whatever part of her luscious body might appeal to a man. But Alice knew that this wouldn't sway Ricardo because there was only one woman who appealed to him, and that was Carol Moore.

"Carol told me that you reminded her of herself when she was your age," Ricardo continued. "She likes your ambition and she likes that you're motivated enough to change your circumstances in life."

Alice was growing very impatient with Ricardo's little sermon. "What are you getting at, *Ricky*?" she said.

Ricardo lowered his voice. "She trusts you, Alice. Carol Moore has been very good to me and I don't want to see her get hurt in any way."

"So who's hurting her? What are you talking about?"

"I know what you're up to, Alice. I've seen you looking through her private files. I've seen you gathering information. I've heard you talking to her authors."

"I'm not up to anything," Alice hissed, "except work. I'm doing my job." Ricardo couldn't know about the novel. Alice had been very, very careful about that. Unless . . .

"Is what you're doing with Vaughn Blue part of your job?"

Alice recoiled as if she had been slapped. She hadn't expected this. She had underestimated Ricardo and his powers of observation. This was a regrettable, but not fatal, error in judgment. He didn't know about what else Alice had been up to. Vaughn was a very small part of a much greater plan.

"Carol needs to know about this," Ricardo said. "But I'm giving you the opportunity to tell her yourself. If you come clean about it, I'm sure that she would still be willing to give you a good reference. A *real* reference."

"You're crazy," Alice said, and laughed. "I'm not going to do any such thing. And neither are you."

Ricardo stood up straight and adjusted the collar of his shirt. "Well, then, you haven't given me any choice but to talk to Carol myself," he said.

"Really?" Alice said. "And were you also planning to tell your wife about Carol?"

Instantly, all the color drained out of Ricardo's face. Alice knew she had scored a direct hit and she took real pleasure in watching the fear flood Ricardo's face like a pale ocean.

"Yes, *Ricky,* I know all about it."

"You don't . . ." Ricardo had to clear his throat and started coughing. "You don't know anything."

"Don't I?" Alice said, and tossed him a big smile.

"Hey, you two!" Jewel stopped in front of Ricardo and Alice. "There's a staff meeting happening. We'd better get going! Hey, Ricardo, what's the matter, you look awful."

Alice regarded Jewel's beautiful face with distaste. There was another one who was going to have to be dealt with soon. For all Alice knew, Ricardo might have already started shooting off his mouth.

"I think I ate some bad clams last night," Ricardo said. "But I'll be right in."

"Okay," Jewel said. "Alice, are you coming?"

"Right behind you," Alice said sweetly. She started to follow Jewel, but Ricardo grabbed her arm.

"Don't you touch me," Alice whispered, pulling her arm free.

"You don't have any proof of anything," Ricardo said hoarsely.

"Ricardo," Alice said, stretching her tongue out over the syllables. "I know everything."

"But . . . how?" Ricardo stammered.

"You said it yourself, Ricky, she trusts me. She confides in me. We're like *sisters*. I've even seen evidence of your, how do I say it, literary prowess? Carol treasures those letters of yours, by the way. I think they're a little juvenile myself, but what do I know of true love, eh?"

Alice let the effect of her words sink in.

"Now, should we go to that staff meeting?" she asked when it became clear that Ricardo was not going to respond. "Carol will start to wonder what's keeping us."

Ricardo looked utterly defeated, which was exactly how Alice wanted him. He turned to go into the staff meeting and Alice followed him. Before they could get to Carol's office, though, Alice paused and added one more little dig.

"Bad clams?" she asked. "Not likely, is it, Ricardo?"

ELEVEN

LUCY WAS AFRAID TO FLY. This was something she hadn't shared with anyone in the office that I knew of. If he'd been aware of it, surely Craig would have informed me before Lucy and I set out on a cross-country flight together. As I adjusted my seat belt and ignored the flight crew's halfhearted flight-safety instructions, I realized that Lucy's trepidation was probably the reason she'd never before taken anyone with her on her many business trips. Lucy hated showing weakness of any kind and never once mentioned her fear to a soul.

She hadn't exactly said anything of it to me, either, but it didn't take a genius to figure out what was going on. Before we even boarded, she started popping Xanax as if they were little candies. I'd picked up the prescription for her a few days earlier and read the Rx on the bottle, which instructed that she take one pill every six hours "for anxiety." From what I could tell, she'd taken at least eighteen hours' worth by the time we got on the plane.

Although she could have boarded before me (Lucy had purchased a first-class seat for herself and one in coach for me), she waited for my group to be called before taking her seat. Her steps were hesitant and jerky as we walked down the Jetway together, as if she were pushing against an invisible force. She fell against me at one point, gripping my arm so hard her fingernails almost punctured my skin.

"I hope you're not planning to sleep on this flight, Angel," she said through clenched teeth. "Because we've got a lot of work to do in New York and this is a perfect opportunity to get caught up."

I glanced at her, mutely nodding assent. The Xanax hadn't taken effect yet; her face was the color of a blank page and tiny beads of perspiration glistened on her forehead. I couldn't help but marvel at her ability to maintain her usual commanding tone while in the grip of a full-blown phobia. I left her in first class, where she was already ordering a hapless flight attendant to bring extra blankets, pillows, and a glass of wine "immediately," and took my seat near the back of the plane, grateful for the space between us.

But as we pulled back from the gate and began to taxi down the runway, I found myself getting nervous, and not because I was the least bit anxious about flying. It was Lucy I was concerned about. It was easy to see Lucy more as a force than a person. This was an image she cultivated. But now I'd seen that spark of naked terror in her eyes and felt compassion for her along with a weird need to protect her. It was as if her fear of flying had made her human, if only briefly, and despite the relief I felt to be sitting twenty-five rows away from her, I wanted to make sure she was all right. We lifted off the ground, all those tons of steel rising in an improbable ascent, and I could feel her fear in my own body. My stomach flipped and adrenaline made my heart race. I gripped the armrests hard enough to turn my knuckles white and attract the attention of the woman sitting to my left, who put down the paperback she was reading and smiled at me reassuringly.

"You'll be fine," she said. "Takeoff is always the hardest part."

"I'm okay," I told her.

"You look a little scared," she answered.

I relaxed my grip on the armrests. "I'm not, though," I said. "I'm not afraid to fly." I sounded like I was trying to convince myself.

"All right," she said, disbelief plain in her voice, and picked up her book. Out of lifelong habit, I looked at the cover to see what she was reading. It was the most recent edition of *Cold!*

"Good book," I said, the words falling out before I had a chance to stop them.

"What? Oh, this?" She waved the book in front of her. "Yes, it's excellent. I've already read it three times, but it's one of my favorites."

"Mine, too," I said.

"He's such an amazing writer." She sighed. "I wish he'd write another book."

"He is," I said, and bit my lip. "An amazing writer, I mean."

"Makes you wonder, though, doesn't it?" she went on as we continued our climb into the sky. She seemed pleased to have the opportunity to chat. "I mean, why *hasn't* he written another book yet? Maybe he can't. Maybe he didn't even write this one. Maybe there isn't even a real Karanuk. It's not like things like that have never happened, right?"

Not only had they happened, but they'd happened in multiples. Fake stories, lying authors, even completely fabricated identities had popped up with increasing frequency, so my seatmate wasn't off-base at all. I knew I should just agree with her, smile, and be done with it, but something seized me, some need to set her straight combined with a misguided sense of hubris, and I couldn't stem the flow of words from my mouth. "I can assure you that there is a Karanuk," I said. "And he is working on another book right now."

The woman turned her head toward me, curiosity lighting her eyes. "Do you *know* him?" she asked.

"No . . . I mean yes, but not . . ." That was it, I realized. I was screwed. And it was going to be a long flight. "I represent him," I said finally, and rather than correcting myself immediately, I let the words linger in the air for a moment, trying them on for size. She'd probably leave it at that, I thought. She was just a reader. Unfortunately, I was soon proved wrong.

"You're his literary agent?" she exclaimed.

"I work for his literary agency," I said. So much for trying things on for size.

"You work for Lucy Fiamma?" Her voice had risen to a level that threatened to alert flight attendants. I was doubly screwed. I'd managed to wind up sitting next to someone who knew enough about the world of publishing to identify Lucy as Karanuk's agent. What were the chances?

"Yes," I admitted. "Yes, I do."

"This is just the most amazing coincidence," she said, excited. "I'm a writer myself. I've recently completed my first book and I was *just* getting it ready to send to your agency."

I was triply screwed. And trapped as well. I knew what was coming next: a detailed description of this woman's manuscript, along with all the reasons it was sure to be a bestseller and probably an encapsulated version of her life story as well. And I'd have to listen politely. I'd have to outline our submissions policy and assure her that I'd pay special attention to it when she sent it in. I hoped to God she wasn't carrying a copy with her, because then I'd be forced to actually read some of it. At least she wasn't aware that Lucy was also on the flight. That knowledge could lead to a truly unpleasant situation.

"How about that?" I said, and hoped I didn't sound too disingenuous. "That really is a coincidence, isn't it?"

"Indeed," she said, and smiled broadly. She extended her hand. "Solange Martin," she said. "But everyone calls me Sunny."

"Angel Robinson," I said, wiping my damp palm on my pant leg before shaking her hand.

"Pleased to meet you, Angel," she said. I waited for her to launch into a pitch of her book, but to my surprise she stopped right there, picked up her copy of *Cold!*, and got back into her reading. I checked her out from the corner of my eye, seeing her for the first time. She was trim and tan, and everything about her was colored brown and gold, from her hair to her eyes to her loose silk pantsuit. It was difficult to determine her age because her skin was smooth and unlined, but her face had an aura of maturity about it. Mid-thirties, I guessed. I studied her more carefully and decided that she was a very attractive woman. She'd look great on a book jacket.

The pilot announced that we'd reached our cruising altitude and that FAA-approved electronic devices could now be used safely. I reached down for my laptop and Palm Pilot. I needed to give Lucy's schedule a once-over while she was far enough away from me that she couldn't change it—again—and then I needed to get back to my ongoing edit of *Blind Submission*. Lucy had been pressing me to get "fifty hot pages" of the novel ready to send to editors. She was planning to pitch it hard in New York, even though I'd told her I didn't think it was ready to go out. Since my blowup/breakup with Malcolm, there had been a few times I'd come very close to telling her that he was the likely author. But Malcolm's vehement denial, difficult to dismiss out of hand, stopped me every time.

What if he was telling me the truth and he wasn't the author of *Blind Submission?*

As difficult as it was to admit that the man I'd loved and trusted for so long could have used me in such a craven display of selfishness, it was a still more frightening prospect to consider that he hadn't. Because if it wasn't Malcolm (and, as G, he wasn't giving an inch), I couldn't think of who would know the intimate details of my life as laid out in the novel—or how that person would have obtained the information.

For her part, Lucy seemed unbothered by the fact that the author was remaining anonymous. All she cared about was that I was working on the chapters as quickly as they came in and that G wasn't going to take the project anywhere else, which I assured her wouldn't happen. I suppose, with keeping Karanuk under wraps for years, she was used to dealing with cloaks, daggers, and quirks.

"Excuse me, are you Angel Robinson?"

I looked up to see a flight attendant staring down at me. I noticed that she was wearing a St. Christopher medal and a silver airplane charm around her neck.

"Yes?" I said, adrenaline surging.

"This is for you," she said, and handed me an instantly recognizable pink memo. Clearly Lucy was wasting no time.

"Thank you," I said.

"You're welcome." The flight attendant knit her eyebrows and gave me a look that fell somewhere between annoyance and pity. I gave her a weak smile in return.

A—Need to discuss. —L.

I refolded the memo and stuck it in the seat pocket in front of me.

On the face of it, the intent of that memo was undecipherable, but I knew her so well it spoke volumes to me: *Get over to first class now and bring a notepad, my schedule, and pitch letters for every project I'm selling. We need to discuss all of it. Now. And in minute detail.*

I gathered all the necessary papers and unbuckled my seat belt. They weren't going to like a visitor from coach in the first-class cabin, but I was going to have to go, anyway. I could only pray that I'd get booted out quickly or that the Xanax would kick in and she'd pass out. I was sitting in the center seat, so I was forced to climb over Sunny to get out. She gave me a warm smile as I clambered over her with all my documents and electronic devices.

"Sorry," I said.

"No problem," she said. I got the sudden sense that she understood, that she knew what I was up against. I found it oddly comforting.

Lucy was holding the glass of wine she'd asked for and leaning against the window, a manuscript in front of her, when I made my way into the first-class cabin. She was still very pale, but the pills had made her face relax so much since we'd boarded that she was looking slightly melted.

"Angel, sit," she said, gesturing to the empty seat next to her.

"You know, Lucy, I don't think I'm really supposed to be up here," I said, sotto voce.

"Just sit, Angel . . . for God's sake. There's nobody sitting here . . . you're not going to stay long." She spoke much more slowly than usual, with big spaces between her words. I wondered if she'd taken more pills since I'd last seen her. "I paid enough for these seats, anyway," she added.

"Lucy, are you okay?" I asked her as I juggled papers on my lap.

"Why . . . wouldn't . . . I . . . be . . . okay?"

"You look a little pale."

Lucy looked down at her wineglass. "Not really much of a drinker," she said, with slightly more briskness. She handed me her glass. "Here, drink this."

I assumed she just wanted me to dispose of it, so I put it on the floor and hoped there wouldn't be any turbulence. "Sweet of you to be concerned," Lucy said, twisting her mouth into a loopy Xanax smile. I offered her one in return, unsure how to respond to this drugged version of Lucy.

"We should go over my schedule," she said.

"Right, I've got it right here," I told her, pulling out the printed version. Lucy was a Luddite when it suited her. My feeling was that she simply preferred live assistants to digital ones. The unpredictability of human emotion was what she thrived on, what she needed.

Lucy looked at her schedule and asked for a pen. But when I gave her one, she dropped it in her lap and fixed me with a look of great sincerity.

"I don't want to talk about this again," she said.

"We don't have to," I told her. "It's all worked out."

"I mean, what I really want to talk about is . . ." She leaned in very close to me. As always, I could smell her Chanel N°5. "Why are you so far away, Angel?"

"I'm sitting right next to you, Lucy."

"But this is totally confidential," Lucy said, and raised her eyebrows in slow motion. I realized that she was probably very high, and the thought amused and frightened me at the same time.

"Okay," I said, and leaned toward her a little more. We were so close I could feel her hair tickle my forehead.

"Karanuk," she said.

"What about him?" I said, and realized that I'd lowered my voice to a whisper.

"I don't know if he's going to be able to pull it off," she said.

"Are you talking about *Thaw*?" I asked her. I'd heard Lucy on the phone, tempting editors with hints and morsels (even though, technically, Karanuk's previous publisher was supposed to get an exclusive first look at his next book), but she'd kept the actual text sealed off somewhere in her office and still hadn't allowed anyone else to read it. I hadn't really thought twice about Lucy's reticence with *Thaw*. I'd always expected that she would want to keep this particular project very private. Plus, I still didn't understand the nature of her relationship with Karanuk and wasn't sure that I wanted to.

"It's not even close to the level of *Cold!*" she said. "But that's not the problem. They'll buy it, anyway. But it's *not good*, Angel. Something's happened to him. It's as if the ability to write has been sucked right out of his being."

I flashed on Sunny, reading her crisp new copy of *Cold!* back in coach. *Why hasn't he written another book?* she'd asked. *Makes you wonder.*

"It's going to need a lot of work," she said, and fixed me in her sights. "It's going to need *you*, Angel."

"Oh." The weight of what she'd just said hit me hard. I eyed her cautiously, wondering if she knew what she was saying.

"So now you know why I haven't sold it already," Lucy continued. "If it wasn't such a mess, I'd have had the deal done the day after the first page arrived in the office."

"Of course," I said, realizing the truth of what she was saying.

"I've brought it with me," she went on, "and I want you to read it. When we get home this is going to be your first priority, Angel. And I don't need to tell you that this is a delicate situation. There's a lot of money at stake here, not to mention reputation." She inhaled deeply. "I don't know how kindly Karanuk will take to your giving him *direction,* so it's going to have to come from me. Do you get my meaning, Angel?"

Of course I got it. I'd do the work, she'd take the credit. It couldn't be clearer, really. But I didn't really care about that. I was far more concerned about Karanuk. I couldn't imagine him writing something *bad.* Not after *Cold!* I wondered if he was one of those fabled writers with just one great work inside him, a work that is almost channeled through him, and after that, it's over.

"Sure, Lucy."

"Good. As long as we understand each other." She pointed to the seat back in front of her. "There," she said. "Take it."

I reached in and pulled out the curled, worn manuscript pages. Lucy had written wild, scrawling notes all over the cover page. I could barely make out the title and Karanuk's name. Lucy leaned back in her seat, breathing very slowly. Her eyelids looked heavy and I was sure she was about to drop off. I looked up and met the eye of the flight attendant who'd brought me the memo. I could tell by her expression that my time in first class was about to get cut short.

"Lucy?" She didn't move or react in any way. "I think I'm going to have to go back to my seat now."

"He was one of the worst lovers I've ever had," Lucy said. Her voice was somnambulant. She sounded like she was reciting a passage from a novel. "Talk about cold! Ha! Great writer. Lousy lay. You wouldn't think it, would you? You'd figure an Eskimo would know how to heat things up."

I realized with horror that she was talking about Karanuk and felt my mouth drop open. I had the same feeling you get when you witness your parents fighting or when you run into a teacher outside of school. It was just wrong—and uncomfortable in the extreme.

"They don't know," she went on, "they don't understand . . . what a *privilege* it is to get published. So many of them . . . don't even deserve it."

"Miss?" The flight attendant was hovering over me, her charms dangling. "I'm going to have to ask you to return to your assigned seat, please."

"No problem," I said, and gathered my things.

"Where are you going?" Lucy asked.

"I have to go—"

"Ma'am, she needs to be in her assigned seat. If you need—"

"I'll tell you what I *need*. Now listen to me, do you know who I am?"

I'd never heard anyone actually use that phrase before and had to stifle the laugh that bubbled up in my throat. I made my exit as gracefully as possible considering the tight space and left Lucy arguing with the flight attendant. I could only hope that she wouldn't make enough of a scene to get us both detained when we arrived in New York.

I climbed over Sunny for the second time, careful to fold *Thaw* in half, and tried to settle myself back in my seat. I was already exhausted and we weren't even an hour into the flight. It occurred to me that I could make good use of Lucy's Xanax myself.

"Everything okay?" Sunny asked me, those notes of comfort and understanding in her voice again.

"Oh, yes, fine, thanks." I looked at her, still expecting her to start talking about her book, but again, she just smiled at me and went back to her reading. Perhaps she was waiting for the right time, waiting for my curiosity to be piqued. I gave a nervous glance down to first class. I hadn't seen any air marshals walking the aisles, so perhaps Lucy had quieted down. I pulled out my laptop again and turned it on. The most recent installment of *Blind Submission* stared back at me. This chapter, along with three others (G had gone into overdrive now), had come in as Lucy and I were preparing to leave, so I hadn't yet had a chance to read them.

There was no question that this manuscript was getting much better as it went along. It was as if G (or Malcolm—damn him) had had some kind of breakthrough after our last go-round and was finally finding his real voice. There was still some work to be done, of course, especially when it came to his annoying tendency to use clichéd and peculiarly awkward metaphors, but the characters were starting to come alive. Alice had found her voice as well, in a manner of speaking. The fact that this voice belonged to another author whose work she was about to steal and present as her own made for an excellent plot twist. Even as it worked on me, *Blind Submission* was getting good.

"Ms. Robinson?"

The first-class fight attendant was back at my seat. I braced myself for her wrath, sure that Lucy had stirred her up again, but was surprised to see her smiling warmly.

"Yes?"

"Would you mind coming with me for a moment, please?"

What could it be now? I wondered as I climbed over poor Sunny for a third time. I had a sudden fear that the flight attendant was only calm and smiling to avoid creating a scene before I was placed in some kind of custody at the front of the plane.

"Is there a problem?" I asked her timidly as we headed toward first class.

"No," she said, "not at all. Your mother explained the situation to me. You can stay there with her for a while if you need to." She graced me with a wide grin. "But I'd personally appreciate it if you'd return to your seat before the end of the flight."

My *mother*? Lord, but Lucy was good. I wondered if she'd promised literary representation as well.

"Thank you," I said. "She—"

"Not to worry, dear." The flight attendant actually patted my arm, which was an awkward maneuver in the tight cabin. "She's already told me everything."

I shuddered to think what "everything" might constitute.

The color and texture of Lucy's skin made her look like a wax replica of herself. She'd applied an overly generous amount of flaming-red lipstick since my last visit, which only served to heighten the effect. I sat down next to her and realized, with horror, that I hadn't brought my laptop or notes with me. I told myself it didn't matter because there wasn't a single piece of business Lucy could bring up that wasn't hardwired into my memory.

"Angel." She leaned toward me woozily, her bright green eyes clouded over. I had another pang of concern about her pill consumption. The flight attendant was attending to a passenger directly in front of us but seemed to be keeping a curious eye on us all the same.

"Mom?" I said, and realized how incredibly strange the word sounded in my mouth, and not just because I was directing it at Lucy.

"Books are like children, you know," Lucy said with great seriousness.

My hair had started to come loose and I blew a strand of it off my face. For the first time in my life, I thought it was a pity that I *wasn't* a writer. I was trapped on an airplane with my crazy-stoned boss, who was claiming to be my mother and who was now going to launch into a discussion about giving birth to literature. It was a situation that was ripe with literary possibilities. "You labor over them, deliver them, and then they're out there in the world," she continued, "and you never know what they'll become."

I'd heard this many times before. I wondered where she was going with it, if anywhere.

"I've midwifed . . . midwived . . . been the midwife for many, many books that wouldn't have been born at all without me." She ran her tongue around her lips, smearing her lipstick slightly. I thought about offering her a napkin to blot her lips.

"So true," I said, wondering why I felt the need to speak.

Lucy stared through me for a moment, her gaze on some unseen point beyond the confines of the first-class cabin. I thought she was going to zone out completely, but then she slowly brought herself back around. I could almost see the thoughts collecting behind her eyes.

"Blind submission," she said suddenly and with great force. "I need it." I looked at her, perplexed, searching her face for more information, and then it dawned on me that she was talking about the manuscript and not giving me an employment directive.

"I've just been reading it," I told her, and I could hear the skip in my voice. "It's really getting better, Lucy. I don't even think the new material is going to need much work. I'm not quite finished reading yet, but I think—"

"Really?" Her voice was in near-monotone, but I could see some animation working its way into her features. "I need to sell that book, Angel. I'd *like* to sell it as soon as possible. How close are we?"

"Close," I said. "I think with the rewrite of the last two chapters and this new—"

"I don't need the details of every sentence, Angel. I want to know *when*. We're hours away from New York. In the morning I'll be having breakfast with . . . with . . ."

"Natalie Weinstein."

"With Natalie Weinstein, and she's still upset about losing *Parco Lambro*. She's ravenous for a hot new project. From me. Can I tell her I have one or not?"

I struggled with what kind of answer to give her. "Well, I think if—"

"Do we have the pages?"

"Only on my computer. But I'm still—"

"On your computer?"

"Yes, because I'm—"

"Still *writing* it?" Lucy gave me a twisted, joyless smile, her smeared lipstick adding to it a touch of the grotesque.

"What?" I asked her.

"Are you still writing it, Angel? Is that why we don't have it yet?"

I knew that Lucy was out of it, perhaps dangerously so, but I found it difficult to imagine that she really thought I was the creative force behind this novel. Unless . . . Staring at her, unable to come up with a response, I realized in a sense I *was* writing *Blind Submission*. Hadn't I been over every word of this thing, changing it, reshaping it, doing my fairy-tale spin of straw into gold? Were the "suggestions" I was giving G starting to become more than that? Was I creating the text before he wrote it? My thoughts started to collapse on themselves in a flash of total confusion. I had the terrifying sensation that she'd found me out, that she'd caught me at something I didn't even know I was doing. I shook my head and the moment passed.

"I'm *editing* it, Lucy. Isn't that what you want me to do?"

"What I want . . ." She stared at me hard, her eyes gaining focus on mine. "What I want from *you*—" The plane gave a lurch before she could finish speaking, and the FASTEN SEATBELTS sign blinked on with its accompanying ring. Lucy cringed and seemed to shrink into herself, an expression of sheer terror flashing across her face. "Fucking airplanes," she said through clenched teeth. I was at a loss, unsure whether to try to comfort her, summon a flight attendant, or search for more Xanax. She covered her eyes with her hands and leaned forward in her seat. I waited for her to speak or change position for five minutes and then I realized that she'd fallen asleep or, more likely, passed out. I reached over and tapped her lightly on the shoulder. No response. I put my hands on her shoulders and tried to lean her back into a more comfortable position. Lucy stirred as I fumbled. Without opening her eyes, she reached up, grabbed one of my hands with her own, and held on.

"It's . . . um . . . Lucy? It's okay. Do you want me to stay here with you?"

Lucy didn't open her eyes and didn't respond. I waited another few minutes until she dropped my hand and it became apparent that she was out cold. It was as good a time as any to go back to my seat, I thought. I caught the flight attendant's eye as I headed back. She gave me a dirty look as she draped a blanket over Lucy's inert form. I knew what she was thinking. *Bad daughter.*

Nor did Sunny look forgiving when I climbed over her for what I hoped would be the last time.

"Do you want to switch seats?" she asked me. "I don't mind. And if you're going to have to get out again . . . ?"

"I hope not," I said. "But if you don't mind switching anyway, I'd really appreciate it."

We changed seats, and in the process of moving all my things, I decided I needed a break. The remainder of *Blind Submission* would have to wait. As excited as I was about how well it was progressing, every time I looked at it I was reminded of Malcolm. And I just didn't want to dwell on him, on what went wrong, or what was never right between the two of us. There were still hours to go before the end of our flight, and if I didn't manage to get back to it before we landed, there were always the wee hours to squeeze in a little work time. And to think I'd always wasted those hours in slumber before I started working for Lucy.

I turned off my laptop, shoved it under the seat, and leaned back. I took out my CD player and tried to relax. Immediately the opening chords of "Angel" by Jimi Hendrix flooded through my headphones. It was Damiano's CD. I pulled off the headphones and hit the STOP button. Damiano was another person I didn't want to think about. It was wrong, in so many different ways, to indulge the fantasies that had been hounding me since the night of Lucy's dinner party. I was upset and confused about my unraveling relationship, I told myself, and so I'd made Damiano the romantic hero Malcolm wasn't. And Damiano was a client. The attention he'd given me was probably nothing more than a gracious expression of gratitude for the work I'd done on *Parco Lambro*. To think there was anything more was to invite disaster. I hadn't spoken to him again since our dance outside the office. He hadn't called me, either at home or at the office, and that was as definite a statement as any.

I opened my eyes, which seemed to have closed of their own accord, and forced myself to focus on something other than the images in my head. Sunny had shoved her copy of *Cold!* into the seat back and was sitting with her hands folded in her lap, twiddling her thumbs. She looked like I felt—distracted and in need of conversation. I felt bad about crawling over her so many times, and I was also more than a little curious about her book, namely why she hadn't tried to pitch it to me.

"So what's your book about?" I asked her.

Sunny gave me a very sunny smile and nodded as if she'd been waiting for me to ask. "It's about astrology," she said. "And tarot."

"Oh." I was disappointed. Metaphysical textbooks weren't exactly hot sellers.

"But it's not a technical book or anything."

"Oh?"

"No, it's about an astrologer who gets involved in solving a series of ritual murders through astrology and tarot. She connects several murders of famous and powerful people through several centuries using these signs and symbols and starts being able to predict when the next ones will occur."

"Sounds interesting," I said. "Like *The Da Vinci Code.*"

Sunny's brow furrowed slightly. "I keep hearing that," she said.

"You haven't read it?"

"Mm, no. But my book isn't a novel. It's a memoir. That astrologer is me."

"Really?" I said, beginning to lose interest. Another memoir. Did anyone write anything else anymore?

"I wasn't going to write about it at first," Sunny was saying. "I didn't want to be like all those other people who take advantage of their media exposure to pop out a book. I wanted to make sure it was authentic. Also, it wasn't a good time for me astrologically. Jupiter is transitting my ninth house now, so—"

"You have media exposure?" I interrupted her, my interest level ratcheting up exponentially. She was an author with a ready-made platform, something literary agents and publishers alike prayed for.

"Oh, sure," she said. "I guess you've missed me on TV, huh? I've been on *Larry King Live,* all the newsmagazines, I've even had a spot on *60 Minutes.* That was something, let me tell you."

"I can't believe I've never seen you," I said.

"Well, you've probably had better things to do than stay home and watch TV," Sunny said charitably. I stifled a laugh. If she only knew.

"So you have a real-life *Da Vinci Code?* That's fascinating. You don't have any of the book with you, do you?"

Sunny's face brightened. "I do," she said. "But I didn't want to bother you with it before. I'm sure that kind of thing happens to you all the time, doesn't it? People must throw manuscripts at you constantly. It seems as if everyone has at least one book in the drawer, don't they?"

"You don't know how true that is!" I said. I liked this woman.

"Right," she said, "and as I said before, it's just perfect that you're here. I was planning to send it your way next week."

"Well, I'm very interested," I told her. "I'd love to read it. Do you have a card?" There was something about Sunny's story that set off a flare in my head, some sort of seventh sense, and as she fished in her purse for one of her cards, I knew I wanted her to myself.

Sunny's business cards were designed to look like the night sky, with white stars and astrological symbols floating against the black background. Her name, phone number, and e-mail address were in silver. I wrote my name and cell phone number on the back of one and handed it back to her. "My direct line," I told her.

"Perfect," she said, and handed me her manuscript.

"*Balsamic Moon,*" I said, looking at the title page. "I like it already."

"Thank you so much," she said. "This is just wonderful."

I glanced down toward first class. All quiet there. For how long I couldn't be sure, but for the moment I was on my own time. I turned back to Sunny. "So tell me some more about your book," I said.

TWELVE

I DIDN'T NEED THE WAKE-UP CALL I'd scheduled for seven o'clock. Lucy rang my room at six and she sounded as if she'd already been up for hours.

"I need you to come to my room now, Angel," she said. Her voice didn't reveal a trace of the grogginess or jet lag I was feeling. I wondered if she had some secret chemical rejuvenator, or if she just produced some kind of enzyme that enabled her to be so functional after a cross-country flight and all the Xanax she'd taken.

"Okay," I said, clearing the gravel from my throat, "I just need to take a quick shower—"

"You're not *awake* yet?" Lucy made impatient clicks with her tongue. "You'd better hurry, then. We've got *no time*, Angel. We'll be late. *I'll* be late. We've got very important meetings today."

"I'll be right there."

"And Angel?"

"Yes, Lucy?"

"I'm sure I don't need to tell you this, but you need to look presentable. I hope you've brought appropriate clothing. This is New York, dear, not *Petaluma*." Her emphasis on *Petaluma* made it sound like a small Third World country.

"On my way," I told her, and hung up.

Lucy's room was several floors above mine. When I entered, I could see that it was bigger and better appointed than mine. Hers had a couch and a coffee table sporting the remains of a room-service breakfast. The smell of the coffee immediately triggered hunger pangs in my stomach.

"I have an extra cup for you," Lucy said, as if she could sense what I was feeling. "But you'll have to wait to eat. I had an extra croissant, too, but I ate it while I was waiting. Early bird gets the worm."

"Right, okay, sure. Thanks." I reached for the coffee, grateful that there was anything here for me to consume at all. I remembered that Lucy's first appointment was a breakfast with Natalie Weinstein and wondered why Lucy had already eaten.

"Natalie Weinstein doesn't eat," Lucy said, reading my thoughts again. "I've never seen the woman put a molecule of food past her lips. Breakfast is just a term she uses for an early meeting." She gave me a blinding-white smile. "There's so much you don't know, Angel." She paused, hands on hips, and assessed my attire. "You look all right," she said. "Unimaginative, but all right."

"Mm," I said, sipping the lukewarm coffee and instinctively smoothing a crease on my pants. Lucy herself was dressed like a stylish undertaker. She was wearing fitted black pants and a black blouse with a mandarin collar. A matching black duster was thrown across the back of a chair. Her hair was pulled back in a tight chignon and a turquoise dream-catcher pendant hung from her neck. Despite the sepulchral quality of her ensemble, she actually looked very good.

"Now," she continued, "I need you to call the office and get Craig on the phone."

I was already punching the numbers on my cell phone when I remembered the time difference. "Do you want me to leave a message?" I asked her. "There won't be anyone in right now. It's four o'clock in the morning in California."

Annoyed impatience danced across Lucy's features. "Very inconvenient," she said. "Well, then, send a fax or an e-mail or something. I need numbers." Lucy's requests were always missing vital pieces of information. What numbers did she need, for example? Where was Craig supposed to send them? I'd stopped asking Lucy for details about these kinds of things long ago, choosing instead to make educated guesses and hope for the best. The longer I worked with her, the easier it got to figure out what she wanted. Still, she was prone to throw a spanner in the wheel just when I thought I'd reinvented it for the last time. I sent a text message to Craig's e-mail address telling him that Lucy needed numbers and that he should call me on my cell phone as soon as he had them. I hoped that would cover all the bases.

"He'd better have that handy. He's been so distracted lately," Lucy was saying. "Must be having problems at home again. That wife of his . . . You should see—" She cut herself off and stared at me hard. "Marriage is a curse, Angel. You should really think about that before you make any big moves with that *fiancé* of yours."

I debated telling her about Malcolm. Although I didn't know why exactly, I was sure it would please her to know that we were no longer together. Fortunately, she didn't give me a chance.

"Get the new one on the phone as well," she said. "Make sure he knows what he's doing with the submissions."

"I've shown him—" I started, knowing that she was referring to Jackson, who apparently hadn't been part of the staff long enough to warrant a name in Lucy's eyes. I supposed it was better than being called "Nora." I wondered, fleetingly, what had become of Kelly.

"Just make sure he knows," Lucy interrupted me.

I looked up at Lucy, who was hovering over me like a dark cloud, and the edge of an image pressing against my brain. I had a feeling of déjà vu, as if something she'd said had triggered a memory, but I couldn't quite grasp it.

"Now," she said, "tell me what I'm doing today. I can't find that annotated list of editors and projects, which was very annoying, by the way, Angel, because I could have gotten a jump-start this morning if I'd been able to *look* at my schedule."

I knew that Lucy had several versions of her schedule with notes and lists attached, but I didn't bother to tell her this. Instead, I reached for one of the many extra copies I had handy and handed her one.

"Now, what about *Elvis?*" she asked me.

"I've got two copies."

"*Two?* What the hell can I do with two copies, Angel?"

"Um, you didn't want to bring more? You said we could—"

"Fine! We'll just make copies as we go, but really, Angel . . ."

It went like this for the better part of an hour—Lucy chastising me for following directives that she'd given me specifically, and me pretending that she hadn't and allowing her to come up with "solutions" to nonexistent problems. I had to wonder, though, how she had managed these trips without an assistant in the past. I was reannotating her schedule for what must have been the twentieth time when she said, "Angel?"

"Yes, Lucy?"

"What are you waiting for? We have to go."

She loaded me up with canvas bags full of manuscripts and lists until I looked like a pack mule. "You should have a briefcase," she said as I struggled under the weight.

I patted my laptop carrying case, which was buried under a *Book Lovers Never Go to Bed Alone* tote bag, and said, "This is it."

"Well," Lucy said, and adjusted the strap of her large black purse on her shoulder, "you should get something more like this." She picked up a small black alligator briefcase and held it out for me to see. "I'm paying you enough now, Angel. Really. You can't cry poverty."

"Right."

"Unless you've spent all that money I've given you already? Have you?"

The question so took me by surprise I was rendered speechless. How could she have known that I had indeed spent a large portion of my "raise" paying off my student loans and accumulated credit-card debt? I'd left enough to cover the taxes I was going to have to pay on her generosity and a little that I planned to send to my mother, who was perpetually without funds and a reliable phone.

But Lucy wasn't waiting for an answer to her question. "We ought to take you for a haircut and maybe a makeover while we're here— spruce you up a bit. I'd be willing to help you with that, Angel. You do represent me, after all."

"Oh. Well, I—"

"Come on, Angel, let's go."

I gazed longingly at the crumbs of food on her coffee table and followed her out the door.

"You should know I don't like taking taxis unless it's absolutely necessary," Lucy said, marching ahead of me in the echoing marble lobby of the hotel. She pushed herself through the revolving glass door at the entrance, leaving me and my bags caught hopelessly between the rotations. I struggled to free myself and I could hear her saying, "Nobody walks in California. Here you can walk!"

I finally freed myself from the revolving doors and broke out onto the street, into Midtown Manhattan. My senses were all immediately overloaded with every kind of sensory information—honking, exhaust, yelling, smoke, perfume, garbage, music, garlic, laughter, daylight, and the vast shadows of tall buildings. It was impossible to take it all in at once.

"Angel!" Lucy's voice reached me through waves of sound and air. "Let's get moving."

⁓⁓⁓

THE TRIAD PUBLISHING GROUP was located ten city blocks from our hotel. I knew this because I counted every single one as I struggled to keep up with Lucy's pace. She was right, this was the ideal city to walk in— every square foot jammed with activity and something to look at—but I couldn't stop to see any of it. I followed as close behind Lucy as possible with all the weight I was carrying. If I lost her, I'd lose myself in a matter of seconds.

I was short of breath and sweating like a horse by the time we arrived. There was a giant concrete obelisk outside the building engraved with the Triad name and colophon, which was the symbol for infinity within a circle, within a triangle, within a square. I stared up at it and felt a chill run through my entire body—the same chill I'd felt the first time I walked into Lucy's office and knew, unequivocally, that I was in the right place, the place in which I was meant to be. This was the center, the beating heart of publishing, the place where everything was about letters, words, books. I loved this world so much it took my breath away. Lucy must have sensed my sudden sense of book-geek awe because she turned to me, eyebrows raised, one corner of her carmine-stained mouth turned up in a sardonic half-smile.

"What?" she said.

"It's . . . um . . . exciting," I answered.

"Yes, this is your maiden voyage, isn't it?" she said. "Well, don't get too carried away, Angel, we've got a lot of work to do." She was all business as usual, but there was a glimmer of recognition in her eyes and her smile broadened. Wasn't my love of this business and everything it entailed the reason she had hired me in the first place? It was a love she had to have felt—had to still feel—herself.

Like the other large publishing houses, Triad had swallowed several smaller publishers over the years, most of which now had their offices in the same building. I was surprised by how sparse and unbooklike the lobby appeared when Lucy and I walked in. Gabriel Press, where Natalie Weinstein ran Weinstein Books, was located on the eighth floor. Over the course of the next couple of days, though, Lucy would have many more meetings here on different floors. C&P Publishers was on the sixth floor, First Wave on the eleventh, and so on. These smaller publishers all had specific types of books they put out (C&P published literary works, for example, whereas First Wave only published mass-market paperbacks—the kind one found in supermarkets and drugstores), but they were all ultimately answerable to and dependent on Triad.

"One has the illusion that there are many options when it comes to selling books," Lucy had once said, "but that's all it is—an illusion." She often bemoaned the current state of publishing, claiming the book business had been so much "spiritually richer" in the old days before massive corporations took it over, but then this kind of complaint was almost de rigueur for anyone who had been in the business for longer than five minutes, from booksellers to literary agents to editors. None of it was stopping Lucy from selling books, however, and none of it was stopping publishers from buying them.

"Don't speak to her unless she asks you a question," Lucy said as we rode the elevator to the eighth floor. "She's very particular about that kind of thing. She's also quite prickly, so just steer clear of her and don't attempt conversation."

"You mean Natalie Weinstein?" I was baffled. I'd spoken to Natalie several times from the office, and unless she was in a state of high dudgeon over something Lucy had done or not done, she was extremely personable and always polite.

"Well, who the hell else would I be talking about? Honestly, Angel, sometimes I worry about the speed of your thought processes."

There wasn't really a need to respond to that statement, so I just followed Lucy out of the elevator. We stepped through glass doors etched with the Gabriel Press colophon (a trumpet) into a waiting area that was as lush and literary as the lobby had been sterile.

There is something about the aroma of fresh books that is totally intoxicating. When I'd worked at Blue Moon, I loved to unpack the cartons when they came in. A new book has a certain clean, crisp smell full of promise that is difficult to define. Sort of like the scent and feeling of just-washed bed linens at the moment you slide your legs between them. The air in Gabriel Press was full of this fragrance—the halls were lined with books, paper, and bound galleys. There were blown-up book jackets on the walls and thick cream-colored carpeting on the floor. And it was quiet—peaceful—the sounds of computer keyboards, phones, and voices all muted in some kind of literary hush. It was, I thought, very much like my idea of a personal heaven.

As we marched through the corridors, Lucy tossed greetings through every open door and cubicle, sending ripples of sound through the calm. It was still early, so the offices were only half-full from what I could see, but Lucy managed to announce her presence to everyone who was there:

"Daniel, I can't wait to show you this scrumptious novel," was followed by, "Susan, I have one that practically came in with your name on it," and then, "Jason, be sure to tell your boss that I am simply dying to see her as soon as she gets in," winding up with, "You're going to love it. . . . You'll love it. . . . You will fall in love. . . ."

Natalie Weinstein was at the far end of the floor, occupying a large corner space. Several semienclosed cubicles, the largest of which belonged to her assistant, encircled her office. The assistant was not at her desk when we arrived and Lucy made *tsk-tsk* noises. "She's had a lot of trouble with assistants," Lucy said. "Personally, I can understand why. She can't be an easy boss, if you know what I mean."

I shrugged so as to give her some kind of response, but again, I was perplexed. Natalie's assistant, Wendy, and I had also spoken on the phone several times, and she'd always seemed not only efficient, but pleasant. She had none of the strain in her voice that I knew *we* all had at the agency.

"Naaaatalieeee," Lucy called. "Helloooo?"

"Come on in, Lucy," came the voice from behind the door, but Lucy was already halfway in and I came trailing behind her.

I assumed that Natalie Weinstein was sitting behind her large lacquered desk, so when she moved away from it to greet us, I was stunned to find she'd been standing. She was minute. Not just short or small-boned, but tiny in every way. I watched as Lucy leaned over and swallowed her in an embrace. She had to be under five feet, I guessed, and her body looked like an assembly of twigs covered with skin. Her hair was platinum blond and cut so short it had a military look to it. She had huge light-blue eyes and her skin was extremely tan. She looked, I thought ungenerously, like an alien.

"Always a pleasure to see you, Lucy," Natalie said. "You look well."

"As do you, my dear," Lucy responded. Lucy continued on with pleasantries for a few moments and I hung back behind her, directing my gaze out Natalie's large corner windows, which offered a spectacular view of the city.

"And you must be the famous Angel," Natalie said, moving away from Lucy and fixing me with her extraterrestrial eyes.

"Famous!" Lucy snorted.

"It's a pleasure to meet you in person," I said, shaking Natalie's small bony hand.

"Likewise," Natalie said, and tipped her head to one side, assessing me in some way I couldn't figure out. Behind her, Lucy was looking at me and shaking her head as if to tell me not to speak.

"Shall we get down to business, my dear?" Lucy said sharply. "I know how valuable your time is."

"And yours, of course," Natalie said. "But wouldn't you like a cup of coffee or something?"

"I think my assistant can handle that," Lucy said, waving her hand in my direction. "Also, if you don't mind, Natalie, I have a manuscript here. . . . I was planning to go out with this in the next couple of weeks, but I know you're going to fall in love with this one. It's the perfect cross between literary and commercial, and I know you've been looking for something Las Vegas–oriented, yes? Anyway, I've just decided now that you must have it. My assistant can make a quick copy for you if you'll direct her to the copy machine?"

"Sounds intriguing," Natalie said, and looked up at me. "Wendy can help you find everything, Angel. Thank you."

"Do you . . ." I started. I could feel that my face was flushed and my ears were burning with the mortification of being reduced to coffee/copy girl by Lucy. "Would you like some coffee?"

"No thanks," Natalie said. "I'm on a green tea diet at the moment. No coffee allowed."

"Well, then, I'd be happy to get you a green tea," I said, and left her office before Lucy could speak to, at, or about me again.

———

MY CELL PHONE RANG as I was negotiating how to get back into the building while balancing the coffee, the green tea, the *Elvis* manuscript, and the muffin I'd bought for myself. I was forced to put everything on the ground to dig into my purse and pull the phone out. The caller ID listed a 212 area code.

"This is Angel."

"We're growing old here, Angel. What could be taking you so long?"

She was calling me from Natalie's office phone. The memory of that old horror flick—*the calls are coming from inside the house!*—flitted through my head and I had to stifle a wild giggle. Kill the babysitter. Kill the assistant.

"On my way now," I said, and snapped the phone shut. It rang again before I could put it back in my purse.

"This is Angel."

"It's Craig. I got your message."

I looked at my watch. It wasn't even seven o'clock in California. "Are you in the office?" I asked him.

"Of course I'm in the office," he said. "How else would I— Can you put Lucy on the phone?"

"I'm downstairs. I mean, she's upstairs. . . . I'll have to have her call you back, Craig. She's in a meeting with Natalie Weinstein."

"Take down these numbers," he said. "Then you can give them to her and she can call me back."

"I can't do that right now, Craig. I'm kind of standing on the street."

"Just tell her 'seventeen without,' then. But she needs to call me back."

"Okay, thanks. Listen, Craig, I need to speak to Jackson when—"

"WHY WOULD JACKSON BE HERE," he screamed into the phone, "AT THIS HOUR OF THE DAY?!" and hung up.

Craig was obviously losing it. Could it be that he was suffering from Lucy-withdrawal and didn't know what to do with his slavish self without her? I mean, really, *seventeen without.* It was like something from *The Rule of Four.* The world was going mad. My corner of it at least.

NATALIE WAS ALONE in her office when I finally made it back upstairs, and she beckoned me to come in and sit down. I looked around for Lucy and I wondered if she'd left me behind to go on to her next appointment.

"Your boss is using the restroom," Natalie said in the same tone that someone would tell a lost child, *Don't worry, your mother will be right back.* "Thank you so much for the tea."

"It's a pleasure," I said. "You have a beautiful office." She smiled at me. "And I just want to say I think that your books are fantastic." I pointed to her bookshelf, which was stacked with Weinstein Books titles. Her books *were* exceptional; they won a disproportionate number of literary awards, but they rarely made it onto bestseller lists. *Parco Lambro* would have been perfect for her. She was exactly the kind of editor Damiano needed, but she hadn't been able to come up with enough money to satisfy Lucy.

"I've known Lucy Fiamma for a long time," Natalie said.

"So she's said." Lucy had also told me, "I knew Natalie Weinstein before she was *Natalie Weinstein*—when she was still taking messages for Gordon Hart."

"She's never brought anyone to New York with her before," Natalie went on. She paused a moment to let this sink in. "You must be something very special," she said, and let out a mirthless laugh. "Either that or you've got something on her."

I laughed politely.

"I'm betting on the former," Natalie said. "That Italian book . . . Lucy hasn't come through with anything like that for a long time. I think you had something to do with that one, didn't you?"

I laughed again. It seemed like the thing to do.

"And I think you have a hand in whatever it is she's got today."

I shrugged.

"Ever thought about moving to New York, Angel?"

"No," I said. "Not really."

"Maybe you should. Think about it, that is. So tell me, should I get excited about that manuscript you're holding?"

I looked down at *Elvis,* which was getting damp and curled from the sweat of my palms. I knew I should tell her that she'd *fall in love* with it, but I was thinking about Sunny Martin and her memoir, *Balsamic Moon.* I'd read part of it the night before when I was too wired to sleep and I really liked it. I knew that it was exactly the kind of book that Natalie Weinstein wanted. "Well, it's . . ." I hesitated, my mouth still open around the words.

"Come on, Angel," she said. "Let's see what you've got. Pitch it to me."

I looked into Natalie Weinstein's freaky eyes and made a decision. I hoped I wouldn't live to regret it, because once the next words were out of my mouth, I'd never be able to take them back. I was taking a big chance. Lucy could walk in on us at any moment and I'd be caught in literary flagrante delicto.

"This is a terrific book," I said, holding up *Elvis,* "but I think I should let Lucy tell you about it. She's so excited about it and I'd hate to ruin it for her. But I have something else. It just came in and Lucy's not— I mean, I'm sort of handling it right now and . . ." My nerve was fading and I looked at Natalie for a sign that I should proceed.

"I get it," she said, giving me one. "Go on."

"The title is *Balsamic Moon,*" I said in a quick rush, frantic to get it all out before Lucy came back. "It's a memoir by an astrologer, but with a great twist. It's a real-life *Da Vinci Code,* which is perfect since everyone wants a new *Da Vinci Code,* but nobody wants another imitator. I think we all know *that* ship has sailed. The subject matter is fascinating— hasn't been done before that I can tell—and the writing is excellent. She's a natural. I know the kind of books you publish and I know you'll love this one."

"Indeed," she said. "And what is the author's name?"

"That's the best part," I said, going in for the close. "She already has great media visibility. Her name is Sunny—Solange—Martin. I'm sure you're familiar with her."

"In fact, I am," Natalie said. "Is there a finished manuscript?"

I was about to answer her when Lucy glided back into Natalie's office on a wave of freshly applied Chanel N°5. The three of us froze in a weird little tableau for a moment, Natalie looking like the cat that ate the canary, Lucy glowering when she saw me seated in front of Natalie's desk, and me, slack-jawed and speechless. It was Natalie who spoke first.

"Well, Lucy, your assistant has just been telling me what beautiful weather you've been having in California. Sounds divine." She looked over at me, smiled, and winked.

"Like Valhalla," I said, and stood to give Lucy my chair.

To: anna.anderson@fiammalit.com
From: angel.robinson@fiammalit.com
Subject: manuscripts/editors/questions

Hi Anna,

Hope all's well. We're back at the hotel for a minute before we head out again for dinner—well, before Lucy has dinner with Susie Parker and I wait for her in the bar—so I've got a minute to send you a note. I know I've already spoken to you about 50x today, but Lucy keeps adding more editors for every project, so I've been continually updating all day. I guess the most important one is *Elvis Will Dance at Your Wedding.* She's been pitching that to everyone, and since I can't copy it everywhere we go, please send a copy overnight to the following editors: Susan Jones (C&P), Lydia Smith (Long, Greene), and everybody who bid on *Parco Lambro* (you have a copy of that list, right?). I'm sure there will be more tomorrow, but that's it for now.

She's really been talking up *Blind Submission* and they're getting excited. It's not ready to go yet, but Lucy wants you to start generating a list. Just put every editor in New York on it and I'm sure you'll be fine. Speaking of *BS,* Lucy wants to know if everybody's read the material. If you could let me know, or maybe send me reader reports, that would be great.

Some random questions from Lucy (I'm reading my scribbled notes here, so bear with me—I had to write this stuff down while I was running along next to her on the way to appointments!):

—Film interest for *Parco Lambro*?
—Permissions backlog for *Cold!*?
—Reading cycle while we're gone? (I think she means is Jackson picking up more submissions?)
—Change hold music. Lucy would like you or Craig to change the hold music in the office (but she also said that she doesn't want anyone to ever *get* the hold music—she called a couple of times

today and the phones went right over to hold and she wasn't happy). Anyway, she wants the music changed to "Some Girls" by the Rolling Stones. (I don't know why.)

I think that's it for now. I'll be here for about another forty-five minutes and plugged in, so if you can e-mail back, I know Lucy would appreciate it.

Thanks!
Angel

To: angel.robinson@fiammalit.com
From: anna.anderson@fiammalit.com
Subject: Re: manuscripts/editors/questions

Hi Angel,

That is GREAT news about *Blind Submission*!!!! Please tell Lucy that I will be MORE THAN happy to put together a list immediately. Does she need a pitch letter? I can do that too. And if she wants me to put the pages together, it's no problem.

As for the list of editors who bid on *Parco Lambro,* of course I have it. I put it together. Anyway, I will get those manuscripts off to the editors ASAP. Although I think you should know that since you've been on vacation, we're seriously short here, so I'm picking up a lot of the slack, including the reading, and I might not get that out until tomorrow morning. I guess that answers one of your other questions about Jackson. He really doesn't seem to be "getting it." Maybe you can retrain him when you get home. Because of this, I haven't been able to get to the permissions (I thought you were supposed to be covering this?) or the film interest for *PL* yet. But please tell Lucy that I am working on it and will hope to have very good news for her when she returns.

Re: hold music. Can you tell Lucy that *Exile on Main Street* is considered by many critics to be one of the Rolling Stones's best albums? If she likes, I can prepare a folder with some of the important reviews for both that album and *Some Girls* and then she can make a final decision.

So, are you having a good time in New York? Have you eaten at Michael's yet? That's where all the literary muckety-mucks hang out. You should go. It must be so exciting to be there—you should live it up, do something outrageous and different. You go, girl, as Oprah would say.

Give Lucy my love.

See ya!
AA

P.S. Speaking of Oprah, can you please tell Lucy that I just learned that my aunt's stepdaughter's friend's cousin is a producer there! Please tell Lucy that I'd be happy to use my connection to try to get our authors on the show.

To: anna.anderson@fiammalit.com
From: angel.robinson@fiammalit.com
Subject: Re: Re: manuscripts/editors/questions

Anna,

I don't think Lucy wants a report on which Rolling Stones album was better received—I'm pretty sure she just wants you to change the hold music, okay?

By the way, I'm not on vacation. I haven't done anything except work since we got here (and sleep—although not very much). Just so we're clear on that.

I'll pass your Oprah news on to Lucy. And I'll get back to you on everything else tomorrow. Have to go now.

Thanks,
Angel

To: angel.robinson@fiammalit.com
From: anna.anderson@fiammalit.com
Subject: one more thing

Hi Angel,

You're probably off having drinks or whatever now, but I wanted to send you a note before I forget to tell you that someone named Sunny Martin called for you today. She was calling about a book. She said you met on the plane? She said you had given her your "private number" but that she "lost" it. She was calling here because she said you told her you worked with Lucy. I must have gotten confused because it sounded like you were offering to represent her. . . . Anyway, I told her that you would be back in the office on Friday and that she could send in the first 50 pages and you would pass it on to Lucy. Just thought you'd like to know.

Also, your old boss from the bookstore called looking for you. I didn't tell her where you were. She said she has your home phone number.

That's it for now. Hope you're having fun! Make sure you take care of Lucy!

AA

To: solange@sunstar.com
From: angel.robinson@fiammalit.com
Subject: BALSAMIC MOON

Dear Sunny,

I just wanted to drop you a note to tell you how wonderful it was to meet you on the plane the other day. What good fortune for both of us! I also wanted to offer you my thanks for being so gracious about having to get up and down so many times—that was really very nice of you. Finally, I must tell you how excited I am about your book. I've read quite a bit of it already and I think it's terrific. I've been meeting with several editors here in New York and I think that many (if not all) of them would be most interested in a book such as yours. I've already mentioned it to one of the most talented editors I know and she's extremely interested—sight unseen! This is the right time for a book like *Balsamic Moon*.

Speaking of sight unseen, I understand you spoke with Lucy Fiamma's assistant, Anna, today? My apologies if she didn't understand who you were. As I'm sure you can imagine, we get scores of submissions daily and many of the authors claim to "know" us to get a foot in the door. Anna may have been a little aggressive in her screening today—my apologies again.

I'll look forward to discussing all of this with you very soon. I'm including my personal phone number, which Anna said you'd misplaced, so please feel free to call if you have any questions.

Many thanks again, Sunny.

Best,
Angel

To: angel.robinson@fiammalit.com
From: jackson.stark@fiammalit.com
Subject: Anna

Hey Angel—

Hope all's well with you. I'm sure you're super busy and I might be totally out of line here, but I thought you should know that Anna's been going through your desk a lot since you've been gone. Well, actually, she's been sitting *at* your desk. And also—I know this sounds a little weird—she's answered the phone a couple of times by saying "This is Angel." She said she just got confused because she's sitting at your desk and that she had to sit at your desk because she has to do all your stuff now that you're gone, but I don't know. Like I said, it's a bit weird. Also, she's been feeding your fish—A LOT. He doesn't look good, Angel. I told her to stop but she said she promised to take care of him for you. I didn't think that sounded right. I think the only thing Anna knows to do with fish is eat them. Anyway, maybe you don't want to know any of this and maybe I'm just overreacting, but I thought I should tell you.

Thanks,
Jackson

To: jackson.stark@fiammalit.com
From: angel.robinson@fiammalit.com
Subject: Re: Anna

Hi Jackson,

I don't think you're overreacting and I appreciate your telling me all of this. Would you do me a big favor and just take my fish over to your desk before she kills it? Tell her I asked you to do it to take some of the load off her. As for the other stuff, yes, please keep me posted about what she's doing. And, not that I have to tell you this, but it's just between you and me, okay? And please make sure that you delete this e-mail after you've read it, okay? Thanks, Jackson.

Angel

To: angel.robinson@fiammalit.com
From: jackson.stark@fiammalit.com
Subject: Re: Re: Anna

Hey Angel,

Not to worry re. deleting and keeping things on the QT. I'm glad you're not mad. You never know around here. . . . One more thing. I heard her on the phone (but don't worry, she didn't know I was listening) having an argument and then crying. Well, weeping actually. Anyway, she was talking to someone named Malcolm. She seemed pretty upset. Isn't your boyfriend's name Malcolm? Not that there's only one Malcolm in the world but still . . .

Speak to you soon,
J.

THIRTEEN

To: angel.robinson@fiammalit.com
From: ganovelist@heya.com
Subject: ?

Dear Ms. Robinson,

I'm wondering if you've received my most recent installment? You are usually very prompt, so I'm a little concerned about what might have become of you! And may I ask what are Ms. Fiamma's feelings about the manuscript to this point? One final thought: I am wondering if either you or Ms. Fiamma have discussed the possibility of film for this book?

Looking forward to your reply,
G.

To: ganovelist@heya.com
From: angel.robinson@fiammalit.com
Subject: Re: ?

Dear G,

I'm sorry that I haven't been able to respond for the past few days, but I've been in New York City with Lucy Fiamma on business and am only intermittently on e-mail. I'll be back in the office on Friday.

I have received your pages and I've just finished reading them. I think that they're very good. This set is really in the best shape of all that you've sent so far. I think the direction you've taken is a good one and I also think you've really hit your stride. I'll be sending back my notes as soon as I return to the office. For now, though, here are a couple of questions I had:

I'm not totally clear on why Carol likes Alice as much as she does. It seems to me that Alice hasn't really offered Carol much to like? I guess the question is, what is Alice giving Carol Moore?

What has happened to Alice's own writing? Is her ultimate goal to publish her own work or just to have her name on a book? I'm not sure where you're heading with this and, while I like the underlying comment you're making about the "business" of books and the role of the writer within that business, it's important that we have an actual story here. Does this make sense? If not, it's probably because I'm getting kind of punchy. It's been a long day.

At any rate, I've shown the pages to Lucy and she's gone over them as well, although she'll be giving a closer read when we return home. But she's very enthusiastic about this book—so enthusiastic, in fact, that she's been talking about BS to editors while we're here and they are all very excited about it. The sooner you can get it all to us, the sooner we can get it out there! We haven't discussed film in any depth yet (it's a bit early for that), but Lucy has, as I'm sure you know, an excellent track record as far as selling her projects in that arena.

I'll have to sign off now as it's extremely late and my day will begin again in a few hours. Just one more thing . . . Between friends (because I do consider you and I to be friends at this point and I hope you feel the same), who are you? I promise not to tell anyone! Well, maybe Lucy! Seriously, G, do you think you might consider revealing yourself pretty soon? It's not like this book is giving away any national secrets or anything. It's a book about books, right? I guess the secrecy thing is kind of fun, but I don't really understand it. We're getting pretty close to the wire here, and if you want us to represent you, we're going to have to know a LITTLE bit more about who you are. Have to know where to send those checks, right?

Soon,
Angel

To: angel.robinson@fiammalit.com
From: ganovelist@heya.com
Subject: Re: Re: ?

Dear Ms. Robinson,

I am quite thrilled on all counts.

I'll look forward to your notes (and I do look forward to them—it's so refreshing to read them—you have an excellent way of identifying exactly what I mean to say, quite a talent), but in the meantime, let me address your questions. What does Carol see in Alice? As Ricardo stated, Carol sees *herself* in Alice and she likes the reflection. As I wrote in Chapter 2, Carol's rise to the top wasn't exactly without some questionable moves, but that was what she had to do to reach her goal. Carol sees the same drive and ambition in Alice. Of course, Alice is possessed by something that Carol is free of and that is the need to write. Alice is a self-loathing writer and clearly not very good at her craft. So her plan is just to take over, to attain as much power as possible, and then take the publishing world by storm. The catch, as I pointed out in Chapter 1, is that Alice wants to be a *legitimate* writer. She wants to write a bestseller, but she wants the accolades, too. She knows that Carol Moore is the key to all of this. As for her own writing—well, I thought I'd made it clear that she didn't deal with rejection very well. Of course, if you're not getting any of this, then I'm not doing my job, am I? Back to work I go.

To answer your last question about my identity, "all in good time," as they say. I have my reasons for remaining anonymous, and as long as Ms. Fiamma is satisfied with my progress, I shall remain so for just a little while longer. As to your considering me a friend—I think we are both more and less than that now.

Here's to you, Ms. Robinson; coo coo coo-choo.

With best wishes,
G.

I was too exhausted to move. I lay on my hotel bed, where I'd fallen a half hour earlier, without enough energy to even pull back the cover, which I knew was laden with the filth of every person who'd lain there before me. I'd pulled back the heavy purple drapes before I'd collapsed on the bed and I could see a sliver of gray-blue New York City sky behind the crowd of brick and concrete walls. My feet and head were throbbing, but the thought of going downstairs to the lobby to buy an eight-dollar bottle of aspirin was overwhelming. It was my last night in New York and my first nonsleeping break from Lucy in days.

She'd gotten herself invited to a cocktail party that HartHouse was throwing in conjunction with HBO for a series based on a book by one of its authors and was going *alone*. In fact, she'd been adamant about keeping me away from any function or meeting that might involve Gordon Hart. And as much as I wanted to meet Gordon Hart, I wasn't disappointed that Lucy left me out of the meetings. I could only imagine the embarrassing things she'd think to say, and would rather never meet the man at all than be humiliated in front of him.

"Why don't you go get yourself some dinner in the Big Apple?" she'd suggested when I left her room after reorganizing her notes, responding to her messages, and preparing her for the next day's meetings. "If you can't find a good place to eat in New York City, you don't know what food is. Or better yet, you can order something in your room and get caught up. I'm sure you've got a lot of work to do." As if any work I had to do was unrelated to her. "Anyway, enjoy yourself—this is your vacation! But don't get carried away. We've got a long day tomorrow and then you'll have to get yourself to the airport."

Lucy had decided to take an extra day in Manhattan without me (which had entailed at least two hours of phone time for me, rearranging her flight and negotiating an extra night at the hotel at the same rate) and had given me no information about why or what she was planning to do. Which was fine with me. I'd never worked as hard as I had in the last two days or been as connected to another human being for such an extended period of time. I marveled at Lucy's energy level. She was unstoppable. She had to tire, had to feel the effects of her mad pace, but she never seemed to show it. I had begun to wonder if she was sucking that energy from me. Despite my suspicion that she was some kind of psychic vampire, though, I was impressed, almost awestruck, by her performance in New York. They didn't always seem (or even pretend) to like her, that much was certain, but every editor and publisher gave her their undivided attention for as long as she was with them. From what I could see, Lucy had no "pals" in New York. Nobody ever spoke to her as if she were a girlfriend or a buddy. Nobody asked about her hobbies, her family, or the details of her life. But every one of them, including the elusive Gordon Hart, wanted to know what she *had*.

And Lucy had something for everyone. She had an encyclopedic knowledge of every editor's history, exactly what kind of books they liked, and exactly how far out on a limb they could go to buy. Often, that limb didn't seem to extend very far, but I only saw Lucy express anything less than brisk confidence once.

We were marching out of Long, Greene, where she'd just finished a meeting with Julia Swann, an editor with a number of adjectives on her stationery (executive, vice president, senior, etc.), but a very limited allowance for what she could buy. Julia had sighed when Lucy told her about *Elvis,* said that it sounded wonderful but that she doubted she'd be able to get it past her board. She was looking for the next *Da Vinci*

Code, Julia said—didn't Lucy have one of those? And what was happening with Karanuk, for heaven's sake? Now, there was something she'd have carte blanche to bid on.

"This is a very difficult time to be in publishing," Lucy said as we hit the street and headed down Fifth Avenue to her next appointment. "Nobody has any imagination anymore and they're all scared to buy anything that isn't incredibly safe or has been done before. I mean, really, how many celebrity children's books do we need? Or prizewinning authors writing *cookbooks*?"

This rare moment of doubt passed as quickly as it had come, though. Lucy was back on her game by the time we reached her next meeting, busily pitching her own celebrity children's books and literary cookbooks (because, of course, she *had* them) along with everything else on her list. It was really quite a sight to behold. Lucy must have known this, too, because, despite insisting that I fetch coffee and make copies almost everywhere we went, she seldom excluded me from her meetings. She wanted me to see her in action. At all times, Lucy made it very clear that I was her assistant, but as we circled New York City like hungry sharks in search of prey, I began to get the sense that she also wanted my admiration. She had it, of course.

After being attached to her at the hip for almost three days, though, I couldn't stand the sight of Lucy anymore. I was sick of her relentless rudeness, of the way she managed to make me look like an ignorant hick at every office we visited, never giving me an iota of credit for doing anything other than the most basic of clerical tasks, and I was sick of carrying her crap, literally and figuratively. But mostly, I was weary and unsettled by how *close* I was to her—of how she seemed to occupy every space of my being, under my skin and inside my head.

I also had the feeling that somehow she knew about my conversation with Natalie Weinstein and was just waiting for the right moment to drop some kind of bomb on me. Although Natalie had indicated that she wasn't about to tell Lucy, my anxiety wasn't entirely irrational. Anna had spoken to Sunny Martin and, for all I knew, had gone straight to Lucy with that information. If Jackson was to be believed (and I did believe him—I had decided that I had to trust somebody), Anna had been acting strangely enough to justify those suspicions and more.

I hadn't figured out what I would do if Lucy confronted me about Sunny Martin. I hadn't even worked out how I was actually going to *sell* Sunny Martin's book with or without Lucy knowing about it. All I knew was that I wanted to sell it. That book was *mine*. The last thing I wanted to do was to give it to Lucy.

I rolled over on the bed and faced the door. My laptop sat on a tiny desk, plugged in and wired into the phone jack, awaiting e-mail messages. The screen threw an eerie blue light onto my suitcase, which looked like it had exploded, spewing paper and clothing everywhere. Keeping Lucy organized required the constant pulling out and reordering of my own things. Taking the time to make neat piles had not been a priority. *Balsamic Moon* sat on the floor next to my copy of *Thaw*. I'd read all of those pages as well, and they were every bit as bad as Lucy had said they were, but I had ideas about how Karanuk could fix them. Despite the scattered story and disconnected paragraphs, Karanuk's prose still held grains of the genius that had made *Cold!* great. I knew I could work with that and I knew Karanuk could work with me. Maybe that was the answer, I thought. I'd try to trade my work with Karanuk and *Blind Submission* for a shot with *Balsamic Moon*.

But, no, she'd never go for it.

After all she'd done for him, Karanuk would never take me over Lucy in any way. And while it wouldn't be as good, *Blind Submission* could probably survive without me. It was likelier that Lucy would just fire me. No, she wouldn't do that, either. If the last few days had taught me anything, it was that I was valuable to Lucy. Not *in*valuable, mind you. Nobody is ever invaluable. But I was valuable enough not to fire if she didn't have to. She'd rather try to make me so miserable that I'd want to quit, and if I quit I'd have to pay back all the money she'd given me in that hellish contract I now knew I never should have signed. And I couldn't afford to do that. So I couldn't quit and she wouldn't fire me. In all scenarios, Lucy came out ahead.

I thought if I could get up and tidy some of the mess in my room, it might help me to gain some clarity, but I was just so tired. It occurred to me that the hollow feeling in the center of my being was probably due to hunger and that I should eat something. I decided I would order room service as soon as I checked my messages. I reached over to the bedside table for my cell phone and dialed my home number first. There was one message:

"Hi, Angel, it's Elise. You never called me back. Are you okay? Have you been eaten by wolves? Or should I say *wolf*? I tried you at work, but that weirdo who answered the phone wouldn't tell me where you were. Listen, Angel, I've been doing a lot of thinking and planning and, well, you always knew that I wouldn't be able to stay out of the book business, didn't you? Anyway, I've decided to go for it again. I want to reopen Blue Moon but"—there was a long sigh—"smaller, more upscale. More, I don't know, geared to a specialty market, although I don't know what that is. I'm still thinking. But the thing is, I was wondering if you'd be interested in putting this together with me. I couldn't afford— I don't know how much you're making now, Angel, but I'd love to have you with me on this. Think about it. I miss it, Angel. And I miss you! I'm going on and on here, listen to me, I'm going to fill up all the room on your machine. Please call me when you can, okay? And I've *still* got something I want to show you. I won't tell you what it is—I'll leave it a surprise, okay? You'll find it very interesting, I can tell you that. Call me! Bye, Angel."

I listened to the message one more time and then erased it. I was in no state to think clearly about what Elise was offering. Part of me was thrilled that she was going back to bookselling, but another part of me was frustrated that she was doing it *now* and offering me an opportunity that I would have jumped at only a few months ago. I missed her as well, but in the way you'd miss a halcyon period in childhood you know you can never return to. The truth was, no matter how difficult it was to deal with Lucy, one day in her office was more exciting than all my years at Blue Moon combined, and I'd become addicted to that rush. I knew that going back to what I'd been doing before I started working for Lucy would feel like a huge letdown. I'd need some kind of rehab to get back to normal—although, now, I wasn't even sure what "normal" was.

Despite this ambivalence, I decided to consider Elise's offer anyway. It was reassuring to know that I could still count on her, and if my behind-the-scenes maneuverings blew up in my face, I knew she would help me pick up the pieces. I made a note to call her as soon as I got home.

I closed up my phone and laid it down on the bedside table. I felt sweaty and covered with grime. What I really needed was a shower, I thought. At least that was one thing that was easily done. With great effort, I lifted myself from the bed, pulled back the cover so that the clean sheets were exposed, and stripped off my clothes. I was almost there, almost under the hot running water, when I heard a knock at my door. Lucy. She'd found something else for me to do or had suddenly decided I needed to come with her to hold up the hem of her dress while she mingled. Typically, she'd found the most inconvenient moment to come looking for me. I grabbed a towel from the bathroom and wrapped it around my body as best I could.

"Lucy?" I said, placing one hand on the door handle. I hoped I sounded as exhausted and unable to muster enthusiasm as I felt.

"Angel? Is that you?"

My heart leaped into my throat. I'd heard and read that phrase so many times, but I'd never really understood it—never truly felt it—until that moment, when I realized that it was Damiano on the other side.

I pulled the door open and the towel fell to the floor. I froze, unable to make any kind of move to pick it up. Damiano walked in and closed the door behind him, and I stood in front of him completely naked. For a long moment, he just stared at me and said nothing. When I raised my eyes to meet his, I saw them shining with frank admiration and desire. But there was so much more behind that. There was empathy, the whisper of sadness, and deep longing. It was as if I were looking into my own heart. It was Damiano I needed. Of course.

He moved toward me until we were almost touching, then stopped. Without taking his dark eyes off mine, he reached out his right hand and slowly traced the curve of my hip as if he were carving it out of soft clay. He moved his left hand up to cup the side of my face and drew me close enough for me to feel his breath on my lips. We stood like that for a small eternity, his hands warm on my skin, the moment before the kiss suspended in anticipation between us. I wanted to stay like that forever and I wanted to grab him and pull him into me. My tension turned to trembling and I felt myself start shaking.

"*Angelina mia,*" Damiano whispered. He put both arms around me and held me tight. He kissed me, his lips light and soft, savoring the taste. I pressed against him, opening my mouth to his, my hands moving wild across his back and arms in a frenzy of exploration. I pulled at his shirt, desperate to feel the smoothness of his skin beneath it. Our arms tangled, our mouths pressed together hard. He lifted me as if I were weightless and carried me to the bed. He tripped, stumbled, and we both fell heavily onto the sheets. He landed on my hair and pulled it out from under him. Something that sounded like a curse fell from his mouth and I laughed. He sat up, yanked off his shoes, and started fumbling with the buttons and buckles on his clothes.

"*Vieni qua,*" he said, pulling me up. "Help me."

I reached around him and lifted his shirt over his head as he managed to free himself from his jeans. There was a moment of awkwardness then, the hesitation that falls between new lovers when they see each other naked for the first time. But he leaned over, softly kissed the racing pulse in the hollow of my throat, and suddenly the entire room seemed to ignite.

Sensation took over, pushing every thought out of my head. I felt myself give way to the weight of his body on mine, felt the softness of his skin and the taut muscles beneath it. I felt my body rise up to meet his lips wherever they touched me—on my thighs, breasts, and belly. I felt myself open and heard myself sigh with satisfaction. I felt Damiano's breath in my ear, heard him whisper, "*Che ricco,*" tasted the salt of his sweat as it mingled with my own. I closed my eyes, using my fingertips and tongue to see. I felt him deep inside me and I lost myself there, buoyed up and away on a long swell of pleasure that went on and on and on.

The room was dark when I opened my eyes again. I couldn't see any sky at all through the narrow space between the drapes, just the reflection of artificial light against the buildings. Damiano lay melded to me, his arms fastened around me. I blinked my eyes to adjust to the dimness and realized that I was covered in sweat and that the sheets and pillows felt damp. Damiano's back was slick and wet under my hands. His breathing was soft and even against my chest, so slow that I thought he'd fallen asleep. I moved my arm, which was pinned under his shoulder, and he raised his head and kissed my mouth.

"Thank you," he said. He traced one finger along my eyebrow, down my cheekbone, and to my lips. "You are so beautiful," he said. "Here." He stroked the inside of my thigh. "Here." He rested his hand on the skin of my abdomen. "And here." He laid his hand gently on my forehead.

"I don't . . ." I began, and had to clear my throat of all the passion that had accumulated there since I'd last spoken. "I don't usually open the door stark naked for men who come knocking."

Damiano laughed, sending a merry echo through the room. "But it was very convenient," he said. "Thank you for that also. I've never been greeted in such a way. I think it is something I'll remember for my whole life."

"I was going to take a shower," I said. "I thought you were Lucy."

"You can still take a shower," he said. "But not yet. Please don't go away from me yet. I have . . . ahh, *Angelina* . . ." He sighed and kissed me again. "I was wondering . . . I didn't know if you would be pleased to see me. The last time, you were so strange. I thought maybe I did something wrong or said something. I don't know. But . . ."

"But?"

"I knew we would be here before I saw you for the first time. I felt you inside me, Angel. Didn't you know, too?"

If I could have spoken, I would have told him that I did, but my lips were trembling too much for me to get the words out. I had started crying, without even knowing why, and the tears were coming fast, spilling down the sides of my face and wetting my hair. I tried to stop, tried to strangle the sobs that were forming inside my chest, but that only made them come harder.

"No, no," Damiano said. He brushed my cheeks with his fingers. "*Non piànge.* What did I say? Why are you crying?"

"I d-don't kn-know," I said. "I'm s-sorry."

"No, no," he said. "Shh. Don't be sorry."

He wrapped me in his arms again, whispering words I couldn't understand into my hair. He stroked my back and my shoulders. And then he leaned over me and kissed the tears off my face.

"*Angelina,*" he whispered. "You see? I drink your tears. Don't cry."

I thought that if I had to die right then, wrapped in his arms, his lips on my cheek, I'd die happy.

I must have fallen asleep, although it couldn't have been for long, because when I opened my eyes again, the lights were on and Damiano was propped up against the pillows next to me, smiling down at me.

"I wanted to look at you," he said. "You are so beautiful, I can't believe it."

I smiled back at him.

"Are you okay?" he asked.

"Yes," I said, and reached out for him, pulling him close to me again.

"I want to make love with you, Angel," he said, "here in this room. Again and again."

I rolled on top of him and stared down into his wine-brown eyes. They were alive with desire. *For me.* "I think I can help you with that," I said, and placed my hands on either side of his head, feeling the bristly ends of his hair under my fingertips. "But first tell me, how did you know I was here? Why are you in New York?" I wanted—no, I *needed*—him to tell me that he couldn't stop thinking about me, that his desire for me had driven him to search me out, to drop everything and cross the country to find me.

"I spoke to Luciana," he said. "She told me the hotel."

"*Lucy?*"

"*Sì.* What's the matter?"

I slid off him and sat up. Out of some belated and now-unnecessary sense of modesty, I drew the sheets up around my waist. "Why would *Lucy* tell you where I was?"

"She told me where *she* was going to be. But I knew you were with her, Angel. I was there at the famous dinner party, remember?" Damiano was looking up at me with a bemused expression, as if he couldn't understand why any of this would be of concern to me. He lifted a strand of my hair and stroked it between his thumb and forefinger. "That was the first time I saw this beautiful hair all free like fire."

"I still don't really understand, Damiano. You called Lucy to ask her where we were staying in New York? Didn't she wonder why you wanted to know?"

"*Bella,*" he said patiently, and raised himself so that we were sitting side by side on the bed. "I didn't call Lucia— Lucy. She called me a week . . . maybe two weeks ago. She told me she was coming to New York. She said it would be a good idea for me to come as well. She said for me to meet my editor? *Capisce,* no? I thought you would know about this. She ask if I can get a ticket to New York and of course I can. We made a meeting with my editor for the day after tomorrow and today I am here with you."

The day after tomorrow—Lucy's extra day in New York. Without me. I'd wondered why Damiano's editor hadn't been on Lucy's list of appointments when I'd scheduled this trip for her, and I'd even asked Lucy about it. "No need," she'd said at the time, and now it made sense.

"I'm going home tomorrow," I said.

"Yes, I know," he said, "that's why I came early." He shrugged as if all of this should be totally obvious to me and started pulling me gently toward him, his eyes sparkling with undisguised lust. "*Ècco. Vieni qua,* Angel. Come here, *amore.*"

"Wait," I said, instinctively moving away from him until I was on the far corner of the bed. There was something about this scenario that was starting to feel frighteningly wrong, some sense that I'd been expertly manipulated into being the butt of an elaborate and cruel practical joke. "How did you know what *room* I was in? Did Lucy tell you that, too?"

"No, no, of course not. I spoke to Anna. She was very sweet. She told me where you were."

"*Anna knows?*"

He missed the alarm in my voice and went on, a smile curving the corners of his mouth. "Don't worry," he said. "I came in very quiet," he said, and chuckled. He lowered his voice to a conspiratorial stage whisper. "Nobody saw me, I promise. I wore dark glasses." He laughed again. "Like a rock star."

"Like Vaughn Blue," I said. My voice sounded distant and hollow, as if it were coming from across the room.

"*Che?*" A worried and ever so slightly annoyed expression passed across Damiano's face and was replaced by renewed desire. He moved over to my side of the bed. "Ahh," he breathed, "so beautiful." He cupped my breasts in both of his hands, leaned over, and formed a kiss on my angel-wing tattoo.

I leaped off the bed, pulling the sheet with me and wrapping it tightly around my nakedness. I backed up as far from him as I could get until I was pressed against the window.

"Why are you over there, Angel? What are you doing?"

I stared at him and tried with all the powers of reasoning I had left to convince myself that I was in the middle of a bad dream. *Who was this man?* He'd become a complete stranger in a matter of seconds. No, he'd been a stranger all along. I knew his words on a page—I didn't know *him* at all. But he knew me, didn't he? Knew just what I'd do, how I'd be, what I wanted, and he *had kissed my tattoo.* He knew everything. It was worse than a bad dream, I decided—it was a bad dream that belonged to *someone else.*

"Angel?"

"I think you should go." I sounded weak and slightly hysterical. In the remote corner of my brain that wasn't full of frightened confusion, it occurred to me that I'd just delivered one of those lines that only works in the movies.

"What? Why? *Che cosa c'é?*"

"I . . . my . . ." I raised my hand to my right breast, instinctively covering my tattoo. "You knew about this. How did you know?"

"Know? I don't understand. Excuse me . . . Angel?"

"Can you just— Can you *please leave?*" The note of hysteria in my voice had sharpened.

Damiano searched my eyes with his. His face went from light to dark with surprise, confusion, disbelief, and finally something that looked like a kind of sad acceptance. He shook his head slightly and started to speak again, but caught himself and closed his mouth, compressing it into a tight line. He got up, more gracefully than I would have expected under the circumstances, picked up his clothes from the floor, and put them on in less than a minute.

He was at the door, one hand on the handle, before he turned to me again. "Angel?" I shook my head, tightening my grip on the sheet, and looked away. *"Mi dispiace,"* he said, and then he was gone.

I waited, suspended, for what could have been seconds or minutes and listened to the sounds of voices and traffic coming from outside the window. The room had gone cold and I was shivering. It was suddenly essential that I be clothed. I didn't want to look at my own naked, traitorous body for another second. I walked over to my suitcase, dragging the sheet with me, and saw that I had an e-mail message waiting on my computer. I was going to wait—to get dressed and read it afterward—but then I saw who had sent it.

To: angel.robinson@fiammalit.com
From: ganovelist@heya.com
Subject: Alice

My dear Ms. Robinson,

A quick question for you.

I've just realized that since Alice's steamy encounter with Vaughn early on, we haven't seen much of the two of them together in the flesh as it were. I'm wondering if I shouldn't write in a quick scene of Alice and her stud getting down and dirty in their favorite hotel (which, incidentally, is the Whitman on East 54th Street—is it a problem if I use the real name of the hotel in my manuscript? I thought it had a nice literary feel to it). What do you think? Personally, I believe it would add a little heat. Sex sells, doesn't it? And the two of them could be very, very hot together, no? But you're the boss—I'll only add it in if you think it would be a good idea.

Looking forward,
G.

I looked from my laptop to the small hotel pad and pen next to it. The curling script on each said *Whitman Hotel.* He knew where I was.

He was watching me.

I stood over the computer, my body paralyzed by fear but my mind alive and swarming with wild thoughts. I had been such a fool to believe, even for a second, that Damiano was involved in *Blind Submission* in any way. My paranoia was justified—the e-mail was hard evidence of that—but I'd made the terrible mistake of directing it at the wrong person. I'd kicked Damiano out, a move as cold as anything Alice could have come up with, after he'd given me so much, and now he was gone. I'd become so unbalanced by this novel that I could no longer tell what was real and what was fiction. I was Alice, all right, and I'd gone right through the looking glass. But my feelings for Damiano had to be genuine. I hadn't dreamed what had happened between us. I'd had him and lost him in the space of an hour and now I didn't know if I'd ever get him back. He was probably thinking about what a mistake *he'd* made at this very moment. And all of this was because of a book—*Malcolm's* book. Of course Malcolm would know where I was. Anna had seen fit to share all those details with Damiano, hadn't she? It would make perfect sense that she'd shared them with Malcolm as well. Like me, Damiano had just been a pawn in the game Malcolm was playing. The game he'd been playing with Anna's help. Anna, who had been sitting at my desk, going through my things, talking to someone named Malcolm on the phone . . .

Was it possible that Malcolm and Anna were working on this thing *together*?

I looked at the clock and subtracted three hours. It was only five o'clock on the West Coast. Everyone should still be in the office.

To: jackson.stark@fiammalit.com
From: angel.robinson@fiammalit.com
Subject: <no subject>

J—

Are you still in the office? Is Anna? What is she doing? Need to know.

A.

While I waited for Jackson's answer, I tried to figure out what I should write back to G. It was clear that I was *supposed* to respond in some way, but I didn't want to risk playing into whatever scenario G was setting up for me next. I didn't have time to get very far, though, because Jackson's response came over within minutes.

To: angel.robinson@fiammalit.com
From: jackson.stark@fiammalit.com
Subject: Re: <no subject>

Hi A—

I'm here, but Anna's gone. She left work early (a couple of hours ago, maybe?)—said she was feeling sick. Why? What's up? What do you need?

J.

Anna hadn't missed a day of work since I'd started and had never taken off early. Feeling sick, was she? If my not-so-far-fetched suspicions were true, she really *was* sick. I didn't take the time to write back to Jackson, reaching instead for my cell phone and dialing the office number.

"Lucy Fiamma Agency, this is Jackson."

"Jackson, hi, it's Angel. Just act like I'm calling about a submission, okay?"

"I'm sorry, she's unavailable at the moment. May I help you with something?" He was good. I felt a small twinge of relief that I hadn't dismissed his intelligence before it was too late.

"I need Damiano Vero's cell-phone number. Can you get that for me?"

"Yes, we'd be happy to look at it," he said. "Anything else I can help you with?"

"That's it for now. Thanks, Jackson."

"No problem," he said.

"I'll fill you in later," I said. "I know you're wondering. . . . Anyway, I'll be back in the office soon and we can talk then."

"Well, we'll look forward to reading that," he said, and as he spoke, an e-mail message from him containing Damiano's phone number appeared on my computer screen.

"Got it," I said. "Thanks again."

As soon as I'd hung up with Jackson, I dialed Damiano's number. I was desperate to find him. I needed to explain everything to him, which I should have done before I threw him out. I had to tell him how sorry I was and beg him to come back. My heart was beating so hard as I dialed the numbers that the phone vibrated in my hand. His name was on my lips, ready to fall, when an automated operator came on the line informing me that the wireless customer I was trying to reach was out of the area. Damiano was gone—just gone—and I was the one who had sent him away.

For the second time that night, my eyes spilled over with tears. But this time the tears were angry ones. I'd been feeling so sorry for myself, as if I'd been the victim of some master manipulation. But what had really happened was that I'd allowed myself to become a character in somebody else's story. The realization that I'd been facilitating it all along made me furious with myself. It might be too late to save what I could have had with Damiano, I thought, but this—I turned back to my computer— I could still control.

It was time to smoke out the author of *Blind Submission*.

To: ganovelist@heya.com
From: angel.robinson@fiammalit.com
Subject: Re: Alice

G—

I don't want to play anymore. I'm done. I've discussed it with Lucy and she agrees. She'll be in touch to let you know how we proceed from here.

Angel

I sat in front of my computer and waited. I didn't know exactly who G was, it was true, but in a strange sense I *knew* G—the entity behind *Blind Submission*—quite well. I knew what kind of notes to give him and how he'd respond to them. Editorially, at least, I knew what he wanted from me—and that was for me to keep going. He liked our little arrangement very well. I sent the e-mail because I knew G would be quite disturbed by the thought that I was quitting *Blind Submission* and would quickly write back to me with some kind of concession or maybe an apology for going too far. Either way, my e-mail would get to him enough for him to reveal himself—I hoped. I was taking a risk, of course. It was possible that he'd contact Lucy himself and tell her and then I'd have to answer for it, but I didn't think he would. G needed me.

When there was no response after a half hour, I got up, put on a pair of pants and a sweater, and sat back down again. After another half hour of staring at the screen, I picked up the hotel phone and ordered a sandwich from room service. It took forty-five minutes to be delivered and twenty for me to eat it and place the tray outside my door. Still there was no response from G. I sat, and then lay down on the bed. I could smell Damiano on the sheets and I buried my face in the pillow to breathe what might be the last of him into my body. I wasn't even aware of falling asleep until the hotel phone rang at midnight, jolting me out of unconsciousness. I was still half in a dream when I picked it up.

"He-hello?"

"Angel! Are you awake?" Lucy's voice shredded the remnants of my sleep and pulled me into full, glaring alertness.

"Um, I am now."

"Good! What's on tomorrow's schedule?"

"Well, you've got . . . um . . ." I couldn't remember the details of her day, and I started to slide off the bed to pull out my copy of her schedule when she stopped me.

"I need you to rearrange my morning, Angel. I want you to move all my appointments to the afternoon."

"But I can't do that, Lucy. It's too late to call—"

"You'll find a way, Angel—you're a bright girl and this isn't rocket science."

I sighed into the phone. It was senseless to argue with her. "Okay," I said. "And is there something you'd like me to schedule instead?" Like a meeting with the mayor, I thought, or something equally impossible.

"We're taking a spa morning, Angel! Hair, nails, the works!"

"What?"

"It just occurred to me that tomorrow is your last day here in Gotham and I promised to get you made over when we arrived. So voilà, Angel, I'm true to my word."

I was sure that, like all of Lucy's "generous" gestures, this one had a catch buried in it, but she sounded genuinely excited at the prospect of taking me with her to a salon and I was too unstrung to try to figure out why.

"Okay," I said. "Great. I'll see you in the morning, then."

Lucy hung up without saying good-bye, something I'd gotten used to from her. It saved time and skipped over any finality. If she hadn't said good-bye, she was still present in some form and one would have to stay at the ready, waiting for the next command. I placed the receiver back in its cradle and got out of bed. The wise thing to do now was to leave messages for the editors Lucy would now not be seeing in the morning, but instead of reaching for the schedule, I sat down once more in front of my laptop. It was still on and plugged into the phone line.

There were no new e-mails waiting for me.

FOURTEEN

MY FLIGHT ARRIVED in San Francisco so late it went over into the next day. By the time I got out of the airport, through the city, and on the road to my apartment, it was close to five o'clock in the morning. I'd been able to sleep a little on the plane, but that only served to stave off total exhaustion. What I really needed was a long night in my own bed. I was so tired I didn't know if I could even stay awake for the long drive home. If you counted the time change, I was twenty-four hours into what had become an endless day.

It had started, as so many of my days now did, with Lucy. After obsessively checking my e-mail only to find my in-box empty and G now apparently playing possum, I collected Lucy, who actually sprang for a taxi to take us to one of New York's finest salons.

"This is where I always come when I'm in the Big Apple," Lucy told me. "They are beyond fabulous here. I've pulled quite a few strings to get you in as well. What they do here is *better* than plastic surgery. You won't believe it. You're going to be *transformed*, Angel Robinson!"

"What am I transforming exactly, Lucy?" I softened my question with a bright smile, but I was starting to get a very uneasy feeling about Lucy's plans for our spa day.

"Well, among other things, your hair," Lucy said.

"What's wrong with my hair?"

"The *color,* for one thing. You shouldn't *be* a redhead in the first place, Angel, that's the problem right there. And the length is an entirely different issue. Mature women don't have long hair, Angel, it's a rule."

I had a painful flashback to Damiano and how he'd run his hands through my hair, how genuinely he'd admired it and how beautiful he'd made it seem. Lucy saw the memory reflected in my face and gave it an entirely different interpretation.

"Don't worry about how to style it, Angel. I've instructed them to cut your hair like mine. This is a brilliant cut and very versatile. And I think my color—well, maybe a shade or two darker—would be *perfect* for you."

That was when I decided that our bizarre girlfriend-bonding moment was over.

"That's extremely generous of you, Lucy," I said, "but I'm kind of attached to my hair the way it is."

"You're not *serious*?" she asked. "If it's the cost you're worried about, don't—I'm buying. Now, let's go, shall we?"

"No, really, Lucy, I don't want to color my hair. I'm not going to color my hair. Or cut it."

She gave me a long look, her irises bright green against her pale skin. "You don't want to look like me, is that it?"

"No, that's not it. I just . . ." I didn't know what to say. Her eyes were begging me to tell her that I would love nothing more than to look exactly like her and that I was overwhelmed with gratitude. I sensed that anything less would actually wound her. But I couldn't find it in myself to give her what she wanted. "I just don't think it would suit me," I said.

"That's where you're wrong," she said. "You don't know what suits you. That's why you look the way you do. I thought I could help you with that, but clearly I'm mistaken."

"I'm sorry, Lucy, I didn't mean—"

The daggers flying from Lucy's eyes cut me off mid-sentence. She moved away from me and toward the salon. I followed her, preparing to go in with her, but she put her arm out to stop me.

"We're done for the day, Angel. You're on your own. Make sure you don't miss your flight."

This, I realized, was Lucy's way of showing that she was hurt.

I stood bewildered on the street for a minute after that, wondering what she expected me to do. Was I supposed to follow her? Apologize? For a second, I toyed with the idea of doing just that. But a second was all it took to realize that I was actually *free* of her for the first time in days, released from servitude and able to go wherever I wanted. I hailed my own cab and went to the hotel. I was going to pick up my things and then I was headed directly to the airport. Because the only place I wanted to go was home.

DAWN WAS BREAKING as I dragged my suitcase up the stairs to my apartment. I'd never craved the comfort of my own bed with such a single-minded intensity. It was all I could think about as I dropped my bags, locked the door behind me, and fell down onto my covers.

Something was wrong.

I sat up and looked around my apartment. All the objects around me were still, familiar, the way I had left them. But there was something different in the air. I got the distinct feeling that things had been moved and then put back in their place. There was a just-settled feeling all around me, a displacement of ions, a faint odor I couldn't place—as if someone had been there very recently. I got up and flipped on the light, although the sun was starting to filter through the window. The feeling of intrusion got stronger even as I failed to find anything that would confirm it. My unrinsed coffee mug was exactly where I had left it in the kitchen. The piles of papers and manuscripts next to my bed were in exactly the same state of disarray. The sink in my bathroom was dry. My bed was made, exactly the way I'd left it. Had I made my bed before I'd left? I searched my memory for the details of that morning and couldn't find them. I'd always been inconsistent about making my bed in the morning, leaving it rumpled half the time when I couldn't be bothered. I grabbed the covers and threw them back, expecting I didn't know what to jump out at me, but of course there was nothing there except the sheets and pillows.

I was very tired, I told myself. This was a reasonable explanation for why I was suddenly so paranoid. Sleep deprivation was the quickest way to get to hallucinating twitchiness. But I'd operated just fine on less sleep. I'd only started feeling this pervasive sense of intrusion since *Blind Submission*.

It took only a minute to pull my laptop from its bag and power it up. There was one e-mail waiting for me. From G.

To: angel.robinson@fiammalit.com
From: ganovelist@heya.com
Subject: An excerpt

Dear Ms. R—

I find myself with an excerpt and I'm looking for a place to insert it. Ideas?

Cheers,
G.

Alice's bed was her sanctuary. She loved the feel of rich cotton sheets and plump down. She took her bedding very seriously. She'd read somewhere that Jackie Onassis had said that people with real wealth and taste only used pure white cotton sheets and Alice had never forgotten it. It had been difficult, in the early days, to provide herself with a bed, let alone white cotton sheets, but as soon as Alice had the means, she'd gone shopping for linens of gradually increasing thread counts.

It wasn't easy to keep such high-quality sheets looking good. They had a tendency to wrinkle at that level. But Alice was willing to sacrifice for her luxury. She ironed her sheets with steam, focused to the point of meditation, until every wrinkle vanished from their surfaces. Then she took great care to lay them on the bed and tuck them in tightly. It was then that Alice could slide herself between those tight, soft sheets of white. In this, Alice's bed resembled nothing so much as a book. The bed-sheets became clean white sheets of paper that she slid herself between, insinuated herself against. And Alice became the text written upon them.

Soft white sheets for her hard dark thoughts.

I looked over at my bed, at my white down comforter and my white five-hundred-thread-count cotton sheets that, until this moment, I had been dying to lie down on and I started to cry.

He was gaslighting me and it was working.

Blind Submission was starting to make me crazy just as Alice was becoming crazy in it.

It was time to tell Lucy. She'd read the manuscript and she'd seen my notes, but she had no idea of the extent of G's personal game with me. I'd kept it from her out of . . . what? Pride? The illusion that I could control both the book and its author? Or was it fear? Fear that Malcolm, my bitter ex-boyfriend, was the real author. It was time to come clean— to tell her about Malcolm and to fill her in on my suspicions about Anna. I didn't know exactly how I was going to do this, but I had a little time to plan it out. By the time she got back from New York, I'd be ready.

I realized that my telephone was ringing. Damiano! I'd tried his cell phone at least a dozen times over the last day and got the same out-of-area message every time. I lunged for the phone, catching it before it had a chance to go to voice mail.

"Hello?" I sounded, both breathless and anxious.

"Angel? It's Jackson." He was whispering.

I checked the time. It was 8:15 A.M.

"Jackson, what is it? What's the matter?"

"Are you coming in?" he asked.

"I just got in," I said. "My plane was delayed. I was going to come in later. . . ."

"I think you should come in now," he said.

"What's the hurry?" I asked. "What's going on?"

"Lucy's about to have a staff meeting. I've only got a second here—Craig's in the bathroom. But Anna's in there already, Angel. She told Lucy that you're not coming in and she's—"

"But how can Lucy have a staff meeting?" I said stupidly. "She's still in New York."

"She's not in New York, she's here."

"But she's staying an extra day—today—in New York. She's not coming home until tonight." *So she can take Damiano to meet his editor and whatever else she's planning to do with him,* I added to myself.

"No," Jackson said insistently. "She's here. And Julia Swann came in with a preemptive offer for the *Elvis* book and Lucy's looking to maybe have some kind of mini auction for it. Didn't you know that?"

"*Today?* But Julia Swann said— I thought she wasn't even going to offer on it. How can Lucy have an auction *today?*"

"I don't know, Angel, but she's going to. I thought you knew. Lucy was expecting you to be here. There's a note on your desk from her."

"What does it say?"

"Angel, I have to go. I'll tell her you're on your way."

How was it possible that Lucy was back in the office when I'd barely landed myself? And where was Damiano?

THE OUTER OFFICE WAS EMPTY when I walked in a half hour later. I could hear voices coming from Lucy's office and assumed the staff meeting was already in progress. I dropped my purse and manuscripts next to my chair and was overwhelmingly relieved to see my angelfish alive and swimming in its bowl. There was a yellow sticky note stuck to the side. *Welcome back,* it said in Jackson's handwriting. Lucy's note sat next to it, waiting for me on my desk. I grabbed it and scanned it as I headed toward her office.

Angel—

Today's top priorities:

1. *Get "Elvis" author on the phone asap—we need to discuss her new direction with her novel!*

2. *Karanuk—see me!!!*

3. *My NY notes are on your desk—please sort!*

4. *What is going on with Blind Submission?!?!*

5. *Prepare list and status of all option books!*

—LF

I was trying to figure out where she'd found the time to even think about the items on the list, let alone organize them as tasks for me, when I walked into her office and saw all eyes in the room immediately turn to me.

"Well," Lucy said, "glad you could join us, Angel. Anna said that you were ill, which I found difficult to believe since I just saw you yesterday and you were fine." Lucy delivered this statement with her usual crispness but didn't seem at all annoyed. She looked well rested and surprisingly chic in a black pin-striped pantsuit. Her hair, a white mist around her head, looked exactly the same as it had the day before.

"That's interesting," I said, shooting quick daggers at Anna, "because I never said any such thing."

"Um, well, I guess I just assumed," Anna said. There was something different about Anna, and it took me a second or two to figure out that she was wearing makeup—too much of it, in fact, and she'd chosen exactly the wrong color (powder blue) to layer on her eyelids. She'd used some kind of greasy product to slick back her hair and was squashed into a pair of khaki overalls. I had no idea what kind of look she was going for, but whatever it was, it wasn't working. She looked like painted lunch meat wedged between Craig and Jackson on Lucy's couch.

"As fascinating as the semantics of your conversation are, Anna, there is business at hand," Lucy said. "Do I need to reiterate that we are extremely short on time today?" Anna's face flushed and she looked down at the floor. Craig, who seemed more sallow and shapeless than usual, was staring intently at the pad of paper on his knees, and Jackson simply looked relieved to see me. I sat down in the only available chair, which happened to be right next to Lucy.

"Weren't you planning to stay in New York today, Lucy?" I said.

Lucy raised her eyebrows and gave me a half-smile. "My plans changed," she said. "If that's all right with you, Angel?"

"I was just wondering," I said, "because—"

"In fact, I was due to meet with an author," Lucy interrupted. "Your Italian man." She gave me one of her laserlike stares. I felt my heart flip and beat erratically against my chest. I couldn't control the flush I could feel spreading to the roots of my hair. I looked down at my notepad in a weak effort to conceal it.

"Damiano Vero," Anna squeaked from her position on the couch.

"Yes," Lucy said. "Damiano Vero. But he never showed up. Which is either the height of disrespect or an indication that something's happened to him."

"But how . . . ?" I began. My overtired brain was trying to work out how Lucy could have been in New York waiting for Damiano a couple of hours ago and be sitting here now. I scrambled for options, but the only ones I came up with were witchcraft and time travel. "Weren't you meeting with him *today*?" I asked before I realized that I wasn't supposed to know anything about their meeting at all.

"Actually," Lucy said, plucking a speck of lint off her pants, "we were supposed to meet for drinks yesterday." She shrugged dramatically. "I gave him an hour and a half. I think that's plenty of time. It was obvious that he wasn't going to make an appearance. I'm assuming he didn't contact you, Angel?"

"Um . . . no." I didn't have to see my face to know that it was beet red.

"Heeey," Anna said, as if something important had just occurred to her. "Didn't you talk to him the other night, Angel?"

I was a deer stuck in headlights and couldn't speak, couldn't move away from the oncoming impact. A look of genuine surprise spread slowly across Lucy's face, and behind that I thought I detected a glimmer of satisfaction. I needed to say something, but my words were frozen and unyielding in my throat.

"What's this?" Lucy asked.

I could actually see Anna puffing herself up like a hideous popover. Clearly, she'd been waiting a long time for this moment. "He called here the other day looking for Angel. He wanted to know what room she was staying in. In New York. I thought he had, you know, a meeting or something." Anna gave Lucy a big fat grin. I wanted to kill her—put my hands around her doughy neck and squeeze until she choked. "Did I do the wrong thing?" Anna said sweetly.

"Did you talk to him, Angel?" There was an echo in Lucy's voice, as if she were speaking to me through a tunnel. I couldn't focus. My heart was beating so hard, my vision was jumpy and blurred.

I cleared my throat and with all the self-control I could muster, I said, "No. I haven't spoken to Damiano Vero for weeks."

"Really," Lucy said. "Well, I can't imagine what happened to him."

"Isn't he, like, a heroin addict or something?" Anna said. "Maybe he, you know . . ." Every one of us turned to Anna then, our faces showing varying degrees of surprise and disgust. Anna sensed that she'd taken her little riff too far and her color rose slightly. "I'm just saying—" she started, but Lucy finally cut her off.

"Find him, Angel," Lucy said. There was firmness and finality in her tone. "But not now. Right now we need to discuss the *Elvis* book. You saw my note? Have you spoken to the author yet?"

"Not yet, no. I haven't had a chance."

"Well, that might be better, actually, although I can't imagine what you have to do that would be more important. The point is this: Julia Swann is very interested in this project. She's offering us a one-hundred-and-twenty-thousand-dollar preempt." Lucy took a dramatic pause and tapped her Waterman pen on her knee.

"That is so great," Anna interjected.

"I thought Julia said that she wasn't likely to get a book like this past her board," I said. "What happened to change that?" I was flooded with relief that we were off the topic of Damiano, and intended to keep steering the conversation away from any other verbal land mines.

"*I* happened," Lucy said. "I see you were paying attention, Angel, but not closely enough. This book has certain elements that are irresistible to Julia Swann and to Long, Greene, and they want it badly enough to offer us a lot of money."

"But what elements?" I pressed.

"Poker," Lucy said.

"*Poker?*"

Lucy sighed as if my question was very tiring to her. "Yes, Angel, poker. And if it's Texas No Limit Hold 'Em poker, that's even better. I don't remember if that's the specific game she's writing about."

"That's because she wasn't writing about poker at all. It's a literary relationship story about modern love, trust, and marriage set against the backdrop of Las Vegas. It's about a road trip. It has nothing to do with poker."

Lucy looked at me, and perhaps it was some trick of light in the room, but I could swear her eyes were twinkling. Her mouth, however, remained set and determined.

"It does now," she said.

"So that's the new direction you want me to discuss with the author?" I said after a pause.

"Exactly," Lucy said.

"But Lucy . . ." I couldn't stop, although I wanted to. After all, it wasn't *my* book, and what did I care if Shelly Franklin rewrote her entire novel to include the game of poker as a central theme? But I couldn't let it go. I didn't particularly care for Shelly Franklin herself and thought she could use both a primer on social skills and a few visits to a good therapist, but I loved her novel and I'd worked very hard to get it in the shape it was in. The thought of dumbing it down and tearing it apart to make it fit the commercial flavor of the moment was revolting to me.

"What if the author doesn't want to take this book in a different direction?" I asked Lucy. I heard the strident note in my own voice and did nothing to soften it.

Lucy waved her hand in the air and smiled. "Please," she said. "Of course she'll *want* to. That's not the concern here. Look, Angel, you know as well as I do that poker is very hot right now. There are plenty of instructional books and collections of fiction, but there isn't really anything out there *like this*. Honestly, do you think this author would rather sell her book to Long, Greene—who, by the way, have plenty of literary cachet if that's what she's after—or some tiny little press with no money to give her and no way to give her book wide distribution? There's a reason she came *here*, Angel."

"I don't know, Lucy, I've been working with her for a while now. I don't know if she can change this book so radically."

Lucy tilted her head to the side and gave me an appraising look. I'd never challenged her this way before and we both seemed to realize it at the same time. What came as a surprise to me, though, was that Lucy didn't seem to mind. In fact, she seemed invigorated by it.

"Well, you'll call her in a minute, Angel, and we'll see, won't we?" Lucy crossed her legs slowly and tucked an errant wisp of hair behind her ear. I noticed that she was wearing a brand-new pair of black alligator pumps that matched the stylish briefcase I'd seen her carry in New York. "But the consideration now," she went on, "is do we accept Julia's preempt or do we take it out and possibly get more? Or possibly less? Julia's advised me that she won't use her offer as a floor, so we'd be starting lower. I've got substantial interest for this book, but you never know how that's going to play out. Especially these days. So which way do we go?"

Lucy's question had a rhetorical flavor, but I answered, anyway. "Shouldn't we ask the author?"

This was, perhaps, one question too many. "Again, Angel, why did she come here? If she could make these decisions for herself, she wouldn't need an agent, would she? She wouldn't need *me*. Does anyone *else* have any thoughts on this? We need to get it settled immediately."

"It would be so cool to have another auction," Anna said. "You're so amazing with those, Lucy."

"Okay," Lucy said. "Any other thoughts?"

"It's a very solid offer from Long, Greene," Craig said. "And I think that if you limit the rights to North America, we could get some decent sales on the foreign side. Then there are the other subsidiary rights. It could do well as an audio book. Then, of course, there are the paperback rights. You could try to work some magic with royalty rates there."

How had Craig gotten this job in the first place? I wondered. He lacked anything resembling a spleen. His little speech was so dull and devoid of passion, he risked boring all of us into a collective coma. Perhaps sensing this, Lucy moved on.

"What about you, Jason? Any thoughts?"

Jackson, clearly unused to being called by a name that wasn't his, hesitated for a moment before answering. I could almost *hear* Lucy's irritation increase.

"Well?" she barked.

"Um . . ." Jackson looked over at me as if for support. "I kind of think Angel's right. Maybe we should ask the author what she wants to do."

"Well, what do *you* know?" Lucy said, dismissing Jackson. "It's after noon in New York. This meeting is over. Let's get to work, people. Angel, you stay here. Get the author on the phone."

Lucy seated herself at her desk as everyone else beat a hasty retreat out of her office. "Use my phone," she said. "And put her on speaker." I punched the numbers and Shelly Franklin picked up after the first ring.

"Hi, Shelly, it's Angel Robinson."

"Hi?"

"I've got Lucy on the phone for you."

"Okay?" On speakerphone, Shelley Franklin's verbal tics were more annoying than usual. The woman was hopeless. There was no way she'd be able to turn *Elvis* into a book about poker. Lucy was in for a surprise and I was going to enjoy it wholeheartedly.

"Hello, dear," Lucy boomed. "We've been working extremely hard for your book. Angel and I have just returned from New York, where we blanketed the landscape with the fruits of your labor." I winced inwardly at Lucy's mixed metaphor. "What do you think of that?"

"Oh?" Shelly giggled nervously. "That's great?"

"So listen, dear, I've got some very exciting news for you. Are you sitting down?"

"Sitting down?"

Lucy looked at me, gestured to the phone, and rolled her eyes. I shrugged. Lucy lifted her hands, palms up, and I nodded my agreement. Just like that, without either of us uttering a word, we'd been able to have an entire conversation.

"We have a lot of interest in your little novel, my dear," Lucy sang into the speaker, "but here's the best part: I have received an offer from Julia Swann, an editor at Long, Greene. I'm assuming you've heard of them?"

There was a long pause before Shelly came back with, "Long, Greene? Oh, yes, I've heard of them. They're . . . that's wonderful!"

"But wait," Lucy said. "The best part is the kind of money they're offering. One hundred and twenty thousand dollars, my dear. That kind of money is almost unheard of in publishing these days. Do you understand what I'm saying?"

"Oh . . ." Shelly said. "Oh, oh, oh . . ." She sounded as if she were swooning.

"Indeed," Lucy said. "But now I want you to listen carefully, all right? We have two options. I can accept the Long, Greene offer right now or you can wait and we take our chances trying to sell it elsewhere. Of course, there are no guarantees that I could get the same kind of money from another publisher. Not to mention the fact that Long, Greene will undoubtedly do a wonderful job of publishing this novel. They are the kind of house that builds their authors. Do you understand what I'm saying? You'd have a future there."

"I want to take their offer," Shelly said without hesitation, the shy, faltering tone completely absent from her voice.

"You don't have to rush into anything," Lucy said. "Although I do have to tell you that I promised Julia Swann I would get back to her today, and well . . . We do have an excellent opportunity here. But would you like to consider the other option and give me a call back?"

"No!" Shelly gasped. "Please call her and tell her that I want to take her offer."

"You're sure?" Lucy asked. She looked up at me and smiled.

"Yes!" Shelly said. "I'm sure. Oh, please call her before she changes her mind."

"I'm thrilled," Lucy said. "Nothing would make me happier. Now listen, dear, there's one thing."

"What? What is it?" Shelly now sounded frantic.

"Julia Swann, who, by the way, is an *excellent* editor, would like you to play up the poker element in your novel. This is very important to her, dear. It's sort of a deal-breaker. Do you think you'll be able to do that?"

"The . . . what? I'm sorry," Shelly said, "I don't think I heard you?" Here it was, I thought, and formed a smile of my own. I doubted Shelly Franklin had ever played the game of poker, let alone considered making it a part of her novel.

"*Poker,*" Lucy said firmly. "The novel needs poker. Texas No Limit Hold 'Em, to be specific." Another long pause on the other end. "Have I lost you?" Lucy said. "Are you already spending your money?" She barked out a laugh. "I do need to call her back, dear, so keep that in mind."

"Okay," Shelly said. "It's no problem. I can do that. I can write about poker."

I felt my heart sink with disappointment and mourned the untimely death of Shelly Franklin's artistic integrity.

"Wonderful," Lucy said. "And really, I think that it's a wonderful new direction to take the novel in. When I speak to Julia, I'll be sure to let her know that you're very excited about it. You're going to love working with her, dear. She's even come up with a fabulous new title. Hold on a second, I have it written down here somewhere." Lucy leaned back in her chair, making no attempt to find anything, written or otherwise, on her desk. After a few seconds had passed she said, "*White Aces and Promises.* That's it. As in 'white lace and promises.' That way you keep the wedding theme."

I heard something that sounded like a stifled groan or a grunt on the other end of the line. Lucy ignored it and went on. "Really, dear, the more I think about it, the more impressed I am with this offer. I hope you know how fortunate you are?"

"Oh yes, yes. I am so very lucky."

"Indeed. Lady Luck has certainly been looking over your shoulder," Lucy said, taking the poker metaphor to its nauseating end.

"Yes, I know, but . . ." Shelly was faltering.

"What is it, my dear?" I noted that Lucy's *my dear* had the same emphasis as *you bitch*.

"I don't . . . I don't know ANYTHING ABOUT POKER!"

Lucy and I both cringed at the sound of Shelly's outburst. What the hell had happened to her? Five seconds before she'd been willing to sell her firstborn for a book deal.

"It's not a difficult game," Lucy said, disgust creeping into her voice. "Just turn on the damn TV and you'll see some tournament on every other channel. Better yet, get a book on the subject."

"But I don't know how to do it. I don't know how to make it a book about poker. I don't know what to dooooo. . . ." Shelly Franklin had started weeping. I was embarrassed for her. Lucy was having a very different reaction.

"You know, my dear, I worked very hard to put this deal together, and as with every deal I make, my reputation is on the line. I didn't sweat my ass off in Manhattan so that you could sit around feeling miserable when a *million talented authors* are out there waiting for me to discover them. So am I to call Julia Swann and accept the offer or am I to tell her that the author has fallen apart and will not be able to write about a game that any eight-year-old can play?"

"Ah, unhh, baa, haaa . . ." Shelly Franklin was falling apart and so was her deal. But I had an idea.

"Shelly?" I said. "Can you hear me?"

"A-A-Angel?"

"Yes. Listen, Shelly, I've been thinking. You know how Michael is hiding his alcoholism from Jennifer and she's hiding her pregnancy? Well, why can't he—or she—also be addicted to gambling—poker, specifically—and then when they get to Las Vegas, of course it all comes out? Michael could leave her to go to a tournament. Or she could leave him and go play. Then he goes to the bar, gets drunk—again—and then they try to hash out their problems, but she's winning and they both get caught up in it. Then you can make poker the central motif. You can have both characters thinking about it all the way to Las Vegas along with all the other things they're keeping from each other. Because—

here's a thought—perhaps they *both* have a secret passion for this game. Can you see it, Shelly?"

There was a crackling silence from the speakerphone. Lucy was staring at me, her eyebrows forming perfect arrows, her lips folded into a thin line.

"I can do that," Shelly said finally. "I can definitely do that."

"So I can call Julia Swann?" Lucy had taken it down several notches now that Shelly was back on the line.

"Yes, I'm so happy," Shelly said. "Please accept. I can do it. I can do what they want."

"They want to publish you!" Lucy exclaimed.

"Of course, of course. Thank you, Lucy. Thank you so much for making this happen."

"Thank *you*, dear. But listen, you'd better let me go so that I can call Julia. Again, I'm just thrilled. Enjoy! I'll have Angel call you when we wrap this up, yes? Bye, dear." Lucy hung up before Shelly could say good-bye and immediately turned to me, her eyebrows still raised.

"Well, that's done."

"Yes. Congratulations."

"Thank you," Lucy said. She waited a moment before delivering her next words, which sounded as if they'd been torn from her. "And kudos to you, Angel. Nice work at the end. You have, indeed, been paying attention." That was clearly all the praise or acknowledgment I was going to receive, and it seemed to have cost her substantially to give it to me. I folded my arms and tried to keep my disgust from working its way onto my face. I'd finally understood why so many of Lucy's authors never wrote second books—she hated writers. And she probably hated me because I didn't.

Lucy stood, brushing the folds out of her pants, looked over at me, and completely misread my thoughts. "I hope you weren't expecting *her* to thank you," she said, gesturing to the phone. "Not that one. Another one who doesn't deserve what's falling into her lap. To think *I* had to convince *her*. It's a disgrace how many of these self-obsessed narcissists get published, get acclaim, while so many deserving writers *never get heard*." She took a deep breath. "They'll let you down if you allow them to. I knew you were an author advocate when I hired you, Angel. It helps. But you get much too involved. You can't separate the writers from their writing. That's your problem." She shrugged and placed her hands flat on the surface of her desk. Her fingernails were painted with a pale opalescent polish. "It's a great pity that one can't excise the author from the book once it's written," she said. "But there you are."

Lucy seemed to drift for a moment, caught up in thoughts she chose not to share, before she bristled, her shell hardening once more.

"Speaking of authors," she said, "I need you to get Karanuk on the phone. You've read his pages, yes?"

"Yes."

"So you've seen the shape they're in?"

"Yes, but Lucy, I think—"

"But I know how we're going to fix this." Lucy paused, forming her hands into a steeple and placing them under her chin. "Karanuk is going to write *Cold!Cooking*." She smiled broadly. "Prose recipes from Alaska. It's a brilliant idea."

She looked at me for confirmation. I tried, and failed, to muster any kind of enthusiasm. It was a god-awful idea, worse than turning *Elvis* into a novel about poker. She could sell it, of course, but it would permanently damage Karanuk's career. Lucy saw the disapproval in my face and said, "What? What is it, Angel?"

"I know that *Thaw* doesn't look good right now," I said, "but I think I can work with him. It's got so much potential, Lucy—he's an amazingly talented writer."

"Fuck *Thaw*!" Lucy snapped. "Get him on the phone for me. He'll write *Cold!Cooking* if I tell him to."

"Okay," I said, and turned to leave her office.

"Wait," she said. "Get me Julia Swann first before she *does* change her mind."

"Okay," I said.

"And Angel?"

"Yes?"

"We've got a lot to do today, so you'd better get going."

FIFTEEN

AS SOON AS I CONNECTED Julia Swann with Lucy, I felt myself breaking into a cold, crawling sweat. Chilled and overheated at the same time, I put my hands to my forehead and pressed. Bouncing between the extremes of lack of sleep, the absolute creepiness of *Blind Submission*, Shelly Franklin's deal, and worry over the missing Damiano, I was on the verge of having a panic attack. Damiano would never intentionally stand Lucy up. It just wasn't his way. Plus, such disrespect wouldn't exactly be a good career move. He was already in New York and planning to meet with her when I saw him. What could have happened between then and the following evening? I glanced at Anna, snake in the grass that she was, and thought about her heroin addict comment. What if my throwing him out had driven Damiano to . . . but no, I was giving myself *way* too much credit there.

So where was he?

"Find him," Lucy had said, and that was good enough for me. I tried his home phone number first. I let it ring ten times before I hung up. I'd discovered during our all-night editing sessions that Damiano had no answering machine or voice mail for his home phone. I tried his cell phone again, but it was still out of area. The last number I had for him was a work number, but even as I dialed it, I knew I wasn't going to find him there.

"Dolce and Pane." At least someone had answered at this number. Someone who might have a clue as to where Damiano could be, even if the gruff male voice on the other end didn't exactly sound like it belonged to a rich conversationalist.

"Good morning. Is Damiano there?"

"Damiano? No."

"Do you know if he's coming in? Do you know when?"

"Damiano? No."

"Damiano Vero, yes. He works there, right?"

"Damiano? Yes, yes. Work here."

"Do you know where he is?" I asked.

"Damiano? No. You try later," the voice said, and the line went dead.

I turned to my computer so that nobody in the office could see the tears stinging my tired eyes. Damiano, wherever he was, did not want to be found. At the very least, I thought, he didn't want to be found by me. I was going to have to get control of myself. My blushing and stammering during the meeting had surely tipped my hand, but becoming a sobbing wreck at my desk would expose me entirely. As if on cue, my computer chirped with the sound of an instant message from Anna.

Are you ok?

I turned around in my chair to face her and saw that she had her fingers on her keyboard and her eyes fixed intently on her computer screen. I stared at her long enough for her to notice me, but she kept up with her ridiculous pretense of looking busy. Behind me, my computer chirped again.

You seem a little upset.

I debated whether or not to send a message back. Somehow Anna had managed to become entangled in every aspect of my life. I wondered when all of that had happened and how I'd missed it. Perhaps *missed* wasn't the right word. *Underestimated* was more like it.

We need to talk, I wrote back. I heard the electronic ping of an incoming e-mail and welcomed the distraction.

> To: angel.robinson@fiammalit.com
> From: solange@sunstar.com
> Subject: Re: BALSAMIC MOON
>
> Greetings, Angel!
>
> Thank you so much for your note. I apologize for not writing back to you sooner, but my computer's been on the blink for the last few days and I've just gotten it back up and running (this always happens to me when Mercury goes retrograde, so you'd think I'd be used to it by now)! At any rate, I'm so glad you got in touch with me. I believe our meeting was most fortuitous—and destined to happen. Of course, destiny and the stars are my business, so my belief in them both isn't so surprising.
>
> I am "over the moon" (ha-ha) that you are so excited about my book and can't wait to discuss the next step. I look forward to hearing from you again.
>
> Regards to you and Ms. Fiamma,
> Sunny
>
> P.S. If you're interested, I would be delighted to send you a copy of your astrological birth chart. All I need is your date, place, and time of birth. Think about it—it might prove to be quite illuminating!
>
> SM

I'd almost forgotten about Sunny's book in all the madness of the last twenty-four hours. This was something else to add to the "tell Lucy" list, which was starting to become very long and complicated. I started to send Sunny a reply, something that would hold her off until I figured out a way to keep her from the fate of Shelly Franklin, but the sound of another incoming e-mail completely sidetracked me.

To: angel.robinson@fiammalit.com
From: ganovelist@heya.com
Subject: Re: Re: Alice

Dearest Angel Robinson,

I fear I've offended you, but I can't imagine why. It seemed that we were working so well together. I've just read your last e-mail (apologies about the delay) and I've taken it to mean that you don't agree with the direction I was thinking of taking here, so after giving it much thought, I've decided to rewrite. I'm attaching the fruits of my labor. I'm sure you'll give it your best consideration, Ms. Robinson. I can hardly believe that you wouldn't want to know what becomes of our Alice.

With my very best,
G.

I leaped out of my chair like an insane woman, ran the few steps over to Anna's desk, and turned her computer to face me before she had a chance to quit out of what she was doing.

"Hey!" Anna yelled, and recoiled as if I'd struck her. The sound was loud enough to alert both Craig and Jackson, who looked at us with matching stares of alarm. I gripped Anna's computer screen and peered into it. Solitaire. She was playing Solitaire.

"What are you *doing*?!" Anna squealed.

I searched for open windows on her computer, for any indication that she'd just sent me that e-mail, and found none. She'd been sitting there all along playing an electronic card game. It was no wonder she never got anything done.

"Is there a problem, Angel?" Craig's voice rumbled through my consciousness and forced me to turn around.

"No, no problem," I said, and walked back to my desk, where my intercom was shrieking.

"Angel!"

"Lucy?"

"My office, please!"

"On my way." I quit out of my e-mail program and grabbed the folders on my desk before heading over. I wasn't about to leave anything behind.

"Angel," Anna hissed as I passed her desk.

"What?"

"What's the matter with you?"

"Nothing," I said in a stage whisper. "Thanks for asking!"

"Well, that's done," Lucy said as I entered her office. "Elvis has left the building."

I smiled. I had to give her credit for that one. "Viva Las Vegas," I said, playing along.

"Indeed," she said. "One hundred and fifty thousand later." She looked at my surprised expression and nodded. "That's right, I got her to go higher. And I got our girl a bestseller bonus, too. Let's hope that the *poker* is still *hot* by the time it's published." Lucy was clearly on a roll.

"Have you called the author back to tell her?"

"Angel, I'm an extremely busy woman. If I spent all my time listening to the billing and cooing of grateful authors, I'd have none left to actually sell their books. Now, *what's next*?" She was moving with her usual sharklike speed, swallowing up everything in her path.

"Karanuk?" I offered.

"Yes, but first we need to talk about *Blind Submission*." Lucy walked around her desk to her couch and sat down. She patted the space beside her. "I can't have a conversation while you're standing there like that, Angel. Come and sit down."

I took a seat on the couch as far away from her as I could get, and placed my papers on her coffee table. A wave of dizziness hit me and I had to steady myself to keep from falling forward. I realized that the overload of adrenaline that had been keeping me awake had just run out. It didn't help that the temperature in Lucy's office, which was usually brisk at best, was quite warm, hovering between sultry and somnolent.

"Aren't you exhausted?" I asked her. "With the flying and the time change and all?"

Lucy smiled at me, showing an excessive number of her gleaming white teeth. "I slept on the plane," she said. I wondered if her remaining Xanax had anything to do with that. "The time change never bothers me. It's only three hours and, as you know, I live on New York time, anyway."

"But you must have taken a red-eye, right? I mean, that's the only—"

"Angel, I appreciate your concern for my health, but onward we go, yes? *Blind Submission*. What's going on with it?"

The very sound of the title made my throat constrict. But I had to tell her. "Yes, I need to talk to you about that," I said. "It's gotten a bit complicated."

For the second time that morning, Lucy seemed surprised. It wasn't an expression I was accustomed to seeing on her face, and it made me very uneasy.

"Really?" she asked. "In what way?"

She waited for me to answer, another anomaly, and I reached for the right words.

"I can't work on it anymore," I said at last.

"And why is that?" Lucy asked.

"Because I think I know who's writing it and I know why."

"Well, I'm most interested to hear about the *why*," Lucy said, "but first, do tell me the *who*." She seemed to be enjoying the conversation immensely. There was none of the usual clipped sharpness in her tone. For once, she seemed content to stay on one topic for longer than five seconds.

"It's Malcolm," I said, and held my breath, waiting for her reaction. I'd prepared myself for several—anger, annoyance, a lack of surprise— but not for what I saw, which was complete and authentic confusion.

"Malcolm who?" she said.

"My ex-boyfriend, Malcolm."

"Your *what*?" I watched as she puzzled it out in her head. Was it really possible that she didn't know who I was talking about? Lucy and I faced each other with mirrored expressions of bewilderment until a lightbulb finally went on in some corner of her brain. "Ohhh, *Malcolm*. The *fiancé*." Her expression changed to one of distaste. "The *writer*," she said with cruel emphasis. "Really, Angel? You're telling me that your fiancé is the author of a novel you've been working on for—how long now?—and that I've been pitching all over New York?"

"He's not my fiancé," I said. "He's not even my boyfriend anymore."

"Is this your way of trying to get me to represent him, Angel?" she said. "Because I can assure you it's not going to work."

"And I can assure you that I'm not," I said.

For a moment I thought I saw the flicker of a smile on her face, but I couldn't tell. Her eyes had gone very bright and clear and were staring right through me. I had the sudden sensation that we were on opposite sides of a seesaw and that the balance between us was about to shift.

"An-gel," she said, stretching the syllables of my name, "you're saying your— Malcolm told you he was the author of this novel? Why on earth wouldn't you have told me sooner?"

"Because I wasn't sure. I'm still not one hundred percent positive, but it *has* to be him."

"And why is that?"

"I think this was his plan all along," I started. I looked at Lucy, trying to gauge her receptiveness. She was waiting patiently for me to continue, with what seemed like genuine concern on her face. That look gave me strength and my words started tumbling out. "He wanted me to work here in the first place," I said. "He figured I'd give you his novel and then you'd represent him. But when that didn't work, he started writing this one, anonymously, so that we wouldn't know it was him and automatically reject it. His writing is all he's ever cared about, not me. And then I broke up with him. That was not part of his plan."

Lucy tapped her fingers lightly on her leg, her impatience returning. "But how is that connected to *Blind Submission*, Angel?"

I hesitated for a fraction of a second while I debated whether or not to tell her about Damiano. That was all it took to decide not to. "Lucy, you've read that manuscript," I said. "Don't you think it's more than a coincidence that the characters and plot are so much like us and this agency?"

Lucy shrugged. "Maybe," she said, "but that's part of what makes it interesting. Part of what makes it *different* from all the other crap out there. But Angel, I still don't know what makes you think it's your—Malcolm."

"There are aspects of Alice," I began, and stopped, searching again for the right words. "There are some very personal details of that character that are identical to me. Nobody but Malcolm would know about those."

"And how would *Malcolm* know about what goes on in a literary agency?"

"Well, I told him things he could have used," I said. "But I also think he had some help from . . ."

"From *whom,* Angel?"

"Anna," I said. "I think he and Anna . . . I think they are or were involved in some way."

"What?" Lucy looked revolted.

"I don't know," I said. "For sure."

"Well, Angel, I have to say I'm very disappointed in you." Lucy shook her head as if to punctuate her point.

"You're . . . ?"

"If you'll recall, you assured me when I hired you that your *personal* life would not infringe on your professional life. This is exactly the kind of scenario I was trying to avoid. You were not honest with me, Angel. And I have to say this hurts me. Really, I feel that I've offered you much more than a job here. I've given you a career, not to mention a salary that is astronomical by publishing standards. And I feel, frankly, like I've been a mother to you, Angel."

I remembered how on our flight to New York Lucy had convinced the flight attendant that I was her daughter. As absurd as it seemed, perhaps she'd convinced herself as well. For an instant, I thought about what it would be like to be Lucy's daughter and found it vaguely terrifying. I promised myself I would call my own mother as soon as I had the chance.

Lucy was still talking. "Do you know how many aspiring writers have come through this office in the guise of employees?" she asked me.

"But Lucy," I told her, "I am *not* a writer."

Lucy raised her hand to stop me. "No," she said, "what you've done is less honest than that. This is a business, Angel. I sell books here. And I now have a book that I have a tremendous amount of interest in, a book that I have staked my reputation on, and now, because of your personal involvement in it, I am supposed to abandon it?"

"No, that's not what I'm saying," I said, grasping for whatever it was that I *was* saying. "I just don't want to work on it anymore."

"Angel, do I need to remind you that you were the one who 'found'"—she made quotation marks in the air—"this novel in the submission pile?"

"Yes, but—"

"Has it suddenly become a bad book?"

"No, it hasn't."

"So the only reason that you don't want to work on it is that your ex-boyfriend is writing it? Because you *did* want him to get published, and that's why you took advantage of your position here, but now that you've broken up with him, you *don't* want him to get published, so you've decided to try your best to destroy his book? Is that right?"

"No," I said. I had to admit it to myself, Lucy's argument was starting to sound perfectly valid. It was true that *Blind Submission* had become a much better book. It was true that I had wanted to help Malcolm. And it was true that I no longer wanted to have anything to do with him. With a few well-aimed verbal strokes, Lucy had managed to make me doubt all of my own motivations.

"I wouldn't have thought you'd want to represent this novel now," I said, "knowing that he's writing it."

"But why wouldn't I, Angel? It's not about *him*, it's about the book."

As soon as the words were out of her mouth, I realized the truth in them. It was always about the book for me. In one form or another, I'd been living inside a book for as long as I could remember. And now I was living inside *Blind Submission*, a book about books, which *was*, in its own perverse way, about me. I'd been living on its pages, shaping it to suit myself. She was right: It wasn't about him at all—for her or for me.

"Do you really think it's that good?" I asked her.

"It will be when you get through with it, Angel. You were there with me in New York. You heard them. They want it."

"They haven't seen it," I said.

Lucy shrugged. "That doesn't matter," she said. "They're going to buy this one and they're going to spend a lot of money. It's going to be big, Angel."

"But what about Malcolm?" I asked her.

Lucy gave me a tight smile and folded her arms. "What if you're wrong, Angel? What if he's not the author? Are we going to let it get away because of your personal problems?"

"Well—"

"But let's assume that he is for a moment. Why don't we let him remain anonymous? Since that's the way he chose to come in. And now that I think about it, that may be the best way to sell him as well, as an industry insider who has to keep his identity concealed." She ran her fingers along the crease in her pant leg, sharpening it. "It's fitting, no? He gets his book sold, but he doesn't get any glory. Everybody wins. What do you think?"

I liked the idea more than I wanted to admit, and I thought that Malcolm would never go for it, which made it even better because he'd have to. And I was the one who was going to deliver the news to him.

"Okay," I said.

"Good," she said. "I'm glad we've got that settled. Now, is there anything else you'd like to get off your chest?"

"No," I said.

"Good," she said. "Then get Karanuk on the phone. No, don't leave, Angel. Use my phone and put him on speaker. You need to hear this."

I was halfway to her desk when I decided to take one more leap into the deep end. "Actually, there is one more thing, Lucy."

"What?" All of Lucy's trademark impatience was back.

I took a deep breath. "I've been thinking, and I know you like us to take initiative, Lucy, you know, be *proactive.*" I tried to smile, although my heart was beating double time at the thought of what I was about to say. "I've learned so much from you, Lucy. I'm sure I could never be as good as you, but I was wondering if . . . you'd consider giving me a shot at selling a project on my own. For this agency, of course."

Lucy was amused. "At what point did I give you the impression that I was interested in adding another agent to my staff, Angel?"

"You've said I've got a good eye, Lucy. I could still do what I'm doing now, but I'd be better, more productive."

"How can you possibly think you've learned enough to be a successful agent, Angel? You're a baby in this world."

I swallowed the insult and moved forward. Still smiling, I said, "I've had an excellent teacher. The best."

Lucy paused, weighing the options. "I'll have to think about it," she said finally.

"That would be great." And enough to move forward with Sunny Martin, I thought.

"This is a good day for you, Angel. Now, if you don't mind, get Karanuk on the phone."

I was halfway to her phone when Lucy stopped me again. "Go get everybody else," she said. "I need everyone to hear this. It's not often one gets to witness the birth of a seven-figure book idea."

"Karanuk!" Lucy shrieked into the speakerphone once we were all assembled once more in her office.

"Yes, Karanuk," he said with his characteristic deadpan.

"My dear, I've got some fabulous news for you," Lucy said, sweeping her eyes over the four of us.

"News," Karanuk repeated.

"I know you've been torn as to what to write next, dear," Lucy said, "and I'm just thrilled to tell you that I've just been to New York and I have come up with a brilliant idea for you."

"I'm writing *Thaw*," Karanuk said. "I sent it to you."

"*Cold!Cooking!*" Lucy yelled into the speaker, unable to contain herself any longer. "Recipes in prose. Or essays and recipes. A new kind of cookbook. It will be stunning, K, just stunning."

The static hiss was the only indication that Karanuk hadn't hung up. Flushed with anticipation, Lucy leaned closer to the phone. "Karanuk? Are you thrilled?"

"I'm writing *Thaw*," Karanuk said finally. "I am working with your assistant, Angel. I'll talk to her. She understands."

Lucy leaped at the phone and picked it up so that Karanuk's voice would no longer be audible to the rest of us. All eyes, I noticed, were now on me. "Listen, K," Lucy said, "this is a good idea. You should consider it. What? Well, in all honesty, *Thaw* needs some work, K. Yes. Yes, she is. Yes, I do. *I'm* your agent, Karanuk, not her. No. Well, I hope you'll reconsider."

Lucy hung up the phone and looked across her office at the four of us. It was impossible to get an exact read on her expression. "He wants to write *Thaw*," she said quietly. "Angel, you'll need to work with him on that."

Nobody spoke or got up for a moment. I got the sense that we were all afraid that if we moved she'd explode.

"Why the FUCK is everyone still sitting here?" she said finally. "Have we run out of work to do?"

Within seconds, every one of us was back at our desks.

SIXTEEN

To: ganovelist@heya.com
From: angel.robinson@fiammalit.com
Subject: Blind Submission

Hello G,

I thought you'd like to know that we've decided that we now have enough text to take your novel out for sale. However, we won't be able to do that until you sign an agency contract. I know you want to remain anonymous, but I'm afraid it's time to "come out." Lucy and I both know who you are, so there's no need to keep this up. There's no harm done, okay? Just give me a call—you know the number—and we'll get this thing going the way it's supposed to.

Thanks,
Angel

It was almost noon on Saturday when I turned on my computer and prepared to check my e-mail. As my laptop booted up, I dialed Damiano's number one more time and listened to it ring a half-dozen times before I placed the phone back in its cradle. It was the fifth time I'd tried to reach him since I'd left work. I'd brought my angelfish home at last and had placed the bowl next to my computer. I ran my hands over the glass as if it were a crystal ball and tried to make myself believe that I hadn't lost Damiano forever. But as I connected with the server and logged onto my e-mail program, I could see immediately that it wasn't going to be a day for faint hopes and half-baked beliefs. There waiting for me was another missive from my author from hell.

To: angel.robinson@fiammalit.com
From: ganovelist@heya.com
Subject: Re: Blind Submission

Dear Ms. Robinson,

Well, it seems we are in the home stretch, doesn't it? I am racing toward the finish—with your help, of course. I don't have time to write you a long note (need to get back to work, don't I?), but I wanted to tell you this:

It's time for a murder, Ms. Robinson.

I've given this a great deal of thought, and while there is certainly merit in writing a bloodless tale, a look at the bestseller list will show you that public taste runs to killing. Death seems to sell. So, a murder. You'll find it within the enclosed chapters. I am working both backward and forward, incorporating your notes and hurrying to finish. My hope is that the next installment will be the last.

Enjoy!
G.

P.S. We'll talk soon.

BLIND SUBMISSION

Chapter 9

Alice was dreading her meeting with Carol Moore. Alice knew what it was about and, although she had plenty of alibis at the ready, she was still a little anxious about making sure that Carol didn't suspect her. Not that there was anything to suspect, really. Carol wouldn't have known anything about her affair with Vaughn from Ricardo—Alice had seen to that. As far as Jewel went, Alice's assessment of her was that whatever intelligence that woman had didn't translate into anything like street smarts. Alice, of course, had plenty of street smarts, having trolled them herself for quite some time. All that time in dark alleys had come in most useful recently when she'd gone looking for the drugs. She'd known exactly where to go and within hours she'd had exactly what she'd needed.

But she wasn't going to think about any of that now. What she needed to do was focus on her meeting with Carol. The agent was distressed and Alice thought she'd even seen Carol wiping tears from her face when she'd heard the news. Well, it was understandable, Alice thought. Carol had barely signed him and hadn't even had a chance to pitch his book and now he was permanently out of the picture.

Vaughn Blue's death represented a substantial loss of potential income for Carol Moore.

Alice pondered this. It was possible, even likely, she thought, that Carol actually liked the man. This was something she couldn't understand about Carol—how she seemed to have genuine feelings for her clients. She got involved with them, suffered through their stupid writer's blocks with them, listened to their asinine complaints about having to sacrifice themselves for their art (as if!), paid attention when they came to her with tales of husbands and wives gone astray, ungrateful children, alcoholism, and on and on. They were impossible, Alice thought, always wanting to talk, talk, talk. And yet Carol had unlimited patience with them and a seemingly endless flow of compassion for their plights.

Maybe she was faking it, Alice thought. If so, she admired Carol even more than she did now, and she *did* admire Carol. You couldn't not admire what Carol had accomplished in the world of publishing. But Alice would have preferred to think that Carol made a show of being so emotionally involved with those writers. Like Vaughn Blue. Could Carol really be that upset over his death? Really, if anyone should be crying it should be her. It had to be the loss of Vaughn's book that was bothering Carol. Well, that was all right, too, Alice thought, because her own book would provide just the remedy.

Alice had made a big mistake with Vaughn—she'd trusted him. Foolishly, she'd told him that the "idea" for her novel had come from another author. Then Vaughn had developed a very unfortunate sense of moral outrage. Damn writers—they were all the same! She had to come clean, Vaughn told her. She was better than this, he insisted. He would stand behind her, help her. He loved her, he said.

Alice had played at being sorry. Fine, she said, she would tell Carol. And then she would tell Carol about the two of them. They'd announce themselves as a couple. They should celebrate, Alice told him. They should do something . . . wild.

Alice shook her head. It had been so easy to convince him. It was as if he'd just been waiting for the opportunity to fall back into the arms of Morpheus. If you thought about it, she hadn't really done anything that he wouldn't eventually have done himself. And she hadn't exactly twisted his arm to expose the vein.

One of the silly office girls, Brie—or Sarsaparilla or whatever her ridiculous name was—nervously approached Alice's desk, interrupting her thoughts.

"What?" Alice said. She'd given up the pretense of being nice to the underlings. Now that she'd become more valuable to Carol, it was no longer necessary, or fitting, to treat them as equals.

"Carol's waiting to see you," the girl said. "She asked me to come get you."

"Get me?"

"Asked you to come see her."

"Tell her I'll be right there," Alice said.

The girl hesitated. Alice gave her a look of impatience. "What is it?"

"It's so sad about Vaughn Blue, isn't it?" the girl said.

"Terrible," Alice said without hesitation. "Very sad."

"He was so talented."

More than you know, Alice thought. "Yes, he was," Alice said.

"And he was so gorgeous," the girl said, sighing.

"Yes," Alice agreed, but, in reality, she couldn't remember. The last time she'd seen Vaughn Blue he'd been the same color as his name and quite dead.

"Tell Carol I'll be right there," Alice said, and dismissed the girl with a wave of her hand.

No, I thought. No, no, no. It was too cruel. Why did he want to torture me like this? He wouldn't—couldn't—do anything to Damiano. The fact that Damiano was missing had nothing to do with this fictional murder and everything to do with the fact that he thought I was crazy. Maybe that was what he meant. Maybe the murder was supposed to be metaphoric. By making me as crazy as Alice, he'd made me "murder" my relationship with Damiano. Had he— Oh God, had he *spoken* to Damiano? Had he found Damiano before I'd had the chance?

There was more—much more, judging from the size of the document—but I had to stop reading. Barely concentrating on what I was writing, I fired off a response and sent it.

To: ganovelist@heya.com
From: angel.robinson@fiammalit.com
Subject: Re: Re: Blind Submission

Look, Malcolm, I know you're writing this book, okay? What are you trying to prove now? Are you trying to scare me with this "murder"? It doesn't even make sense in the context of the book. Don't be an idiot. Are you trying to get back at me? Lucy knows, okay? She knows.

Within moments, a reply appeared in my in-box. He was obviously online just waiting to see how I'd react. I couldn't get over the sheer gall of him—I didn't know where he found his nerve.

To: angel.robinson@fiammalit.com
From: ganovelist@heya.com
Subject: Re: Re: Re: Blind Submission

The question, Ms. Robinson, is not what I'm trying to prove, but whether or not this is good fiction. What's your opinion? If you're scared by my murder, it must mean you think it works.

To: ganovelist@heya.com
From: angel.robinson@fiammalit.com
Subject: Re: Re: Re: Re: Blind Submission

I didn't say it scared me, I asked if it was supposed to scare me. I know who "Vaughn" is supposed to be and I know what you're trying to imply here. Don't ask me to believe that he's dead and that I'm somehow responsible, because that's not going to work. I was going to play along—I have been playing along all this time—but I don't want to do this anymore. I'm finished with your charade.

I punched the SEND key with so much force that my laptop slid backward on my desk. I waited for Malcolm to send me another poisonous e-mail and dialed Damiano's home phone number one more time. No answer. I told myself that it didn't matter, that this manuscript was merely the product of Malcolm's clearly bitter mind. It had nothing to do with reality. I had to stop, had to pull myself out of the pages of this book and . . . It was a *book,* that was all. "You're nothing but a book," I said out loud, and wondered where I'd heard the same line. The memory floated just out of reach for a moment and then I grabbed it. *Alice in Wonderland.* That was it. *Who cares for* you, Alice says at the end of the story, *you're nothing but a pack of cards.*

I got up and stretched my legs, trying to ease some of the tension in my muscles. I tried not to stare at the computer, tried not to hit the REFRESH icon more than once a second, and tried to keep the edge of fear from cutting into my consciousness. Finally, after several more minutes of waiting and watching, I couldn't stand it anymore and took a long, almost scalding shower. I toweled my hair dry and got dressed. Still no response from G.

"This is ridiculous," I said out loud, and grabbed the telephone. I was sick of playing along—I was just going to call him.

"AANNGGELLL!!!"

There was an inhuman wailing coming from outside my apartment, along with fists pounding on the door. "Damn it, bish! Open the fuggen door!" It was Malcolm—not on my computer but at my doorstep—and by the sound of it, he was out-of-his-mind drunk. "Aaannngel! Open it!" He pounded again. As I got up and walked over to unlock the door, it occurred to me that *now* was the time to be frightened. The crazy-drunk-ex-boyfriend-pounding-at-the-door story never had a happy ending. I opened the door knowing that legions of women who'd done the same before me often wound up as statistics. But I was completely calm. There was desperation, not violence, in Malcolm's voice. And he was making an infernal scene outside. If I didn't let him in, there would be police at my door within minutes.

Malcolm looked like the wreck of the Hesperus. Bedraggled didn't even begin to cover it. His hair was matted and dirty and plastered to one side of his head. He was wearing a pair of baggy torn jeans I'd never seen before and a stained gray T-shirt that said *Canada* in faded red letters. His clothes looked as if they'd been wet and then had dried on him while he slept in them. He was unshaven and unwashed and there was a still-raw scrape down the side of one cheek, as if he'd slid his face along a gravel road. His eyes were bloodshot and dark with patent misery. And if all that wasn't enough, he stank—of liquor and cigarettes and a few other substances I didn't want to identify.

"What happened to you?" I said.

Malcolm looked at me, fists still raised to hit the door I'd just opened, and started to cry. "Bish," he whimpered. "You ruined my life."

I stood aside and let him stumble through the door. "What is this?" I asked him after I'd closed the door behind him. "What have you done to yourself?"

Malcolm staggered toward my desk to sit down, but he was too drunk to negotiate something as complicated as lowering himself onto a chair. He missed it, sliding to the floor, catching my computer cord on his way down so that I had to leap over him to save my laptop from crashing onto his head. When I replaced the computer on the desk, I saw that I had another e-mail. It was the response I'd been waiting for.

To: angel.robinson@fiammalit.com
From: ganovelist@heya.com
Subject: Re: Re: Re: Re: Re: Blind Submission

Are you so sure it's a charade?

Doesn't art imitate life?

Malcolm was sprawled out on the floor, making feeble motions to try to right himself. "Annnggel," he moaned. "I fugged up."

I leaned over him, peering into his face. The fumes coming off him were toxic and I had to stop myself from gagging. "Malcolm! Listen to me. How long have you been here?" Even as I asked the question, I knew that the answer didn't matter. He was here now and couldn't possibly have sent me that e-mail. My hands and feet had gone cold and a chill was spreading up my legs and arms to my spine.

"I dunno," he said. "I had shome drinksh."

"Some drinks?" I said. "You think?" I stood up, reached over to my laptop, and hit REPLY. *Who are you?* I typed. *What are you doing?* I pressed SEND and waited.

"Anngggellll," Malcolm wailed at my feet.

"Malcolm, get up and tell me what's going on."

Malcolm raised himself to a sitting position. "You ruined my life," he repeated. "Why, Annggell? Why'dja have to do that?" He hiccuped and put his hand to his head. "I think I'm gonna be sick," he said.

"No!" I yelled at him. "Don't you *dare* throw up in my house now! Malcolm, for God's sake, tell me what the hell you're talking about."

Malcolm covered his mouth with his hand and hiccuped again. "You told her . . . she told me . . . never going to have a career . . . gonna be a waiter for the resht of my life . . . your fault, Angel. No angel. Thass you. No fuggen angel."

As he was finishing his slurred diatribe, another message appeared on my computer.

To: angel.robinson@fiammalit.com
From: ganovelist@heya.com
Subject: Blind Submission

Angel Robinson wrote:

Who are you? What are you doing?

Dear Ms. Robinson,

I am writing a book, which you've been editing (quite well, I might add) for literary representation by Ms. Fiamma. And while it's obvious that you've read *some* of what I've recently sent you, I don't think you've finished. I urge you to continue—I think you'll enjoy it. And while our little flurry of messages has been most entertaining, I think it would be remiss of me to take up any more of your time with pleasantries. We both have work to do, don't we? I'll sign off now, but

I promise to be in touch soon. I'm almost certain that I'll be able to finish the book within the next day or two.

Until then,
G.

"Never should've got you that job," Malcolm was saying. "Woulda had better luck on my own . . . My angel . . . left me for a guy with a book deal. Ruined my career . . ." He started to laugh and started coughing. "Really bad country song," he said. "She warned me . . . I shoulda listened."

"Who warned you?" I asked him. I kept my voice quiet and calm but firm enough to get through his drunken haze. "Who warned you about what?"

"Lucy," he said. "Told me you didden really care about my career."

"When did Lucy tell you this? *Why* would she tell you?"

Malcolm whimpered. "I screwed up, Angel. I never shoulda . . . I thought she believed in me."

"Never should have *what,* Malcolm?"

"Don't you get it?" he asked me miserably. "I screwed her. She's the one who told me about you and that Italian guy. I knew it, but I didn't wanna believe it."

"You *had sex* . . . with *Lucy?* Is that what you're saying?"

"She told me I had talent," Malcolm wailed. "She told me you were cheating on me."

I looked at him and knew he was telling the truth. I thought about how flustered and familiar he'd been with her at her dinner party and how she'd looked at him as if he were another piece of meat at her table. He'd known how to get to her house not because he'd followed me to work but because he'd been there before. Then there were the flowers, asking forgiveness for things he'd never felt the need to apologize for before. It all made sense. I was starting to feel sick. Bile rose in my throat.

"How long—" I started, and had to swallow the bitterness in my mouth. "You're not still . . . ?"

"It was a mis-mistake," he hiccuped. "I love you, Angel. Always loved you."

"Sure, Malcolm. That's why you screwed my boss."

"She wasn't anything like you, Angel."

"That's disgusting, Malcolm."

"I know," he said. "I'm disgusting. Take me back."

I looked at my computer and then back down at Malcolm. "Anna . . ." I said, more to myself than to him. "Malcolm," I said, leaning over once again so that I could see into his eyes, "did you have sex with Anna, too?"

Malcolm stared up at me, my question working its way through a sea of alcohol to his brain. I saw it register and watched as a look of shame cut through the bleariness in his eyes. "Sort of," he said.

"Sort of?"

"I was drunk," he said. "She tried to . . ." He shook his head slightly and winced at the pain the motion caused him.

"She was nice to me," he said finally.

"Lucy?"

"Anna. She understands . . . what it's like."

"Are you working on this book together, Malcolm?"

"What book?"

"Blind Submission."

"She told me—" He stopped and tried to lick the dryness off his lips. "You shouldn't be so mean to her, Angel. She just wants to *be you.* You gotta feel sorry for her."

"I should feel *what?*"

"You don't know, Angel," he said. "You think you do, but you don't know *anything* about what it takes to be a writer." He fell over again and attempted to pound the floor with his fists. I could tell that it was supposed to be a dramatic gesture, but it was just a weak slap against the wood. "Angel," he said, "I loooove you." He wrapped his arms around my legs, throwing me off balance.

"Listen to me, Malcolm. Let go of me and get up. I'm going to get you some coffee now and you're going to drink it and sober up. We're going to talk. And then I'm taking you home. Do you understand?"

He lay still for a moment, his head resting on my feet. Then he sighed and released his grip on my legs. "Okay," he said.

"GOOD LORD, ANGEL, I thought I'd never see you again!"

Elise stood in the doorway of her small, shaded San Anselmo house and regarded me with a look of kind concern.

"Can I come in?" I asked her, smiling.

"Oh hell, I'm sorry, honey, I didn't mean it to come out that way. I'm so pleased to see you." She wrapped me in a tight hug. "Come on in. Let's get you something to eat. Have you had lunch?"

"You know, I haven't," I said, following her into the house. "It's been quite the morning."

"Honey, you're gonna have to tell me about it." Elise looked better than I'd ever seen her. She'd cut her long hair into a short, loose style that made her look ten years younger, and she'd traded her bookstore pallor for a light golden tan. She'd obviously been exercising, something she'd never had time to do before, because her body was toned and tight. All around, she looked the picture of health. Not working— or at least not working at the bookstore—seemed to be agreeing with Elise.

"You look good, Elise."

"Thanks, honey, but I have to say you've looked better. Well, maybe *healthier* is a better word. You're a little pale."

"Yes, well, I don't get out much these days," I said.

"I imagine you wouldn't," she said, "working for *her*. Come into the kitchen. We'll get you something to eat and then you'll tell me all about it. Best room in the house, the kitchen. It's the heart and soul of a home, don't you think?" She led me by the hand as she prattled on. "Nourishment, the nurturing that comes with cooking. Women used to have their babies on the kitchen table in the old days."

"Elise," I said, smiling, "women did *not* have babies on the kitchen table in the old days."

"How do you know?" she said, sitting me down in a comfortable cushioned chair at her own kitchen table. "It's a little-known fact. Good things happen in the kitchen."

I pushed the hair out of my face and sighed. I could believe good things happened in Elise's cheerful kitchen. I felt comforted and safe and I could see myself sitting there forever.

"Elise," I said as she took a tin of loose tea from her pantry and filled the kettle with water, "it's so good to see you. I've missed you."

"Me, too, honey," she said. "I'm very glad you called."

"I should have called you long ago. You know, before you left me that message. I'm sorry about that. It's unforgivable."

"Angel, please don't apologize. There's nothing to be sorry for at all. I can imagine how busy you've been. . . ." She stopped and stole a glance at me. "Anyway, you're here now, that's the important thing." She opened the fridge and cupboards, clattering plates, cups, and silverware.

"Thanks for letting me come over today," I said. "I know it was short notice."

"Don't be silly, Angel. You can come over any time you like. Hang on a minute now, I'm going to get you set up here."

As Elise busied herself putting food on plates and preparing tea, I felt my body begin to relax. It wasn't the sleepy kind of unwinding that comes at the end of a hectic day, but a kind of yogalike awareness. It was as if I were slowly coming back to myself.

"There," she said, placing a steaming mug in front of me, "drink that. It has great restorative powers."

"What's in it?" I asked.

"Plain old ordinary English Breakfast," Elise said. "Nothing like it." She pointed at the mug. "Remember those?"

I turned the thick white ceramic mug around and saw the words *Blue Moon Books* written underneath a cobalt gibbous moon. Years ago, in one of her efforts to increase sales, Elise had ordered several cases of those mugs for the store. We'd sold very few of them, as I remembered, but almost all of them had disappeared.

"You managed to save one," I said. "I haven't seen these in forever."

"I thought you'd get a kick out of it," Elise said, and put a full plate and fork next to the mug. "And here's some *homemade* carrot cake for you. That's right, I made it. Been doing a lot of cooking lately, actually. All that time selling cookbooks and I hardly ever checked them out. Anyway, eat, Angel." Elise sat down next to me with her own cup of tea and watched as I picked up my fork and started eating. I hadn't realized how hungry I was until the first delicious bite, and then I couldn't stop, wolfing it down as if it would vanish if I didn't get it into my mouth as fast as possible.

"Good?" she asked.

"Amazing," I answered, my mouth full of cake and raisins.

"Well, there's plenty more," she said, "so keep eating."

In the middle of my second slice, I took a breath and leaned back. I traced my fingers over the moon on my mug. "So you're really going to try this again?" I asked her.

Elise shrugged. "The bookstore? I have to. You always knew that, didn't you, Angel? It's in my blood. What can I do?"

"But you seem so relaxed. I mean, it must be nice not having to worry about the store all the time. The books . . ."

"Yes, that's true, it's been great. I wasn't intending to get back into all of that mess again, Angel, that's the truth. But . . . Well, here's what tipped me over the edge. I was in a certain bookstore, which shall remain nameless," she said with mock seriousness, and then laughed, "and I was just snooping around. You know, old habits die hard. Anyway, here's this kid who obviously needs a book for school and he asks the clerk, who, by the way, can't be much older than the customer and looks as if he'd rather be anywhere else, doing anything else, than wandering around a bookstore, if it could even be called a bookstore—I mean, they've got everything but plumbing supplies, I could practically do my grocery shopping there. . . . Anyway, the kid's got a piece of paper with the name of the book written down and he says to the clerk, 'I'm looking for a book by Victor Hugo called *Less Miserable*. Can you tell me where to find it?' And the clerk, in his infinite wisdom, says, 'Uh, I've never heard of it. But why don't you try the self-help section?'"

I chuckled and Elise joined in. "We laugh, Angel," she said, "but really, it's so sad. I mean, there's dumbing down and then there's *dumbing down*, you know?"

My laughter turned into a long sigh. "Ah, Blue Moon," I said. "Those were the days."

Elise smiled at me. "I'd love to try it again with you, Angel. I don't know if you've given that any thought. You know, after I left you that message I realized how presumptuous it was to ask you to even think about giving up your job to take a chance on something as foolhardy as a bookstore. I just thought, well . . . I guess I've really missed you, Angel."

"I've missed you, too," I said. "I've been thinking about it, Elise. Looks like I'm going to need a job, actually, and probably a loan, too." I looked down at the table, at my crumb-filled plate and my empty Blue Moon mug, and I could feel angry tears brimming in my eyes. I blinked hard and folded my hand into a fist. Elise reached out and gently covered my hand with her own.

"What's going on, Angel?" she asked. "Is it Malcolm? Is he okay?"

He would be, I thought, once he cleaned himself up and slept off his drunkenness. I'd taken him home right before I'd called Elise and driven over to her house. After several cups of coffee, he'd been sober enough to get himself into his apartment, but he was still wasted, ugly, and ranting about how I'd ruined his life. Out of some vestigial need to take care of him, I waited in my car until I saw him unlock his door and go inside. But as I watched him disappear, I found myself wondering how it was possible that I'd wanted to marry him, that I ever believed I loved him.

"We've broken up," I told Elise.

"Oh, honey, I'm so sorry," she said.

"Don't be," I told her. "It's definitely for the best. He . . . God, Elise, I don't even know where to start."

Elise got up and put more water in the kettle. "Why don't you start at the beginning, Angel? There's no hurry now, okay? We've got as long as you need."

I opened my mouth then and the words came pouring out. I left nothing out, no detail about Lucy, Malcolm, or Damiano or anything that we'd done with or to one another. I told her about the books, the sales, and what went on in the office. I told her about Lucy's hellish contract with me, which I'd have to break because I couldn't possibly work for her anymore after what had happened. And I told her, chapter by chapter, about *Blind Submission*.

I didn't stop talking until the daylight faded and the kitchen grew dark. Elise turned on the light and I blinked, my eyes adjusting to the electric glare. The table was littered with cups and glasses from the un-ending rounds of tea, coffee, and water that Elise had prepared for both of us. She pushed them together in the center of the table and started to carry them to the sink.

"So you think *Anna's* the one who's been writing this mystery man-uscript?" she asked.

"I'm not sure what I think anymore, Elise. I'm thinking now that it has to be the two of them. That's the only way it makes sense—the only way either one of them would have enough information." I told Elise how, after two cups of Italian roast, Malcolm had been coherent enough to tell me that he and Anna had spoken on several occasions. Some-where in there Anna took Malcolm's selfish attempts to extract infor-mation as some kind of romantic attention and made a play for him. Then he'd dumped her as quickly as Lucy had dumped him, which ex-plained the tearful phone call Jackson had told me about.

"It's not even so much what Malcolm did," I told Elise, "as how she sat there while I told her that whole story about Malcolm with that dis-approving look on her face. Butter wouldn't melt in her mouth, Elise—it would freeze."

"Let me say this first, Angel. I'm not upset that you're through with Malcolm. I'm sorry for your sake that it got so ugly, but I never liked him. Never thought he was right for you."

"I wish you'd told me," I said. "Why didn't you?"

"Some things you have to discover for yourself, Angel. You know that." She paused, taking time to formulate her words. "I could have told you about Lucy, too. I've always known that she was a . . . difficult woman."

"Putting it mildly," I said.

"Well, I didn't really know the extent of it, that's for sure. There have always been rumors, but you know . . . But what good would it have done to discourage you, anyway, Angel? And I'm glad I didn't."

"You are? Why?"

"You don't see it yet, do you?"

"See what?"

"How good you are at what you do. Look how far you've come in such a short time. You've found your true calling, Angel, even if it came at a certain cost. I mean, Karanuk! Would you ever have thought you'd have a . . . a literary relationship with one of our most famous authors?"

That stopped me short and I couldn't think of how to reply to her. Elise washed her hands and dried them with a bright lemon-colored dish towel. She walked over to me and put her hand on my shoulder. "Damiano sounds like a good man," she said. "Much better for you than Malcolm. I'm so glad you found him, Angel. And I can't wait to read his book." She paused, considering something. "Maybe you can get him to consider appearing at my new store when it comes out."

"But . . . you don't think . . ."

"That you've scared him off? That he really is Vaughn Blue?" Elise gave a breathy delivery to the character's name and grinned.

"Well, when you put it that way . . . I know it sounds ridiculous, Elise, but I've been trying to reach him. . . ." I couldn't stop the quick sob that escaped from my throat. "What if . . . if . . ."

"He'll turn up, Angel," Elise said. "And sooner than you think. I'm quite sure of it."

"How do you know that? Have you also got some special information I'm not aware of?" I smiled at her as I said it to let her know that I was kidding, but her face had become very serious.

"What?" I said.

She took a deep breath. "Angel, do you remember I told you I had something to show you?"

"Oh, right," I said as it came back to me. "Now I do. What is it?"

"Hold on," she said. "Let me go get it."

"Is it bigger than a breadbasket?" I joked as she left the kitchen. I waited, rubbing out the wet circles of condensation on the table, until she came back a minute later holding an old, beaten-up paperback book.

"I thought this was just funny when I found it," Elise said, "and that's why I didn't make a big deal out of it. I thought you'd get a kick out of it. But it's taken on a whole new meaning now. You'll have to decide what you want to do with it. Here." She handed me the book.

I looked at the cracked spine first and noticed that the book was so old its publisher no longer existed. I turned it around and saw that the cover, probably once a garish purple, had faded over time to a grayish puce. The title, *Flaming Heart,* was printed in large block type and surrounded by orange flames. Below that, in hot-pink script, were these words:

A novel by Lucy Fiamma.

I held it in my hands for what seemed like a very long time, staring at the letters until they blurred, and then I turned it over again and read the back cover.

> *She was born to a life on the streets but was destined to rise above them to the mansions she saw every day. . . .*
>
> *Eden Summer was no ordinary prostitute. With the face of a goddess and the sex appeal of a centerfold, she was desired and pursued by rich and powerful men from around the world. Using her wiles and wisdom, Eden played her men for money and position. She was poised to marry the wealthiest man in the world and live a life of power and influence, and then came the day when she was betrayed . . . by her flaming heart.*

I opened the book and found a small black-and-white photo of a much younger but instantly recognizable Lucy on the inside cover. The title page had been torn or had fallen out, leaving the dedication as the book's first page.

> *For the Eden inside every woman.*

I flipped through the brittle, faded pages and stopped at random.

> *Eden used her body like a knife to cut through the heart of a man's desire. She loved to hold them hostage, to withhold, then give of her sex until they were trembling and helpless with passion.*

I closed the book and looked up at Elise, who had been standing statuelike over me. I pointed to the cover.

"Well, they certainly got the color right, didn't they?" I said. "Prose doesn't get any more purple than that. Where did you find this?"

"Buried in Blue Moon," Elise said. "I found it when I cleaned out. Angel, I hope you know that if I'd known what was going on with you, I would have found a way to get this to you much sooner."

"Of course you would have," I said. I looked again at Lucy's name on the cover to make sure that it was still there. "Obviously pre-Karanuk," I said.

"Obviously. *Way* pre-Karanuk. She has no idea I have this . . . this opus of hers. I'm quite sure she'd want it back if she did."

"God*damn* her!" I spat. "I should have seen it, Elise. I should have been able to figure it out."

"How?" Elise said. "How could you have put yourself in *that* mind?"

"And to think I was worried about getting fired," I said. "Can I keep it?" I asked, holding the book up.

"Of course," Elise said. I stood up and, very carefully, placed the book in my purse.

"You know, Angel," Elise began, "*Blind Submission* really does have quite an intriguing concept behind it." Her voice was sly and conspiratorial, as if she were sharing a particularly juicy secret.

"Well, she's certainly got a lot of interest in New York," I said. "But Elise . . ."

"With the right pitch," Elise went on, "and of course, with your editing . . . You could sell it, Angel." I looked up at her and saw her nodding sagely. "You can make this work for you, Angel."

"But I can't work for Lucy anymore. And if I quit, I have to pay—"

"Honey, you're not going to have to pay a thing. Think about it, Angel. I mean really think about it this time. I'd love to work with you again, but I don't think that's really what you want, is it?"

I looked up at her and smiled. "What an amazing piece of luck it is that you're in my life, Elise."

"And I'll always be, honey. Now, you should go home, take a hot bath, and read that manuscript again. You'll be looking at it with fresh eyes. It's all going to come to you, Angel. You'll see."

I stood and picked up my purse, holding it gingerly as if it contained a bomb. In a sense, it did. I leaned over and hugged Elise hard. "Thank you," I whispered into her hair, "for everything."

"You're okay, right?" she asked me. She reached over and tucked a strand of hair behind my ear. "I don't need to worry about you?"

"I'm fine," I said, and kissed her lightly on the cheek. "In fact, I'm better than I've been for a long time."

But Elise still seemed unconvinced. "You sure about that? You seem a little too . . . calm."

"Really, I'm okay, Elise," I told her. "I'm going to go home. I'm going to call my mother. I'm going to take that hot bath. And then we'll see what happens after that."

SEVENTEEN

BLIND SUBMISSION

Chapter 13

Alice sat down at Carol's desk and laid her tools in order. There wasn't much to contemplate: a bottle of fine, single-malt Scotch, an unopened package of razor blades, and a small sheaf of correspondence from one of the country's most prestigious publishers. Although Alice knew the contents of this file better than she cared to admit, she opened it one more time and leafed through. There was the original letter of interest in "her" novel. Alice read that again for the slight thrill it could still give her, despite her growing numbness.

"We are very excited about this book," the letter read, "and feel that the author's voice is truly unique. This novel is certainly one of a kind."

That Alice knew the truth behind the novel's creation mattered not a bit to her. She felt the same slow flush of triumph that had come the very first time she'd laid eyes on that letter. Below the letter were several handwritten notes describing the details of the sale. Alice read through those carefully as well. She marveled again at Carol Moore's ability to put together the perfect deal. A copy of the actual book contract lay beneath the notes. Carol had made sure that this contract had been drawn up and signed in record time. Alice couldn't bring herself to look at it again. What did it matter if she, as the author, had gotten everything Carol had asked for? It was all over now. The contract had been canceled, nullified. Not only was the publisher refusing to print the book, but they were taking legal action against Alice and Carol both. That was the final piece of paper in the file that Alice held in front of her.

"We are deeply shocked and disturbed," the letter read. Alice scanned the page, which practically burned her fingers with the heat of its outrage. "Literary theft is egregious in itself," the letter went on, "but to abuse the good faith of this publisher is beyond heinous."

Alice felt no hint of remorse. Everything she had done had been justified in her mind. What really hurt, what tore at her soul, and why she was sitting at her desk with Scotch and razor blades, was that her book was not going to be published. Now she would never see her name on the spine of a book. She would never be able to walk into a bookstore and gaze at her own image on a dustcover. Not now, not ever. And worse still than that, she would never, ever be able to bask in the glow of legitimacy that came with being a bestselling author. And it would have been a bestseller, Alice knew. As had Carol.

Carol could have played this differently, Alice knew, but the bitch was caught up in her own damn ethics. Carol had been the one who discovered that the novel belonged to another writer. She'd been sly, as had Carol. She hadn't told Alice about her discovery until after she'd contacted the publisher.

Bitch!

Of course, Carol was a smart bitch. She didn't know, could never prove, that Alice had had anything to do with Vaughn's death, but she suspected something foul. Clever. Had Carol confronted Alice before this all became a publishing scandal, Alice would have seen to it, somehow, that Carol never opened her mouth.

"I'm deeply disappointed in you," Carol had said. "I put such trust in you. To think I even made you an associate agent in this office. You had such a promising career, Alice, and now you've thrown it all away."

Carol had been "kind," allowing Alice to take her things and leave the office without making a scene. Well, Alice had plans for a much grander exit.

Alice closed the file and placed it neatly in Carol's in-box. It was time. She uncorked the Scotch and took a long slug from the bottle. The liquid flamed as it ran down her throat, but Alice kept it down. She needed the warm courage the booze would provide as soon as it hit her stomach. As Alice opened the razor blades and held one in her slightly trembling fingers, she was struck with a final inspiration. Rising unsteadily from Carol's chair, Alice plucked a sheet of paper from the fax machine. Using a fat, permanent marker, Alice wrote, "I did it for Vaughn. I loved him and he loved me. Now we'll be together in heaven." Let the bitch find *that* when she stumbles on my body in the morning, Alice thought.

Alice took one more slug from the bottle and sat down heavily. The office was quiet and dark. Alice smiled to herself. Carol had had no idea that Alice had an extra key made. Nobody knew that she was here, in the middle of a Sunday night. Tomorrow morning would provide a real Monday surprise for the famous Carol Moore.

How strange it was, Alice thought as she dragged the razor blade up each wrist, it didn't even hurt. But there was more than enough blood to make a fabulous mess of Carol's office. Alice was surprised at how much. She held her arms up slightly and moved around in the chair, coloring Carol's carpet crimson. Soon, very soon, Alice was no longer able to move. Her eyes were closing and her thoughts floated, disconnected. She remembered something, dimly, as she began to slip away, and it made her want to laugh.

It was something someone had once said about writing . . . that it was so easy . . . all you had to do was sit down . . . and open a vein. That was it, open a vein. Alice's lips curved into a half-smile. Who was it who had said that? It was clever, Alice thought as the darkness closed in on her. So very, very clever.

IT WAS THE BRIGHTEST, clearest Monday morning I'd ever seen. The sky held a deep range of blues, from cool sapphire in the west to golden azure where the sun was just rising. Heading north on the Golden Gate Bridge, I could see the greens, reds, and browns of the Marin Headlands ahead of me. The bridge stretched out, a perfect design of flame-colored lines and curves, so beautiful in the clean light of morning.

The traffic on the bridge was surprisingly light for a Monday morning and I was making good time. I considered this a positive sign of things to come. I planned to get to the office early enough to beat the rest of the staff, but it wouldn't make any difference when they showed up. I was going to have my time with Lucy regardless.

My fingers went to the hollow of my throat and I touched the small golden angel hanging there. I smiled as I felt the tiny points of its wings under my forefinger. "For protection," Damiano had said when he'd fastened it around my neck. "An angel for an Angel."

When I'd left him less than an hour before, at the door of his North Beach apartment, he'd kissed my throat just above the charm. "I knew it would be perfect," he said, touching the chain with his fingers. "It was made for you."

"I'm going to need it today," I said, kissing his lips, soft and warm from sleep.

"Are you sure you don't want me to come with you?" he asked me then, concern creasing his forehead. "I can be ready in five minutes. *Dai*, Angel, let me come with you."

"It's okay," I told him. "It will be fine."

"You will call me?" he asked.

"I will."

"And I will see you?"

"Later," I said. "You're going to meet me there, right?"

"*Sì,*" he said. "I come early."

"Okay."

"I don't want to let you go again," he said, holding fast to my hand.

"And I don't want you to," I said. "But it's not going to be for long."

"Okay," he said, and pressed his cheek against mine in a gesture more intimate than a kiss. "Angel," he whispered, "*ti vòglio bene.*"

"What does that mean?" I asked him. "It sounds so lovely."

"I'll tell you later," he said, and then he let me go.

I touched my guardian angel again, drawing strength from its small weight. He'd given it to me late Saturday night as we sat in the bay window seat in his living room. We were drinking small glasses of dessert wine and eating almond biscotti that he'd baked himself. The sweet taste of the fruit was heavy in my mouth. He reached into the pocket of his jeans and pulled out a small red box. The angel was inside.

"I got it in New York," he said. "After . . . I never should have left you there. It was a mistake."

"You didn't know," I told him. "You couldn't have known."

Elise had been right about Damiano, although I'm sure she didn't expect him to reappear as soon as he did.

I'd come straight home after I left her house. I'd called my mother and the two of us had talked for the better part of an hour. Then, as Elise had suggested, I'd taken a long, hot, full bath. I put Damiano's CD of angel songs in my stereo, turned it up loud, and submerged myself in bubbles up to my neck, holding the pages of *Blind Submission* above the edge of the tub so as not to get them completely soaked. I couldn't remember when I'd last taken a bath. Since Lucy, I hadn't allowed myself time for anything as luxurious. Elise was right about *Blind Submission*, too. Now that I knew who was writing her, Alice finally made sense to me. And as I read the last few chapters, it became clear to me how I was going to change the ending, not just of the book, but of my own story.

Halfway through the third rotation of Damiano's CD, as if summoned, my phone rang and he was on the other end.

"Angel, it's Damiano. Please don't hang up."

"Oh, Dami . . ." I could feel tears of relief stinging my eyes. "I tried to call you so many times. I didn't get an answer. I didn't know where you were."

"I was in New York," he said. "I just got back this afternoon. I was afraid to call you. . . ."

"You stayed . . . in New York," I said. I couldn't stand up anymore, my knees had gone liquid and weak, so I sat down on the edge of my bathtub, the phone pressed against my wet ear. "I'm so glad to hear your voice."

"But Angel . . . *Non capisco.* I don't understand."

"Lucy said you never showed up for your meeting with her," I said, the words coming fast and high. "She said you never called her, that you just didn't show up. It was right after we . . . and I thought . . . but now I know . . . oh, Dami . . ." I sighed deeply.

"She said I didn't show up?" Damiano sounded confused. "I had a meeting with my editor in New York. *Porca misèria,* Angel, I wish you were there with me. I didn't know what I was doing." He blew out a short puff of air in irritation. "I had to go by myself," he said, "because Luciana wasn't there. She called me to tell me that she had to go home early. She said she had an emergency." I pressed the phone to my ear as if I could push him through it. "I was worried about you," he said finally. "You were so upset. . . ."

"I'm sorry," I said to him. "I'm so sorry about that. I need to explain it to you."

"*Sì,*" he said. "Can I . . . Can I come to see you?"

I looked around at my unmade bed, stacks of manuscripts, and unwashed cups on the table. I hadn't even washed out the coffeepot from the last round I'd made for Malcolm.

"No," I said. "Let me come to you this time. Tell me where you are."

It was late by the time I arrived at his apartment, set amid a throng of restaurants. The air smelled like garlic, rain, and espresso and was bright with neon. The noise of diners, revelers, and car horns echoed off the street. Damiano waited for me outside his building, leaning against a wall, a cigarette in his hand.

"I didn't know you smoked," I said by way of greeting. It was suddenly awkward to be seeing him in the flesh after what had happened between us. I didn't know where we were supposed to pick up or what level of intimacy we'd reached. And I suspected he didn't, either.

"Only sometimes," he said, grinding the cigarette out under his shoe. "When I'm nervous."

When we got upstairs, Damiano poured the wine and we talked, hesitantly at first, then comfortably, gradually moving into a conversation that was quiet and tender. I told him everything I could about the events of the past week and everything I should have told him in New York. Damiano spoke little while I told my story, saving his own thoughts and feelings until I stopped. He didn't touch me until he clasped the angel around my neck. We'd been talking for hours.

"It's so late it's early," I said then, looking out the window at the violet lines starting to break in the sky.

"You should sleep," he said, and led me into his bedroom. In the center of the room was a king-size bed covered with a simple olive green comforter and two large pillows in matching fabric. There was one bedside table with a lamp and a shallow dish of change. On the far wall, there were three floor-to-ceiling bookshelves filled with books of every size and shape in English and Italian. I wanted to study them right then, to look at every title, but I was suddenly so weary I could barely stand up.

Damiano sat me down on his bed and leaned over to take off my shoes. *"Vieni qua,"* he said, patting a pillow. "Lie down, Angelina." I did and he lay down next to me, taking me gently in his arms and resting his head close to mine. I was asleep in seconds. When I woke up the window was flooded with daylight and Damiano was smiling at me.

"Shall I make you breakfast?" he asked me.

"No," I said. "Make love to me." And then neither one of us spoke again for a very long time.

Much later, the two of us ate dinner together by candlelight.

"So, of course I am going to fire her," Damiano said. "Don't you think?"

"You can't fire her, Dami. I mean, you *can,* but she'll always be the agent on *Parco Lambro.* She sold it. It's hers."

"No," he said. "It's your book as much as mine."

"It doesn't matter," I told him, covering his hand with my own. "There will be other books. She doesn't own the rights to *you.* Or to me."

"But I have to do something," he said.

"I have a plan, Dami," I told him. "But let's not talk about that now. Let's . . . I'm sure we can find better things to do until I have to leave in the morning."

"*È vero,*" Damiano agreed. "I think we can."

I SIGHED CONTENTEDLY as I followed Highway 101 to the San Rafael exit. I could still feel the touch of his fingertips stroking my face and could still smell the faint scent he'd left on my skin. Neither one of us had gotten very much sleep the night before, but I felt as refreshed as if I'd gotten a full eight hours. When I checked my reflection in the rearview mirror, I saw that my skin was fresh and glowing, as if I'd spent the day in a spa. *But love can do this, too,* I thought, and wondered where I'd heard the line before. It took me a minute to realize that it came from Shelly Franklin's novel.

As I wended my way through the streets of lovely San Rafael, I felt the familiar flip in my stomach that I got every time I got close to Lucy's house. But this time it was anticipation, not fear, that was giving me butterflies.

I pulled in to Lucy's driveway and saw that I'd judged my time well. I was the first to arrive. I took a moment to gather my wits and take a few long, deep breaths, and then I picked up my things and went inside.

The office was cool and much neater than we'd left it on Friday afternoon. Lucy had obviously spent some time over the weekend going through everybody's desk. Periodically, she was wont to do this kind of "cleaning up" after we left for the day, and we'd come back to our desks in the morning to find them completely rearranged. It was another way of letting us know that everything in her domain, including her staff, was controlled by and belonged to her alone.

I had a flash of my first day in the office, a visceral memory of how I felt in those initial moments. I felt again the fight-or-flight response I'd had standing there, surrounded by the sound of telephones and voices and the silent, pressing demands of all those words, written, typed, and printed, coming at me all at once. I'd thought I was in over my head then, like Alice falling into Wonderland. Alice. There was that name again. It turned out I'd been closer to the truth then, on that first day, than I would get until this moment.

I walked past my desk and went straight to Lucy's office. Her door was open and I stood at the threshold, looking in. She wasn't there, but the lights were on and a cup of still-steaming coffee sat on her desk. Behind it, the door that led into the main part of her house had been left ajar. I looked at the slice of white light coming through the crack and realized that never once had I seen Lucy leave this door open. I walked over to Lucy's side of her desk and sat down. She'd see me as soon as she walked in, but I would see her first.

I didn't have to wait long.

"Angel!"

I'd expected her to jump or startle at the sight of me, and I was slightly disappointed that while I'd certainly caught her unaware, my sudden presence in her office hadn't given her any kind of fright.

"How nice to see you here so early," she said. "At my desk, too. Very industrious of you. I hope your colleagues don't think you're trying to kiss up to the boss, hmm?"

"Hmm," I answered. Lucy sat down in the chair opposite me, the chair that I normally sat in, and reached over for her coffee. She took a sip. I noticed that she hadn't taken the time to style her hair this morning. It was pulled back and pinned up behind her, giving her face a severe, slightly strained effect. She was wearing a black catsuit, the kind that had become so popular in yoga studios of late, over which she'd thrown a filmy white duster that tied in a bow at her décolletage. Her feet were clad in a pair of shiny silver ballet flats. All in all, a ridiculous outfit, I thought. Classic Lucy.

"Well, I assume that you've been checking my call list for the day," she said, "since you're sitting at my desk." She gave me a pointed look tinged with curiosity. "Shall we discuss?"

"Actually," I said, "what I'd really like to talk about is the reading I did this weekend."

"Oh?" Lucy leaned back in her chair, an enigmatic smile spreading across her lips. I couldn't tell what she meant by it. My heart was beating wildly and my mouth felt dry. I lifted my hand to my throat and ran my fingers across the angel. I could feel warmth and confidence returning to me. The gesture caught Lucy's eye and she said, "That's an interesting little charm, Angel. Is it new?"

"Yes," I said, and I could hear new strength in my voice. "A friend gave it to me when he came back from the dead."

Lucy's eyes narrowed to emerald slits as she studied me, waiting to see what I'd come up with next.

"I found a fascinating little book over the weekend," I said. "A real gem." I leaned over, reached into my purse, and pulled out *Flaming Heart*. I held it up for her to see. *"Les jeux sont faits,"* I said. *"You're* the author of *Blind Submission*."

Lucy's face was a study in conflict. Surprise, discomfort, relief, and excitement all battled one another in her eyes. She started to speak several times but kept stopping herself, the words dying in her throat before they had a chance to escape her mouth. For the first time since I'd met her, she was tongue-tied. I knew it couldn't last long because, surprise or no, Lucy was still Lucy, and so I stayed silent, savoring the moment, until she folded her arms across her chest and said, "Well, I must say, it took you long enough, Angel."

"That's true," I said. "There were enough clues along the way, but I suppose I just chose to ignore them. It was so much easier to believe that Malcolm had set this all up, but I know now that I was giving him much more credit than he could ever deserve. At one point, I even thought that *Anna* had authored the book, if you can believe that." I took a breath and went on. "The tattoo was a nice touch, Lucy." I raised my hand reflexively to my breast. "I suppose you saw mine that night at your party. Unless Malcolm told you . . ." I shuddered at the grotesque images that appeared in my mind's eye and went on. "It was the *why* of it I didn't get, though. Why me? Why paint *me* as Alice when Alice is so clearly you?"

Lucy regarded me with interest so intense it bordered on lust. "And?" she said, expectantly. "You worked it out?"

"Your dedication in this book is what did it," I said, holding up *Flaming Heart*. "'For the Eden in every woman,'" I read, and gave Lucy a long, searching stare. "Alice is both of us, Lucy. You needed me in order to write her and I needed you in order to become her. No, to become the *better* part of her."

"The better part of her?" Lucy asked.

"Well, I'm not a writer," I said. "If you think about it, that's what really screws Alice up, isn't it? That's her fatal flaw."

"You're more like Alice than you know," Lucy said. "You've been shaping her in your own image."

"I'm not you, Lucy," I fired back.

Lucy's eyes were glittering. She placed her hands, palms down, on her desk and pushed herself up to a standing position. "And I'm no *angel,* is that it? Let me tell you something, my dear, you can't get to where I am by being a sweet little angel. Success isn't about being *liked,* it's about being tough. If you haven't learned that by now, you never will." Lucy leaned over me, her face darkening. "This has all been very illuminating," she said, "but it's time to get to work. Unless you've got something else you want to say?"

I stood up and walked around to meet her on the other side of her desk. "I'm not going back to work for you, Lucy."

"Really?" Lucy didn't sound at all surprised. This was something she'd prepared for. "You're so morally outraged that you're going to quit? Planning to take off into the sunset with your Italian man—yes, I know all about it—and live happily ever after on his royalties?"

"Not quite," I said.

"I'm very disappointed, Angel, but then I'm often disappointed in people." She gave an exaggerated sigh. "So be it," she said. "You'll owe me some money, of course, as per the terms of your contract. You can see Craig about that. And I expect to be paid immediately. In addition, you

BLIND SUBMISSION | 321

may not use any of the contacts you've made in this office in the future. If you think you're going to continue your relationships with any authors or editors you've met through me, you are mistaken. I will sue you, Angel. I will ruin you. In fact, if I were you, I would consider an entirely new career because it will be *impossible* for you to work in publishing again." Lucy paused to let her words take effect. "But," she said, "I am a magnanimous person. I'll allow you to reconsider, Angel. Do you want to change your mind?" Lucy gave me a big smile. She was expecting that I'd fold in fear and awe. No, she was *counting* on it. Out of the corner of my eye, I could see two figures in her doorway. Jackson and Anna had come in and were hovering, listening to every word.

"No," I said, "but I'll allow *you* to reconsider."

"What?"

"*Blind Submission*," I said. "I've finished it. It needs a lot more work, Lucy, but I can get it to where it needs to be. It could sell now, but you and I both know that it wouldn't be the kind of success you want it to be. It can be a great book, Lucy, but not without *me,* and you know it." I picked up *Flaming Heart* and held it in front of her. "Of course, you could always write a sequel to *this.* But I don't think that's what you want. I don't want your authors, Lucy, or any part of your"—I gestured to the expanse of white in her office—"empire. I only want what's mine. You're going to release me from that contract and you're not going to stand in my way." I heard a quick gasp coming from the doorway.

"Is that so?" The color had drained from Lucy's face, but her voice was still strong and vibrating with anger. "And what makes you think I'll do that?"

"Because you need me, Lucy. And, as a gesture of goodwill, I'll even help Karanuk finish *Thaw.*"

"You can't touch Karanuk!"

"I don't want to touch him, Lucy. I said I'd help him—help you."

"Clearly, I'm going to have to think about this," Lucy said.

"I really need to know now," I answered.

Lucy clenched her fists and set her jaw. She strode over to her desk and fell heavily into her chair, slamming into her desk and rattling her collection of pens and notepads. "Well, then, you'd better get over here now, Angel, so we can work out the terms of this—whatever this agreement is."

A faint but unmistakable sound of soft clapping came from the doorway. Lucy and I turned our heads to look at the same time, but they'd vanished into the recesses of the outer office. Lucy turned to me and glared.

"When did you become this *person*, Angel?" she asked. "How did you get the nerve?"

I walked over to her desk and sat down opposite her. "Like I told you before, Lucy, I had an excellent teacher."

EPILOGUE

BOOK NEWS WEEKLY

JUNE 13–JUNE 19

Real Deals

Hot deal for Cold! *author:*

The biggest news in publishing this week, and no doubt for many more to come, is the sizzling sale of a new book by reclusive, elusive **Karanuk,** author of the award-winning, mega-selling phenomenon *Cold!* Quelling the seemingly endless speculation as to what Karanuk might do for an encore, **Gordon Hart** announced early this week that **HartHouse** will publish *Thaw* next spring as (no surprise) a lead title. Hart won what he described as "a stunning follow-up" from Karanuk's longtime literary agent, **Lucy Fiamma,** after a heated auction involving at least ten publishers. "We are absolutely thrilled," Fiamma said from her Marin County office. "Second acts are always challenging, but Karanuk had an especially difficult task after the enormous success of *Cold!* He took his time and he has created a unique, inspiring book that was well worth waiting for." Fiamma has good reason to be thrilled; the sale is reported to have topped out at seven figures. "We are extremely excited to be working with Gordon Hart," Fiamma added, "and we are confident that HartHouse will do a beautiful job with this very important book." No word yet on whether or not the mysterious Karanuk will make any appearances to promote this book when published, but Fiamma won't rule out the possibility. "We are discussing options at the moment," Fiamma said. "Expect the unexpected."

BOOK NEWS WEEKLY

JULY 11–JULY 17

Real Deals

An "angel" gets her wings with first book by star-watcher:

Astrologer and first-time author **Solange Martin** got news this week that even she couldn't have predicted. That news was that her memoir, ***Balsamic Moon,*** had been sold to **Natalie Weinstein** of **Weinstein Books** at **Gabriel Press.** Weinstein bought world rights for the book with a six-figure preemptive offer. Weinstein described the memoir as a "real-life *Da Vinci Code* with an astrological twist" and hails the author as "a major new voice in nonfiction." What is perhaps bigger news than this, though, is *who* Weinstein made the deal with: brand-new literary agent **Angel Robinson,** formerly of the **Lucy Fiamma Literary Agency.** "She has a great eye and a wonderful book sense," Weinstein said of Robinson. "I'm really looking forward to working with her." Could Robinson be a major new voice in the world of agents? It seems that she's well on her way. Although Robinson isn't naming names, her assistant, **Jackson Stark,** claims that the agency is inundated with submissions and recently signed at least one "very big" author.

Book News Weekly
JULY 18–JULY 24

Bookselling News This Week

Blue Moon rises again:

When **Elise Miller** closed the doors of her well-known but often-struggling bookstore, **Blue Moon,** last year, she planned to "relax, garden, and forget about the high-stress world of bookselling." Fortunately for her devoted customers and the authors she helped support, Miller just couldn't stay away. This week she announced the grand opening of **Blue Moon 2,** a smaller but no less diverse store nestled in the heart of Marin County, California. "Our goal is to carry titles that are varied enough to attract readers looking for a change from the same old thing," Miller said. "I've found that most people are hungry for recommendations beyond the bestseller lists. There's no substitute for human exchange. We want to provide a place where people feel comfortable asking questions." The original Blue Moon was a popular stop for both touring and local authors, and Miller plans to continue that with the new store. "We've got an amazing lineup of authors already," said **Anna Anderson,** the store's events coordinator. "This is going to be a really exciting year." Anderson claims to have booked several well-known authors as well as some hot newcomers, including **Damiano Vero,** whose forthcoming book, ***Parco Lambro,*** is already garnering rave reviews. Anderson also hinted about "a very major literary event" to come but remained mum about what that might be.

BOOK NEWS WEEKLY
AUGUST 15–AUGUST 21

Real Deals

Fiamma's Angel agents the agent:

It's a story that could only happen in publishing, folks. Hot on the heels of her first big sale, **Angel Robinson** of the **Robinson Literary Agency** scored again this week with the phenomenal sale of ***Blind Submission,*** a novel by none other than her ex-boss **Lucy Fiamma.** In a further literary twist, the novel is about, yes, a literary agent and her assistant-turned-writer. Who said the book world was self-absorbed? Robinson generated enough enthusiasm to cut short several summer vacations for what she called "a very lively auction." **Triad** was the winner of this one, with publisher **Julianne Davis** personally making the deal with Robinson for an undisclosed sum. "It's a fabulous book," Robinson said, "written by a talented and deserving author who obviously knows the territory well." Triad plans to publish in the spring.

Book News Weekly
NOVEMBER 14–NOVEMBER 20

Real Deals

Robinson gives thanks:

The unstoppable **Angel Robinson** announced the sale of an important project this week, just in time to make Thanksgiving a very happy one. Robinson's special deal was for an author who is, literally, very close to home for the agent. The book, sold on a proposal, is titled *Fringe: A Study of Witches, Goddesses, and Other Women on the Edge of Normal,* and the author is **Hillary Robinson,** the mother of her own agent. **Gordon Hart** made the deal for **HartHouse,** outbidding two other publishers. **Kate Small** will edit. *La mère* Robinson was unavailable for comment, but her daughter told us this: "Hillary has an encyclopedic knowledge of these groups as well as direct experience. This is going to be a stunning book on an extremely important topic but will be accessible to all readers."

Spoken like a good daughter.

BOOK NEWS WEEKLY
MARCH 13–MARCH 19

Bookselling News This Week

Surprise appearance makes Blue Moon 2 the hottest ticket in town:

Patrons of **Blue Moon 2** bookstore were rewarded for their loyalty last Monday when none other than renowned *Cold!* author **Karanuk** gave an impromptu lunchtime reading of his new, already mega-selling book, *Thaw,* to a lucky crowd of readers. Because Karanuk has been so reclusive in the past, he was able to browse unrecognized in the stacks until store owner **Elise Miller** made the announcement that he was there. Wearing a baseball cap, blue jeans, and a Lakers sweatshirt, Karanuk took a seat on the small stage at the far end of the store and read for thirty minutes to a rapt audience. Word spread quickly that Karanuk, who has never before given a public reading, was in Blue Moon 2, and by one o'clock the store was full to capacity.

"We knew he was coming," events coordinator **Anna Anderson** said, "but of course we respected his request that we not broadcast this information to the media. This is a once-in-a-lifetime event and we wanted to do it the way he wanted." Anderson reported that she'd ordered "hundreds" of both of Karanuk's books, but that the store sold out almost immediately.

Karanuk's publisher, **HartHouse,** denies that he will be touring for *Thaw.* So what was behind Karanuk's surprise appearance? And why Blue Moon 2? San Francisco power-agent **Angel Robinson** may have something to do with it. After his reading, Karanuk thanked Robinson for "beginning the thaw that led to my vernal equinox." Robinson, a long-time friend and colleague of Miller's, was in attendance with her husband, author **Damiano Vero.**

"She can read the heart of a writer," Karanuk said of Robinson, "and understand what she finds there. And that is something only an angel can do."

ACKNOWLEDGMENTS

FOR THEIR LOVE, encouragement, support and patience, I would like to offer huge thanks to: my family, especially my sister Maya, who gets an additional lifetime thank-you for being the only person to have read everything I've ever written; G, Gabe, and Gabriel; Shaye Areheart (and everyone at Shaye Areheart Books), for giving this book such a welcoming home; my literary agent, Linda Loewenthal, for taking such good care of me; my inestimable editor, Sally Kim, for making so many wonderful things possible.

ABOUT THE AUTHOR

DEBRA GINSBERG is the author of the memoirs *Waiting, Raising Blaze,* and *About My Sisters.* This is her first novel. She lives in Southern California. Visit her at www.debraginsberg.com.